Keys
to the
Captive
Heart

BOOK THREE IN THE KINSMAN'S TREE SERIES

Keys
to the
Captive
Heart

TIMOTHY MICHAEL HURST

ISBN-13: 978-1-7916903-3-5

Dedication & Appreciation

Isaiah 61:1 (KJV) The Spirit of the Lord God is upon me; because the Lord hath anointed me to preach good tidings unto the meek; he hath sent me to bind up the brokenhearted, to proclaim liberty to the captives, and the opening of the prison to them that are bound;

To my lovely wife, Brandi – Wow! Just...wow! What a help you have been throughout this entire adventure. We're only getting started, and I'm happy to know we'll be together at the finish.

To my mother – Thank you for your encouragement and for believing in the calling of God upon my life.

To my father – Thank you for always telling me how much you love me and how proud you are of me. I miss your face and the sound of your voice.

To Bev, Brenda, Sandra, and Judy – Thank you for being my cheerleaders, no matter the weather.

To my greater family in Christ – I thank you once more for all your prayers and support.

Glossary

General Terms

Ægle (EH-gul) – A race of large raptorial birds

The Eben'kayah (EH-ben KAI-yah) – A group of Etom who preserve the prophecies of Elyon

Endego (EN-de-goh) – Nida and Nat's home town

Etom (EH-tom) – A race of small, semi-insectoid creatures

Etma (ET-ma) – A female Etom

Etém (eh-TEM) – A male Etom

Malakím (ma-la-KEEM) – The radiant servants of Lord Elyon

Nihúkolem (nee-HU-koh-lem) – The shadowy wraith army of the Empire

Sakkan – An Etom village far northeast of Endego

Shedím (shed-EEM) – Fallen, rebel Malakím

Sprig – A race of tree-like beings

Terábnis – A great city of Men in the desert wastelands of the North

Characters

Dempsey – A young etém leader among the Kinfolk of Endego

Gael – An æglet; Sayah's sister

Iver – A contentious, hard-hearted etém opposed to the Kinship of the Vine

Kehren – Rae's mother and a pivotal figure among the Kinfolk

Makrïos (MACK-ree-ohs) – A Man, and a former Captain in the Empire of Chōl's army

Miyam – A Sprig at full leaf who tends to the needs of all in Sanctuary Endego

Nat – A young etém, first to join the Vine among the Kinship of Endego

Nida (NEE-da) – Nat's mother; a brave and selfless leader in the Kinship of Endego

Pikrïa (PIK-ree-ah) – Nida's Great Aunt; a wealthy and solitary etma

Rae – A young etma; Nat's best friend and a gifted member of the Vine

Glossary (cont.)

Characters (cont.)
Sayah (SAI-yah) – An æglet; a Kin transformed by the power of the Spirit
Shoym – A kindly gentletém who now serves the Kinship as a leader
Tram – Rae's father; a merchant a leader in the Kinship of the Vine

The Supernatural
Astéri (as-TER-ee)—A messenger of Lord Elyon
Elyon (el-EE-awn)—The Creator of the universe and so much more
Gaal (GAWL)—The Kinsman
Helél (heh-LEL)—The villainous leader of the Shedím

The Nihúkolem
Belláphorus (bel-LAF-or-us)—A close comrade of Mūk-Mudón
Cloust—A close comrade of Mūk-Mudón
Imafel (EE-ma-fel)—A close comrade of Mūk-Mudón
Mūk-Mudón (MOOK muh-DAWN)—The Emperor of Chōl

Prologue:

~As the oil of anointing, the Spirit of Lord Elyon rests upon me, that I may deliver good news to the poor, healing to broken hearts, and, to those held captive in darkness, a proclamation of freedom from imprisonment~

An aging stone-faced etém reclined against the wall just outside the warm wedge of light that poured into his cell. The young, pale blue etém had left his door ajar a crack before bounding down the walkway to pound on the door of a more willing escapee.

The elderly gentletém moved not an inch while with eyes closed he listened with care, filling his barrel-shaped chest with long, slow breaths as he waited. Before long, the din of the captive exodus subsided, and all was silent within the obsidian walls of the stout tower. Still the figure did not stir, and from the soft, unlabored rise and fall of his respiration, he seemed to slumber.

Half an hour or so passed before his eyes flicked open, glinting with bright awareness, as he arose in smooth coordination. Though large for an Etom, he moved with unhurried economy to pull open the door without so much as the scuffle of feet to betray his actions.

With continued alacrity, the grizzled lump of an etém stepped from his cage to survey his surroundings. Through squinting eyes set in a square, seamed face of olive-green, he absorbed the aftermath of the escape.

Along the walls of the tower's sterile storeys, the shadowy doorways of open cells yawned in the stillness. Once loosed, those set at liberty had demonstrated little care for their confines in their hurried departure.

As it should be. As it should be, he thought, a smile of considerable warmth creasing his leathery face.

The smile disappeared, though its glow yet brighten his countenance as he reminded himself, *Now to the business at hand.*

With light, lively strides, he descended the tower, traversing its walkways to the top of the first stair, beside which stood the last

7

remaining door, closed fast. A flicker of frustration darkened the etém's countenance for but an instant. Rather, he took heart, recalling a snippet from the prophecies of his people.

But as for you, be courageous. Do not let your hands grow weak, for your work will have a reward if you don't give up.

He peered over the walkway rail across the arbor floor, scuffed with dusty evidence of the multitude's passage. A cloud passing high overhead dimmed the sunshine streaming through the skylight for a moment. With the return of the sun's radiance, the etém's eyes caught a brassy gleam on the floor near the far wall.

Could that be it? he wondered and sprang down the stairs to investigate.

Sure enough, a single key lay flat amidst a scrim of dirt on the floor. Bending down with the same smooth economy as before, the brawny etém swept up the key. Between thick fingers, he held the key before him and read its markings: 2-XXX.

His desire for continued stealth restrained a shout of joy. Instead, he dashed for the locked door atop the stairs. Without hesitation, he slipped the key home and gave the handle a turn.

With ease, he swung the door open, his shadow stretching long before him amidst the luminous frame of sunshine pouring through. While the light reached the far wall of the cell, much of its interior remained in darkness, and so he ventured a hoarse whisper into the murk.

"Hello?"

No response.

He stepped into the chamber's shadows, closing his eyes in the darkness while in his mind he counted off several breaths while allowing his vision to adjust.

...eight...nine...ten.

Opening his eyes to look about the room, he found his vision somewhat improved, if not altogether lacking as before. He stooped in the corners and dangled his hand near the floor to sweep the length of the walls in search of the 'patient' he knew to occupy the room. Returning to the door, he gripped its inward edge as it lay open into the darkness, and set his heavy head against its cool, metallic surface in consternation.

Could the others have taken him? he wondered, then dismissed the thought. *No. Then why would they have locked this door alone?*

Doubt stretched forth with spidery hands, seeking some hold by which to overthrow his flinty confidence. The etém shrugged off the assault, opting instead to call on the Creator for help.

Elyon, he spoke from his heart, *I know You hear me, and that You would not ask me to abandon my friend here. Please guide and help me, so I may carry him from this place.*

The etém's prayer was short and simple. He'd never been known for flowery words and knew with confidence that the effectiveness of his plea was not in his own eloquence, but rather in the power and the goodness of the One to which he appealed.

Eyes lifted heavenward, he gripped the door, straining against it in expression of his fervency. To his surprise, the door encountered springy resistance and a weak moan met his ears. With exaggerated urgency, he pulled the door partway closed to peak his head around it, his eyes wide and excited.

Behind the door lay his friend, another etém of similar age, though by all appearances he'd fared far worse under Scarsburrow's experiments. The rescuer's elation failed him when he saw the damage done his friend, who could scarcely lift his head. The captive lay in a ragged heap, fitting with room to spare into the meager space between door and wall.

Sniffing back tears of compassion and indignation, the burly etém bundled up his friend in his arms, taking care not to allow the frail, ashen figure's lolling head to strike the doorframe as they departed the despicable cage. His emancipated friend seemed light as a feather, so diminished was he.

The large etém felt some guilt that he'd managed to maintain his strength and health during his stay in Scarsburrow's twisted asylum. Yet he saw in their circumstances Elyon's hand preparing the way to carry them both beyond this moment and into a future not defined by their imprisonment here.

With watchful care, he bustled his friend down the stairs and out the main doors, taking care to veer away from the clamorous melee he detected down the road. Although they met a few Etom on the way out of Sakkan, all of Scarsburrow's enforcers were yet busy in pursuit of the others.

Those Etom they encountered had no desire to stand in the way of the massive etém who barreled through their streets with a vague, grey Etom-shaped bundle in his arms. He looked angry, determined, and more than capable of flattening any Etom of usual size without so much as breaking stride.

Soon, they were clear of Sakkan and on their way through the darkening woods east of the village. Though he was far more fit than his companion, the larger etém was nonetheless weakened from his stay with Scarsburrow. Once they had put some distance between them and their captors, he set his friend down and rested a moment.

From his seat atop a stone, he oriented himself, and at last decided on a vague northeasterly course. Danger lay that way, but so, too, did their people. The Eben'kayah – they could help nurse his friend back to health.

He went to retrieve his friend, hoping the poor soul might stand and hobble along on with some support. As he draped his companion's arm across his shoulder, out of the corner of his eye he spied his friend's dangling hand, engulfed in the horrendous Stain. The sickly, black filth had progressed a great deal since they had first entered Scarsburrow's clinic.

The big fellow's concern for stealth disappeared, and he at last broke silence.

"Come along, then. You need to get stronger, or this journey will take us forever. It's not too far if we keep moving. We'll get you some proper food and medicine yet."

The grey and wispy etém swayed a tad before settling on unsteady feet beside his friend. He peered at the larger etém through wincing eyes and offered a wordless smile of gratitude.

His burly companion responded, "That's alright there. Happy to help. And look at you! Standing on your own two feet! Don't you worry, Killam. We'll have back up to full health in no time."

And in halting fits and starts, they set out for their destination.

Chapter One
Still Before the Storm

Basking in the peaceful glow of Sanctuary Endego, Nat sat atop an arching root, reclined against the knotted bark of the Tree that stood in place of the Eben'kayah's beloved olive tree. He followed the crystal-clear flow that sprang from the Tree. The waters had filled the pit left behind when the Nihúkolem uprooted both tree and temple, then had overflowed its eastern bounds, sending forth a tributary to intersect with the Üntfither.

Nearby, Shoym read aloud from the solitary scroll the remnant of the Eben'kayah had salvaged from their temple before the Nihúkolem had destroyed it. Miyam, a sister in the Vine, had planted herself in place the olive tree, and by a miracle Elyon had transformed her into the Tree of Sanctuary Endego. Since then, the elderly gentletém had made a practice of proclaiming the prophecies of the Kinsman each day beneath the protective boughs.

Most days, many of the Kinship would gather their rhema in the morning and sit to listen while Shoym read. Even among those Etom of Endego new to the Vine and to the prophecies of the Eben'kayah, Shoym's recitation piqued a hunger they'd heretofore not known to exist. And as at mealtime, Shoym's reading now proved the perfect counterpoint to Nat's ruminations in the Spirit.

"Look! With righteousness, our King will reign, and in justice rulers will rule..."

Stirring, Nat shot a wistful gaze up the length of the trunk, marveling at the great transformation his friend Miyam had undergone that fateful night. He missed the Sprig and wondered if any shred of her awareness peered out from amidst the branches, but soon relented from his musings at the Spirit's behest.

Do you believe she regrets her sacrifice for a moment? his Comforter chided. *I assure you her reward in Elyon's Kingdom exceeds even her knowledge that in fulfilling her calling she saved her friends from the Nihúkolem.*

Nat frowned in confusion, aware of his ignorance on the topic of the Kingdom. Though he'd grown more familiar as he communed with the Spirit, he'd heard something of the concept among the Eben'kayah before they had departed Endego in search of the Kinsman. What he learned was scattered throughout diverse prophecies and told of an eternal and unbroken fellowship with Elyon under His rule.

The young, pale blue etém shook his head with uncertainty. The intensity of his experience with the Spirit to this point made difficult imagining just how much better or deeper a fellowship might exist between Creator and His creatures. But was that not Elyon's intent for the faculty of imagination? He had purposed it not for flighty musings on fanciful things, but rather for the inspired expansion of the mind in attempting to fathom His immensity and that of His plans.

The exercise caused Nat to consider, too, the abiding peace he possessed, even as he looked eastward beyond the luminous borders of Sanctuary Endego toward the forces of Chōl amassing there. The midday sun illuminated indistinct and innumerable figures churning about in busy preparation for an inevitable assault.

They were coming for Nat and those he loved, yet no anxiety touched his heart. What trouble might come, would come. Nat had entrusted himself to Elyon's plan and would not be afraid. If anything, his real concern was for his friends and family, aware that their suffering would injure him more deeply than any mortal weapon might.

However, they had placed their confidence in Elyon as well, and would share the same ultimate fate. In this, and their shared bond through the Vine, they were united. The Kinship would not falter in their commitment.

With a grunt, Nat arose to look out over the clearing of Sanctuary Endego, that space in which the Spirit made His glory manifest. Not in light alone, but also in life did the unbroken springtime beneath the bower display His glory.

From the eastern edge of the Tree's pool, an overflowing rill of the pure, invigorating water had etched a course to pour into the Üntfither. Along the downstream shore Nat observed verdant life even amidst the deepening chill of late autumn.

He spied, too, several clusters of Etom engaged in conversation and activity about the bower. And with ginger steps, the two foxes, Blithewit and Whisperweave, wove through the Etom as they meandered toward Nat.

A number of Kin bore the responsibility for the security for the village, and today, the duty fell to Nat, who awaited the early scouting report the foxes brought from about the village. Their quick, light forms equipped them well for the task of collecting information from the Etom sentries stationed at Endego's perimeter. What might have taken a number of the smaller creatures a good deal more time, the vulpine pair accomplished in under half an hour.

The burdensome lives of servitude to the dark Nihúkolem lifted from the foxes was now manifest in the carefree strides that carried them along their way. No more clear evidence of their newfound freedom was present than in the playful challenge that the silvery elder, Blithewit, had issued his fire-flocked cohort at their departure earlier.

"Last one back to the bower takes the evening patrol alone!"

"You're on!" called back Whisperweave as the pair frolicked toward Galfgallan Road, where the two had parted ways.

The memory of the morning's interplay elicited a gentle smile from Nat as the foxes approached, and he hailed them with an upraised hand. Blithewit, the more winded of the pair for his age, panted while Whisperweave offered the report.

"No movement or activity along the northern, southern, and western borders," she began. "Besides the steady stream of reinforcements to the enemy camp, all's the same on the eastern front."

"Good, good. Thank you for the report, Whisperweave," Nat replied, then looked to the recovering Blithewit to ask, "And who won today's contest?"

Blithewit's foxy lips curved into a grin, "Why, I believe that honor goes to me."

With an exasperated sigh, Whisperweave rolled her eyes, and responded, "If, and I mean *if* you won, it was by the length of a mere whisker!"

"Our dear friend here disputes my obvious victory," Blithewit explained to Nat, "even though I was clearly ahead at the finish. By a nose. At least!"

Whisperweave batted playfully at the smug, silver fox, and added, "And here I thought it was a *friendly* contest, not a death match! You almost killed yourself to earn the win!"

"Aha! So, at last you admit I won!" Blithewit returned, his eyes gleaming with cheer. "Well, I'm not a sore winner, after all. I'll give you another chance. Same time again tomorrow?"

Whisperweave prodded him, a mischievous smile crossing her snout, "Ever the chivalrous one, eh, Blithewit? Giving the poor young vixen another chance? Alright, then. I'll take you on!"

Entertained by the exchange, Nat couldn't contain the chuckle that escaped him. Turning in a slow, tandem swivel, the foxes faced him, mock predatory seriousness sharpening their features.

"Did we say something funny?" Whisperweave intoned, her face slack and solemn as she towered over Nat, who looked back and forth at the two, his smile tinged with uncertainty.

One side of Blithewit's mouth opened in a sneer as he growled an aside to Whisperweave, "I daresay he finds us amusing."

Nat's golden eyes widened amidst the momentary tension, which broke when the foxes collapsed in fits of laughter at their prank.

Nat exhaled a heavy breath and chided the cackling pair, "You two are *hilarious*. Did Sayah put you up to this?"

Struggling to speak through tapering chuckles, Blithewit wiped a streaming eye and responded, "No, no. Although he did tell us of when you met. The poor fellow looked so remorseful, we couldn't help but laugh."

"And, well..." Whisperweave huffed as she arose, her expression sobering, "well, we just wished we had a special memory of meeting you, too."

Her eyes rounded, softening as Nat replied, "I can't think of a better way to have met any of you but under this Tree. I can't imagine a more memorable beginning to our friendship."

The sudden solemnity of the moment took all three by surprise, and tears stood in their eyes at the fast connection the Spirit had forged between them in so short a time. The bond was nothing less than a miracle of Elyon's grace, a loving kindness given those who could never earn it.

The experience warmed them like the sunbeams that poked through the swaying boughs of the Tree Nat had once known as his friend, Miyam. He pondered again her role in establishing Sanctuary Endego and wondered if the Spirit might object if they honored her sacrifice in some way.

A boastful voice arose from the westward perimeter, shaking the trio from their shared meditation, and they swung about to identify the disturbance – an etém of deep orange crossing the bower with a shrouded figure in tow.

"Iver," Nat growled, his chagrin apparent in the frown that strained his face.

Nat had hoped they might have seen the last of the troublemaker after he slipped away three nights prior, but, alas, it was not to be so. The Spirit warned Nat's heart against the danger Iver's return heralded, and against the subtler danger of bitterness that threatened the youth from within.

Since his adoption into the Vine, Nat had learned that though they must protect one another from their enemies, the aim was ever to bring even these into the Vine. As such, the Spirit would brook no unforgiveness in the hearts of His own, even against those who had brought their members grievous harm, or even death.

The cornflower youth filled his lungs, then exhaled, breathing a prayer for a love drawn from the Spirit's vast wellspring. Before setting out to intercept the interloper, Nat turned back to the foxes, who stood ready with eyes quick and bright as the etém forewarned them.

"I know you two just got back, but something about Iver's return has put me on edge," Nat began.

"The Spirit is urging caution, as I expect you also sense. If you're up to it, I would ask you to warn the sentries to be on the lookout for anything suspicious. We will send reinforcements as soon as we're able. We need more eyes at each post. I believe the enemy will soon be upon us."

Blithewit shot a glance to Whisperweave, who nodded her assent, and then barked with enthusiasm, "Without delay, young sir!"

At that, the pair whisked away, bounding side by side across the bower until again they parted ways – a bolt of quicksilver in one direction, a streak of wildfire in the other. Nat smiled, giving thanks for such allies then steeled himself for his encounter with the oft-unpleasant Iver.

Iver's noisy reappearance caught the attention of a good many Etom taking shelter in the bower, and a large crowd began to gather around the malcontent and his unknown companion. At the center of this gathering stood Ënar, who barred Iver's further advance into Sanctuary Endego with his great, dark bulk.

Over the many speculative voices, Nat heard Ënar's deep and sonorous tones warning the two away.

"You are not welcome here, Iver!" he blared. "Now, begone!"

A few at the edge of the clustered throng noticed Nat's approach, and made way for him, tugging on the sleeves or tapping the shoulders of those in front to prompt them to clear a path.

Though a humility cultivated throughout Nat's short life insulated him against pride, Nat nonetheless marveled that these had accepted him as a leader. He stepped with care into the wedge that opened in the crowd as they made way for him. Whispers of encouragement from met Nat's ears from all sides, further affirming him as he drew near the unwelcome confrontation.

Across the way and near the Üntfither, Nida was busy directing the stream of Etom that ported supplies over Potter's Arch. Shouldering a large bale of twigs and bracken over the bridge, Dempsey's yellow cheeks glowed a rosy orange as he huffed with exertion. Dempsey's eyes met Nida's, his gaze speaking more than a patient request for instructions before shifting into the distance and growing troubled. He set his burden down at once and pointed a yellow finger past Nida.

"What's happening there?" he asked in a voice strained with urgency.

Nida whirled about, her long, pink zalzal whipping around her as she did, and just caught sight of Nat's familiar blue form before he disappeared into a growing multitude near the bower's western edge.

"Oh, no," she gasped, certain the scene spelled trouble, a fact confirmed by the Spirit within.

She turned to Dempsey, who nodded toward the crowd, then offered, "I'll find someone to take over here, then I'll be right along behind you. Now go!"

Without hesitation, Nida set off, not quite running for the panic she might cause, but walking at the briskest clip she could manage. As she hurried, she mouthed a silent prayer to ward off the dread that threatened her peace in the uncertain moment.

Nat waded toward the discussion in progress, taking in the scenario before he joined the conversation. Ënar glowered down at Iver, who with smug, unmoving patience listened to his opponent. A couple steps behind Iver stood the mysterious, hooded figure, who from her clothing and bent posture Nat determined to be an elderly etma. But with her face obscured beneath a great shawl, the question remained – who was she?

One thing at a time, the Spirit prompted. *You must tell Ënar that Iver is allowed here in Sanctuary. Degenerate though he is, Iver must be given the opportunity to experience the glory of Elyon among His people. Nowhere else is His glory thus apparent.*

Nat took a deep breath, then stepped forth and laid a gentle hand on Ënar's great shoulder. In mild surprise, Ënar at once ceased his tirade and turned, looking down into Nat's great, golden eyes.

"Please, Ënar," Nat pleaded. "No more. We know you mean well, but the Spirit says Iver and his guest are welcome. Search for yourself. You'll find it's true."

Gazing at the earth in introspection, Ënar's jet black brow furrowed, at first with consternation, then with concern as he sought the Spirit's will.

"Oh, my..." the large etém gasped, grief in his voice and tears in his eyes when he raised them to Nat. "You speak true, Nat. I see that now."

Without delay, Ënar apologized to Iver, "I am sorry, Iver. May the Spirit grant you the same grace as He has to all in the Vine. You are free to pass."

Ënar swung a wide hand, pointing along the open way Nat had traversed to indicate Iver could be on his way.

Rather than accept Ënar's invitation, the etém of burnt orange leveled his gaze at Nat, and returned, words dripping with disingenuous courtesy, "Thank you, Ënar. However, the one I seek here has found me."

Nida arrived just as Nat was establishing some ground rules for Iver and his companion. With what gravity the young etém could muster, he conveyed that the pair could remain so long as they were respectful. While Iver nodded his agreement in feigned compliance, Nida narrowed her eyes in suspicion and took a hard look at Iver's shrouded companion.

"Iver?" she broke in. "My apologies, but might you introduce us to your friend, please?"

Iver cocked a brow and tilted his head toward her to answer, "Ah! Nida. Why am I not surprised?"

He gestured to his companion, and continued, "I'm sure you'll be pleased to find that no introduction is necessary. You and my guest are already well-acquainted..."

Nida twisted her face in perplexity as she looked first to Iver, then to the hooded figure, who, with wrinkled hands upraised, drew back the heavy shawl.

Nida's face fell slack with shocked recognition, and a single word escaped her trembling lips, "Pikrïa."

"Why! Hello, there, Nida," Pikrïa wheedled in a false and reedy tremolo that shook the surprised Nida.

The impact of Pikrïa's sudden appearance doubled when Nida saw the depth of her Great Aunt's deterioration since their estrangement – the Blight had made a helter-skelter mess of Pikrïa's countenance.

"Wha – what are you doing here?" Nida responded, overcoming her startlement at last.

"I came out to see what all the commotion is about," Pikrïa returned.

"You wouldn't refuse me the opportunity, would you?" she continued, waving a hand over the wreckage of her face. "I've heard wondrous things about this place from my new friend, Iver."

Iver, Nida seethed, narrowing her eyes at the unscrupulous fellow. She opened her mouth to banish the scoundrel from Sanctuary before Nat interjected with a careful smile.

"Mom, you might not believe this, but I think we're supposed to let them stay."

While Nida loved and trusted her son, she doubted his practicality in this matter. She was preparing a reply to such effect until at her lips the Spirit hoisted a gentle blockade. With a deep inhale through her nostrils and a concerned frown on her face, she relented. Whatever the

Spirit's reason, He purposed that these two should be allowed in the bower.

Through gritted teeth, Nida offered Iver welcome, and addressed Pikrïa as she passed.

"I would like very much to catch up with you, Great Aunt Pikrïa. If you might have the time, that is."

With lids slitted over unkind eyes, Pikrïa answered, "We shall see, Nida. I will be very busy here, I assure you."

With a dramatic about-face, the elderly etma turned to leave, and found Nat obstructing her way.

The youth beamed with good cheer, his excitement obvious as he introduced himself, "Great Aunt Pikrïa?"

"Or maybe I should call you *Great*-Great Aunt?" he ventured with a cheeky grin and extended a hand in greeting.

"I'm Nat! My mother has told me so many wonderful things about you. You've no idea how happy I am to meet you at last!"

Pikrïa declined Nat's proffered hand, looking down at it in apparent disdain. In the awkward pause, Nat's hand fell, though his countenance did not."

"That's right!" he exclaimed with a chuckle. "Why all the formality? We're *family!*"

To Nida and no doubt Pikrïa's surprise, Nat lunged at Pikrïa to throw his arms around the stiff old etma, who failed to recoil from his embrace in time. A lifetime of training under Rae's indelicate constrictions had prepared the youth for very this moment, and Pikrïa stood no chance of escape until Nat emancipated her from the constriction of his grasp.

Once released, the breathless Pikrïa exclaimed in indignation, clutching a weathered hand to her chest.

"Well! I never!"

Without delay, she bustled over to join Iver at the edge of the crowd, grumbling as she went. Meanwhile, a bemused Nida pondered the abject panic on Pikrïa's face when Nat had taken hold of her – a panic that for an instant had devolved into brittle, trembling fragility before the old etma summoned once again her haughty mask.

Oh, Lord Elyon! Nida prayed, *Did I see her heart for a moment? May You reach beyond her stony façade to touch her.*

A sudden, hot tear rolled down Nida's cheek as she confessed, *Somehow...somehow, I still love her, even after all that's passed.*

Pikrïa and Iver meandered away on what seemed an aimless course, though Nida suspected some unsavory scheme was afoot. A comforting hand on her shoulder drew Nida's attention, and she turned to find Nat gazing up at her with kind eyes.

How does he manage? Especially after the way Pikrïa treated him? she wondered, then reminded herself. *Lord Elyon has forgiven us our every offense. It's right to forgive her. Maybe that's just what Nat's chosen to do. Love her no matter what.*

"Mom?" Nat began, "Don't you think Great Aunt Pikrïa seems a bit sad? Like she's let no one love her for a long time?"

"I think you're right, son," Nida replied, trying not to choke up at her son's tenderness. "We must remember her in our communion with the Spirit, mustn't we?"

"Definitely!" Nat exclaimed.

A shining figure fluttered into Sanctuary, a burst of radiant white feathers gliding in amongst the sunbeams. Sayah folded his wings and dropped to the earth before Nat and Nida, his sharp talons touching down with a delicate grace that belied the ægle's relative inexperience in flight.

"Nat! Nida!" Sayah squawked. "There's movement in the enemy camp. Looks like an advance party of their swiftest with the rest falling in right behind them!"

Nat, Nida and those within earshot swiveled toward the front, where through the trees an undulating wave of bounding, bestial forms was visible on approach. Beyond these, the taller forms of Men marched and behind them, the lumbering forms of the greater Beasts formed up to trundle toward Endego. At the rearmost, mahouts were visible, bouncing in their perches atop armored War-Elephants as they guided their juggernaut steeds.

"An all-out assault," Nida breathed. "They're throwing all they have at us."

Nat whipped his head at the sound of his mother's worried voice, then back to the army bearing down on them. Every natural instinct and rational thought told Nat they were doomed. Nevertheless, deep within, the Spirit yet spoke His tranquil assurance.

"We stand on the side of Elyon and all that is right," Nat asserted. "He shall not fail us now."

"I hope you're right, Nat," Nida replied, "Or the Empire may well wipe Endego off the map, and us along with it."

Chapter Two

The Depths of Deliverance

"To arms! The enemy is coming! To arms!"

The battle cry resounded throughout Sanctuary Endego as Etom scurried to secure their defenses. Meanwhile, down near the pool surrounding the Tree, Nat knelt with eyes closed to dip his fingertips into the sacred waters. As the etém sought the will of the Spirit, Sayah stood beside him, ever the vigilant guardian to his friend, who was closer to him than any sibling.

From the edge of the clearing, Rae pelted toward them, her long and oft-buoyant pink zalzal now gathered back into a thick and manageable braid.

"Nat!" she cried, "What are you doing down here? The Empire's coming, and you don't even have a weapon!"

Nat's face remained serene except for a gentle, lopsided smile as he tarried there. Rae drew a sharp breath to shout again but caught herself when Nat arose to face her.

"Rae, would you do me a favor?" Nat inquired, his voice low and steady.

A confused frown on her face, Rae nodded, "Of course, Nat. But make it quick! If you didn't notice, there *is* an army on the way to destroy us after all."

Nat nodded, "I know. I know. That's why I need your help. We need to gather the others here right away."

"Here?" she asked, incredulous. The pool was the least-defensible position they had, and most Etom had headed for the relative safety of the trees.

"Yes, here," he answered, then turned to Sayah. "I'll need your help, too. Will you both trust in Lord Elyon with me?"

The Spirit resonated through Nat's words and in answer, the ægle offered a short nod, then sprang into the air, the beat of his wings almost toppling his smaller friends.

Once aloft, Sayah began to cry, "To the Tree! To the Tree! Everyone gather at the Tree!"

The ægle circled the bower, repeating the proclamation, and Nat returned his attention to Rae, who yet stood at Nat's side, her eyes wide.

With a gentle glance, Nat pleaded, "Please, Rae. I don't quite understand either, but I need your help."

"Okay," she answered, "Where do you need me?"

"You bring everyone from the east side of the clearing," he waved in the direction from which she'd come. "I'll take the west side."

"Will do!" she responded, dashing off at once.

As Rae sprinted away, Nat called after her, "And see if anyone else will help you! We need everyone here! NOW!!!"

Without breaking stride, she extended an upraised thumb high overhead and began shouting for the attention of any Etom nearby. Nat, meanwhile, set off on a tour of the bower's west side, likewise clamoring for all to join him at the edge of the pool as soon as they were able.

In a stroke of providence, Nat encountered Blithewit and Whisperweave near the Üntfither. On their backs, the pair of foxes carried a contingent of sentries from the edge of the village. Nat hailed them as they crossed the Üntfither with an agile leap.

"Hey there!" Nat shouted, waving a hand for their attention.

With lithe, vulpine grace, the foxes diverted to intercept the young etém, Blithewit calling ahead as they approached, "Nat! What are you up to? Why aren't you with the others?"

Nat came to a stop and explained, "I'm calling everyone to the Tree, and could use a hand, or a paw, if you will. I believe Elyon intends to stand in our defense."

The foxes were new to the Kinship of the Vine but had already experience enough in the Spirit to discern His resonant call.

Without delay, Whisperweave heeded Nat's youthful voice and stooped to ascertain how they might be of use, "How can we help, Nat?"

"If you help carry Etom to the Tree, that would be great," Nat suggested. "You might want to look first for those too elderly or too frail to get there without assistance."

Nat called up to address the foxes' passengers, "You lot could hop down to spread the word around the clearing!"

"On our way!" Blithewit agreed, who let his riders down before bounding away.

Nat continued his circuit of the bower and before long, a perplexed multitude stood clustered at water's edge near the foot of the Tree.

While ever more trickled in, Nat returned and addressed those already assembled, "Listen! I know you're uncertain why I've called you here, but I assure you I have good reason."

The Spirit enriched and amplified Nat's piping, childish tones to carry his words over and through the crowd.

"Just minutes ago, I knelt at this shore to seek the will of our Creator, and I believe He has responded. I don't understand His entire plan, but I know He desires we trust Him. Let all who are in the Vine now enter these waters. Let us celebrate His goodness with the confidence He will again supply our salvation as He has in the past."

A murmur arose from the crowd, and some complained against Nat's proposal. Regardless, in that moment the Spirit spoke to many hearts. Those who listened accepted Nat's words, and began to shuffle down into the water with Rae's parents, Nida and Dempsey leading the way. The resistant few, finding difficulty in again entrusting their fate to Lord Elyon, nevertheless broke free from their stubborn fixtures along the shore to join those wading into the water.

Nat surveyed the scant group that remained outside the water, Iver and Pikrïa among them, and advised, "The rest of you may remain in the bower, though I recommend you move to the far side of the pool, away from Empire's forces."

These grumbled yet relocated as Nat had suggested while he scrambled down to join the others. He soon took his place among the members of the Vine, who formed a great ring in the water, waist-deep to an Etom. On one side he held Rae's hand, and on the other, Sayah draped a shining, silvery wing over his shoulder. The growing rumble of the approaching army sent shuddering waves across the otherwise placid surface of the pool, and those gathered looked to Nat.

The young, pale blue etém released Rae's hand to kneel in the water, which came now to his chest. Without hesitation the other Etom followed suit while Sayah, Whisperweave, and Blithewit inclined their heads in reverence.

Nat clasped his hands together, bowed his head, and began to pray.

"Before You, our Lord Elyon, we bow. You are Father of us all, and the namesake of every creature and kind in heaven above and on the earth below. According to the vast abundance of Your glory, we pray You grant us strength through Your Spirit, Who resides within us as a comforting presence that we may know the Kinsman, Gaal.

"So that, rooted and grounded in Your love like this great Tree, we together are able to understand just how wide and how long, how high and how deep. Reveal to us the love of Your Son, the Kinsman to us all, so our comprehension sails beyond simply knowing and into the promised land of Your fullness so that we may be filled."

"To our great and mighty Creator, able to accomplish more than we might ask or imagine in proportion to the power of Your Spirit working among us, be the splendor of the Kinsman and of His Tree from which we in the Vine depend as mere branches. For all ages of this world and those beyond, may it ever be so!"

Nat, who faced the western edge of Sanctuary Endego toward the Üntfither, raised shining, golden eyes to see the tawny forms of ravenous wolves on swift approach through the trees. Flashes of orange and flickers of white among the underbrush revealed foxes not far behind. With a gentle nudge, the Spirit directed Nat's gaze to where the overflow of Sanctuary's waters met the Üntfither, and overhead, the sunlight radiance of the day grew brighter and purer.

Though none heard the words with natural sense, those in the Vine nonetheless caught a single phrase, and the water shook with its unlabored might, *How wide.*

Without a splash, the waters of the pool transmitted the will behind the words to the Üntfither, which stretched at once into the distant North and South, a sudden and quiet broadening of the waters beyond the limits of even Sayah's vision.

Indeed, the ægle's cousins in the far North, the bearded vultures, were surprised at the sudden appearance of a narrow, shining ribbon at the foot of the Cold Vantage. The Kinship gaped about in wonder, and as Nat looked across the Üntfither where the marauding Beasts were scant yards off, he thought he saw a flash of doubt cross their threatening eyes.

But then the wolves were closing, their lank limbs splashing through the Üntfither while the Kinship brandished arms and braced for battle.

Again, the shimmering waters, now a lengthy channel, shuddered at a second utterance, *How long.*

Though they felt no movement, Kinship and Tree with eerie speed receded from the Üntfither's western banks, the crystalline waters stretching to place a serene and shimmering sheet a near-mile across between them and their foes. Looking about once more in awe, they saw the channel had become a sea that stretched North and South into the horizon and split the village of Endego in two.

In the distant North, Hollowback and the rest of her bearded ilk squawked from the Cold Vantage, alarmed at the great silver beam that split the world below in two.

Back in Endego, the activities of the enemy were clear to none but Sayah at such a distance. The ægle, standing tall with focused gaze locked on the eastern shore, reported to the others as his sight enabled him.

"They've stopped at the water's edge. They all look spooked, but a large, black wolf, their leader I think, is sniffing at the water. Now he's dipped a forepaw in."

After a brief delay, Sayah growled in frustration, "Argh! He's alright!"

"I was kind of hoping something dreadful might happen to him," the ægle whispered to Nat in an aside, then returned to his duty, the Kinship hanging on his every word.

"They're advancing again!" Sayah shouted. "Seems the water's no deeper than it is here. Might slow them a bit, but..."

An agitated voice hectored them from behind, "What good is all this water if they can just splash on through? It's no more than a great puddle!"

Nat turned to address the complaint and was less than shocked to discover its source was Iver. Pikrïa stood at the angry orange etém's side, her eyes bulging in disbelief at the wondrous spectacle that had divided not Endego alone, but the entire visible world.

Nat spoke up for all to hear his answer, his voice calm and confident though sparkling, joyful tears streamed down his face, "We've just begun to see the deliverance of Lord Elyon. Let us not lose our confidence in Him who sent His own Son to perish in our stead. He is not done with us yet!"

Heads nodded among the Kinship and joyful cries of agreement arose. The reaction amongst Iver's cohort was muted by comparison, but at least they fell silent in their grumbling.

The members of the Vine turned to face their enemies, and in a low voice, Dempsey started to sing. The others picked up the verse until their chorus rang out across the water,

"Elyon is our Sanctuary and our strength,
a presence of succor in our affliction.
Therefore, we take courage,
He alone is our courage.

"Though the ground beneath us falls away,
and mountains are cast into the depths.
Even if the ocean roars and seethes,
and the peaks shake at its surging,
yet I will take heart.
Yes, still I will take heart."

Across the expanse, Sayah spied a raptorial legion take wing over the enemy camp, and his keening cry cut through the melody, "Aerial forces inbound!"

For a moment, their song faltered, and some suggested they take to the Tree to fend off the flyers.

Stand firm, the Spirit spoke.

Dempsey rallied them with cheer, "Let us sing, you Kinship of the Vine!"

And picking up where they had left off, they renewed their praise,

"There is a river in whose streams
delight the children of our Lord,
that holy abode of Elyon.

"His presence fills those who are His,
and they will not be moved.
No, they will not be moved!

"Though empires rage,
and nations totter,
the world melts at His word,

"'Still your heart, and know that I am Elyon,
revered through all creation,
and worshipped to the ends of the earth!'"

Although into silence their song fell, their spirits rose, and, thus enheartened, Nat nodded to Sayah for an update.

"Advance ground forces are maybe halfway across with most all the main force now in the water," the ægle reported, his voice steady and serious.

Peering now into the sky, Sayah evaluated the approaching raptors, "Several casts of kestrels at the forefront with a loose convocation of ægles right behind. The kestrels are flying a tight formation and look disciplined. I would guess they're the better-trained and more dangerous of the lot."

"Doesn't surprise me the ægles aren't in formation," he added. "Most are just too independent for it."

The brilliant white ægle gasped, and Nat guessed at the reason, "Is it your family?"

Lowering his head in sorrow, the ægle responded in a shaky voice, "Yes, Nat. Mother and Father are with them, though I don't see Gael."

"I'm sorry," Nat offered, unsure what else he might say.

Sayah straightened, his tone once again steady as he cautioned, "The raptors are closing fast. They'll be here well ahead of the main force."

Nat nodded, then looked up at the Tree, its strong limbs spread wide and swaying in the breeze while its leaves, ever green, rustled peacefully. The fierce cry of an enemy kestrel tore the tranquil sky high overhead, and Nat discerned the arrow shapes of enemy formations as they tipped downward, taking aim at the Kinship. Behind them, the ægles one by one furled their wings, rolling over with lazy grace to begin their diving raid.

Beside Nat, Rae squeaked, but did not shriek, and the congregation took a collective breath as they anticipated the onslaught.

How high!

The Spirit's words stirred the leaves, which fluttered in a sky devoid of wind. Then the first branch struck out at a swooping chevron of feathered forms, jabbing at the kestrels where they flew. The gnarled shaft knocked two members of the lead formation out of the sky, reducing the remnant to a cackling mess that flapped and fluttered in panicked evasion of the forking branches as they sprouted from the bough in pursuit of the attackers.

Then the Tree exploded in every direction, branches waving and foliage swatting at the airborne figures as they struggled to escape. Several fell into the surrounding water with a splash a fair distance from the Kinship, and many did not move after. A few, however, arose and with feeble limps, hobbled away in retreat.

From where they stood beneath the swelling Tree, Nat, Rae, and Sayah marveled up at the network of branches. Before their eyes the Tree had grown to form a verdant lattice that threatened to crowd out the heavens. With such a shield before them, none might approach them from the sky, and though they might have tried, the remaining raptors at last surrendered in defeat, unwilling to hazard the bower's defenses.

The crowd of tiny Etom and their few larger friends shouted with victory. Even Iver and his bunch stared in amazement at what they'd witnessed, Pikrïa included. Nevertheless, Nat looked to the army that marched toward them, the elephantine rearguard of their forces now well along their way through the shallows.

In the defense Elyon had mounted on their behalf, Nat sensed now the answer to his earlier prayer. Elyon's actions to this point cast a looming shadow over those who aggressed against His children, and while he felt no fear for himself or the Kinship, Nat was filled with dread for their foes.

Alongside the foreboding yet in Nat's mind, the Spirit planted two words, *How deep.*

Without warning, the shallow sea became fathomless depths, and the whole of the enemy's forces slipped all at once beneath the water. They had neither opportunity to cry out nor to struggle against the plunge, and heavy arms bore them down, down, down into the darkening deep.

The Spirit sighed in sorrow and relief, His breath a wind that stirred the Tree, which in a blink retracted to usual proportions. Without delay, the westward shore returned, and likewise the pool's former northern and southern limits were restored.

In the stillness of the aftermath, not one in the bower dared to move. With eyes open and unblinking, each one pondered the fearsome nature of their Protector.

Chapter Three
Aftershock

In the somber silence following the eradication of their enemies, the Kinship did not stir. None found expression sufficient either to celebrate the magnitude of Elyon's intervention or to mourn those sent to destroy them. The Creator had unleashed His might on their behalf, and they were grateful even as they wondered at the fate of their foes.

"What was *that*?!?" Pikrïa shrieked, her usual patrician demeanor disintegrating under unusual circumstances.

Nida turned to face her Great Aunt and responded, "Today, you have seen the power of Lord Elyon, Maker of heaven and earth. In defense of His children, He has waged war against the Empire. Quite successfully, I might add."

In her uncertainty, Pikrïa could only gape. In her youth, bitterness had first seasoned the outpouring of her heart, its petty, spiteful savor likewise tinging her confidence in the Creator.

Like a stubborn mule yanking against Elyon's gentle and persuasive hands, Pikrïa's unbelief had carted any semblance of faith away, keeping the hopeful prisoner captive at a safe distance, ever out of reach. Today, however, the Creator's grasp had lengthened to take hold of her recalcitrant bridle in one hand, while with the other He held forth the promise of miraculous deliverance as a pleasant and alluring aroma.

Furthermore, though Pikrïa had anticipated the dismay with which Nida had greeted her, she had also expected a great deal of hostility. But the absence of Nida's animosity had given Pikrïa pause.

Determined to shield herself from the pain of familial affection, Pikrïa had laid brick by spiteful, wounded brick until the crypt in which she'd sealed herself was complete. Nat's enthusiastic welcome had cracked the foundations of her tomb, and not in a long, long while had light reached its dank interior. With the warm glow of a sunbeam, Nat's arms had encircled her, evoking within the bitter old etma sweet memories of young Nida doing the same.

Pikrïa found it peculiar that neither Nida nor Nat had offered any vitriol, though in her shrewd estimation it would have been warranted. Indeed, Pikrïa had braced herself against their hostility, fletching in advance a quiver of pointed insults for retaliation.

Instead, Nida had just expressed an interest in catching up, and Nat had greeted her with sincere excitement, having heard "so many wonderful things" from Nida. Not a list of past offenses or a record of wrongs. Not a jagged and resentful recollection of hardships at Pikrïa's hand. Just "wonderful things."

Her darts blunted by the kindness shown her, Pikrïa had faltered in her tactics, and Nat's arms around her had disarmed her of all but fusty indignation at his familiarity. To pull herself together and dart away had been all she could do. And, now, this – undeniable proof that something or someone had intervened to save all their lives. The elderly etma was for once grateful that her Blighted mask concealed her emotions.

"What is this rubbish you speak?" Iver mocked in answer of Nida's assertions.

The scene had stunned him as well, if for but a moment. Now he'd recovered himself and intended to enact his plan.

"Elyon's children?" he asked, incredulous. "And what have you done to earn the right to call yourselves *His* children?"

"We've done nothing," Nida retorted, "and there's nothing we or any other could do to earn such a privilege. We've merely received the gift He offers us here: Freedom from the Stain. Unity with Him by His Spirit and in the Vine. A life transformed in the abundance He offers.

"Why! He even welcomes *you* to receive this gift, Iver!"

"Yes! Please, Iver!" Dempsey beckoned from beside Nida.

He opened a canary hand, waving it over the water in invitation, "Please. We'd love for you to join us."

Momentary misgiving flitted across Iver's eyes before he narrowed them in suspicion and rebuffed, "No, thank you. Seems in all your bathing here, you've washed away all your sense as well. I know the prophecies. If this Kinsman you proclaim has come, then where is He? Shouldn't He be leading us against the Empire? Taking up His rightful crown? Hmmm? Again, I ask, where is He?"

Breaking from sober meditation at last, Sayah lifted a shy gaze to Iver and in a still, small voice explained, "Wherever two or three come together in His name, there will He be, too, present in authority as King, for *we* are His crown."

"Ugh!" Iver exclaimed in disgust.

Covering his ears, the brick-faced etém grumbled, "How can you stand that bird's infernal squawking?"

Nat patted Sayah's alabaster side to reassure his friend, in truth unsure if Iver couldn't comprehend the ægle's words. In hindsight, he couldn't recall an instance when the two had direct interaction. Shrugging off uncertainty, he chose to encourage his friend.

"Don't listen to him, Sayah" he consoled, then looking around the gathering he shouted, "We all heard you just fine, didn't we?"

"That we did!" came the response, this time from forthright if not eccentric Hezi. "And you speak truth, brother!"

Eyes boggling once more, Pikrïa restrained the cry of amazement that threatened to pass her lips. She'd heard the bird *speak*! The ægle, shining in the dappling drift of sunlight streaming through the canopy, had answered Iver, though the orange etém seemed incapable of comprehending the noble words.

The wasting dowager's mind spun in dizzying circuits, each revolution freighted with the significance of not just the message, but of the messenger, and of its means of delivery.

Where am *I?* she wondered, seeing as with eyes unveiled the peculiarity of their setting, and of the assembly therein.

Here rested a pair of foxes, there the strange white ægle (and who had ever seen a pure white ægle?), and about the clearing any number of Etom familiar from passing acquaintance. Besides these, however, a great many stood out, their exotic dress and coloration uncommon to the region marking them as likely foreigners in Endego. And not a hint of Stain on a one of them outside Iver's surly lot.

Moreover, the Tree around which they rallied was unlike any she'd ever seen, and seemed to exude a light of its own, distinct from the sunlight even at midday. Strangest of all was the stream of water that poured as a fountain from the crux of its great boughs to form the mirror-sheen pool that surrounded the base of the nut-brown trunk. A substantial tributary ran from the pool to the Üntfither nearby, and beyond the confluence grass, flower, and tree grew tall, green, and vital alongside the stream whereas the landscape withered in the latening fall.

Denial raged in impotence, its rancor growing distant while a sweet whisper beckoned Pikrïa near. Brittle doubts creaked under the weight of childhood memory, the ancient tales of Gan in all its harmonious vitality pressing hard against the bulwark of her incredulity.

A golden recollection stood illumined in Pikrïa's mind – a moment of wonder in her fourth or fifth year that followed a governess' recitation of such a story. Pikrïa's young, tender heart had sensed the affection of her Creator in the understanding that she was *His* creature. Just one creature among a great many, yet somehow special and lovely in His sight.

Oh! How she had wished for the paradise of Gan in that instant. To know her Creator and commune with Him! As with the fierce, unyielding grip of a hatchling's plump fist, she had seized on the hopeful desire. After many years deferred, this hope, and that abandoned in her estrangement from Shoym, nonetheless contributed to the sickening of her heart.

Yet today as she looked around the bower, her old eyes perceived glimmers of that old hope, ascendant as a twinkling star and reflected in the gazes of these peculiar folk. Until, that is, her eyes met those which did not merely shine with such a light, but blazed forth in a radiance that staggered Pikrïa, leaving her breathless.

Shoym! What is he doing here? she wondered.

Indeed, the elderly gentletém stood mere steps from Nat and Nida, his ashen cheeks smoldering with the intensity of cooling lava. The excitement that suffused him when he recognized Pikrïa was evident in the blood that now suffused his countenance.

Unable to contain himself, Shoym took a quick step toward her and called, "Pikrïa?!? Is that truly...you?"

Past the trees of Endego, the surviving airwing of the Empire descended over the neat pavilions of their encampment. In silence, the kestrels exchanged glances across the worried skies that separated their now scant formations. Behind them, what remained of the ægles glided onward with eyes fixed dead ahead, their characteristic cool indifference displaced by vexation manifest in frowning brows.

At the start of their so-called engagement, their wing commander, a kestrel named Pennaflot, had been knocked out of the sky, a thrusting limb breaking both her wings and a leg all at once. Floundering in the shallow water, she'd had no chance once the depths had swallowed her and her unfortunate comrades. Then the earth itself had seemed to pave them over, and all those surviving in the sky counted themselves fortunate to have escaped, though they were beyond shaken at what had occurred.

Neither did the few left in authority look forward to offering an explanation to Imafel, for they were uncertain just what had happened. No doubt their Nihúkolem overlord would be unhappy at any such report they gave and might destroy them on the spot.

Sayah would have been happy to know that his parents, Windspanne and Stromweise, were among these, though their survival now was dubious. As the pair fell in along with the rest on their way to Imafel, they wished now they'd been able to distance themselves from this whole mess.

One small blessing that comforted the ægles during their probable deathmarch was the knowledge that Sayah and Gael yet lived. Sayah they had both seen for themselves on their failed assault, and each in secret had marveled at his transformation.

They had heard Gael's ravings when she'd returned from her reconnaissance of the enemy. Their daughter had come back to them unbalanced, her mind teetering on the edge of sanity while with the unblinking certainty of a lunatic she related what she'd seen. For the implausibility of her report, Her parents might be forgiven their skepticism thereof, a skepticism they shared with Imafel.

The Nihúkolem had growled in disappointment when Gael presented herself but chose not to eradicate her. Instead, he sent her far West to a prison post where for all her instability she might still be of some use.

Memory joined the flow of current circumstance as they assembled before Imafel in the confines of his tent. He'd yet to recover his form entire, though he stood with his back to them in relative completeness but for his head. And meanwhile, the slow click of the ebon grit that constituted his physique continued as individual grains slipped upward along his form to take their places atop the stump of his neck.

"Report," Imafel commanded, his voice lazy.

He was growing weary of his post at this backwater and resentful that none of his peers had been likewise assigned. His irritation increased as he sensed Mūk-Mudón, Belláphorus and Cloust turn their attention to the conversation at hand.

Stöttcrest, a gruff and greying male kestrel and the vanquished wing commander's second, stood forward, "Sir! It appears the enemy has...unanticipated resources. We lost nearly half our wing, including Commander Pennaflot."

His headless form whirling to face them, Imafel demanded, "Indeed? And what cause have you to return, then? Would it not have been better to perish alongside your comrades on the ground than to suffer this disgrace?"

Aware their fates might well turn on his answer, Stöttcrest paused in thought, then responded, "That's just it, milord. *All* the Empire's forces are destroyed. We alone survive."

Conscious that Cloust, Belláphorus and Mūk-Mudón observed the interchange, Imafel was embarrassed at the unthinkable losses suffered under his command.

All present perceived his agitation in the buzzing, static intensity with which he exclaimed, "All! ALL?!? Do you mean to tell me that none of our ground force survived? And what of the enemy's casualties? Surely, at such a heavy cost, we must have decimated them!"

"Sir, we can't account for a single enemy casualty," came the meek reply. "They were ...untouchable."

A sudden, stifling stagnation replaced Imafel's earlier turbulence as he seethed through his shame, "How? How did this happen?"

"I don't know that I can right describe it, milord," Stöttcrest answered, spreading plaintive wings.

The swelling rasp of Imafel's ire proved sufficient goad nonetheless and the kestrel stammered, "Tha-that is, I will do my best, sir.

"All was according to battle plan at the start. As designated, we kestrels flew formation at the lead with the ægles at the back, and we were on schedule to reach the enemy before the troops on the ground. Our orders were to engage the enemy before the main force and throw the enemy into disarray. The swiftest on the ground, foxes, wolves and the like, had similar orders.

"When we alit from camp, we knew right away something was out of place – what seemed a narrow river appeared, running through the village and from North to South as far as the eye could see, straight as a beam. Next thing you know, it was a lake a mile wide, and Alpha Wolf was at the shore sniffing around."

"Something right strange was brewing, but, no matter, Alpha Wolf took to the water in a flash with all the packs behind him. From how our troops just splashed on through, the water looked no deeper'n a puddle, so we just stuck to the plan. We'd be there a bit before the wolves and all, but didn't think anything of it, considering our enemy's forces."

Stöttcrest shook his sorry head side to side and lowered his gaze to the ground in reflection before continuing, "We couldn't have been more wrong. We arrived at the Tree before the others were even halfway across the water and descended to engage."

The old bird looked up at Imafel to plead, "Please, sir, what I'm about to tell you sounds unbelievable. I cannot believe it myself, but the rest here can testify to it, too."

Despite his famished patience, Imafel suffered his subordinate, "I assure you I will hear you out. Now, do tell."

A touch emboldened, the kestrel recounted, "We were almost within striking distance ourselves when the Tree struck out at *us*! It was all branches and leaves poking and swinging to bat us out of the sky. That's how we lost the Commander. Would've lost the whole wing if she hadn't sounded the retreat from where she'd fallen in the drink."

For the kestrel's kind, no greater nightmare existed than being grounded, bound to the earth. The thought of so many spattering about the water below brought the instinctive horror he'd felt at the time swirling back to mind and paralyzing him in a cyclone of terror. Unaware of his own transfixion, Stöttcrest fell silent.

"Well?" Imafel growled, "then what happened?"

Shaking his head at the counter-shock of Imafel's voice, the kestrel, his eyes blank and unfocused, began anew, "Yes, sir. Yes, sir. Where was I? Ah! That's right.

"We turned when Commander Pennaflot called the retreat, looking to get some distance between us and that Tree. I was confident we'd be able to slip back in to recover our injured, but before we could, the rest of our ground troops were in the water. And that was the end for them. All of 'em."

Imafel raised a sooty, querulous hand to ask, "Wait. What? What do you mean 'that was the end?' What happened? Explain yourself, soldier!"

"That's just it, sir. They disappeared under the water. Every last one. In an instant. Like the puddle all at once turned as deep as an ocean, and then the world closed back over them like they'd never been there. Just...gone. You wouldn't know an army had ever even been there but for the grass they'd flattened along the way."

Imafel brooded in seeming silence while in he awaited Mūk-Mudón's reaction, the tension of the moment straining like an archer against his bowstring awaiting release.

At last, Imafel addressed the collection of raptors, his tone now flat and perfunctory, "You are dismissed for now. Set watch over the camp and keep an eye on the enemy. I'll have orders for you later."

With a smart bow, the relieved Stöttcrest replied, "Sir! Yes, sir!"

At once, the kestrel led the grateful procession away while Imafel returned to his inner conference with the other Nihúkolem.

Belláphorus, upset his plan had failed, expressed his disappointment, *If these birds are to be trusted, who could have predicted such a defense? It's unheard of!*

This development is most peculiar, Cloust offered. *What do you suppose is the source of this strange power?*

Mūk-Mudón growled, his reluctance to converse betraying a foul mood. Not that his generals were surprised.

Imafel, his injured vanity somewhat assuaged in the shared puzzlement of the others, speculated, *All our difficulties seem to arise from that Tree. Could it be...?*

His interest piqued at last, Mūk-Mudón interjected, *Yes? What is it, Imafel?*

The Tree, milord, Imafel explained, *Not this one, but if you'll recall the Kinsman's execution. Could there be some connection?*

All at once, Mūk-Mudón went from interested to dismissive, *And what connection could there possibly be? That wood was involved in both cases? I see no relation at all!*

Certainly, milord, Imafel deferred.

He, Cloust, and Belláphorus noted Mūk-Mudón's sudden evasiveness and wondered to themselves what their glorious Emperor might be hiding. The whole business of the Kinsman had troubled them from the start, but only because Mūk-Mudón had insisted that His murder would liberate them all from their restless existence. Yet, here they were, still in service to His Majesty's caprice. Imafel decided at once to investigate the matter further but determined to keep his own counsel until he had something of import to share with Cloust and Belláphorus.

And what are your orders regarding Endego? Imafel inquired. *I presume another assault is out of the question. Would you have me station a squad in the area to report on the enemy's movements?*

Mūk-Mudón was inattentive but replied with a grunt in the affirmative before disappearing from their shared awareness, no doubt to confer with his dark patron.

Cloust and Belláphorus were anxious to press Imafel for details, but he quelled them with a preemptive declaration.

I am as curious as you two are and will lead a small force to investigate the site of the Kinsman's execution.

What do you suppose he's hiding? Cloust asked.

Belláphorus sniffed, then grunted, *Whatever it is must be significant, given Mooks' reaction.*

Imafel barked in unexpected laughter at the reemergence of the old nickname, while Cloust snickered. None of them had referred to Mūk-Mudón in such familiar terms since his ascendancy from mere Warlord to The Western Sorrel. Time, however, had tarnished the patina of Mūk-Mudón's mysterious charisma. Likewise, the three generals cared much for the Man he'd been, but little for the obvious charade he presented them now.

The slight insubordination felt good, and tame enough that the three savored it without worry it might develop into disloyalty. Thenceforth and by tacit agreement, they renewed "Mooks" as Mūk-Mudón's moniker in their private gatherings. Even as they departed their shared psychic space, it served as a small insurgency to remind Belláphorus, Imafel and Cloust of the freedom they'd once enjoyed. The complication of such freedom, however, is its flavor – a taste acquired with ease and quite intoxicating, even in small measure among those who have long gone without.

Though in his vanity Imafel was disappointed that his form remained incomplete, he nonetheless took pleasure in learning he was again capable of that mode of travel common to the Nihúkolem, his dissolute being propelled by the power of the air. With some hesitation and within the private confines of his tent, he had tested his capability. He hoped at last to leave this backwater, to him a confluence of disasters that had conspired against him and his forces.

Though their defeat was shameful, naught remained to do in Endego for the time being, and Imafel at his departure felt relief and an eagerness to revisit the place of the Kinsman's execution. The headless hunter swept about the camp issuing orders, for once more excited than agitated while the keen sense of interest percolated within him. Decades had passed since anything had so intrigued him.

Command had fallen in natural order to Stöttcrest, who earlier represented the airwing before Imafel, and it was to him that Imafel entrusted a small squad for continued surveillance of the village Endego and its troublesome inhabitants.

In his musings, two particular raptors had come to Imafel's mind, a faint memory triggering their selection to accompany him on his journey northward. Recollection had served to earmark the pair, Windspanne and Stromweise, notable not just for their distinctive progeny, Gael, but also for their recruitment from the region where they'd slain the Kinsman. Imafel suspected the far-sighted ægles might know the very spot for their acquaintance with the area.

Concern that the distant reassignment of their daughter might impact their enthusiasm traversed Imafel's callous mind, and he came close to dismissing the thought. Upon reconsideration, Imafel nonetheless determined that their disappointment might well be the fulcrum he leveraged into zeal. Perhaps tossing the token promise of Gael's return onto the balance might even make them grateful for the opportunity. Not everything ought to proceed from high-handed demand, and Imafel felt a tad magnanimous from the warm and lingering conviviality shared with Cloust and Belláphorus.

Though the flurry of their activity never ceased, kestrel and ægle alike shared startled glances when Imafel struck up a tune. So disconcerting was Imafel's good cheer as he flitted about the near-deserted camp humming an old hunting song of the Hadza that his subordinates made several blunders. Even more wondrous was the fact Imafel either failed to notice or neglected to punish their mistakes, and the group scrambled to the assistance of those responsible to ensure it remained so.

Per Imafel's earlier consideration, the pair of ægles pounced at the opportunity to assist him in his search, their helpfulness increasing in good measure after learning their performance might earn Gael's swift return. For all their seeming indifference toward their offspring, Windspanne and Stromweise displayed concern through this, their earnest desire to complete their assignment and see Gael home safe.

Besides the diminished airwing, a few Men and pack animals were all that was left of the great army the Empire of Chōl had assembled against the wee denizens of Sanctuary Endego. These were the logistics and support division, responsible for transportation of equipment, meal preparation, medical care, and other sundry items. A few of their number, most of them medics, had been engulfed with the other lost souls, leaving the better part of their division intact to dismantle and transport the encampment back to garrison.

Amidst the bustle of the activity, the kestrels and ægles sorting and reorganizing for their reassignment and the rest breaking camp, Imafel departed with Windspanne and Stromweise. The Nihúkolem swept northward from among the tented pavilions, trailing dark, gritty tendrils as he bounded up into the air, then burst into a dense and swirling black cloud.

Reduced now to a dank and airborne stream carried skyward on the wind, Imafel sped on his mission, flanked on either side by the swift, raptorial forms of the ægles. Imafel was well aware that Mūk-Mudón might be watching and hoped he might find some clue before the Emperor noticed. Windspanne and Stromweise meanwhile flew in silent contemplation of their duty and reward with just the lonely whistle of the wind in their ears.

Chapter Four
Duties of the Living

In yonder western wildlands, at the edge of a dank and tangled wood beyond which lay the sea, the sunrise blush caressed a rusty cage hanging from the branch of a great and twisted tree. The cage itself was just large enough for a small bird, its base a rough circle of hard wood. Its walls consisted of several vertical flat iron strips bent inward to form a dome. Three bands of iron encircled the cage at regular intervals to give it an overall cylindrical form but for its rounded top.

Whence the strips met at the top of the cage, a corroded hook protruded to loop through the last links at either end of a likewise degenerate chain wrapped around the bough. All about the dilapidated enclosure, creeping vines had taken hold, their long, lank tendrils twisting down from the limb overhead to drape the pen in irregular green ribbons.

In the pleasant morning breeze, the cage swung and twisted in mellow convolutions, its various aged joints creaking and verdant skirt swishing with the easy motion. Around two sunward slats, a pair of small hands protruded, curling dark blue fingers about the rusty frame. Out of the cage's shady interior, a face of matching color emerged to reveal an etém, rather unkempt in his captivity. With eyes closed, the small and scruffy prisoner pressed his cheeks against the slats on either side of the gap, seeking the greatest measure of warmth and light.

The etém's skin was the blue of deepest sapphire seas, though after a moment in the sunlight, his cheeks and forehead flushed a deep plum. From the instant he appeared, a contented smile had curved his lips. The smile broke just long enough for the etém to utter a long and satisfied sigh, then returned at once.

At last, the captive opened eyes red as candied apples to scan the eastern sky. He hadn't eaten since evening the day before, when his warden had last delivered a meal, and his stomach growled in anticipation of breaking the fast. Hunger notwithstanding, the smile yet graced his countenance, and his good-natured forbearance was soon rewarded when he spied a distant silhouette traversing the sky.

With a practiced hand, he pulled from the front of his tattered vest a dented brass pocket watch. The watch had a been a gift from his best friend, given at their separation, and his friend would have parted with it for no other, for it had belonged to his father before him. An enduring token of their brotherly affection, the pocket watch yet told the time through a crystal that remained as clear as ever, despite its battered case. He slipped it away again to await the arrival of his visitor.

Before long, the captor's cry met the prisoner's ears, and the etém chose to interpret the ægle's petulant shriek as a friendly salutation. A ragged cluster of grapes depended from one of the ægle's talons as she swooped toward him, her wings spread wide and cupped to slow her descent.

The ægle banged into the top of the cage, sending it swinging in wild arcs, and the etém was happy he'd gripped the slats in advance. He'd been taken by surprise by the ægle's arrival before and still had the bruises to prove it. The ache of these earlier encounters added to that of his exertion as he gripped the cage to avoid further injury.

Once the cage had regained a relative equilibrium, the etém exhaled in loud relief and released his hold to look up at his visitor. Overhead, the ægle gripped the top of the cage with one talon while with the other she shoved grapes through the narrow gaps in the frame, in the process bursting most of the half dozen or so that she had brought.

A wee, solitary ellipsoid survived intact, falling at the captive's feet amidst the slimy mishmash of grape flesh yet raining down around him. Unperturbed at the callous disregard the ægle demonstrated for his meal, the etém waved at the bird, expressing sunny gratitude for the delivery. Given the language barrier, he knew it might be a futile gesture, but offered it just the same.

"Thank you!"

In response, the ægle glowered at the prisoner with predatory greed, her desire to consume him apparent.

The way her pathetic Etom prisoner greeted her during each visit irked Gael, whose temper already stood on edge at her assignment here to these backwoods of the Empire. Perhaps it was his demeanor, uncowed in Gael's presence, that irritated her and reminded her of another of these bugs, and a blue one at that. Furthermore, she'd yet to taste Etom flesh, and though her duty was to the continued survival of this insignificant insect, she considered it fortuitous for both of them that the cage prevented her access as much as it did his escape.

So, in lieu of sating her ravenous hunger on the little blue beast's flesh, Gael had resigned herself to rattling his cage upon arrival each visit. But the clever thing had figured out her game, and now braced himself against the wall every time she came. Her instinctive antagonism for smaller creatures was disappointed, though on some level, Gael respected the Etom for his fortitude and courage.

The etém tried again, "Thank you, friend! May Lord Elyon bless you for your kindness!"

Gael did not begrudge the critter his desire to avoid injury and thought it odd he continued to attempt communication with her, given the great divide separating their kinds. Nevertheless, it was clear his overtures were friendly, which just added to her annoyance. And something in his last statement, unintelligible though it was to her, sparked her already short fuse. Gael's claws gripped the cage ever tighter, the rusted joints and rivets complaining under the strain. Still, the deep blue etém below just looked up, that stupid smile on his face. That smile...

Gael's fury flared, and her wings exploded in a flurry, her talons shaking the cage in wild whipsaw. Her captive bounced around the enclosure, his body careening about in a battered ball, and the one intact grape flew out the side of the cage with the slop she'd made of the rest. Gael's sharp eyes spotted a single, substantial droplet of blood as it arced out of the cage, and her better sense at last took over to quell her rage. If the prisoner died, then so would she.

The ægle's rage now subsiding, she breathed shaky, adrenaline-laden breaths and peered through the vine-entangled cage at her prisoner's still form. Gael was familiar with all manner of corpses, and this Etom did not sprawl as one dead. Instead, he held himself curled on one side in a protective position, blood trickling from various wounds about his body. He held himself thus for several long moments, and Gael would have questioned her initial assessment but for the slow undulation of the Etom's breathing that her keen vision detected.

Regardless, the ægle began to wonder if her captive hadn't succumbed to some grievous injury that had left him in a swoon so profound he might as well have been dead. The conjecture generated concern equal to that over the creature's death, and Gael dipped her head, pressing the side of her head against the cage for a closer look. One great yellow eye bulged through the slats to peer down on the prisoner's motionless form. And, still, he did not move.

Anxiety snared the ægle, its heaviness a stone accruing sudden magnitude and threatening to ground her with dread possibilities that abused her mind. A pleasant smile notched the etém's bloody profile then, and a twinkling eye snapped open to appraise Gael before the captive sat up to address her.

"Had you worried, eh?" the Etom called, then yawned, stretching arms wide to either side.

Gael recoiled with an involuntary sniff. Although the creature's chirpings were indecipherable, she'd read his body language and tone aright. He was mocking her!

The Etom's brazenness almost sent Gael into fresh paroxysms of fury, but something in his demeanor stopped her. He arose, lifted his hands in a gesture of placation, then limped toward a scant smear of grape matter left on the floor of the cage. Wincing with pain as he bent at the waist, the captive collected what he could with a quick sweep of the hand. He took a small nibble, then lifted the meager and semi-translucent handful of grape flesh to her in gratitude.

With a quick bow of the head, he called again, "Thank you, kind ægle. May Elyon bless you for your service!"

How hateful his words sounded in her ears! But Gael could find no fault in her prisoner's conduct, and the schism between his conduct and the reaction it evoked in her was an enigma to Gael. With a bitter scowl, she frowned down at him, uncertain at his continual attempts to befriend her. At last, she grew weary of the prisoner's manifest kindness, and departed to slake her bloodthirst elsewhere. Nevertheless, she carried off a growing puzzlement at the Etom's behavior, and a determination to see the mystery solved.

Waving a small, blue hand, the Etom bid the ægle farewell, then hobbled to the edge of the cage where he sat to rest against the rusty iron. The grape juice stung his split and swollen lips, but the prisoner smiled as with thanks to the Creator he consumed his breakfast. Grateful as he was for the food, he likewise gave thanks for the ægle who had delivered it.

He counted himself blessed for the opportunity to share his own blessedness, even with one who antagonized him. His body would recover from aches and pains, and he counted the cost worthwhile in extending friendship to his captor. That she'd not shaken the cage again after his little joke was encouragement enough, though he'd have again borne injury with gladness.

A though occurred to him, eliciting a chuckle and subsequent wince from the pain amusement caused. Here he was, confined to prison, yet free in profound ways his captor was not, her soul burdened by heavy chains she couldn't see. The gravity of his contemplation sobered him, and he fell at once into prayer, beseeching Lord Elyon for the ægle's freedom.

With the elimination of their enemies, a deep sense of responsibility came to the Kinfolk of Endego. They'd witnessed the might of the Creator on their behalf, and His ferocity in defending them from destruction. Their thoughts now turned to the implications of all they had learned of the Kinsman, grounded in the prophecies of the Eben'kayah.

What seemed clear was that the Spirit intended creatures of every kind be joined in the Vine as a means of putting an end to all hostility between them and their Creator, which the Stain had provoked. Likewise, and as evinced by the conjoining through the Vine of ægle, fox, Sprig, and Etom, the Spirit sought to restore a harmony between all kinds not experienced since the time of Gan.

Indeed, Elyon's miraculous deliverance of His people in Endego had caught the attention of many. From all about their settled grove, the Etom were soon visited by those whose fascination had overcome their misgiving such that they drew near to investigate. At first, it was a couple of field mice, then a hare or two, then a pair of quail with their numerous chicks trailing behind. More and more came to the Tree, and most joined the Kinship, even the eventual weasel, raccoon, and the like.

The impact of the Tree on these predatory creatures in particular compelled a pronounced sacrifice of their instinctive desire to consume flesh, such as Sayah had experienced on the Cold Vantage. The omnivorous Etom also felt the keen loss of meat from their diet, though all under the Tree found the rhema satisfied them in ways no other meal could.

The additional insight the Spirit gave into the speech of fellow creatures elevated the act of consuming one another to the level of murder. One couldn't very well justify such an act when the victim protested in their own voice, a fact that proved unappetizing to any such potential perpetrator.

They were well aware that devouring one another would be disruptive to their harmonious coexistence, and each committed to the endeavor without complaint. The Spirit in various measure supported each one's obedient cooperation with His will to deepen a sense of satisfaction in the rhema and of disgust at indulging in bloodlust.

Of course, none could altogether disregard the manner in which Lord Elyon had saved them from their foes, and tender-hearted Nat in particular wrestled with the tension between the Spirit's affection for His Kin and the abject destruction visited on the Empire's army. How could Elyon both desire goodwill and compassion for some creatures and yet pour out such wrath on others?

Nat couldn't reconcile the seeming paradox, and often returned to it in his communion with the Spirit of Lord Elyon.

What have we done to deserve Your mercy in place of judgment? he inquired from a broken heart, leaning hard against the Tree's rough bark.

A gentle breeze stirred the leaves of the Tree in peaceful susurration as the Spirit answered, *You have done nothing to earn My favor, other than receive it. As for those who sought to destroy you – do I not have the right to protect My children?*

Of course, You do, Nat replied, *and I am grateful You did. I'm thinking of the ones among our enemies who might have joined us as Blithewit and Whisperweave did. How many such friends did we lose?*

You have such a heart for others, which is as I've made you, the Spirit responded. *Consider this, however. Do you truly believe that your concern for these exceeds My own? I've an entire universe to tend to, and every living being to care for. I assure you that My judgments are just, and that I alone am sovereign over all Creation.*

You need only concern yourself with your own being and with those I have entrusted to you. That is sufficient for any creature and is more for your sake than it is for Mine. Anything more you cannot bear, and will prove a detriment to your joy in Me. I am Lord over all.

Something rankled in Nat's heart at such authority, but the etém understood and accepted the Spirit's rebuke. The issue was not altogether settled for Nat, however, but the doubt clamoring for attention fell quiet amidst the youth's redoubling confidence in the Spirit. No matter the question, his Comforter would ever be with him in difficult conversations.

Now, the Spirit prompted, *you should all prepare to receive those who are returning home. They will need the utmost care, and not all will be ready to hear the good news of the Kinsman. Persist in your love for them, and they will come around.*

Nat leapt from his place near the Tree at once to share the exciting news with the others. He anticipated the return of many old friends from among the Eben'kayah and was pleased to know that many among them had likewise received the same message from the Spirit. Those who hadn't nevertheless resonated with the good news to the harmony of the whole body of believers.

United thus in the Spirit and in purpose, the Kinship didn't delay in organizing a warm homecoming. Immediate need dictated they form a new council of elders to confront the challenges before them, with each candidate selected with the endorsement of the Kinship and at the behest of the Spirit. Among these were Agatous, Alcarid, Shoym, Hezi, Nida, Dempsey, Tram, Kehren, and Blithewit. The fox at first had balked at the suggestion he take a position of leadership, but many encouraged him, with the Spirit affirming, to persuade him otherwise.

While Nat, Rae, and Sayah had more than proven their devotion to the Kinsman, neither of the youths sensed the Spirit's leading to commit to the council. Indeed, they each believed their commitment lay elsewhere, though for the time being, they left their convictions unspoken.

At last, a dozen total came before the Tree, surrounded by the witness of the Kinship for confirmation as leaders. In the waist-high, tranquil water, a great circle of the larger community stood facing the appointees at the center. All those within but Blithewit, who sat on his haunches, stood in a smaller circle facing out toward the others as they gathered to seek the blessing of Lord Elyon.

From his place amidst those appointed, Dempsey, under the power of the Spirit, called out in song:

"How good! How pleasant it is!
When Your people dwell united.
As a precious oil, anointing the head,
and running down our faces
and sprinkling on our raiment.

Together, we reveal the Son
and by the Spirit,
we give His body form.

For among us, Elyon founded
His blessing of life eternal."

Although Dempsey fell silent, his final note hung, soft in the air. Whence the water met his waist, a rippling ring pulsed, sending continual, circular waves across the pool. At his side, Nida's mouth stayed closed, yet nonetheless another voice, her voice, arose in harmony with the tone yet reverberating through the bower. At the same moment, the water around her began to pulse as well, and where the waves about her joined Dempsey's, the crests grew a bit taller and the troughs a bit deeper.

Beside Nida, Kehren's voice arose to join the polyphony and start another set of concerted waves. Within moments, similar waves radiate from each member of the circle within, their voices rising together though none with their mouths uttered a sound. The ripples, concentric to each one, joined in constructive intensity as they spread to reach the outer group.

By this time, the waves had grown substantial enough that some of the smaller folk swayed under their influence. Those on the outer perimeter joined hands, or in the case of Sayah and Whisperweave, they stood as supports to the Etom nearby. Within their deepest beings, each one anticipated the Spirit's movement with excitement.

At once, the outer ring of the Vine exploded in a song that swelled to produce a surge of surf that spread beyond the clearing and sound that echoed beyond Endego. Connected to the pool by a tributary, the Üntfither likewise overflowed its banks to send life-giving rills of water into the village.

The Kinship had scant time for amazement, for over top the council, the Tree brought forth from pink bud to pure white blossom a fragrant cluster of flowers. While many exclaimed in surprise at their appearance, Nat and Sayah did not – until they realized these were of the very kind that had adorned the Kinsman's crown at His resurrection.

The silken, white petals, now unfurled in full blossom, shone in heart-stopping radiance over the gathering. Hearts beat afresh as the flowers then folded in on themselves, twisting down into inverse spires where Sayah's eyes spied golden, gravid droplets forming at each florid tip.

The shower of sprinkles fell to land on the upturned faces of the council below, sending a freshet of delectable fragrance washing over the crowd. Each tiny drop settled with uncanny accuracy on the foreheads of their recipients and spread to enshroud them in delicate, golden light. The subtle glow subsided, but within the outer congregants an unspoken understanding grew that the Spirit had set apart these twelve in their midst as leaders.

Shoym stepped forth from his place among the Council of the Vine to address the rest, his voice carrying across the now-placid water.

"We have seen the will of the Spirit enacted in our appointment today, and already know His desire that we should be ready to receive the many still scattered abroad in our search for the Kinsman. I hear His wisdom, also, in the possibility that they may return with fellow captives of the Empire.

"So, let us set to the task before us with all our strength, as though we do it for Elyon Himself, and let us not grow weary in it. For a great harvest yet awaits us among the friends and family we long to see again, so long as we do not lose heart."

At that very moment, the community of the Vine as one departed the waters and set to work. The Kinship soon recognized that, though together all bore the burden of preparation with joy, some were gifted to a particular task at hand. A few were quick to identify and to prioritize the various physical needs of those returning, while others took the lead in organizing the other Kinfolk to accomplish the work. Still others were excited at the prospect of teaching the new arrivals about the Kinsman, while another contingent considered the procurement and allocation of resources and where they'd be of greatest benefit.

All in all, those in the Vine sensed the Spirit at work in and throughout their entirety of their fellowship to orchestrate their movements. It was a beautiful and glorious sight to behold, though such glory was not always apparent in the obvious or majestic, but rather in kind-hearted compromise or in gritty, sweat-soaked labor.

As youth, Nat, Rae, and Sayah put themselves at the disposal of the community to expend their youthful energy wherever they might be needed. For an instant, Nat had been considered for Council, but a halting dissonance in the Spirit removed him from such consideration. He felt no disappointment in the matter when the Spirit reminded him of the adventure that awaited them beyond Sakkan.

Thus, it was that, though their usefulness among the Kinship was without question, the trio became convinced the Spirit was calling them out of Endego. A few short days after the anointing of the Council, before any others had returned home, the three found themselves drawn together just after nightfall around a low fire in the clearing.

An itchy restlessness among them stood in tension with the deep tranquility each held in their hearts as they hunkered around the fire, their skin and feathers painted amber in the glow of flickering flames.

As was often the case in such matters, Nat was first to speak, "I think you both know why we're here. The Spirit brought us back to Endego, and I'm happy. I think you are, too."

With slow, almost-imperceptible nods, Rae and Sayah agreed, and Nat continued. "I've never felt so at home anywhere, not even among the Eben'kayah, and I'm excited to welcome everyone back. But..."

In concert, Sayah and Rae whispered, finishing Nat's sentence, "...but it's not where we're supposed to be."

Nat stood, his eyes gleaming in the fire as he looked to his best friends. No! They were more than friends. They were family! They were Kin!

"Then you both know we can't stay here. The Spirit's calling us north, past Sakkan, and we don't know what awaits us there."

"No matter what, we're with you," answered Sayah.

Rae followed, her face awash with devotion, "Yes, Nat. Always."

Something in Rae's gaze caused Nat to flush, and he had to swallow hard before he went on, "Thank you both. We know what we need to do, then. Rae and I need to speak with our parents. In truth, if our desire to depart is of the Spirit, then He, too, will speak on our behalf. Even so, we should pray now that He makes our departure an easy decision for our families."

At that, they fell to prayer, their hearts coming together in agreement as one in the gentle ebb and tide of the Spirit. Afterward, they spoke sober goodbyes, and each headed to his resting place.

With all their time spent on the trail, both Rae and Nat now found it strange to sleep in their own homes, and even their beds had become a foreign comfort. And, while any of the Kinship would have welcomed Sayah into their home, the ægle was still more comfortable outside.

Tonight, as he nestled amidst the Tree's leafy crown, he surveyed the dark contours of Endego and its surrounding lands, and a sigh of soundness in his new home escaped his beak. The utterance spoke a belonging he felt among these he once had thought estranged to his kind.

Perhaps you should reconsider what is meant by 'kind,' the Spirit interjected, grabbing Sayah's attention.

What do you mean? the ægle asked.

The creature looks to external appearance, but I look within.

A memory of Miyam came to mind, her words traversing his mind in parallel with the Spirit's speech, *If you are grafted into the Vine, you are a new creation. The old has passed away, and look! The new has come.*

The Spirit continued as Miyam trailed off, *Your friend, the Sprig, spoke truth, and her words were Mine. You, and all those in the Vine, are the new creation. That is your kind now, and the kind of everyone who receives the gift of new life in the Son.*

Sayah sensed the truth of it resonating throughout his being and identified it as the cause of his sudden incorporation among those with whom he shared so little in the natural sense. He thanked His Creator for the revelation and fell to sleep in the assurance that, wherever he went with Nat and Rae, he took his home with him.

Chapter Five
What They Found There

A dark and foreboding comet streaking across the sky, Imafel flew onward to his destination with Windspanne and Stromweise flanking him on either side. The Nihúkolem was preoccupied with the prospect of what awaited them and with the possibility of Mūk-Mudón finding them out.

The distracted Imafel did not note the worried glances Windspanne and Stromweise passed between them as they flew. The ægles did not care much for this particular assignment, which brought them into close proximity to one of their loathed oppressors, and much too close to the volatile and capricious Imafel for their comfort.

The ægles likewise sensed Imafel's desperation in his furtive and sudden departure, and they wondered what kind of mission Imafel had recruited them to. On their current course, the Nihúkolem would lead them straight back to their aerie, which added to their anxiety. Ægles weren't hospitable to begin with, and the prospect of bringing Imafel back to their nest was unthinkable.

Windspanne and Stromweise had built their home atop the lofty tree not long before their first clutch of eggs had arrived. This particular tree had theretofore stood out for the gray and deathly depression it left in the canopy from above.

Nevertheless, at some point, the tree had straightened to stand tall over all its peers, and its branches flourished with fresh and leafy life. Stromweise, in readiness to mate, had been first to spot the tree, which had drawn the pair once she pointed it out to Windspanne.

Without hesitation, the couple had decided on the tree for its attractive vitality. Upon further inspection they likewise concluded that the great stature of the tree made it ideal for spotting prey and defending their hunting grounds. Their new aerie enabled them to view both land and sky for many miles around, adding to its allure.

In an act that ran contrary to the ægles' protective instincts, they now conducted Imafel to the home they'd built together, and

Windspanne and Stromweise grew ever more uncomfortable as they drew near the aerie. Thus, Imafel and the ægles, under such a gathering thunderhead of anxiety, approached the Kinsman's Tree, which alone stood green and at full leave amidst the autumn wood. The ægles, as of yet ignorant to the Tree's transformative role in the world, nonetheless breathed a sigh of relief when Imafel showed interest not in what stood above, but beneath its branches.

Without concern, Imafel dove through the surrounding woods. The various grains of his aggregate form pelted the bare boughs, a dark and heavy hail that more often than not stripped any foliage that remained away and left the impoverished branches swaying in its passage.

The ægles proceeded with greater care for both their environs and themselves. They had desire neither to injure themselves nor disrupt the natural order, and so flitted through what gaps they could find to follow Imafel.

Windspanne and Stromweise were of courageous stock, but regardless a sense of dread met them as they floated in to land behind the dark and yet-incomplete figure of Imafel. The Nihúkolem brooded outside the low hedge that encircled the Tree, his agitation apparent in the static, particulate buzz that emanated from his sooty form and reverberated in the ægles' minds.

I know this place, Imafel growled, *and I hate it*.

Windspanne mistook Imafel's statement as meant for them, and inquired, "What is it, sir?"

The irritated drone intensified to that of a hornet's nest when kicked, and Imafel's head, diminished yet possessing now a face, swiveled in a swift circle to cast a baleful glare. Windspanne fell silent and asked no more.

For her part, Stromweise hadn't ceased to scan the bower, her quick, sharp eyes taking in every detail of the Tree and its surroundings. The Tree's vital strength yet drew her as it had when, in their ignorance, she and Windspanne had selected it to support their nest. Or had *it* selected *them*?

She shook her aquiline head at the confusion the question presented. Silly, that thought. A tree did no choosing that *she* knew of, yet the warm, golden glow the Tree's branches cast was...familiar.

Stromweise gasped as she recalled the strange Tree that loomed over Endego, the very Tree that had struck so many of their fellows from the sky. This Tree could have been its twin. No! For all its timeless maturity, this Tree rather seemed the ancestor of the other. Surely, they were the same, seed and stalk.

"No..." she groaned, drawing a forbidding glance from her mate.

"Quiet, dear," he hissed, then tipped his beak at Imafel. "We needn't any more attention from *him*."

She bore the reproach, and with greater care, whispered to Windspanne, "Doesn't this look – doesn't it *feel* – like the Tree in Endego?"

At once, Windspanne knew the one of which she spoke. Dumbstruck, he, too examined he Tree, its spreading branches, the strange spring pouring from within. He'd not looked so close at it before, but now he did, it was plain as day.

Imafel recognized it, too, and not just from his dissolution in Endego. No, he was acquainted with this site, where he and the Nihúkolem ordered the execution of the prisoner, Gaal. This whole place stank of Him, and of the strange, incorruptible power He embodied.

What is this Imafel?!?

The question struck him like a blow, a surprise ambush of the mind at the hand of Mūk-Mudón, who seethed across their psychic link.

Imafel at first wilted within himself, then arose to his own defense, *Milord, it would seem our holdouts in Endego have something in common with this place – a Tree just like the one on which we hung the rebel, Gaal.*

Windspanne and Stromweise, though unable to hear the exchange, recognized something was afoot, and held their peace, as did Imafel while Mūk-Mudón ruminated on this new information.

Hmmm...but he told me nothing more would come of it, Mūk-Mudón muttered to himself. *What is the meaning of all this?*

Imafel listened without interrupting, certain his old friend betrayed more than he intended through his musings.

Yes. Yes, Mūk-Mudón continued. *But we* must *do something about this, mustn't we?*

With some horror, Imafel realized that the 'we' Mūk-Mudón spoke of seemed less and less to include Cloust, Belláphorus, or himself. Or anyone else he'd seen or might be aware of. Perhaps Mūk-Mudón had gone mad?

Mūk-Mudón startled him again with a sudden, decisive bark, *Imafel! You've disobeyed a direct order, and for that you deserve punishment. However, what you've uncovered is both sensitive in the extreme and very valuable to the Empire.*

I might be willing to overlook your indiscretion so long as you can ensure the total containment of this information. Besides you and I, none *may carry the tale away. Do we have an understanding?*

With ever so slight a shift in his position, Imafel glanced at the watchful ægles who now stood beside him. Any other creature might have missed the movement, but the exceptional vision of the ægles caught it – and the subtle, compact coiling of Imafel's shaded form.

Heightened awareness saved Windspanne and Stromweise, who sprang back from Imafel with wings upraised for flight. The Nihúkolem was too quick for them, however, and struck the nearer of the two, Windspanne, with a lashing tendril that broke one of the ægle's wings.

Windspanne grunted in pain and with a graceless spin fluttered to the ground. Stromweise was more fortunate, and began to climb out of Imafel's reach, raking the air for altitude that she might escape.

The absence of her mate distracted her from flight, however, and a glimpse down at the broken Stromweise cost her a moment she did not have. Imafel burst skyward in a swirling sphere to surround the ægle. He swirled all about the bird, generating such a turbulent current that she could not fly and smothering her within the stifling, static charge of his frenetic motion.

The ægle's strength failed as Imafel closed around her and together they plummeted to the earth. With eyes forlorn, Windspanne watched his lifemate fall, and shambled over to break her fall, his broken wing dragging on the ground behind him.

Windspanne got under her just in time, though how much he lessened the impact was unclear. Imafel, however, erupted in an ebon cloud when he met the ground, and it took him a moment to coalesce again into useful form.

Windspanne choked on the lingering dust of the collision, but recognized Imafel's delay for the opportunity it was. He needed to spirit his stunned mate away, but where? And with a broken wing, how?

The ægle looked to the old, rugged Tree, its clear waters sparkling in the bright and mellow glow beneath the bower.

Please! Windspanne's heart cried unto the heavens for a Creator he had scarcely acknowledged.

Just let us pass!

As an enemy of the Tree, Windspanne was aware that in all likelihood a well-deserved destruction awaited them but grasped the slim and hopeful thread of sanctuary before them notwithstanding. He limped toward the hedge, dragging a broken spouse on one side and a broken wing on the other.

Imafel composed himself in time to spot the ægles staggering toward the Tree, and his furor erupted in a deep, sawing roar. So enraged was he that his outmost layer ejected an arm's length in all directions to dance a hazy tarantella around him.

Don't you dare! Imafel howled, advancing on the ægles.

Stromweise stirred from her daze, taking in their predicament as her senses returned.

"Oh...no, no, no," she whispered in disquiet.

Windspanne set his eyes on their finish line, the hedge that circumscribed the clearing, and ignored the whipping frenzy at their backs.

Whether I look back or not, he thought, *if he catches up, we're dead.*

With gritting talons, the ægle tore the earth for traction. Pulling with all he was worth for uncertain safety, Imafel's cry rang immense in Windspanne's ears when the ægle reached the stout wall of foliage.

"We don't mean to go in there?" Stromweise whispered, then replied to her own question. "But what choice do we have? We must go."

Windspanne raised a talon to begin the climb over, lamenting the time it would cost them even as he pressed on without hesitation. Before his talon met the outermost leaf of the hedge, however, the verdant snarl yielded and spread to either side to make way for them. The ægle had heretofore remained in motion, resolute in getting Stromweise to safety, but the opening of the hedge gave him brief pause.

Struck with wonder and some misgiving, he stared into the vibrant land before them, impressed again with the sense of untamable energy at work in the Tree. An urgent nudge from Stromweise animated him, and then, with her at his side, they stepped into the light.

The hedge closed behind the ægles, who receded beyond Imafel's grasp just as he reached them. At the last instant, the Nihúkolem pulled up short, unwilling to touch the barrier he knew would scatter him to the four winds once again.

Oh! How Imafel raged and raged outside the Sanctuary the Kinsman's Tree had established. Unable to transgress the boundary, he had failed his mission, and his embarrassed awareness that Mūk-Mudón watched just kindled his anger more.

Imafel swore murderous oaths against the ægles, desiring even the paltry satisfaction of their acknowledgment. But, no, they didn't seem to hear him, nor did they appear concerned any longer at his presence. Wounded, the ægles shuffled onward to the Tree, and not once did they look back.

Chapter Six
Bed & Breakfast

A supportive Nat accompanied Rae home, encouraging his friend in advance of the discussion that awaited her at home. He intended a like conversation with his mother when he, too, arrived home. His plan was thwarted, however, when the young pair discovered Nida and Dempsey chatting with Kehren and Tram in the parlor of Rae's home. The four had just come from a prayerful meeting with the Council and were enjoying some fellowship and tea while they relaxed.

After perfunctory salutations, the youths looked to one another, unspoken prayers in their hearts, and the decided to broach the subject with everyone at once. Nat nodded toward Tram and Kehren as the signal for Rae to begin. With rare hesitance, Rae declined, and instead responded with gesture of her own – a pressing elbow to Nat's back that forced him to step forward.

The quartet of adults saw that something burdened the youths, and Kehren gave voice to their common concern, "Yes, dears? What is it?"

Discomfited, Nat nevertheless pressed on, clearing his throat before he began, "Well, the thing is...that is, Rae, Sayah, and I have been praying about where the Spirit might best use us..."

Nida put her tea and saucer down to devote her full attention and inquired, "Yes, son. And how has He answered you?"

Tram and Kehren also set their cups aside while Dempsey set a half-eaten tea biscuit down, brushing a crumb from the corner of his mouth and leaning forward in his seat. Each set of their unblinking eyes were fixed on Nat, and he took a deep breath, praying for the wisdom and courage to continue.

"All three of us believe we're to go North – past Sakkan," he blurted.

Skeptical, Kehren asked, "And do what, precisely?"

Rae, feeling disloyal for making Nat bear the brunt of the parental interrogation, leapt to her friend's aid, "We don't know just yet, but we sense the Spirit drawing us there."

"We think it may be a quick trip, really!" Nat asserted. "We'll fly there on Sayah's back. It's just a few days' journey as the ægle flies."

Kehren and Nida sat stunned at the emotional impact of the proposal, while Tram mused aloud, "North of Sakkan? Why, there's nothing up there but..."

He looked to a likewise perplexed Dempsey, then gasped in horror, "No! You don't mean...?"

The four adults erupted in an anxious clamor while Nat and Rae looked on in total confusion. That Dempsey and their parents perceived some great threat in their destination was apparent, as was their own ignorance of the danger. Nat and Rae were unable to decipher the concern until the adults had stilled somewhat.

At last, Nida raised a hand to quiet the rest and asked, "Nat? Rae? Have either of you heard of Terábnis?"

Both children shook their puzzled heads.

"The Desert Jewel? Seat of ancient empires?" Nida inquired.

She was not surprised when they again shook their heads.

"And I suppose you want to take the Dimroad there as well?" Kehren interjected. "You know, where that great ghastly Nihúkolem nearly made æglet jelly of our friend Sayah on the bridge?"

Nat and Rae knew the place well, though they'd never heard anyone give a name to it.

"Terábnis is a city of Men, my dears," Nida explained. "You're asking us to let you go to quite possibly the most dangerous place in the world for an Etom."

An exasperated Kehren jibed, "And you didn't even know it. Unbelievable."

Nat considered his response for a second, unshaken in his confidence that the Spirit desired the three friends venture forth regardless but unwilling to disrespect any of the adults in his insistence. In the momentary pause, the Spirit Himself provided Nat with the appropriate words, and Nat hoped they would resonate among the adults.

"It's true, what you say," he answered in a quiet voice, ushering in a hush as the others strained to hear.

Nat looked into the eyes of his audience, and resumed, "It *is* dangerous. We know that. But *everywhere* is dangerous for us now. The Empire of Chōl has marked us as enemies, and while we'd like to believe that the safest place for any of us is in Sanctuary Endego, we all know in our heart of hearts that's not true.

"Lord Elyon has protected us our entire lives. He didn't just start now. He kept us alive on our journey to Sakkan, guided me to the Kinsman's Tree, and afterward rescued you all from Scarsburrow's clinic. And how did He accomplish all of this? He *spoke*. To each of us. And we listened. We heard, and we obeyed. No more. No less."

Nida, Dempsey, and Tram absorbed Nat's words, though Kehren objected, "But, Nat. That was different. We were following the prophecies, and..."

She circulated a hand across the quartet before finishing her argument, "And *we* were with you."

"Kehren," Nat implored, his eyes deep golden pools, "You are like a second mother to me, and I intend you no dishonor, but I *must* disagree.

"We were together until I escaped the clinic, alone. And alone I picked up our search anew, and alone discovered the Kinsman's Tree. Alone, but for the guiding hand of Elyon. He has ever been, and always will be our guide.

"It was under the power and direction of the Spirit after I had bathed in the streams of the Tree that Sayah and I mounted your rescue from Sakkan. And it was the Spirit who delivered us to Sanctuary."

A ragged sob tore from Kehren, "And you and Rae almost died! Have you children already forgotten?"

Tears fell from Kehren's downcast face onto her clasped hands, and a shuddering whisper escaped her, "You *both* almost died."

At last, Rae joined the conversation to encourage her mother, "No. We haven't forgotten. But maybe we're supposed to focus on how Elyon saved us, even when all seemed lost."

Offering his support, Nat added, "And the Spirit has rescued us twice now from the might of the Empire. For what it's worth, I can't think of anywhere safer than in His will."

He looked again to Tram, Dempsey, and his mother before addressing Kehren again, "Which is why we want to go. We believe it is His will. Won't you all at least pray about it? Please? Whatever you four decide, we will do."

This last bit was a gamble, and Nat knew it, but he didn't see any other way to honor both their parents and Lord Elyon. He prayed the Spirit would make a way. A nervous Rae cleared her throat next to him, and he glanced at her, happy she was at his side.

Tram lay a gentle hand on his wife's shoulder and offered her his handkerchief. While she wiped her eyes, he whispered something in her ear that the two youths couldn't hear, and Kehren nodded without lifting her gaze.

His earthy brown face resolute, Tram at last answered Rae and Nat, "We will pray about the matter. If it's Elyon's will for you to go to Terábnis, we will not stand in the way."

Nida had waited to respond, prepared to answer as Tram had, but desiring not to sway the others' decision. She, too, agreed to pray about the issue, although she already sensed the Spirit urging her to let the trio go. A mournful tugging in her heart compelled her either to lie and keep them in Endego or accompany them, but she knew she would do neither.

However honest she'd been before grafting into the Vine was now further reinforced by the constant influence of the Spirit's presence. She couldn't lie. She also knew the compulsion to keep Nat in Endego would stunt his growth, and she very much desired to see what all he might accomplish for Lord Elyon if she would just let her son go.

Nat, Nida, and Dempsey departed Tram and Kehren's estate, leaving the other family to sort through the emotional events of the evening and try to get some rest. Compelled to see Nat and Nida home safe, Dempsey accompanied them along the Sylvanfare in thoughtful silence. An easy survey of their surroundings revealed the dramatic change the village had undergone in the last week or so. A free and tranquil breeze seemed to have replaced the stifling oppression that had blanketed Endego when they first returned. The peaceful trek provided Dempsey the opportunity to reflect on Nat and Rae's request.

Though he shared the same anxieties as Nat and Rae's parents, Dempsey had remained quiet throughout the interaction. While he enjoyed profound connections with both children, he was parent to neither and felt it wasn't his place to object.

Perhaps it was this distinction in relations that enabled his varied perspective, since, besides any worry he felt over sending them into danger, he felt, too, admiration. The kids had guts. A chuckle escaped Dempsey at the thought, breaking the relative silence to draw Nida's bemused gaze.

"And what, pray tell, is so funny?" she probed through curved lips.

By now, Dempsey had Nat's interest as well, and he ruffled the youngster's now-lanky zalzal with affection, then attended to Nida's question.

"I just think these kids are great. Nat, Rae, Sayah – I can't imagine doing half of what they've accomplished at their age. They're amazing. Each one."

Dempsey's words touched Nida's nurturing heart and complemented her earlier introspection over letting the youths leave. Nida fought back tears that threatened to overrun deeper sensibilities in favor of the instinctive fervor she'd nourished for her son. She'd felt the tension before, in the moment she'd commanded Nat to escape from Sakkan and leave them behind. That separation had been against her will, but Elyon had used it to free them all. Perhaps His plan for the children now would bring forth even greater things.

Dempsey, having become quite adept at reading Nida, extended timely encouragement, "Nat was right, you know. They're no more secure here if they're outside the Spirit's will. If He desires them to leave, we best not stand in the way."

Nat feigned disinterest in the grownups' conversation as Nida responded, "You know me too well, Master Dempsey. Though it pains me, I also believe the right course is that they leave."

Aware that Nat also listened, she issued a caveat, "Nevertheless, I withhold final judgment until tomorrow. I would at least like to sleep on the matter."

They arrived at the narrow grass-fringed lane leading up to Nida and Nat's home beneath the rubber tree. Nat took a few steps up the walk, then turned about to call his lagging mother homeward. Something in the way she and Dempsey lingered together at the foot of the path dissuaded him, however.

A sudden awareness of their resurgent romance blossomed in Nat's mind, manifesting in embarrassed violet blooms that enflamed his cheeks as he turned away. Over his shoulder, he bid Dempsey a hasty farewell, his feet bidding them one even hastier. After a clumsy, clattering fuss with the keys, he managed to slip inside the house, puffing a great sigh of relief as he fell back against the closed door.

Outside, Dempsey and Nida stifled snickers at Nat's awkward exit. Their laughter was not unkind but erupted rather from surprise at the otherwise mature young etém's reaction. Nat had grown up in so many other ways that they took his innocence regarding romance for granted. No matter that Nat's naïveté suited an etém his age.

The momentary levity warmed the pair, and Dempsey looked deep into Nida's shimmering eyes with longing. She was bare before him but for the hesitance revealed in a wince when he leaned in for a kiss.

Dempsey's advance was more forward than usual, and he stammered a shamefaced apology as he turned away. Before he could, Nida caught him by the arm, her weeping eyes imploring him to stay.

"Please," she gasped, then wrapped him in her arms. "I'm sorry. Don't go. Not yet."

The tense anxiety in Dempsey's form melted away in her embrace, and he rested in the comfortable press of her body against his. The chirp of crickets counted off long moments as they held one another in the moonlight.

When at long last they separated, they did so without a word, though their hands spoke volumes. Dempsey's fingertips trailed down Nida's arms, drifting across her open palms where they each squeezed the other's hands in reluctance at their parting. Bashful smiles were their best goodbye, and they wore them long after, Dempsey all the way across Endego to his home.

Nida, for her part, fell asleep in the gentle contentment of the intimacy she and Dempsey shared. At last, she was free to rest in the possibility of renewed romance and of a potential partner in her life. In the blessedness of their lives, she was certain Lord Elyon smiled on them.

Nida awoke the following morning to the bright chill of a late-autumn morning in Endego. Sunlight streamed through a window hedged with frost, the delicate white etching an intricate reminder of the Creator's order. Sliding pink feet into her slippers and wrapping herself in a thick robe, she steeled herself for the cold, anticipating several shivering minutes in front of the stove as it warmed the kitchen.

Nida swung the door of her bedroom open to confront with mild shock her son at the table, already dressed for the day. On the stovetop, a kettle chuffed with the merry promise of tea not long to follow, and a pleasant wave of warmth struck her face. Her son had been busy this morning.

Nat greeted her, "Good morning, mother!"

The eager gleam in his eye caused Nida to question the youth's motives in taking on the chilly chore of starting the morning fire and putting on the kettle. She went to the kettle, a charred and brassy thing, and went about the commonplace alchemy of preparing her tea.

The infuser fell into her teacup with a dull tinkle as she cocked a sidelong glance at Nat to ask, "You wouldn't, by chance, be trying to influence my decision on your little adventure?"

With brazen cheek, her son replied, "Why would I ever need to do that, mother? I'll let the Spirit speak for Himself. I just figured it couldn't hurt to show you just how responsible I've become."

Nida's retort was cut short by a curious rustling at their door.

She frowned and inquired instead, "You weren't expecting anyone this morning, were you?"

With a grimace and a shrug, Nat shook his head, then started for the door. Before he could get there, his mother screamed, a clatter arising from her teacup as she set it on the saucer with shaky hands. Nat whirled at once to see what the matter was, his wariness dissolving into amusement when he saw a great golden eye framed in their kitchen window.

"Sayah!" Nida shrieked with an irritation reserved only for cold, groggy mornings.

The ægle blinked and retreated from the window as Nat burst from the home to salute his friend.

"Sayah!" he called, ducking the sweep of the ægle's feathers as Sayah swiveled to reply.

Nida, on the other hand, was on Nat's heels with some choice words for the ægle.

Her face was stern and cross as she scolded him, wagging her pink finger in his beak, "Sayah, you do not come to an etma's home first thing in the morning and peep through her windows. It's just rude!"

To see such a great thing shrink before one so small might have been funny if not for the honest confusion and hurt in Sayah's eyes. The ægle peered out from behind a protective wing, and in that moment, it occurred to Nida that Sayah knew nothing of the social conventions of Etom-kind. After all, did nests even have windows?

Concluding that she'd overreacted, Nida desisted from her criticism to apologize, "Sayah, I'm sorry. You didn't know any better."

Nida splayed a hand against her chest and with a nervous chuckle confessed, "And you really scared me!"

"Yeah, he did," Nat agreed with a sly smile.

The pain disappeared from Sayah's eyes when Nida apologized, but the confusion persisted, exacerbated by Nat's amusement. Nida crossed her arms, and turned gorgon eyes on her son, whose smile petrified at once.

"If you were looking to show me just how much you've grown up, *son*, then I recommend you stop the shenanigans. *Now*."

"Yes, ma'am," he complied, nodding soberly.

"There's nothing fu – fu-huh funny a – abou..." Nida struggled along in parental seriousness, then burst into a fit of laughter.

She couldn't contain it, and the contagion spread at once to the Sayah and her son. Nat brayed aloud from behind his hand, while Sayah laughed – noisy hiccupping squawks that made him sound more than a little distressed.

Nida and Nat, unacquainted with the ægle's laughter, at once grew still and gawped at Sayah out of concern. Sayah persisted in his spasmodic jubilation until, comprehending the sudden stillness that had fallen over the Etom, he grew self-conscious and likewise ceased.

Eyes yet streaming with jovial tears, Nat and Nida all at once realized Sayah's strange, convulsive cawing had been the ægle's laughter. With great guffaws, mother and son resumed their hilarity, drawing Sayah back in with cords both joyful and irresistible. The ægle's renewed paroxysms spurred Nat and Nida on, producing in Sayah a reciprocal effect. And for many minutes, the trio were thus unable to escape the seeming mechanism of perpetual emotion.

At last, when they had exhausted themselves with cheer, their shared jubilation melting away any earlier contention, they recovered themselves. Arising from where she'd fallen to lean against the doorpost, Nida straightened while Sayah and Nat stood from their happy sprawl on the forest floor.

Although they had addressed Sayah's earlier impropriety, the thought recurred to Nida that she'd not gotten an answer as to the purpose of the ægle's early morning visit.

Thus compelled, she asked at last, "So, Sayah, what brings you here so early this fine morning?"

Sayah directed an expectant gaze at Nat, who returned it with a subtle and forbidding shake of his flushed and violet-blue head.

With one curled and bashful claw, Sayah rubbed the other, and struggled for a response, "Well, you see...I thought. That is, I understood, that we might...er...have our answer soon. You know, for the journey North."

Irked, Nida turned an unblinking stare on Nat, the heated creep of blood climbing her neck to redden her bright pink skin.

"Is that so?" she answered Sayah, as meanwhile her piercing green eyes pinned her squirming son in place.

Nat shifted in discomfort, aware of his impertinence, but determined to give an explanation, "Mom. Mother. Ma'am. I'm sorry. I know it was wrong to presume you'd have an answer for us right away. But, please, hear me out."

Nida crossed her arms, her face skeptical and foot tapping with impatience as she returned, "I'm listening."

"I just figured you were so in tune with the Spirit that you'd have an answer right away. That's it. And Sayah here insisted that we both have your permission before we go."

Nat's words cut Nida to the quick as she realized the clumsy honor these juveniles had conferred on her: Nat in assuming the best of her, and Sayah in seeking her surrogate approval in the absence of his own mother's. In their bumbling way, they touched her, and she desisted in her ire.

Instead, she chided them with an upraised finger and a smirk playing at the corners of her mouth, "I won't answer either of you until I've had my tea. And breakfast!"

This last Nat met with enthusiastic action, and at once he dashed inside to busy himself preparing a porridge of grains, nuts and dried fruits while Sayah waited outside. Leaving the front door open allowed Sayah a glimpse inside, though to do so decreased the temperature in the homey kitchen. Notwithstanding, Nida thought the warmth of the ægle's presence more than offset the cost.

They all conversed while Nida sipped a fresh, steaming cup of tea and Nat served up the porridge. Though at first strange to Sayah, he soon found the aroma of the Etom's breakfast intoxicating, and watched with keen, greedy eyes as they drizzled honey over the hot cereal. After the first couple bites, it became difficult for the Etom to ignore the quiet interest with which the ægle watched them eat.

It dawned on Nat how rude it was not to have offered Sayah some as well, and he begged the ægle's pardon.

"Sayah! I'm so sorry! I didn't think to make some for you, too. Honestly, I've never seen you eat anything but rhema, so it didn't even occur to me. Would you like something to eat?"

Sayah's pupils pinned with excitement. He clicked his beak in hungry expectation and replied, "I would. Very much so. Do you have more of…whatever that is?"

Nida and Nat chortled with pleasant understanding, and the etém arose to prepare more while disclosing, "This is called porridge. Sometimes, it's just grain boiled until soft enough to eat, but today, I added nuts and some fruit for extra flavor."

Nat hurried to fill their largest pot, a deep and dented thing, at the nearby brook and put it on the stove to boil. He would make Sayah an extra-large portion. Soon, the water danced with soft, hot bubbles, and Nat stirred in the ingredients and a healthy mound of salt, then tapped his wooden spoon against the edge of the pot before setting it down in the trivet.

Before long, a steamy, hearty aroma filled the kitchen and wafted out the door to tease the ægle's nares. Out of politeness, Nat and Nida both elected to wait until everyone was served to break their own fasts. While Nida was content in the meantime to sip her tea, Nat's stomach rumbled with angst, though his face remained impassive.

The etém's young body would not remain quiet at the delay and complained with ever more frequent insistence. Sayah's gut concurred, and soon their stomachs engaged in a contest of whinging against the wait. After the passage of interminable minutes, the meal was done, to the delight of the hungry young males.

Looking to Sayah, Nat asked, "Honey?"

His one hand cradled the jar of sticky sweetness while the other gripped the wooden end of the submerged dipper.

With a fervent nod, Sayah assented, "Yes. Please!"

Nat leaned the lip of the jar against the battered edge of the pot and tipped it sideways, coaxing the thick, amber-gold liquid in from the mouth of the jar and into the pot. He was quite generous with the honey and with a free hand poured it over top the porridge until its surface was almost covered.

Brandishing his wooden stir-spoon, Nat folded the honey, now thinning with the heat of the cereal, into the porridge with slow, steady beats. Satisfied he'd mixed the sweet liquid into the cereal with sufficient care, Nat again tapped the spoon against the edge of the pot and replaced it in the trivet.

The etém at once wound a thick tea towel over his fingers and gripped the hot handles on either side of the pot to carry the meal to the threshold for Sayah. The eager ægle was just going to dig into the hot porridge, but a cautionary upraised hand from Nat gave him pause.

"Careful," Nat intoned with grim seriousness. "It's hot. Maybe you might blow on it a bit?"

As all Sayah's food heretofore had been uncooked, the idea of hot food was novel to him. Nevertheless, he huffed and puffed over the porridge in the threshold until he saw how much dust he was sending into the Etom home. Nat and Nida sat at the table, their eyes wincing from the brief windstorm and arms hovering over their bowls to protect the contents.

"Sorry," the ægle offered with sheepish remorse, then hooked his beak through one of the looping handles to tug it aside.

Once clear of the doorway, Sayah resumed his cool ministrations, which proved twice as effective in the chill autumn morning. This cooked food thing was a lot of work! The amount of steam rising from the porridge had diminished in large part, and the ægle thought it proper to at last sample his meal.

Sayah dipped a narrow pink tongue into the warm, sweet cereal. The pot was not wide enough to fit his beak, but Sayah made the best of it. Turning it this way and that, he scraped the inside of the pot with his tongue until all but a morsel was left. It was tricky getting at the sticky glob, which was located dead center at the bottom of the deep pot, but Sayah thought he could manage.

With ginger delicacy, he grasped a handle in one talon and rolled onto his back, spreading his wings as great snowy blanket to steady himself. With some difficulty he hooked the other handle with his free claw, but so he did. He then lifted the pot over his upraised and open beak, tongue stiff and eyes hunter-deadly as he focused on retrieving the gobbet of porridge with gravity's help.

The tip of his elongate tongue had just brushed the morsel when Sayah detected a soft stirring nearby. Freezing in place, Sayah turned a sidelong eye toward the sound. There, stacked atop one another as they craned around the doorjamb of their home, were the bemused faces of Nat and Nida, who for some time had been watching Sayah with interest.

With slow dignity, Sayah first removed his tongue from the pot and closed his beak, then lowered the vessel to the ground. In the back of his mind, he imagined the disgust his parents might have expressed at his unseemly display. He turned over with the greatest decorum he could manage, grateful that his feathers rendered undetectable the embarrassed blush he felt in his skin.

Sayah looked to Nat, who had stepped from the doorway to approach him, and discovered again amusement on the etém's face, but also kindness.

Nat pointed to the pot next to Sayah and with a cheery smile asked, "Would you like some more?"

Gratitude flooded the ægle's heart, and he thanked Elyon for such friends as these. Yes, they had found him in unflattering circumstances, and, yes, they thought it entertaining. But, at their core, Nat and Nida were to him the family that had never been, the family that had loved him, even before the Spirit had remade him. In reflection, Sayah decided he might just be taking himself too seriously and rejected the practice to favor community with his Kinfolk.

Instead of shame, the ægle felt now joy at his acceptance, and answered Nat with a smile of his own, "Yes, Nat. Please!"

"Sure thing, boss bird!" Nat fired back, running to collect the pot. "Just gotta wash this out, OK?"

While Nat set about preparing Sayah's seconds and Nida returned to tea and breakfast, the ægle pondered the depths of joy he had experienced since joining the wee blue Etom in Sanctuary what seemed so long ago. Life in the Vine was in truth a spectrum of delights Sayah suspected was inexhaustible – a way of life in the Spirit that transformed even deepest suffering into pleasure unshakeable. And, leading them along this way, He likewise transformed His children.

As Sayah huffed and puffed anew over his replenished pot of porridge, the thought recurred, and he mused, *Perhaps that is how the Kinsman changes the world. One transformation at a time.*

Chapter Seven

Coming or Going

Breakfast was over, and, while Nat and Sayah hadn't mentioned the matter of her answer again, Nida sensed their longing regardless. With practiced, unhurried motions, she dressed for the day, beseeching with whispers the wisdom of the Spirit. Nida did not want to crush the hopes of either youngster outside her door. Neither did she desire to place undue pressure on Tram and Kehren. For this reason, she prayed, confident Lord Elyon would speak some tender solution to her quandary as she issued from her bedchamber.

The keen gleam in Nat and Sayah's eyes betrayed their question before it left their mouths. Anticipating their interrogation, Nida raised a hand to stop them.

"Just a moment, please, before you ask again," she preempted. "I've a proposal, if you will hear me out."

Ægle and etém nodded in agreement, and Nida continued, "I would like for us three to go to Tram and Kehren this morning, and I would like to speak to them *alone* before I give my answer to you. Until then, I don't want to hear another word on the matter. Is that acceptable?"

Again, they nodded, this time with enthusiasm, and a bright-eyed Nat asked, "So, when ar – ?"

"Ah! Ah!" Nida interrupted. "Not another word, remember?"

Nat took a deep breath and replied, "Yes, ma'am."

"Fantastic!" Nida exclaimed. "Well, then! Let's go!"

Nat joined Sayah outside while Nida locked up. She forbade them not their exultant cries of "Hooray!" and didn't dissuade the ægle's flapping, though she might insist on a few of his feathers for a new duster to help clean the house later.

She turned in the doorway to peer back into their home, oft-missed during their adventure. The sunlight framed her, its rays illuminating the discreet particles that yet floated in the wafting air. After all Sayah's puffing over the porridge earlier, and now his flapping about, the home was a right dusty mess.

No matter, Nida considered with a smile, then closed and locked the door. *It was worth it.*

Nida followed Sayah and Nat down to the Sylvanfare, trailing behind at such a distance that she lost sight of them for an instant when they hooked behind the screen of straw along the road. She quickened her pace to catch up, likewise turning to follow a familiar course to their friends' estate.

She pulled up at once, obstructed by the upturned fan of Sayah's great tailfeathers, and uttered a startled cry. The ægle lowered his tail, and Nida spied Nat atop Sayah's back, gripping the raptor's shining, white neck. Both Nat and Sayah looked back at her, Nat freeing a hand to beckon while Sayah jerked his head to welcome her aboard.

Nida was unprepared for flight but could think of no reason to refuse the invitation. She'd never ridden Sayah before, though she had permitted Nat to do so, and was a tad intimidated. Shaking her head, she resolved to give it a try. She'd climbed tall trees and even cliffs before. This couldn't be so different.

Besides, she reasoned, *It will get us to Tram and Kehren's that much faster.*

A little uncertain at how to mount the ægle, she asked, "Just how do I do this?"

"Just step around my tail and hop on," Sayah called back over his shoulder. "You can grab my feathers to climb up behind Nat. Don't worry! It doesn't hurt."

Doing as Sayah had instructed, Nida circumvented his tail and gathered herself before leaping at his back. She sprawled, her fingers raking into the short, fan-shaped feathers for purchase.

"AAAGH!!!" the ægle cried out, as though in pain.

Concerned she'd injured him somehow despite his reassurances, Nida yelped, "Oh, no! Have I hurt you, Sayah?"

The ægle turned his head again, a cheeky grin curving his profile while Nat stifled impish giggles in Sayah's feathers, his frame convulsing with pent-up amusement.

Sayah winked a golden eye and apologized, "My apologies, ma'am. Just a little joke. Some humor to lighten the mood before our flight."

Before Nida could ready a dry retort, the ægle flipped his tail into the air, leveling his frame and bouncing Nida closer to Nat, who straddled Sayah's neck. These two were getting out of hand!

Nida decided not to force the issue, electing instead to scoot up behind her son, who leaned forward to encircle Sayah's neck with his arms.

Nida looked around with some anxiety before asking, "And what do I hold on to?"

"Me! Hold onto me, mom!" Nat shouted with excitement.

She embraced his frame at once, and in response he cheered, "Yeah, that's it!"

Sayah hollered, "Everyone ready back there!?!"

Nida braced herself and looked about once more, uncertain if she was, indeed, ready.

Sayah didn't wait for a response, but sprung from the earth, beating the air with great sweeps of his wings. Nida gulped while the ægle carried them upward, lunging with each thrust as though ascending invisible steps in the air.

Soon, they were high over the treetops, and Sayah wheeled eastward, his eyes picking out their destination through the foliage. Sayah leveled out to glide toward Tram and Kehren's home, and Nida enjoyed the serene sense that she was unbound from the earth with the wind flowing around and lifting them along their way. The sensation did not last long.

The trip was a short one, and soon Sayah was hurtling downward, his wingspan narrow and tight while Nat whooped and hollered. Nida gripped her son so tight she wondered how he had breath left for exultation. Her apprehension grew as she realized how close the ground had come, and the ægle had yet to slow his descent. At the last moment, Sayah snapped his wings open, wide in braking form, and the force of sudden deceleration pressed his passengers down into the cushion of his feathered back.

With a powerful grace, the ægle alit upon Tram and Kehren's lawn, mere steps from the doors of the manor. And with a bit less grace, Nida draped her legs off one side of the ægle's back and slid down the sleek, snowy feathers to land with a jolt. Years of climbing experience informed her movements, and she landed in a semi-crouched position to absorb the impact. She brushed tiny, white tufts from her jacket and took stock of herself in the aftermath of her first flight.

"So?" Nat asked, as he, too, slid from Sayah with the carefree ease of youth. "How was it?"

"If it's all the same to you two," she answered, "I'd prefer to stick to walking. No offense, Sayah."

"Hey there!" a cry arose from the direction of the house, and Rae leapt from the porch, clearing all the steps in a single bound as she hurried to greet them.

Nat prepared himself for Rae's embrace, bending his knees and dropping his hips low to brace himself for impact as he held arms out to catch her. He would not be caught unawares this time.

Rae collided with Nat at full speed, and the etém redirected the force of the encounter to whirl her around. Together, the young Etom twirled, their eyes locked as time seemed to slow around them.

In revolution thus prolonged, Nat saw something new in the glint of Rae's eyes, a force that drew them into its center and closed the gap between them. A scan of kindred memories blurred through Nat's mind. His friend matured before his mind's eye from sassy schoolmate to devoted friend, the gleam in her eyes ever present and intensifying, though all the while escaping his notice – until now.

The realization kindled a strange warmth deep in Nat's belly, and brought a violet blush to his cheeks. The speedy sweep of their circuit slowed to a dance of concerted pivots, and Rae, spotting the blooms of color on Nat's face, mirrored him. They stopped altogether, and something inside Nat turned over, stoking warm embers into a blaze.

The sudden, penetrating heat of the moment soon discomfited Rae and Nat so that, releasing one another, their dance devolved into an awkward dither. They stood with faces flushed and downcast, neither unwilling to lift embarrassed eyes.

Sayah and Nida witnessed Nat and Rae's brief but expressive display – the former with naïve confusion, the latter with informed interest. Nida clucked her tongue and shook her head with an incredulity borne out of her surprise. She'd not expected such a turn in Rae and Nat's relationship so soon.

"Alright, alright. That's enough of that, you two," Nida declared, inserting herself between the gawky youths.

Taking Rae by the shoulder, Nida spun the young etma about to face the mansion and compelled her forward with a firm hand at her back. Nida was eager to meet with Tram and Kehren and hoped that a change of setting would bring the youngsters back to their senses.

"Rae, dear," she began, "where are your parents, please? I would like to speak to them if they're home."

Recovering from her daze, Rae blinked, and replied, "They're both home. They should just be finishing up breakfast."

With a self-conscious hand, Rae rubbed her other arm and confided, "They were a both down a bit later than usual, but that's because they were up so late last night. I suppose that's our fault, isn't it?"

Nida felt for the etma and slid the hand on Rae's back around her shoulder to give her a sidelong squeeze, "There, there, Rae. Don't feel too bad about it. We live in dangerous times as it is, and now you're asking to leave home for a bit. It's a worrisome enough business, parenting, although the more practice I have of it seems the worrying doesn't help anyone a whit."

They mounted the steps to the porch and Nida, presuming Nat would have followed them, glanced back to find he and Sayah yet lingered on the lawn.

Employing her most commanding and matronly tone, Nida shouted for his attention, "Nat! Son! You and Sayah come keep Rae company on the porch. I'll have a private word with Rae's parents while you wait."

The unlikely pair scampered to catch up while Nida left Rae at the wide swing on the veranda.

Before stepping into the home, Nida stopped to ask Rae, "May I?"

She gestured to the door, and Rae nodded, "Yes. Please, let yourself in. You know the way to the dining room?"

"Yes, dear," Nida responded. "And don't you worry. If they're following the Spirit, all will be well."

Rae gave a reluctant nod, and Nida turned to go inside. She stepped into the palatial home and gathered her bearings before setting out for the dining room. The layout of the house was simple and elegant, yet expansive. While her destination was not too great a distance away, the trek was sufficient that Nida had opportunity to pray along the way. She believed the Spirit had spoken to her and hoped Tram and Kehren had likewise found agreement.

Nida approached the dining area, clearing her throat to announce her imminent arrival. With soft, cautious steps, she crossed the threshold, meeting Tram and Kehren's attentive gazes. They hadn't expected such a visit this early in the morning, but Nida had given sufficient warning that she'd not caught them altogether unawares.

The large bay window at Tram and Kehren's backs admitted the cool morning sunlight, which played with delicate grace across the all-white décor. The lighting flattered Kehren's lemon-yellow skin, and Tram's chocolate brown, but could not altogether mask the dark patches and tired lines beneath their eyes.

Nida greeted them, "Good morning. I'm sorry for dropping by unannounced. I was hoping to catch you two before you began the day's business. I hope you don't mind that Rae let me in."

Tram stood to motion her to the table, "Not at all, Nida. You're always welcome here. Would you care for a bite? Or perhaps some tea?"

Nida took a seat opposite the couple and a cup of tea to warm herself after the chill of her inaugural flight. Settling in, Nida noticed that Kehren stared obliquely at the wall, her plate untouched before her on the table.

Unaccustomed to seeing her friend so distracted, Nida initiated conversation to see if she could draw her out.

"It's a beautiful morning, isn't it?"

Kehren shook her head as if from a daze, her eyes darting to meet Nida's and then away again. She fidgeted in her seat and then just looked down.

From her downcast face wafted her reply, "I suppose it is, yes."

Nida attended the first, silent tear to fall on Kehren's lap, and was at her friend's side before the subsequent torrent had commenced in full. She wrapped an arm around Kehren's heaving shoulders, consoling her as she peered around the etma for Tram, who wore the same pained expression as his wife.

"Oh, you poor dears!" Nida commiserated. "Look how troubled you are. Have you been praying? Has the Spirit delivered you an answer?"

"That's just it!" Kehren sobbed. "We knew at once what He desired. It's His answer that wounds us so!"

"So, you're letting Rae go?" Nida enquired, all at once hopeful and dismayed.

"I can hardly bear to say it, but...yes," Kehren breathed, while Tram nodded in somber affirmation.

Nida, in solidarity with her friends, revealed what she, too, had learned, "I have my answer, as well. Nat will go with Sayah and Rae. Whatever the Spirit has planned for them must be important."

"We know. We know," Tram returned, his face growing stern and determined.

A flash of insight, a whisper from the Spirit, revealed to Nida that Tram was resolute in his obedience, and that his current pain was in sympathy with his wife.

Kehren stanched her flowing tears, her mouth trembling as she spat with tempered bitterness, "But how could He send them out alone? At this age? They're just *babies!*"

Kehren's grief wrenched at Nida's maternal heart, for she'd endured the same internal argument now a number of times. She struggled for mastery over the tears that threatened beneath the looming stormfront of separation from her son, and at last blinked them back behind the brimming levee of her determination.

"Kehren," she began in a low and sturdy voice, "We've no assurance of their safety out there. But, we know that whatever He commands, every mission the Spirit assigns us is significant."

Kehren shook her head, and retorted, "I don't know how you can be so calm."

She shot Tram a resentful look and continued, "*Both* of you. I can't stand the thought of our children in harm's way. I'm even worried about Sayah. The three of them out in the wilderness and us here with no way to help them."

"We know Lord Elyon will send them whatever help they might need," Nida encouraged. "Regardless of where *we* are, He will be there, and that's most important. Think back to every moment of peril, of doubt, on our journey to find the Kinsman, and you'll find He walked there with us, every step of the way.

"Throughout our escape from Endego and our search for Him, through Rae's injury and our imprisonment, He was alongside us. And consider, too, Nat's adventure alone. He didn't find the Kinsman's Tree alone, and he didn't come back for us alone. Even when my son was on the brink of death, Lord Elyon held him in His hands and sent him on ægle's wings to be healed in the springs of life. None of us could have done the same, which is why He is Lord, not us.

"And while you may imagine some terrible fate for Rae in the wilderness, I can imagine none more terrifying for Nat than a safe and meaningless life here in Endego because *I would not release him.* I daresay you feel the same, if you have thought it through."

Nida watched as Kehren breathed in the words to tonifying effect. With her each passing breath, Kehren, once bent with sorrow, straightened to sit erect with shoulders back. The etma's eyes, alight with faithful flames, stared beyond current circumstance into a future ideal, and a flinty grin touched her lips.

Her good cheer having returned, Kehren looked first to Tram, then Nida, and spoke, "Ok. Let's give the children our answer."

While the adults decided their fate inside the house, Rae had some interesting news to share with Nat and Sayah. This morning, she'd headed out to the stables before dawn to groom the chevrotains. At this hour, in the early tranquility of the day, Rae found stillness enough within herself to commune with the Spirit, undistracted.

Today, however, had proven different. As with meditative care she had brushed one of the deer-like creatures in his stall, a voice had sounded from across the way.

"Aaahhhh! I bet that feels nice, doesn't it? I hope I get a turn today, too."

The unprepared Rae had shrieked with fright and thrown her brush up in the air. The hard, wooden implement by chance fell atop the head of the creature she'd been grooming, a young buck named Acorn, eliciting a wounded cry from the animal.

"Ow! Ow! Ow! That smarts!" Acorn protested. "Do be careful, please!"

Rae, in the rarest of occasions, was stunned into silence.

When she'd regained her voice, she sputtered, "Y-you can talk? Can all of you, then?"

Acorn was stunned as Rae had been when he realized that not only could the etma understand him, but he likewise understood her. Oh, the chevrotains had a rudimentary comprehension of Etom speech, as do many creatures trained to do the bidding of those they serve. This, however, was a chevrotain of a different stripe altogether and Acorn was a moment in processing the revelation.

Rae asked again, "So can all of you speak? Acorn? Acorn!"

The young etma's persistent intensity at last broke through to Acorn, who replied, "Yes, yes, yes! Of course, we all speak. To one another at least. This, though...this is something new."

"And how did it come to be that we can understand one another?" an inquisitive voice called from the adjacent stall.

It was Acorn's neighbor, Chickpea, a sweet doe not much older than Acorn. Since Rae's first startled outcry, Chickpea had remained quiet, listening to the conversation next door until an opportune time.

Rae bustled out of Acorn's stall and stood back from him and Chickpea, her eyes flitting back and forth between the two as she answered.

"Well, you see, a long time ago, Lord Elyon promised He'd send someone to save Creation from the Stain, the Kinsman, if you didn't kno–oh-OH-AAAGH!"

While backing away from Acorn and Chickpea's stalls, Rae had put herself in reach of one of their neighbors across the way, whose snuffling nose against the back of Rae's zalzal had evoked her violent reaction.

"Yeah, yeah," the newcomer drawled. "We know Elyon's plan. Don't everyone? Been talkin' 'bout it long enough now. Like *thousands* of years already."

This time, it was Walnut, an oft-sulky, older buck who made a habit of begging Rae for sweets.

"Didn't know this'd be part of it, though," Walnut droned. "The talking to strange critters bit, that is. No offense to any strange critters present."

This last was paired with a pointed glance and nod at Rae, who chuckled in reply, "A *critter*? *Strange*? Me? That's too funny. You all are the cri – "

The statement died on Rae's lips as she realized now the depth of division the Stain had drawn between the kinds. Indeed, Walnut's next words drove the point home.

"That's right, isn't it, folks? Everyone in Crittation is a critter what Elyon crittated...or am I wrong?"

"No, no," a melodious voice intoned, joining a chorus that now swelled to fill the stables as the rest of the chevrotains assured Walnut.

Another doe, this one more mature than Chickpea, poked her head around the edge of Walnut's stall and added, "Not wrong at all, Walnut."

"Elyon *created* all *creatures* in *Creation*," the matronly doe, Pralíne, offered gentle correction in the emphasis of her words.

Walnut flapped his lips at Rae along with a half-lidded retort, "See? Toldya."

Rae was both flabbergasted and fascinated that these creatures among whom she'd found such joy in life also had in common the remembrance and recognition of the Creator and His plan. These *creatures* had been her friends since before she'd met Nat, and fond recollection, draped in sepia, overwhelmed her in a nostalgic wave: her father, setting her atop a mellow steed, her mother teaching her to brush the chevrotains' short fur, the family bundled up together in a sleigh pulled by...by these *friends*.

Oh! And the Stain! She daren't let these poor creatures go another day without her sharing with them all the Kinsman had accomplished on behalf of "Crittation."

A bemused chuckle escaped Rae as she recalled Walnut's earlier declaration. If anything, their voices endeared them even more to her, which, as Rae reflected, might just be the Spirit's purpose in giving her such a gift.

Rae had spent the early hours of the morning with the chevrotains, pampering them and spoiling them with treats while she chatted with them and got to know them even better than she had. It wasn't long before she'd let them all loose of their stalls on the solemn oath of each that they'd not caper or attempt to escape.

"You needn't worry 'bout us, missy," Walnut shared. "We know it's cold out there, and in here we've got a whole lotta food, too."

"Yes. Rather," Pralíne enjoined. "If anything, we might prefer the stalls were gone so we have a bit more room to stretch our legs from time to time."

"Like a really nice barn?" Rae asked.

Pralíne snorted at Rae's crudity, then nodded, "Well, yes. If you must call it that. Like a...*barn*."

The word dripped from Pralíne's lips as if it were a strand of dangling slobber she couldn't quite shake. Nevertheless, Rae had a clear idea on how she might make the chevrotains more comfortable in their dwelling, and a tale to tell Sayah and Nat.

She wished her new friends a good day and closed the main stable door fast behind her, then set off for the porch swing to await visitors she was certain were due any moment now.

After Rae recounted the story for her amazed friends, they peppered her with questions while they waited on the adults to bring forth their decision. Rae, Nat, and Sayah were thus engaged in full until the creak of the front door alerted them the moment had arrived at last.

The trio of adult Etom stepped out of the great home to meet the trio of youths outside, and the latter were giddy with anticipation. Sayah's sharp eyes darted to the main door as it opened, and Nat and Rae sprang up from the porch swing to stand at attention at once. Each one was hopeful they'd be allowed to undertake the mission. With such hopes in their hearts they turned to their parents in a moment burdened with expectation.

When neither Nida nor Tram at first spoke up, Kehren looked to them with some doubt. They both replied without a word and rather nodded at the young ones. Kehren took a deep breath. She'd not expected impromptu appointment as spokesetma but fell back on her years as Headmistress in the Bunker to address the eager youths.

"Well, as you know, we three parents have been seeking the Spirit's will since our conversation last night, and we've arrived at a decision. It was a difficult choice to make, but not because we found it difficult to perceive the Spirit clearly."

Kehren turned shimmering eyes on Rae, Nat, and Sayah in turn, then shared, "You should know how precious each of you are to us. Even you, Sayah. You were born a child to none of us but have become like a son to us all. We are family, which is why I, in particular, had such a hard time deciding...deciding...to..."

She could no longer hold back the tears, and her voice hitched with emotion before she regained herself to finish, "...to let you go!"

Even the gravity of the occasion could not altogether restrain Nat, Rae and Sayah's glee, though all three managed somehow not to jump or, in the case of Sayah, flap, for joy. The two Etom shouted and the ægle crowed, and their eyes shone with excited delight. They were going on a mission!

"Children! Children!" Nida shouted for their attention, and they soon stilled themselves to listen to her.

"The question now is a matter of *when* you might depart. Now, we daren't delay you any longer than necessary in the Spirit's mission but thought it prudent to bring the issue before the whole Council of the Vine. Not so much for permission, mind you.

"We believe they'll find the matter settled with the Spirit as we have, but we wish to ensure the whole community is prepared for your absence. Each of you brings something special to our number, and we will all feel your absence in one way or another. Will you accept the Council's decision regarding the time of your dispatch?"

"Yes, ma'am!" Nat and Rae chimed in synch and Sayah bobbed his snowy head in emphatic agreement.

"Now that's settled, I suggest we take you to Council immediately for their answer," Nida proposed, scanning Tram and Kehren for a response.

Rae's parents were of the same accord, and, having all adorned themselves for the crisp autumn weather, they departed at once. Though Sayah might have carried a couple of the Etom at a time with greater speed than their legs could, Nida insisted they travel by foot. There would be time enough for the young ones to fly once they had embarked on their adventure.

Chapter Eight
Ready to Launch

The party of six took their morning walk at a brisk pace, as though the Spirit Himself compelled their steps. The five Etom puffed along, their breath frosty in the cold air while Sayah sauntered along, his long legs enabling him to keep up with the others without much effort.

Nat's mind was abuzz with a trembling, luminous melody that sang in him a hopeful chorus. He sensed the Spirit moving them along at a terrific speed and did not anticipate that the Council would much delay their departure. He rejoiced, too, that it the Spirit was rewarding his obedience and that of his friends. They had neither defied their parents nor allowed themselves to be dissuaded from the path appointed them.

Amidst all his youthful, energetic experiences, he couldn't recall another so exhilarating. His being seemed to crackle with a quickening charge. When he could no longer contain the energy, the etém dashed up a bowed root, his feet swift and sure as he ascended. With a great whoop of joy, he bounded from the root's highest point, flipping and turning as he descended.

The outburst took none of his companions by surprise for the Spirit coursed through each of them. At the moment Nat darted forward, Sayah had shot straight up into the air with a single, great burst of his wings. At the apex of his ascent, the ægle tucked his wings and arched back in a tenuous roll. Sayah's beak tipped back, back, back until he faced straight down, a diving missile in trajectory perpendicular to the earth.

Rae had cartwheeled sideways behind Nat before she turned on a graceful spring of the hands, pouring herself forward in a smooth, liquid arc to land on both feet. Charged with momentum, she didn't stop her forward motion, but skipped with lengthening, playful strides, then sprinted up the root after Nat.

Overhead, she heard Sayah's keening call, and, reaching the pinnacle of the root, called in response, "Sayah, catch me!"

Without breaking stride, she leapt straight out, arms extended in miniscule emulation of the ægle. Breaking from his dive, Sayah opened his wings wide and fanned his tail, sweeping forward in a streak of flashing light. His looming form eclipsed Rae just as she began to fall, and he extended talons to encircle either arm with gentle care. The pair floated to the ground, where Nat awaited them with a wide grin and shining face.

Tram, Kehren, and Nida had not been idle, though expression of their sudden empowerment had taken a somewhat milder turn. While the youth cavorted, the adults jogged on in wonder, concerned more with losing sight of the youths and their spontaneous acrobatics than with joining in the performance.

They approached the gaggle of children, and Nida noted the depth of the bond Nat, Rae, and Sayah shared. The three of them belonged together, and Nida couldn't think of anyone else she'd rather see at Nat's side for their journey. Dangerous though the adventure might be, she knew that these three would lay their lives on the line for one another should the need arise.

The six of them soon arrived at Sanctuary Endego and spread out to gather the Council of the Vine. Since three of the Council's members were already involved in the search for the others, their task of finding the remaining nine was accomplished in short order.

In the later hours of the morning, the twelve members of the Council encircled Nat, Rae and Sayah beneath the Tree to discuss the matter at hand. They entreated the wisdom of the Spirit to open the meeting, then set to the discussion of when the young trio should depart.

Even the temporary loss of Nat and Rae was incalculable. Their contributions were in large part spiritual, and thus the loss was not easy to define. They would be missed, as would Sayah, whose worthy contributions were of a less abstract nature. He was a stalwart sentry and a mighty ally in combat, whose mere presence lent great comfort to the community as a whole.

In the end, the Council distilled their concerns down to a single point: Sayah's absence would diminish the security of Endego by great measure. His reconnaissance abilities alone would make him sorely missed, his other qualities aside.

Unaccustomed to being the focus of conversation, Sayah retreated to his own reflections while the discussion continued. The Spirit nudged his meandering mind, and Sayah's thoughts turned to a recent phenomenon in the aftermath of the Empire's defeat.

Afterward, the Etom here or the wee creature there approached the bower, most often with a timid eagerness to which Sayah had at once related. They came with the same hope in their hearts as any other, though they would have been hard pressed to articulate the unspoken hope with lip, beak, or maw.

Regardless, the Kinship recognized the need to welcome these into their midst and so conducted them to the brimming, shimmering pool at the foot of the Tree should they desire. These first non-Etom the Kinship greeted with some hesitancy, uncertain how to share the good news of the Kinsman with those not of their kind.

Again, however, Lord Elyon provided. From amongst the Kin, a number soon came forward to assist as the Spirit enabled them with new gifts. While the various kinds already in the Vine enjoyed uncanny communication with one another, such as between ægle, fox, and Etom, this was not common to those not yet grafted in.

Ever since the Sunder, the harmonious connection all creatures had once shared with one another was severed. Afterward, the utterances of each kind became unintelligible to those who differed and prevented the universal understanding all creatures enjoyed at the beginning.

Nevertheless, those the Spirit empowered with this particular gift were able to converse with any type of creature that ventured near the Tree. Sayah was counted among their number, and, as she had demonstrated upon meeting Astéri, Rae also displayed such a gift for communication with outsiders. Proving to be a hospitable hostess, Rae strove to be present when newcomers trickled.

In any case, it was the newcomers that Sayah contemplated, and ere long he recalled several birds of various sizes and persuasions that had come to join the Vine. For a long moment the Spirit suffered the young ægle to consider the implications before he struck the right one.

"Oh! That's it!" Sayah exclaimed, oblivious he'd interrupted the ongoing deliberation of the Council.

All eyes turned to Sayah, none irritated, but all expectant until at last Shoym urged him, "Yes, Sayah? What is it?"

A glowering bashfulness threatened, but Sayah swept it aside to answer, "I'm sorry. I didn't mean to interrupt, but I believe the Spirit's already given us the answer."

A broad smile curving his beak, the ægle looked about the gathering, unaware he'd failed to give said answer. Again, they all looked to him, though now bemused smirks danced at the edges of a good many mouths. Most covered their grins with a polite hand, hoping not to embarrass the ægle.

Shoym wheeled an ash-colored hand in forward motion to prompt Sayah, and, when this cue failed to coax out the critical information, resorted to another inquiry.

"Sayah, my dear ægle, we're all ears. What's this answer of which you speak?"

"Don't you see?" Sayah asked, his head twitching from side to side with excitement as his gaze darted about his audience.

"It's birds!"

Even after such dramatic escalation, not all of Sayah's audience managed to follow the ægle to his conclusion. Several shook their heads in confusion, and at least one groaned in disappointment. Nat, however, just looked down at his feet, chin in hand, until confident he perceived the thrust of Sayah's assertion aright.

"Ok, hold on!" Nat shouted, coming to his friend's defense. "I think I see what Sayah's after here. Will you give me a second with him, please?"

Nat turned, whispering to Sayah as Rae leaned in to listen, "Sayah, do you mean to say that we should recruit some of the birds who've joined us as replacements for you?"

Sayah gave a fervent nod, and blurted, "Yes! Yes! That's exactly it!"

"That's not a bad idea, Nat," Rae offered. "I've met nearly all of them. They probably want to help out anyhow, and this would solve the Council's problem."

"Ok, then," Nat agreed, and chuckled at his ægle friend before hooking a thumb over his shoulder at the Council. "Do you mind if I tell them?"

Eyes wide, Sayah shook his head, relieved to relinquish the burden of public address to Nat.

Nat turned around and raised a hand for the Council's attention, "Sayah has what I would call an inspired idea, if you'll hear us out."

As always, his Etom friend's use of inclusive terms warmed the ægle's heart. Even amidst his family, he'd not often been counted as part of the 'us.' In silence, he thanked Lord Elyon again for His gracious invitation into this great family, this Kinship.

Agatous spoke up in response to Nat, "Please, tell us, dear."

"We believe we can enlist the aid of our new feathered friends to secure the village in Sayah's stead," Nat proposed.

A collective sense of rumination fell over the Council, expressed in lowered, introspect stares and by way of pensive frowns, punctuated with short nods of affirmation. A few Etom murmured to one another while, to the contrary, Blithewit lounged with face impassive and bushy tail flicking the air. Sensing the Council was near a decision, the fox turned to the young trio and sent a cockeyed nod and a wink their way.

With his back to the youths, Shoym conferred with the Council until at last he turned to address them, "We believe your plan might work, but would like to see how well it does before giving a final decision. Would you three consider helping us put together the new team? Sayah, we would rely on you for their training."

Nat appealed to Rae and Sayah for confirmation, "What do you say? Can we wait a few days before we go?"

"Sure!" Rae replied at once.

Sayah was a bit slower to respond, but also agreed, "I think it's for the best. After all, it doesn't seem right to leave the village vulnerable when we go."

"We would be happy to help," Nat told Shoym with a smile. "When can we begin? We would like to start right away."

"Well, I should think we ought to gather those creatures amenable to the duty first," Shoym answered. "After, we need to screen our candidates for suitability."

He waved an open hand to Sayah, "That's where you come in, Sayah. We'll need your insight to pick the right ones."

Now committed to the task, Sayah pressed on past the limits of his self-consciousness to assent, "I will do my best, Lord Elyon willing."

Shoym clapped his flinty hands, then rubbed them together as he exclaimed, "Fantastic! Then let's get going!"

Out of necessity, the youngsters broke into two teams, one comprised of Sayah and Nat, and the other of Rae and Blithewit, who offered his services after the meeting ended. Communication and speed were critical to their current mission and were the two factors foremost in their consideration when pairing off.

Rae and Sayah were the two able to speak with and understand their potential recruits and were thus placed in separate teams. Nat's knack for navigating misunderstanding made him the best partner for the often tongue-tied ægle.

Rae could handle herself in a negotiation and required nothing but the swift feet of the sprightly old silver fox to carry her and his predatory assets to ward off potential attackers along their way. Sayah would likewise provide Nat protection and lend swiftness to their search amidst the sky.

Before long, naught remained but to depart, one pair to the east and the other to the west with each group planning to return in the afternoon to confer. In their final act before embarking, the two Etom sat astride their respective steeds, all their heads in humble inclination whilst they prayed the Spirit's blessing.

The prayer was little more than a few spoken words, but the wind caressed their prostrate forms, the Spirit stirring their hearts and suffused their actions. With a smart switch of the tail, Blithewit bounded away, Rae calling farewell from his back. Sayah, meanwhile, gathered himself then burst upwards through the leafy canopy, and they were off.

To term their adventure perilous would be to overstate the case. In truth, all went as well as any could have planned. Better, even. Each team encountered the first of their recruits over wary moments that resolved almost at once. Those fowl who had visited Sanctuary Endego at once recognized Sayah and Blithewit in particular, as did a good many Rae.

A silver fox and pure-white ægle were an uncommon enough sight in the region, let alone these who did not treat their diminutive peers with predatory scorn. Rae, too, had made an impression. Her welcoming presence at the Tree was well-remembered, and Nat alone found himself forced to make frequent introductions.

In each instance, the separate pairs discovered many birds great and small willing to assist those earthbound near the Tree. Another help these also offered was the expedient dissemination of the Kinship's need. Sparrow and jay, mockingbird or crow, none was above the task of carrying the word to others of their kind: those who had brought new life and light to the land now requested aid.

When Nat and Sayah returned to Endego near noontime, they found a veritable flock of the feathered variety under the bower. The vixen, Whisperweave, and the other Etom had at first been apprehensive when birds began to arrive in force. The Council had anticipated a substantial turnout, but the sheer number of recruits was alarming, though they soon acknowledged the enormity of the enlistment as the endorsement of Lord Elyon.

Although for the most part the Etom hung back from the assemblage of larger creatures, they were nonetheless grateful for the fowl and marveled at the Creator's provision. Some Etom the Spirit had gifted both the tongues of their feathered friends and the courage to wield them. These brave few ventured forth from the fringes of the gathering to engage the burgeoning flock.

A concerted effort between the Etom thus gifted and those birds already in the Vine produced among the gathered flow a good many new Kin. Before Nat and the others had returned from their errand, a baptismal parade was making way through the springwaters of the Tree. Indeed, the triumphal procession had continued throughout the morning until every bird who answered the call to help had likewise answered the call of the Kinsman.

The warmth and enthusiasm of the reception Nat and Sayah had earlier received aside, the sight of the multitude they encountered now encouraged them in their endeavor. Nat had never seen such a great variety of birds together in one place and couldn't identify many of them.

Fortunately, at his side he had Sayah, who was well-versed in the diversity of his kind. From their perch in a willow at the perimeter of the gathering, the ægle relayed the nomenclature of the fowl with short descriptions.

"The large black bird there is a raven, and the two smaller black birds are crows. They are known to be quite clever, though a bit cheeky."

"The loud, gray one near the water is a francolin, a distant cousin of the pheasant and partridge. Not great flyers, but excellent on the ground. You wouldn't want to tangle with one due to their spurs."

"Strange to see a hornbill this far north. You see him there beyond the francolin with the great, hooked beak. Must be a male. The females are quite preoccupied with rearing their young, and don't often roam."

Sayah tipped his head left and right before waving a wing at an arching tree root, "Don't know if you can pick him out, but just past the root on the left, you might see him. A hypocolius. Not known as social, but dear creatures all the same. He's still as stone, that one, but watching every move."

"Over here, you'll see a pair of goshawks. The heavyset ones standing there. Interesting lot, the goshawks. They're smart enough, but don't have much initiative of their own. They often lurk about while others hunt and pick off the strays."

"Note the cluster of wee, dark birds at the center? The ones with a metallic gleam to their feathers?"

Nat nodded, and Sayah returned to his instruction, "Those are starlings, what you'd call a gregarious lot. They're wonderful in their own way but can't seem to mind their own business. Might be useful in communications."

And thus, Sayah continued to describe the various types already present, and those that yet teemed to join the burgeoning flock. Soon, it seemed every available inch of the bower was packed with plumage, and rows of fowl lined every branch.

A disturbance at the western bounds of the bower signaled the return of Blithewit and Rae, who paraded through the parting crowd in search of Nat and Sayah. The scant clearing that opened around fox and etma gave opportunity for Sayah to carry Nat to their side.

With a sweeping flair of his beating white wings, the ægle dropped down into the crowd. Sayah stooped low to let Nat disembark, then stood erect, his dynamic entry and stately, shining form drawing attention as a hush fell over all. In the quietude, the quartet whispered a quick conversation, determined not to make their guests wait long.

"Do you see how many came?" Rae asked in amazement, her pink cheeks rosy with excitement.

Even cool Blithewit was affected and an uncharacteristic enthusiasm colored his speech, "It is, indeed, a spectacle unlike any other I've seen."

"Our efforts have certainly been rewarded," Nat affirmed.

Eyes closed in reverence, Sayah offered, "Lord Elyon is with us, and has filled our wings with the wind of success."

The three others blinked, then turned to stare at the ægle, who was not often prone to such flowery statements.

Nat cleared his throat, threw a friendly jab at Sayah's soft breast and complimented the ægle, "There's poetry in you yet, brother. You surprise us all at times."

The etém craned his neck all about for a moment, then asked the others, "I suppose the main thing is deciding who will speak to them all. I've no aversion to the task, but I don't know that I have the same knack for their speech as you, Rae, or Sayah. What say you all? Who should do it?"

Blithewit gave a curt shake of the head, and declined, "I'm pleased to help you gather everyone here, but I'm not suited to this particular deed. How about Rae? She's well-spoken, it seems, no matter the tongue."

Rae considered the issue while with a pensive hand she pet the braided zalzal draped over her shoulder.

"I'm willing to do it, but don't know what it is we'd like to tell them," she responded at last. "Honestly, I think the only one here who knows how to direct them is Sayah. He's the one that's been doing the job the Council is asking them to do, and he'll know best what to tell them."

Aghast at the prospect, Sayah balked, his great golden eyes round and pupils pinning with agitation while he sputtered, "I...I can't do *that*. Wha – ?"

He whipped his snowy head around to the murmuring crowd, then back to his fellows to protest, "What do I say? I can't for the life of me think of anything."

The ægle gulped, then began to breathe in shaky, ragged breaths. Sayah's friends spied his panic at once and Nat moved to stand before the ægle to grip the front edges of the bird's folded wings in his tiny, blue hands. With a forceful, downward tug, Nat prompted Sayah to lower his gaze to meet his own.

Nat smiled at Sayah as he had at their first meeting, as he ever did when greeting a beloved friend, and spoke strong, low words to him, "Sayah, *you* are the one to do this. We all know it. *You* know it.

"The Spirit within you has decreed it and has prepared you for this moment. We three believe He is at work within you, and there is none here more qualified for this task. You alone here know the assignment, and what is required."

"Now," the etém exhorted, waving a hand over the crowd, "Tell *them*!"

The unsteadiness left Sayah's frame, and he stood tall, fixing blazing eyes straight ahead in his resolve. Nat stood aside and the ægle strode forth to look over the crowd, the Spirit emboldening him with each forward step.

Others there stood taller, yet none struck a more noble figure than the ægle, all the more so for the singularity of his pure, snowy plumage. No longer timid, Sayah swept his gaze across the crowd, assessing the light in each eye before daring to utter a word.

"Friends!" he called. "Comrades in arms! We've come together today in common cause, but not in cause alone.

"What drew you today was not our shared enemy, the Empire of Chōl, that barren carcass that terrorizes our lands – no! The entire world! Rather, we have sensed the tug of something greater, the hand of the Creator extended to us in kindness."

With a low, flat extension of the wing, Sayah gestured back toward the fox and Etom, "But know this – it was these that carried this light into our dark and harried world. Into the prison of our oppression, these tiny Etom cast the rays of their lamps, and showed us the way of our escape through Him who bore away the Stain that permeated our existence.

"Instead of the Stain and its promise of death, we have now a clean countenance before the Creator and the promise of a life connected with Him through the Vine. However, the Vine connects us not with Elyon alone, but also with one another, even across the gulf between our kinds."

Sayah's head bent beneath the weight of emotion as he waved again at Nat, Rae, and Blithewit. His voice choked with the overflow of tearful thanksgiving that percolated within before he could resume his appeal to the enthralled audience.

"While I was yet an enemy, a threat to their very lives, these Etom invited me into their midst. And, now, by the power of Tree, I count them as Kin closer than those to which I was born. I pray now as you search your own hearts, you find the same Kinship there, and that you will join with these around Sanctuary Endego for the protection of the village.

"We know the Empire will not desist in the destruction of Endego, especially now they've suffered a defeat. They cannot afford to. They *will* return. So now I ask – under threat to life and limb, will you risk yourselves in defense of these, your Kin in the Vine!?!"

Sayah's voice rang out over the quiet crowd, the words finding their mark in the hearts of those assembled. The fowl deliberated in the stillness, the ægle growing a bit nervous at the delay until a voice piped up behind the feathered bulk of the goshawks."

"I don't know about these others, but I'm game!"

Even Sayah's prodigious vision was incapable of seeing through solid objects, but nonetheless he squinted in direction of the cry. The crowd bustled about in search of the speaker, and from amidst the commotion a smallish bird emerged.

The creature's plumage was blue-grey in color but for it much darker wings, and Sayah was a moment in identifying the bird as a thrush, and a male at that. The thrush sauntered toward Sayah, tipping his head to the ægle in respect though his fearless eyes never left the raptor's.

"May I ask your name, friend thrush?" Sayah inquired, returning a bow of his snowy head.

"Pteetya is my name," came the stout, whistling reply before the thrush raised his beak to call, "and I'm proud to commit my wings to the cause!"

At once, the ægle loved bold Pteetya, who had shown greater courage than even those larger and better-armed than he among the assemblage. Heartened at Pteetya's response, Sayah followed the thrush's lead to challenge the rest.

"Who else here is brave enough to heed the call of your Kin?" Sayah pressed, his penetrating gaze raking the crowd. "No one? Just this solitary thrush?"

"Good sir!" implored the hornbill. "Please, sir! That's enough."

A raven crowed from amidst his conspiracy, "More than enough, I'd say."

"Aye, Master Ægle," honked a cormorant, a long-necked seabird. "Ye've cut us to the heart, that ye have. Some of us are just a wee bit slower than the thrush. A right trig feller, that one, and speaking for meself, I be with ye."

The rustle of many bobbing, feathered necks filled the bower as the congregated fowl nodded their agreement. Nat and Rae thought they'd never seen anything so wonderful and peculiar. Sayah just gaped in amazement and the narrow eyes of sly Blithewit widened an intrigued and subtle sliver as each one in his heart searched the lore of his people for such an historic event.

But none could recall such an assortment of kinds in concerted agreement outside Man's coercive domination since...well, since before the Sunder. Yet of their own accord these creatures had rallied to the aid of those outside their own race. And in the hearts of those who recognized the miracle and its magnitude, thanksgiving swelled.

Chapter Nine

The Cup

From where he stood in the small clearing amidst the assorted fowl, Nat's golden eyes climbed the Tree's nut-brown trunk. A recollected vision of the Tree Ha Datovara in the vital fullness of Gan cast itself as a net across his gaze to capture past and present in a single instance. Seizing Nat's imagination, the Spirit expanded the young etém's capacities that he might comprehend what was to come.

For like a veil descending over Nat's eyes, the hand of Elyon drew down a third vision atop the others. Against the background of the other two this last stood foremost, and the central figure thereof saved Nat from confusion in the trebled concurrency.

Stamped over top the first two layers of Nat's vision was the Kinsman, no longer nailed to the bent, accursed Tree Ha Datovara. And behind Him stood the ancient Tree, as it did now and forever in Sanctuary, righted once and for all and never again to suffer the twisting perversion of Stain and Blight. And at the forefront, Gaal welcomed all with arms stretched wide, ever radiant and adorned in the blinding white robes of His coronation.

Nat marveled at the Kinsman's majesty while perceiving again the strange, shrinking sensation of self he recognized from earlier encounters with the presence of the Creator. Thus diminished, Nat wondered that such a Being might take note of him, and at that moment felt the heat of Gaal's gaze fall on him.

Never before had Nat experienced such frightful magnificence as Gaal's blazing eyes searched him inside and out. The tiny etém bowed, wracked with fearful heat and pressure in the holy crucible of Gaal's glory, and in that moment cried out for respite. The Spirit assured Nat, comforting him in his affliction and fortifying him against the urge to withdraw. In his pain, Nat clung to Him who had ever proven Himself worthy, although he was uncertain of the meaning of his suffering.

Nevertheless, the Spirit offered Nat escape if he so chose it. The Etom cried out in anguished refusal, resolved to endure the Kinsman's examination. At last, the flames subsided, and the crushing weight lifted from Nat, who, still bent from agony, assumed the eyes of Gaal had passed on.

Lifting his head once more, Nat was surprised to discover the Kinsman still looked at him with eyes aflame. Something had changed within his own being, of that the Etom was quite sure, for now he saw beyond Gaal's burning gaze a tender, warm affection.

The loving-kindness in the Kinsman's eyes drew Nat in, and thus transported into His inner being, the Etom detected a greater closeness with Gaal than ever before. And he drew still nearer at the invitation of Gaal's hearthstone glow, confident in his approach until he found himself beyond the pleasant warmth.

At once, Nat stood ashore unfathomable depths that lapped at his feet with slow, rhythmic constancy. It was dark but for a deep blue luminescence that permeated waves, shore, and cavernous ceiling overhead. Besides the gentle whisper of waves washing against the brittle and porous stone of the shore, Nat heard a faint, steady drip echoing across the expanse.

A golden glint beside his foot prompted Nat to examine the shore, and he lay a hand upon the shining artifact, an ornate, bejeweled chalice. The treasure he held befit a king, and even in darkness it was brilliant.

Compulsion overwhelmed Nat, who knelt at water's edge to dip the chalice beneath the placid surface. He clasped the brimming vessel at his chest, staring into the draught while a single drop slipped from the rim to touch his lapping hands.

Upon contact with the waters, a sudden, boundless grief filled Nat's soul, and images of every kind of abuse came unbidden to his mind. Murder, theft, deceit, and torture drowned his senses as heart of both perpetrator and victim murmured a bitter and broken deluge. From amidst the lamentation Nat picked out a common chorus, a litany of selfishness. Each voice sang the song of self-determination, and each heart purposed a universe centered on its own desires.

With shaking hands, Nat forced the cup away, his weeping eyes cracked open in appraisal of the brew.

Tears! It's tears! he managed through the cacophonous flood. *And that's only what touched my hand.*

He cast his gaze across the waters, and surmised, *How deep His pain must be.*

The Kinsman's voice carried over the waters, which trembled at the sound, "Can you drink of my cup?"

Nat eyes started for the chalice with wary shock, his mouth drawn down in an unpracticed frown of consideration.

What is this?

The Spirit, meanwhile, whispered in counterpoint to the murk that threatened Nat's faculties until revelation as the rays of dawn illumined the Etom's understanding. From Eternity past, the Son enjoyed a will in full concert with Father and Spirit, their existence a triune community of love and perfect submission. Until the rebellion of Helél and the Sunder that followed, all Creation had likewise submitted to the will of the Creator.

Lord Elyon stood as the center of the Universe, the only One of sufficient weight and worth to conduct the grand symphony in its complexity. Life flowed from Him, the very Source of Life, poured out along the untainted and unbroken streams of Tree Ha Kayim that saturated Gan.

With tacit understanding, all creatures obeyed the Creator in the knowledge of their utter dependence on Him. That is, until Kessel and Pethiy introduced a subversion of the life-giving order. They chose their own way. They chose to disobey.

Their disobedience infected all, manifesting in the virulent Stain, an inescapable fracturing of the pristine channels through which Elyon's blessing flowed. But the Stain was a mere representative of the chaos with which Man had infected the world. And beneath it lay the root cause, a will that neither knew nor cared to submit to the Creator.

All creatures became as planets disowning their sun to career through the cold darkness, bereft of a single point of orientation sufficient in warmth and gravity to bring them into regenerative orbit. And in their futile attempts to set themselves up as such a center, many collided with one another – to the great misfortune of all. Others, meanwhile, spun off into the lightless murk in search of other masters and there found none worthy.

The tragedy of selfish will offended the Creator, who ever intended life and pleasure for His dominion. At first, Nat had mistaken the sea of tears as the well of Creation's sorrows, but now saw in them the immense grief of the Creator Himself.

There is more, the Spirit pronounced as the ocean of sorrows cast up a single droplet from its depths.

It arced toward Nat, who watched on in anxious expectation as it flew at him, the dim light catching the drop to reveal its color – red.

Blood? Nat wondered right before it struck, splashing its misery across his broad and hapless brow.

The droplet of blood enveloped Nat's vision entire, then at once receded to pinprick size as he was launched backward past fragrant, unfamiliar foliage. He landed in a painless, backward somersault and rolled to a stop in a moonlit garden.

What met the Etom's eyes transfixed him, for before him knelt the Kinsman Gaal, who prayed, face upturned and hands clasped before him on a great stone.

"My Father," He pleaded, "If it be possible, allow this cup to pass from Me. Nevertheless, not My will, but Yours be done."

Nat spied again the droplet of blood from which he'd sprung into the vision. One among many that now stood out on Gaal's anguished brow, the drop traveled down to mingle with the falling tears that spattered against the stone.

The scene dissolved before Nat, who yet stood at water's edge, cup in hand and contemplating his answer. In his heart, the Spirit awakened ever greater understanding.

The Kinsman had suffered the temptation of His own will, perhaps the one and only time between Son and Father that contention had threatened. Nonetheless, the Son had submitted to the Father, though pain unspeakable awaited Him at the Tree. Pain as what awaited in the chalice Nat held.

In His obedience, even unto death, Gaal made a channel of Himself as of those flowing from the Tree Ha Kayim, a Way to restore the life-giving order Lord Elyon established from the beginning. From the Kinsman's reversal of deathly self-determination sprang a fount of new life and the means of all Creation to partake in it.

The sea before Nat contained every sorrow of the Kinsman's heart, including the torment of His self-denial. A created being dared not set foot therein, only the Begotten One. To do so would overwhelm any heart but that of the Divine. Pulled down by the weight of despair, even the stoutest in Creation would slip under the surface to drown beneath the heavy waters.

Regardless, the Spirit spoke the revitalizing potential of any creature willing to follow the Kinsman, to emulate His sacrifice, and brought to Nat's mind the moment Miyam gave herself over to establish Sanctuary Endego. Hers was a seed that had sprouted to bring both life and protection to all who put their hope in the Kinsman. *She* had drunk of His cup.

This last realization was enough to convince the Etom, who with trembling breath gave action as his answer. He downed the draught in one go, its bitter, salted savor proving almost too much for him to swallow. Nevertheless, he finished the cup to its dregs, staggering back a step as frightening sobriety shook him.

Impressions and images persisted in their grievous refrain and again the Spirit comforted Nat's soul with a melody at once sadder and more joyful than any he'd heard before. Nat discovered clarity in the song, a resolution of reality's deep conflict that life itself should be both bitter and sweet.

The drink worked outward from Nat's interior, breaching first his heart, then skin, nostril, tongue, eye, and ear with a crisp and glassy snap. With senses sharpened thus, he peered across the cavernous expanse to discover a distant heap of smoldering coals peeking up through the surface of the waters.

Steam and smoke roiled about the pyre, obscuring it in part, though now Nat could see its glowing foundation plunging down, down, down into the yawning brine past his ability to trace its fulminating roots. He likewise perceived now the approach of vapor and fumes wafting toward him over the water, their drift heretofore undetected by Nat's sensibilities before the draught had tempered them.

None but the slightest tendril crossed the void to reach the far shore, the remainder of the chuffing cloud dissipating over the breadth of the salted sea. The ringlet of smoke curled before Nat's nostrils, and the Etom, accepting the invitation, inhaled the fumes.

At once, Nat sensed anew the now familiar heat of Gaal's holy gaze intertwined with His indignant fury. The Kinsman was angry! Not just angry but incensed. Nat trembled at such a wrath and fell against the abrasive shore, scraping hand and cheek as he caught himself. As before, the Etom sensed fire and crushing pressure, though this now seemed to threaten his destruction. A weight and fury as of the blazing sun fell upon his shoulders, and Nat cried out in fear.

Be still. Be still, the Spirit spoke. *This is just a lesson.*

The Spirit's words removed from Nat much of his terror at Gaal's wrath, but he tasted still the stinging pain of His sorrow at every offense and abuse in Creation now coupled with His anger. The Creator, just and holy, could not forever abide the injustice committed in the heart and at the hand of each and every creature. Nat shook ever harder, recalling his own iniquities, and recognizing he, too, deserved judgement. All had fallen short of their Creator's glory, and none could meet His perfect standard of holiness.

"Then what hope is there for us?" Nat groaned aloud. "Please tell me there is a way!"

"Do not be afraid," rumbled the Kinsman's voice from all around, "I *am* the Way."

In an instant, Nat stood again before the trebled vision of the Tree. However, now the vision pressing to forefront was of Gaal, nailed in all His affliction to its crooked trunk. While relieved at the absence of the crucible heat and pressure he'd been under, Nat was riveted to the enactment of the Kinsman's passion that lay before him.

Straining to lift His eyes toward heaven, Gaal implored, "Father, forgive them; for they know not what they do."

It struck Nat at last that no greater transgression against the Creator existed than this, the murder of His Son. And, yet, at the apex of offense, the Kinsman had begged for the forgiveness of not only those present, but of all whose misdeeds had made necessary His sacrifice.

The dark and deadly vision receded, giving eminence once again to the shining vision of Gaal in royal raiment before the rectified Tree as He spoke, "This is the loving-kindness of the Father, that all who place their trust in Me are forgiven. They are as those purchased out of slavery at the price of My blood and by adoption redeemed forever as sons and daughters, as the Kin of Lord Elyon!"

Reaching wide, the Kinsman in His right hand took as one might a curtain, the vision of the past, murderous and dark. In His left, Gaal gripped that of the present with all its crowding throng, and before the Tree drew the two together with a thunderous clap of His hands. The visions of past and present met, coming together in the glorious future promised in the Kinsman as a shaft of blinding white light pierced Him through, reconnecting Heaven and earth in irrevocable reversal of the Sunder.

In that very instant, the Kinsman likewise revealed Himself to all present in Sanctuary Endego. In shock at Gaal's sudden appearance and in trepidation of His majesty, many squawked or crowed in alarm and fell back, bowled over altogether. Others hid themselves behind a cloaking wing, peering out between trembling feathers for a glimpse of the One to whom they owed their lives and freedom.

Blithewit and Rae gasped in reverence with joyful, streaming eyes affixed to Gaal's brilliant, form. As Nat watched, the others began to reclaim themselves in His presence, His glory drawing all eyes heavenward. Sayah alone stood from the start, bold and fearless before the Kinsman, his wings upraised and aflame in reflection of Gaal's brilliance.

In wordless worship, the ægle bowed himself low before Kinsman, his wings spread prostrate at Gaal's pierced feet. In adoration, Sayah raised eyes and wings aloft, and in humble devotion, he lowered them again. And again. And again, his golden eyes shining and overrun with tearful adulation before his Savior.

The Spirit compelled Nat to the side of his friend, his brother in the Vine, and there, beside the ægle, the pale blue etém flung himself likewise on his face. Next were Rae and Blithewit, rushing to join them. Soon Etom, bird, and every kind of creature gathered was dashing to the Kinsman's feet. In concerted waves of adoration, the entire congregation arose, wings, paws, or hands uplifted only to fall prostrate over and over again before their King.

The Kinsman favored them all with a smile, His good pleasure apparent, and ascended along the shining beam that yet ran Him through. Over Him, Nat saw now the palace of Lord Elyon, with its gleaming, alabaster towers, descending to meet Gaal. At its gates stood the Tree Ha Kayim, its leaves and bark aglow with quickening fire as its broken streams found again their Channel in Him who had restored the Tree Ha Datovara to glory.

The life-giving flow cascaded from on high, pure water falling into holy light shining to comingle in Gaal as He arose. Inextricable in their passage through the Kinsman, the sacred elements combined in falls to overturn the Sunder, and their interplay sent prismatic light dancing over the land.

The moment announced to all present the good news that longer would the fall of Mankind prevail over Creation, but rather the downpour of grace, shed upon the world in every drop of the Kinsman

Gaal's blood. Suspended between Creation and the palatial seat of Elyon's cosmic authority, the Kinsman Gaal embodied the perfect conjoining of the two.

His voice boomed overhead, carried by the Spirit deep into the hearts of the Kinship below, "The Father has granted all authority in Heaven and throughout all Creation to Me. Go, therefore, into all the world and proclaim the good news that My Kingdom has arrived, and that My rule will never end.

"This is the Father's heartfelt invitation to every creature because He loves the world: that whosoever believes in Me need not perish, but by My finished work upon the Tree, they may be grafted into the Vine and so enjoy the gift of life everlasting.

"Therefore, bring all who receive the good news of My Kingdom before the Tree, baptizing them in the name of the Father, and of the Son, and of the Holy Spirit, and teaching them to follow My instruction, My example, and My Spirit. And behold! I will be with you always, even until the end of all days."

Along the shaft of light, Gaal arose to stand beside the Tree Ha Kayim and then was gone. In the bower below, all stood in shocked and dumbfounded silence, though in each one's breast the Spirit fanned ablaze a passionate desire to share the good news of the Kinsman's reign. The Stain, the Blight, the cruelty of life after the Sunder, the oppression of the Empire of Chōl – none present nor those that they loved had escaped these calamities unscathed. Now, however, a new hope had dawned over Creation, and the Spirit inspired each one to rise in the Kinsman's glory as a shining sun in the lives of those they cared for.

Overcoming their awe, those assembled began to wonder, their amazed whispers a fair complement to the rustle of mounded, fallen leaves stirring in the autumn breeze.

"Did you just see what I saw?"

"That *was* the Kinsman, right?

"...and where do you suppose He went?"

Compelled amidst the speculation of his Kin, Nat spoke out, "What we have seen here today is a sign that Elyon has restored His connection with the world, a deposit of His glory that begins with us, His people. His life-giving Spirit now abides in us to effect His restoration, and among us, He is King over all kings. If you share His mind, as I believe you do, you sense the upswell of His strength filling us that we might expand the borders of His Kingdom here in this dark world.

"So, let us do as He commanded, following Him in the example of His love, and carrying forth the light with which He has filled us to oppose the darkness that had at one time overwhelmed us and that yet envelopes the rest of Creation. Now go!!!

Thus enlivened, each one set to work in quiet and fierce determination, some to spread word of what had happened beyond the borders of the village and others to make ready for those who would return. Likewise inspired to their mission abroad, Sayah began preparing those who would guard Endego while Nat and Rae gathered provisions and planned their journey.

In hushed, reverent tones, word of Gaal's appearance spread throughout the Vine, the eyes of those who had not beheld Him illuminated by the resonant witness of the Spirit within them. And from all about Endego, Etom-kind and otherwise streamed into the bower, drawn by rumors of the hope that seemed beyond all hope.

Chapter Ten
The Lot of Leaders

For Rae, Nat, and Sayah, the following three days were a blur, and each was hard-pressed amidst the rigors of preparation for departure. Wherever the pair of young Etom strayed in provisioning their adventure, they found audience with the numerous Kin who sought them out to bless their journey and express heartfelt affection for the youths. These frequent delays Nat and Rae endured with a supernatural patience and constancy that belied their meager years, though they longed to make ready and depart forthwith.

While the many interruptions were exhausting, Nat and Rae soon developed a means of working in concert, a dance that made certain each one they entertained knew they appreciated the love and blessings. Often after preliminary salutations, Rae would be first to engage the well-wisher with a hospitability that Nat thought admirable. He would then step in to offer some encouragement, matching his exhortation in intensity to the distress of their guest of their departure.

And across this waltz of sociability, Nat would sometimes glance Rae's way, often communicating with soundless expression as their eyes met to speak in wordless phrases.

Are you okay?

Yes, Nat, just a little tired.

I would love to just leave. Right now. You?

Yes, you silly etém, but just look how precious these Kinfolk are. We simply must *say our goodbyes.*

You're right, of course. Nothing to do but press on.

Then they would return to the task at hand, often shuffling on toward their destination with what seemed to them slow and graceless steps, oblivious just how full of grace their steps were. And sometimes, Nat would catch Rae unawares, his gaze resting on her smiling face, brilliant and welcoming as she greeted yet another caller.

Again, the moment would seem to slow as it had when he'd greeted Rae outside her home, and he'd sense the reprisal of warmth within, a glow as pleasant as the rosy blush on Rae's happy cheeks. Most times, he caught himself and returned to the present with a jarring jolt.

Once or twice, though, Rae spied him watching, her emerald eyes growing softer and brighter and cheeks burning all the hotter while she brushed a stray zalzal back over her shoulder. In these instances, it was all that Nat could do to snap his eyes downward at once and stare at the ground in discomfort until he was certain she'd looked away.

He was thankful that on each such occasion, they'd been surrounded by a crush of visitors, the next in line to greet him salvaging him from embarrassed introspection. A flicker of his golden eyes in Rae's direction assured him the moment had indeed passed, though not from his memories. Nor hers.

Thus determined, the pair arrived three days later at the eventual end of their labors, exhausted and well-equipped for the journey. They were ready at last.

As commander of Endego's emergent airwing, Sayah found his challenges in training his recruits a bit more complex than those Rae and Nat faced. While the ægle did not have to navigate the social intricacies of the Kinship as the Etom did, a mighty task stood before him notwithstanding, and he would need the Spirit's help to accomplish it.

The ægle had the unenviable duty of first planning and then organizing full reconnaissance in defense of the village. To pivot from directing himself alone to employing a large contingent for complete coverage of the village put the ægle out of his depth.

Recognizing the difficulty Sayah faced, the silver fox Blithewith offered himself as an advisor. In service to the Nihúkolem, he'd gained plenty of experience in coordinating multiple skulks of foxes for such a task. In fact, his last such accursed assignment had been to command the surveillance of the very folk he'd now joined.

The old dog chuckled to himself, then called for Sayah's attention, "Sayah, a word, if you will."

Sayah had yet stood in frozen preoccupation before the jabbering mill of assembled wildfowl in the aftermath of the Kinsman's ascension. He looked now to the fox with gratitude before turning to his audience to excuse himself.

"Hello, there, everyone!" the ægle keened, "I need just you to wait a while, please, and then we'll get started."

"Yeah!" crowed...well, a crow, "Let's get started already!"

Sayah nodded to the sleek and shiny black bird and trod over to Blithewit, who awaited the ægle with cool patience.

"Yes, Blithewit?" Sayah asked, "What is it?"

"Might I offer you a bit of advice?" the silver fox began, his tone sage and confident, "I've done *quite* a bit of this work."

Sayah's eyes widened with grateful relief, "Yes! Please!"

Just as Blithewit was about to speak, his fiery cohort, Whisperweave, sauntered up to them, her eyes gleaming with excitement.

"What a crowd here, eh?" she interrupted. "What do you plan to do with them, Sayah?"

His mouth half open to council the ægle in this very enterprise, Blithewit stopped. He closed his mouth, now seamed with a wry smirk, and just looked at the vixen before clearing his throat.

"Oh!" she exclaimed in horror. "Am I interrupting, then?"

With a light nudge of the shoulder, Blithewit replied, "Not at all. Not at all. I was just going to answer that very question. Or at least give Master Ægle here some suggestions."

"Yeah!" Whisperweave affirmed, throwing a playful jab back at Blithewit, "You'd be perfect for that, you old fox!"

Aside to Sayah, she confided, "He's done *quite* a bit of this work."

Losing a smidge of his cool, Blithewit sputtered, his open mouth working as he gaped at the saucy vixen.

"That is *literally* what I just told him," Blithewit snarled. "Were you listening in?"

Ears standing pointed and sharp atop her head, Whisperweave wrinkled her nose and squinched her eyes into a smile before answering.

"And if I was? You know I always keep an eye on you, you old dog. Someone has to keep you out of trouble. Besides, you know more than most how tough a job this'll be."

She tipped her copper snout toward the waiting mob, then continued, "This lot hasn't a lick of discipline to begin with, and they're likely to peck at one another as keep watch. You two need all the help you can get."

Sitting back on her haunches, she curled a forepaw and pressed it to her breast, "That is, unless you two fellows would rather spend several more days or even weeks getting them ready?"

Sayah shrugged, uncertain, and Blithewit shook his head in resignation. He knew the vixen was right, and that she was just stubborn enough to insist on helping.

With an exasperated growl, Blithewit relented, "Argh. Alright! You're right. We *could* use the help, and you're best-suited, after all."

"I'm happy to have you both," Sayah interjected. "Now, Blithewit, what were your suggestions?"

The fox collected himself afresh, and proposed, "You've plenty of troops to work with, but you've got to get them organized. First, you'll need them to cover designated areas – quadrants, maybe – so nothing slips through undetected."

"Sayah, you've been up there. We've really got no idea," Whisperweave added. "Do you think divvying up the coverage into quadrants will work best?"

Sayah nodded as he considered the question, then looked over the crowd at the variety of fowl. There were those with sharp vision not unlike his own, others quiet and observant, though nearsighted, some well-suited to flight, and still more not at all. A few were quite large, like the cormorant or hornbill, but the majority were pretty small with several somewhere in between.

"I wonder," Sayah murmured, then turned to the foxes, who awaited his response. "What do you think of rings?"

"Rings?" Blithewit sniffed. He'd dealt with only homogeneous groups consisting of foxes, so didn't quite follow the ægle's lead at first.

"What do mean, Sayah?" Whisperweave inquired with a bit more understanding, "Why rings?"

"Well, I was just thinking that our friends here are all so different," the ægle began. "Maybe we need to sort them by what they can do. Or by how big they are. I don't know."

Sayah shook his snowy head in perplexity, but Whisperweave grew excited, "I think I see what you mean. Like maybe we put the ones with the best eyesight near the center of the village?"

Blithewit caught the idea, and carried it forward, "That just might work. And I imagine some of these fellows might be better than others in a fight?"

Sayah, encouraged at their support, continued with growing zeal, "That's just it! They're all a bit different, but maybe we can use the differences to our advantage!"

The three of them continued in this vein of discussion for several minutes, carried along by momentum until Blithewit recommended, "I think we have a rough sketch of where we might deploy our teams, but perhaps now we should talk about *when* you'll want on duty."

The ægle looked askance at the old silver fox, unsure how to respond, though at last he did manage, "Wha – when? I thought we would want them on watch *all the time*."

Whisperweave jumped in to clarify, "Ah. Yes, I see what you mean, but what you might not have considered is that these creatures have *lives*, dear. If they're all here, *all the time*, then when will they sleep, eat, care for their mates or their chicks?"

"That is to say, my young ægle friend," Blithewit added, reinforcing Whisperweave's point, "We ought to schedule separate teams to different times of the day – shifts, or watches, if you prefer."

"Three watches per day should be plenty," Whisperweave suggested to Sayah, who nodded in silence as he absorbed the information. "Maybe dawn to afternoon, afternoon to midnight, and midnight back to sunrise. Those are the watches we set, you know...before."

"It sounds reasonable," Sayah replied his brow furrowed in contemplation. "This is a complicated business, isn't it?"

"Indeed, it is!" Blithewit returned, "But the three of us will make quick work of the matter. Now, last, we'll want to appoint an acting authority over each shift, a Commander of the Watch, if you so please."

"They would need to be clever. Able to think for themselves should the need arise," Whisperweave submitted.

"And not afraid to stand their ground for what they believe in, or get out in front of their troops, even when it's dangerous," Blithewit advised, then proclaimed, "Leaders! We need leaders!"

At once, Sayah recalled the wee blue thrush, Pteetya, and he told the others, "I have at least one in mind. Who would you recommend?"

Blithewit directed his gaze to a tall raven standing alone just beyond the jabbering conspiracy of his peers. Ashy-grey painted the raven's feathers in a jagged streak that ran beneath his jaw and twisted down across one jet-black wing. Unlike the other ravens, who often bent their renowned intellect toward pert criticism, this one seemed more interested in assessing his surroundings in silence.

"What say you to that one?" the old fox asked.

"I don't know him," Sayah replied. "Why do you ask?"

"What I know of ravens is that they're often smart, but..." Blithewit trailed off, at a loss for words of sufficient kindness to convey his meaning.

A straightforward Whisperweave was less hesitant to offer, "But they're also notoriously difficult and unruly."

"Right..." Blithewit sighed, "That. What I noticed during your speech earlier, Sayah, is that all the other ravens either quipped at your words, else were busy whispering amongst themselves. This fellow didn't join in with them. He just watched and listened. A rare trait among his kind."

"Hmmm..." Sayah considered the possibility of such intelligence uncoupled from the ravens' characteristic sarcasm.

"Let's put him down as a 'maybe' for now," Sayah concluded. "Who else?"

Whisperweave had wandered off several steps while Sayah had contemplated his response to Blithewit's nominee, and her attention was affixed to a large group of starlings perched along a long, level branch of the Tree.

"Hey, Whisperweave!" Blithewit barked. "What have you got there?"

The coppery vixen circled around with a graceful swish of her tail, and jerked her head back toward the starlings, "You should see this. Might be another candidate. Well, a pair of them, that is."

Sayah and Blithewit sidled up next to the vixen, and the three of them gawked up at the starlings, who were too preoccupied with their own business to notice their audience below. More than a dozen or of the birds shuffled side to side along the branch or darted about it in an apparent competition for a position of prominence on the limb.

Although the trio on the ground would have been hard-pressed to define the starlings' criteria for prestige, after a moment of listening to the creatures overhead, they garnered some understanding. Unsurprised, the foxes nodded acceptance as Sayah explained that such a group of starlings was called a murmuration. The starlings were a chatty lot.

"No! No!" one slight starling of brown plumage contested while shuffling in his place closest to the Tree's knotted stalk, "Nearest the trunk is best. Closer to the Kinsman, I say!"

"Reeediculouuuus!!!" trilled another, as she flitted to the far end of the branch, just past the next farthest bird. "This end is best. The leaves are the liveliest part, and just look how close to the *leaves* I am!"

Staying within a wing's breadth of her nearest cohort, she stretched her neck out to put her beak in near-contact with the foliage, though she didn't quite dare to touch it. Her neighbor, an older and heavier male, took umbrage at her cheek.

Slapping the back of her head with a stiff wing, he rebuked her, "Nay, you wee whippersnapper! How dare you approach the leafage of the Tree? You *know* it to be the most sacred portion of the Tree. Why, you only just said it yourself!"

Cowed at her elder's reprimand, the young female desisted in reaching for the nearby leaf just in time to resume her taunting, "But look! LOOK!!! I'm still closest to the leaves!"

In her distraction, however, she did not detect her elderly neighbor hopping past her to perch just a little farther out on the branch. A smile of smug satisfaction spread over his plump and swelling breast.

At once, and in quite the superior tone, he turned to inform the young lass, "Well, who is closest *now*?"

The younger starling puffed in startled indignation, and then a fresh bout of jockeying for position began. At the other end of the branch, closer to the trunk, a similar scenario also played out.

It was strange behavior, and Sayah noticed something more curious still: no matter how close to crux of the Tree or tip of the branch the outermost starling might go, they would always stay within reach of their neighbor. Likewise, the starlings shuffling back and forth along the limb seemed to do so to more evenly space out the ever-increasing distance at either end of their murmuration.

"There!" Whisperweave exclaimed. "Look at those two there."

Near the middle of the branch, a couple of starlings perched abreast, unmoving amidst the bustle of their kind with one wing around the shoulder of the other. The pair looked only at each other, tender affection apparent in their eyes, though bemusement at the helter-skelter hubbub around them played along their beaks.

"Just look at them," the vixen whispered, then turned to the ægle. "So? What do you think?"

"Well...errr...I guess I don't know," Sayah replied. "What is it we're seeing here, Whisperweave? I don't get it."

Exasperated, Whisperweave remarked, "This is why you boys needed a female's perspective. They're the only ones not bickering up there. The only ones just enjoying this place while the others tussle."

Sayah knew starlings to be social in the extreme, and soon came to see what Whisperweave was driving at. The fact that these two among the whole lot weren't involved in the rivalry spoke a great deal to their priorities. They were here for the Kinsman and for each other. Not just that, but they hadn't chosen to isolate themselves from the rest of their kind to enjoy their peace and quiet.

The ægle wondered if this meant they had some sense that their presence might influence the other members of their murmuration to rest among the Kinship here as well. While uncertain, Sayah was determined to see if his suspicion bore out.

Stepping forth from the foxes, the striking, ivory ægle cried out to the starlings above, "Hello, there!"

With tandem expressions of mild shock, the couple looked down at Sayah, then each in concert pointed to their own breast with the wing free and unentangled in embrace.

Together, they called down in eerie symmetry, "Us?!?"

"Yes, please," Sayah answered, "do you mind coming down to speak with us a moment."

The pair of starlings looked to one another with identical inquisitiveness, shrugged an identical shrug, then gave again their weird, stereophonic assent, "Sure! Be right down!"

In perfect synchronicity, the couple hopped from the branch, descending in a flurry beat of wings that Sayah might've argued were also in precise time with one another. He began to wonder if he'd made a mistake. But then it was too late. They were already there, standing before him and eager to chat.

To his left, Sayah thought, stood the cock of the couple, who was a tad thicker and plumper than the other. They both had dark plumage, mottled with white spots, but otherwise, they looked the same to him. In the meantime, they had each slipped a wing around the other again. They almost seemed one inseparable creature. A tad nervous, the ægle just looked back and forth at them a tick until he overcame his hesitation.

"Well..." Sayah started, at first uncertain, then seizing on what he'd learned of etiquette among the Etom. "First, perhaps, introductions?"

The starlings nodded in time, their indistinguishable smiles pleasant, and Sayah continued while Whisperweave and Blithewit watched with some disquiet.

"My name is Sayah," the ægle offered. "I was responsible for watching over the village, so I could warn the Etom of any threats."

The starling on his right (the hen?) waved a free wing to reassure him, "Oh, we know who *you* are."

This one's voice was higher-pitched than the other, so Sayah surmised he'd gotten it right.

"Too right," the cock jumped in, pointing up toward the murmuration, "We might be in the Vine now, but we've had a vine of another kind for ages now. A grapevine, that is. Told us all about you."

"Ah! Yes!" Sayah barked in awkward reply, then inquired, "May I ask who you are?"

"Of course!" they cried together with glee, "Why, we're the Darlings!"

"Ahem," Blithewit interjected, "I'm Blithewit. Pleased to meet you both. Am I to understand that you're the, ahem, the Darling starlings?"

Whisperweave stifled an unexpected snort of laughter, managing to keep her peace while the Darlings answered in enthusiastic conformity, "Yes, we are! Nice to meet you, Blithewit! And who is this?"

Whisperweave pulled herself back together, to return, "My name is Whisperweave. How do you do?"

"Quite well, thank you!" they replied.

In an attempt to ascertain their individual names, Sayah turned to the male, "And how should I address you, sir?"

"Oh, you silly goose," the hen stepped in, "he's just *my* Darling. Aren't you, dear?"

The cock replied, "Right you are! And you're *my* Darling."

Cheek to cheek, the pair sighed with contentment, then answered together, "That's right. We're the Darlings, and we're quite at your service, young Master Ægle."

Realizing he was making no headway in the matter, Sayah turned the conversation to the happenings amongst the starlings overhead.

"Maybe you could explain to us what's going on up there?" the ægle waved a wing at the branch the Darlings had dismounted.

The Darlings shook their head in disappointment, and the hen began, "The poor, confused dears..."

Master Darling picked up where the missus left off, "We love our kind, you understand?"

Missus Darling interjected, "But they're not always the wisest sort."

They continued in this back and forth as they explained, each one finishing the other's thought.

"We have a strong community, you see. Very sociable, we are."

"So much so that most don't even know how to think for themselves."

"You don't say?" Blithewit muttered aside to Whisperweave in a tone less kind than he intended.

"Anyhow, after the Kinsman appeared to us, we all got together..."

"...as we always do..."

"We all got together after to discuss what had happened."

"Things stayed pretty level-headed for a while, but then wild speculation began to take over."

"As it always does."

"Yes, as it always does."

Sayah's neck began to ache from turning to one or the other to follow the conversation, yet he managed to interject, "Why is that?"

Missus Darling answered with an upward roll of her eyes, which settled toward Master Darling as he spoke, "Well, it seems to be a weakness among us that the one who grabs the most attention..."

"...is seen as the most important."

"Whoever comes up with the most scandalous theory might find themselves attacked on all sides..."

"...but they get everyone's attention. Before long, everyone forgets how crazy their ideas are..."

"...and just sees how popular they are. In short order, the rest copy the crackpot..."

"...until another starling comes up with some other hare-brained scheme."

Both Darlings started at once, each putting up a guarded wing while with wide, shocked eyes, they apologized, "No offense to any hares around here!"

"We really must be more careful now, my Darling."

"Too right, too right, my Darling."

"Well..." Whisperweave began, her voice dry, "that was enlightening. You two didn't seem to be joining in up there. Why not?"

"We were just so..." the Darlings started.

For the first time since the other three had met them, the two Darlings spoke across one another.

"...amazed," said one.

"...happy," said the other.

They looked at each other and giggled, exchanging words once more.

"Happy."

"Amazed."

The pair looked into each other's eyes, and fell into a contented and silent snuggle, their feathered breasts first puffing, then deflating as they sighed. Recalling their own overwhelming joy and wonder after Gaal's ascension, the ægle and foxes likewise held their peace. And as he watched the starlings in their devotion, Sayah thought they were indeed quite darling.

Blithewit again cleared his throat, prompting Sayah to resume their impromptu interview.

"So, you were just too busy to get involved in all the bickering up there?" he asked, drawing the Darlings out of their shared reverie.

"No, not exactly."

"It just didn't seem right."

"All the arguing..."

"...the jockeying about."

"We're happy just to be here, you see?"

"Yeah, none of that other mess matters."

"And we didn't think telling the rest to relax would work, but..."

"...but we thought it might settle them down if we just stayed put, happy-like."

"Exactly."

"Precisely."

The two gazed once more into each other's eyes, and began to nuzzle their beaks back and forth until Whisperweave interrupted in a loud voice, "So, Sayah? What do you think? Should we ask them?"

Sayah looked the couple over as he sought the Spirit's guidance. Detecting the resonant thrum of approval within him, the ægle nodded, then asked.

"So how might you two feel about helping us out as leaders of a sort? We would need your help overlooking three separate teams."

"Oh my!"

"Dear me!"

"You don't intend to separate *us*, do you?" came the incredulous reply.

"No, no, no. We wouldn't *dream* of it," Whisperweave answered in mock horror, then whispered aside to Sayah, "I should think we keep them together, yeah? The pair of them over one watch?"

"That's a brilliant stroke, if I might say," inserted Blithewit as he sidled up between them. "The two of them together...they practically share one mind as it is."

"But we still need to cover two shifts," Sayah objected.

"True," Whisperweave returned, "but we still have the raven, and..."

"...and your mystery candidate!" Blithewit finished in eerie imitation of the Darlings.

Whisperweave narrowed her eyes at him in uncertainty, *Just what is the old dog playing at?*

She had no time to speculate before the ægle was announcing his decision, "Yes, let's see if the Darlings will do it. Together."

"What say you, Darlings?" Sayah asked, his eyes flinty as he enjoined the starlings with a smile. "Will you accept our offer? Will you, together, command a watch?"

"We'd be honored!"

"We'd love to!"

Without additional fanfare, Sayah requested the Darlings be back first thing the following morning, then set about tracking down the raven they had spotted earlier. After some searching, Whisperweave found him leaning back against a tree outside the bower, staring up at the sky.

Upon locating him, the vixen greeted him, "Hello, there. My name's Whisperweave. My friends and I were hoping to speak with you, if you don't mind."

The raven straightened, and gave her a short, stiff bow. The gesture showcased the streak down his long, dark body while he introduced himself in a rich, quiet brogue that Whisperweave could scarce understand.

"Hullo. Bhean Dealanach Ris, atchyer disposal."

From afar Sayah had seen the vixen had found the raven and fetched Blithewit at once. Now the pair trotted up to join Whisperweave.

"Sayah. Blithewit," Whisperweave greeted them with distracted perplexity, "This here is..."

"Aye, ma name's a full mouth, but wi'it comes a tale," spoke the raven. "Ah will say it agin, fer ye three – Bhean Dealanach Ris. Ye ken call me Bhean fer short."

The three listened, intent on hearing the fellow aright, though in the end, they were still uncertain as to his name. To their ears, it seemed he'd said, "Ven," or something like, which is just about how Blithewit now spoke it.

"Bhean, is it?" the fox ventured.

In the back of Blithewit's mind, he wondered what the Spirit might do to help them when they all seemed to be speaking the same language, but someone's accent was so thick, they still couldn't understand them.

"Aye. Ah suppose it's close enough, tho' it don' sound quite right t'northern ears," Bhean assented.

"Well, then, Bhean," Sayah inserted, "I'm Sayah, and this here is Blithewit. I assume you've met Whisperweave already?"

"Aye, that Ah did," Bhean replied, adding, "An' a fair lass she is fer a vixen, if ye don' mind me sayin'."

Bhean's rough charm took Whisperweave by surprise, and the 'lass' tipped her head in response to his flattery.

"Yes. Well. Thank you for that," Blithewit interjected, somewhat ruffled at Bhean's rather forward comment to his colleague.

"Shall we, then?" the silvery fellow prompted Sayah.

"Ah! Yes," the ægle answered. "Bhean, we're wondering what you thought of what happened here today."

Bhean paused a moment to collect his thoughts before responding, "Was a right glorious sight, wa'nt it? Ne'er seen anything the like. Amazing."

The raven put his head down and fell silent, and Sayah was stunned at the great tear that ran down Bhean's long, dark beak. Perhaps it was just Bhean's personality to stand off from the rest of his kind, or perhaps he'd already possessed a proclivity to do so.

Whatever the reason, Sayah saw now that the Kinsman had touched this raven deep down. It was all the more cause to pursue Bhean as a candidate once Sayah perceived the somber moment had passed.

"Bhean, why aren't you with the other ravens?" the ægle asked.

Bhean looked up, attempting to overcome his loss for words, "Hoo do Ah say it? Ah've never been one ta talk so much as me kin. An' there's the tale of me name in it, too."

"What tale is that?" Whisperweave inquired, curious. "You mentioned it before."

Bhean brightened at her interest and leaned in toward his audience with a conspiratorial air as he began his tale in a voice deep and graveled.

"Ye canna understand without hearkening back ta me nest, an' me jes' a wee egg high oop inna pine. The day was bright an' sun shining wi' da an' ma away huntin'.

"All a'sudden, a grea' dark storm came oop o'er oor tree. Wi' a crack, a bolt a'lightning hi'it. Near split off oor branch an' singed me shell.

"When Ah hatched, Ah had this streak upon me. An' so, me ma an' da gi'mme the name Bhean Dealanach Ris. It's like to 'lightning touched 'im.' E'er since then, Ah been a bit strange ta me kin. Not talkin' so much, they say Ah'm maybe a touch slow, but Ah dinnae ken if Ah agree wi' 'em."

Fascinated by Bhean's story and by the telling of it, the trio shook their heads in disagreement at this last bit. They thought the raven endearing and found the oft-stinging wit of his kind tempered by his humility.

Sayah decided he'd seen enough, and, looking to Blithewit and Whisperweave, asked, "What do you think?"

Without hesitation, Whisperweave answered, "He has my vote."

"Er, um, well, that is, he has mine as well," Blithewit bumbled, flustered at Whisperweave's ready reply.

"Mine, too," the ægle added, then turned again to Bhean.

"Bhean, we have need of your help, if you will," Sayah declared. "Would you consider leading a contingent of this flock to watch over Endego?"

His eyes grave and introspective, Bhean gave thought to Sayah's proposal.

Seconds later, the raven turned a clear gaze on the ægle and responded, "Ah would like very much ta help. What is it ye need a' me?"

"Well, first of all, can you be here at dawn tomorrow morning?" Sayah requested.

As Bhean nodded, the ægle offered, "I'll explain the rest then if that's alright."

The raven nodded again, and Sayah added, "Very nice to meet you, Bhean. Tomorrow, then!"

The foxes likewise said their goodbyes while with sharp eyes Sayah scoured the area far and wide for the thrush he intended for their final candidate.

"Whatchya lookin' for?!?" arose the question from Sayah's side.

At the sudden sound, the ægle jumped in his shock-pimpled skin, his feathers ruffling as a result. He looked down at his side and barked an awkward guffaw when he discovered the very bird he sought.

"Pteetya! I was just looking for you!"

"You alright there? Did I startle you?" the thrush inquired. "You look a tad...well, pale's not the right word."

"I'm fine. I'm fine. Just not used to being caught off guard like that, you cheeky pipsqueak," the exasperated ægle retorted.

"Pipsqueak? Pipsqueak!?!" Pteetya rejoindered in mock offense. "I'll have you know I'm the largest of my clutch!"

Pteetya's voice grew shriller as he objected. All at once, he realized his ever-squeakier utterances contradicted his assertions and cleared his throat to growl in a modest alto.

"And the stoutest, too!"

Though he keened laughter at the thrush, Sayah's affections for the smaller bird grew, and he soon apologized through mirth-teared eyes for any offense he might have caused.

"You kidding me?" Pteetya replied with a smack of his short wing to Sayah's snowy flank. "That's nothing. You should see how the ravens over there ribbed me after I stood up at the meeting."

"Now," Pteetya began, cocking his head to deliver an incisive stare up at the ægle, "it seems you had some business with me. What is it you need?"

In deference to the foxes, Sayah appealed to the thrush's patience, "Just a moment, if you don't mind, Pteetya."

He then raised a great wing to wave for his cohorts' attention, calling as he did, "Blithewit! Whisperweave! I found him!"

"More like *he* found *me*," Sayah muttered to himself while he awaited the foxes.

They were there in a flash, or, in Blithewit's case, just a tick longer than. Whisperweave declared herself winner in their ongoing contest with a sly look, but the detached Blithewit gave her no satisfaction.

The silver fox ignored the vixen to greet Pteetya instead, "Pleased to meet you. I am called Blithewit."

"Pteetya's my name!" the thrush exclaimed with a short bow, his eyes never leaving Blithewit's. "Nice meeting you."

Pteetya didn't wait for Whisperweave to introduce herself but swung at once toward her to offer a much lower and more sweeping bow.

"Mistress Vixen, the pleasure is all mine," the thrush declared. "Pteetya, at your service."

A smile of mild amusement across her snout, Whisperweave accepted Pteetya's introduction and responded with a much more restrained version of her own.

The niceties now aside, Sayah delved into the matter at hand. He and the foxes soon determined that Pteetya was a qualified fit for leading a watch. The thrush had wit and spine to spare and to no one's surprise he volunteered at once.

"I'll be here at first light tomorrow," Pteetya confirmed, then said his goodbyes and fluttered off on some other urgent business of his own.

Sayah explained the general plan to all birds gathered and thanked them for their patience while he and the foxes had worked. He asked everyone to return at first light the following morning, which elicited complaints from a number of their recruits, many of whom were crows and ravens. Nevertheless, most who had answered the call departed with cheery hearts, and from the songbirds among them came a comforting melody that drifted away as they flew off into the night sky.

The recruits having departed for the night, Sayah and the foxes retired to a substantial distance from the bower to discuss plans for the following day. A variety of factors were at play, which the trio reviewed at length. After some time, the discussion had borne little fruit, and Sayah decided it might be best to wait until morning to see what kind of turnout they had before planning in advance with too much specificity.

Their conversation was not altogether fruitless, however. With Whisperweave and Blithewit's expert guidance, Sayah soon learned the fundamentals of reconnaissance.

The distillation of the foxes' collective wisdom and training produced a list of seven such guiding principles:

Continuity, or maintaining unbroken vigil over the village and surrounding area.

Commitment, the maximal usage of all available units during a given watch.

Focus, the directive of the Watch Commander to prioritize under chaotic circumstances and meet the watch objectives.

Communication, an emphasis on clear and immediate reports to the Watch Commander to enable a coordinated effort.

Maneuverability, or the ability of engaged units to move as the situation demands.

Prolongation, the directive that any units in contact with the enemy should maintain contact so as to derive as much information as possible from the enemy force.

Assessment, an on-the-spot determination any engaged unit must make on contact with the enemy regarding the magnitude of the threat and any implications thereof.

With such resources to direct their sensibilities in selecting and preparing their troops, Sayah grew more confident. Though the ægle wasn't altogether certain as to the number and capability of their contingent, he sensed the Spirit at work. In his heart, he submitted their plans to Him who planned and upheld the universe by His power, and worried no more.

Chapter Eleven
Training Day

Before daybreak the following morning, Sayah met with the foxes beneath the Tree to await the arrival of their forces. Before long, Pteetya made an eager appearance, with the Darlings not far behind. A smattering of others arrived before they saw Bhean, and even though the raven seemed especially gloomy at the early hour, he was present when the sun arose.

A good many others were not quite so punctual, a fact that did not escape the notice of Blithewit and Whisperweave. The two foxes remembered Imperial discipline, and with each late arrival they cringed at the thought of what unpleasantness might have befallen them if they had been tardy upon muster.

Addressing them both at once, the Spirit spoke, *You are no longer slaves, but children of promise, and heirs of My kingdom.*

The proclamation grounded them both in the love with which they'd become acquainted in recent days and renewed their state of mind. With eyes transformed in this renewal, they looked again over the growing crowd, detecting fresh potential among even those who came late. These were children of promise as well, which made them brothers and sisters, or Kin among the Kinship.

The foxes' earlier anxiety melted away, and they began to attribute advantages to their new Kinfolk that the cloud of fearful judgment had earlier obscured. Without the foxes' knowledge, the Spirit had taken Sayah on a similar internal jaunt. When he came alongside to join them in overseeing the swelling flock, he spoke in parallel with their thoughts.

"I was disappointed at first when I saw some arriving late, but now..."

Whisperweave finished his trailing sentence, "...now you're thinking the Lord Elyon made them so for a reason."

"Exactly!" the ægle responded.

"These ones might best serve on the late watches," Blithewit suggested.

With a crack and a rustle of leaves, a large and rumpled brown owl broke into the clearing. Her great, round eyes had diminished to drowsy half-moons, and she almost flew smack into a thick bough of the Tree. At the last moment, her eyes flew open, and she dove to safety with a refreshing splash in the waters below.

"Especially that one," the silver fox offered in a dry voice.

Ægle and fox alike burst into laughter that ceased when a tittering outburst exploded beside them.

Once again, Pteetya had evaded Sayah's prodigious vision to approach unnoticed, and the ægle wondered aloud if the thrush's stealth was a talent particular to his kind.

"Golly, no!" Pteetya replied. "How do you think your smaller cousins survive? Not everyone is a 'lord of the sky' like yourself."

"So, there are others as..." Sayah hesitated, not desiring to offend. "Well, as sneaky as yourself?"

"You betcha! And I'm probably not the best in stealth here!" Pteetya exclaimed before extending a wingtip to point out a rough stand of grass a little way off. "Look into those stalks with those fantastic ægle eyes of yours."

Sayah glimpsed a faint, low silhouette in the grass that might have been a clod of dirt or a rock, but at first couldn't identify anyone there. That is, until he spied the dark glint of unmoving eyes peering from the stand.

"There's someone there!" he blurted.

"A hypocolius, my friend," Pteetya confided. "They're like ghosts, still and hidden in the underbrush. Watching."

"And there are more like this one?" Whisperweave inquired.

"Maybe not quite as well-hidden, but, yeah. Sure," Pteetya answered with a shrug. "Like I said, we little guys gotta stay out of sight. You either get good at it, or you..."

The thrush drew a wing across his throat to pantomime the death that awaited all such unwary prey.

Blithewit jumped in, "We can definitely use their skills to our advantage. And we'll need to sort the latecomers out of morning duties."

The Darlings hollered as they drew near, "Oooh! We *love* mornings!"

At the mention of the word 'love,' however, they devolved into a saccharine exchange that brought them to a halt.

"Not as much as I love you, dear."

"No! Not as much as *I* love *you*, sweetie."

Soon, they were reduced to unintelligible murmurs passing between their nuzzling beaks until Sayah cleared his throat.

"Oh! Our apologies!"

"That's...that's alright," Sayah consoled, though already somewhat weary of the starlings' interplay.

"You were saying you preferred mornings?" Whisperweave prompted, eager to return the conversation to something productive.

"YES!!!" the Darlings replied, their eyes wide with shared enthusiasm. "It's our favorite!"

"What? You're my favorite!"

"No! You'r – "

"Right!" Blithewit interrupted, "So it's a good time of day for you both. Now that's settled, perhaps we ought to collect Bhean as well?"

Before the starlings could initiate a fresh round of...whatever it was, the others started off toward the raven, who had propped himself against the low bole of the nearby willow. His dark head was down, and his were eyes closed. He looked, for all intents and purposes, asleep.

Despite appearances, Bhean lifted his head when the detachment was still several steps off and saluted them with a nonchalant wave of his wing.

"Hullo, there! Jes' givin' ma eyes a wee rest."

"About that," Sayah began, spotting the opportunity, "We were wondering which of you would be best-suited to lead the night watch?"

"Mos' me kin would na' do it," Bhean explained, "but Ah could. Been a bit strange tha' way ma whole life. Perhaps it was the lightning, but Ah canna say."

"Is that right?" Sayah asked, marveling at Elyon's providence in bringing this particular raven to them. "Then it's good you're here with us, isn't it?"

Without a word, Bhean inclined his head in slow reply, and Sayah looked about the crowded clearing, which was almost full by now. From various points, the lone nightjar here and owl there arrived. Besides that, no others were yet incoming.

The ægle decided the time was near to begin. Beckoning to the four fowl and the pair of foxes with open wings, he explained the plan in broad strokes. The starlings would command a watch over the early hours of the day into the afternoon, and Bhean would preside over the late hours until morning. The watch from afternoon to midnight, more or less, fell to Pteetya by default, and the thrush was happy to oblige.

Sayah, with the help of Whisperweave and Blithewit, also described how they intended to utilize the unique strengths of the different types of birds to cover the area most effectively. All seemed well until the prospect of the night watch arose, eliciting questions.

"Your strategy should work great for the two day-watches," Pteetya commended, then pointed out, "but you all realize everyone on the night watch has to be nocturnal, yeah? Like owls and such?"

Sayah and the foxes had not considered this critical point, and now lamented the apparent dissolution of their best-laid plans.

Pteetya, however, did not permit them to despair, and at once proposed an alternative, "Wait! Wait! Don't get yourselves in a twist, now. We got plenty of owls here, some nightjars, and I thought I saw a coupla night-herons. With the right placement, they should do the trick."

"Ay, it's a canny plan," Bhean concurred.

After a hurried exchange over the particulars of the species at hand for the night watch, Sayah regained confidence. Returning to the point from which they'd earlier departed, they laid out a rough schematic for deploying their troops.

In short, they would implement reconnaissance in zones with some posted in fixed positions and others roving to best employ their natural abilities in watching over a large, circular region with Endego at its center. Coverage of the village and the surrounding area was more or less comprehensive, and altogether an improvement over a single ægle flying sentry, no matter how sharp his eyes were.

Sayah, his two advisors, and the four Watch Commanders at once gathered the diverse flock, mustering them in neat rows on the flat, open grasslands outside the village. By kind, they had the birds line up with the shortest in front, then ascending in height until the tallest of them stood at the back so that the ægle could see them all from the head of the assembly.

A few, the smallest in particular, trembled in fear at the passing shadows of clouds overhead. A lifetime of successful survival instincts informed their anxiety, but none stepped out of formation while the seven made their inspection.

Soon, Sayah and the other six had a count, and without delay developed a list of assignments for the respective species. On long-range overflight patrols were the vultures, buzzards, and cormorants, and on mid-to-short range of the same were the crows, ravens, shrikes, tchagras, and thrushes. Ground patrols would be conducted by francolins, prinias, and quail, while serins, starlings, and woodpeckers took up fixed posts as sentries. A roving gaggle of geese would patrol a varied route on land and in the sky.

Meanwhile, a few of the smaller, sneakier birds, such as the hypocoliuses and cisticolas would deploy to unfixed forward posts as stealth sentries. And over the village on the daybreak watch, a contingent of goshawks would employ their prodigious vision to spy distant threats or relay important communications. Falcons, who also possessed powerful eyesight, although better suited to twilight hours, would fulfill a similar role in the next watch.

Nighttime presented its own challenges, and the reduction in available troops for the watch necessitated a contraction of the broad concentric circle the other watches enjoyed. In total, the group of nocturnal fowl numbered nineteen: nine owls, seven nightjars, and three night-herons. With fewer birds on hand relative to the daytime watches, the area the night watch could cover was a great deal smaller.

Nevertheless, it was better than no help at all, and most of the nocturnal creatures could fly in near-total silence, which would lend them an advantage at night. Just four of their recruits, the night-herons and one of the owls, did not possess this capability, though they had others that would prove useful.

Of the owls, three were earless owls, two were scops owls, one a great eagle-owl, two more eagle-owls of the spotted variety, and a single large brown fish owl. This last was the dozy latecomer who had almost crashed upon her entry to the bower.

The earless owls and the great eagle-owl would fly a circulating ring around the village at medium range using their fantastic night vision and hearing to locate potential threats while the scops owls would do the same, but at a greater distance due to their expansive flight range.

The couple of spotted owls, a mating pair, would patrol the edge of the grove, finding perches at the perimeter for observation. At last, the brown fish owl, who alone among the owls did not possess a silent flight profile, would circle high over Endego for overwatch as did the goshawks and falcons during the day.

The stealthy nightjars were assigned to flit from the village perimeter to investigate anything unusual that might have escaped the notice of the owls. While active at night, they were restless creatures that preferred to stay on the move, so sporadic flights between Endego and the surrounding area were perfect for their temperament.

At last, they came to the night-herons. Sayah, familiar with the iconic form of their daylight brethren, had anticipated a tall, long-necked creature with spindly legs. He'd been surprised to discover the nocturnal variety was in every respect much stouter than he'd expected. While still rather tall, the night-herons were about half the height of those herons the ægle had seen before.

The night-herons were nonetheless very clever birds, and quite adept hunters. Sayah soon learned they would often stand quiet in the water and toss insects or other bait onto the surface to lure fish and other creatures nearby. At the appropriate moment, the night-heron would spring their ambush, gathering prey with a quick snap of the beak.

The night-heron's method required stillness, patience, and watchfulness – all attributes they could apply when stationed around the village as sentries. Sayah and his team did their best to determine where their three night-herons should go with the knowledge that the night watch would rely much on the team's awareness and the ability to conform on the fly to the demands of hostile contact.

With teams now sorted, Sayah set each group to the task of running a simulated watch under the supervision of their respective Commanders. The task of each Watch Command was first to position their troops about a fixed point on the open grasslands to represent the center of the village. Each watch squadron staked out separate areas of operation to conduct their simulations, and soon the sky around Endego was aflutter with fowl of many kinds.

Before sending Pteetya, Bhean, and the Darlings to their duties, Sayah, Blithewit, and Whisperweave in short order had conveyed the seven fundamentals of reconnaissance to each one. Now, the ægle and foxes meandered between the various staging areas to assess how well the Watch Commanders recalled, conveyed, and trained their subordinates in those principles.

Continuity and commitment were most important at the beginning stage. Without a constant, unbroken vigil, an enemy might slip through, and the participants in the exercise needed to learn how to endure both the rigor and monotony of their duties. It was difficult, boring work that also required focus, yet another fundamental of the duty.

Sayah and the foxes observed the Darlings as they monitored their squadron, the pair darting into action to chide a distracted francolin that had wandered off his route. Though the starlings traded back and forth in delivering a rapid-fire critique, they did so with a light touch. The francolin did not hang his head as he marched back along his patrol, but strode with confidence, his eyes fixed forward with determination.

However, it wasn't long before the Darlings were back at it again, cajoling a hesitant hypocolius who had failed to advance to his post. Satisfied for the time being that the starlings had the situation in hand, Sayah, Whisperweave, and Blithewit looked to Pteetya's squadron.

They at first had difficulty in locating the thrush, but Sayah eventually found him, a blue streak dashing to and from the various posts and patrols of the watch.

"He's going to wear himself out like that," Blithewit breathed with concern.

"Maybe," the more hopeful Whisperweave answered, "but let's watch a bit longer before we decide to jump in."

Sayah focused on the thrush, whose small form was too distant to overhear, and soon recognized a pattern in Pteetya's movements. First, the thrush would approach the patrol or post to greet the troops. Second, the thrush either flew the route with the other bird or hunkered beside a sentry for a moment to inspect their general field of vision. Last, Pteetya conversed with his subordinates, from gestures and body language appearing to suggest improvements before departing each one with an approving pat on the back.

There was also some method to Pteetya's migrations, and the ægle realized the thrush was visiting each of his troops in turn. Once Pteetya completed his circuit, he took up position at the center of their "village" to rest and observe the operation. Where Sayah and the foxes had detected chaos and laxity when they arrived, they now perceived order, discipline, and a certain ready tautness to the activities of Pteetya's watch.

"Well, I'll be..." Blithewit conceded.

"He's done well with them," Whisperweave granted. "A born leader."

Sayah agreed, and the trio left to see how things were going with Bhean's watch. While on the way, the ægle wondered aloud to Blithewit and Whisperweave if they should have the Watch Commanders confer to share what had proven effective in training their troops.

"Certainly!" Blithewith concurred. "It's mandatory Imperial practice, though I imagine our folks will want to do so even without threat of court martial hanging over their heads. Now, let's see how Bhean and his squadron are getting on!"

The three arrived at the night watch's area of operations and were soon perplexed at the seeming absence of Bhean's squadron. In fact, none of them could locate a single member of the watch except for Bhean, who circled at a substantial distance from the center of their mock village.

Sayah quelled a surge of disappointment, not wanting to rush to judgement against Bhean, and asked the foxes to wait a moment while he flew to the raven to ascertain what was going on. The ægle prayed for guidance as he neared Bhean, who searched sky and earth with desperate twitches of his head.

Sayah's recognition of the raven's distress softened the ægle's approach as he hailed Bhean.

"Hello there, Bhean! Is everything alright?"

"No. No, not a wee bit right," the raven replied. "Ah canna find a single one!"

"Let's join Blithewit and Whisperweave on the ground," Sayah suggested. "Maybe they can help us figure out what happened."

They landed near the concerned foxes to discuss their conundrum.

"Did you get a chance to give your troops instructions?" the ægle inquired.

"Ay. Ay. That Ah did, bu' then..." Bhean waved his wings in the air in a tired gesture, "then *poof* they were jes' gone."

Curious, Whisperweave questioned the weary raven, "Did you notice anything strange about them before they left?"

"Well, they dinnae say a thing the whole time Ah was talkin,' bu' Ah jes' thought maybe they were a wee scunnered at ma bletherin.'"

"You see which way any of them went?" Blithewit asked.

"Tha's the way those spotty owls went. I dinnae see th'others," Bhean responded, raising a dark wing to the north.

"I'll be back as soon as I can," Sayah declared, launching skyward with a great dusty gust.

Wheeling to the north, he scanned the open sky, which was empty, then raked the scrub beneath him. It was several minutes before he found the spotted owls, who stood huddled in a sparse thicket.

He descended at once beyond the thicket and peered through the bare branches. The pair had taken no notice of him, so, before greeting them, he circled around them for a clearer view.

"Agh!" he cried in soft surprise when he realized what they were doing.

Leaning together, cheek-to-cheek, the couple slept, their speckled breasts rising and falling in peaceful rhythm. Of course! Every last one of these birds were nocturnal, and it was more than probable they'd all been too exhausted to listen to Bhean, let alone conduct a simulation.

After momentary consideration, Sayah looked again to the slumbering owls, then came to a sudden decision.

"Right!" he said aloud, then again climbed skyward for his return to where the others yet awaited him.

"I think I've solved the mystery of the missing watch," the ægle told Bhean and the foxes while still gliding to a stop.

Bhean bobbed in mellow circles, almost asleep on his feet, but Whisperweave at once probed, "Why? What did you see?"

Bhean opened his lazy eyes as Sayah gestured toward him and replied, "Well, just look at our friend, the raven, here. He's falling asleep as we speak, so how did we imagine it might be different for any of the others? They're all out there, sleeping!"

"Ah! Yes," Blithewit returned. "Now you say it, it seems rather obvious, doesn't it?"

"And we foxes are supposed to be clever folk..." Whisperweave lamented before sending her gaze across the grasslands.

"Do you suppose they'll be safe out there?" she asked, her voice full of care.

"Ah canna say," the raven drawled, lurching a short step in the vixen's direction.

Sayah caught Bhean before he could stumble any farther, and exclaimed, "Now, then! Maybe we should get you somewhere more comfortable to rest."

With one wing draped around Bhean for support, Sayah led him back toward Endego. A few steps off, the Spirit prompted the ægle to call back to Whisperweave and Blithewit.

"Can you ask Pteetya to bring his group to train here? They can keep watch over our friends while they rest."

"Will do!" Blithewit complied.

Whisperweave watched the strange pair as they tottered away, the snowy white ægle and jet-black raven side-by-side in unthinkable comradery.

With a gentle sigh, she shared, "That's a great idea, bringing Pteetya's watch over here. Might even be a good exercise to have his crew find those who are sleeping."

"So long as they don't disturb them," Blithewit chuckled. "We need them fresh tonight since they couldn't train today."

"There's time enough to whip them into shape," Whisperweave asserted. "Right, Blithewit? We've trained worse, and these *want* to be here."

"Indeed," the old silver fox answered in abrupt solemnity. "We'll stand with them as long as they need us."

"Right," the coppered vixen agreed. "That we will."

That evening, the owls, nightjars, and night-herons trickled into Endego in a less than triumphal and somewhat sheepish return. Sayah and the foxes reassured them all and conveyed their understanding of the situation. Bhean had yet to awaken, but Sayah had determined to let the raven rest as long as he needed. He even intended to stand in as Watch Commander if necessary.

Meantime, however, the night watch milled together around the waters of the Tree, getting to know each other. The nocturnal creatures were energized afresh now they marched in cadence with the circadian rhythm Elyon had established for their kinds and were almost unrecognizable when compared to their daytime selves.

Even now, a lively conversation arose that Sayah would have never imagined among the dreary lot he'd seen earlier in the day. After some time, the ægle decided that Billbaste, a night-heron, had earned every bit of his namesake. Sayah wondered that the name, synonymous with a beak sewn shut, hadn't served as a warning to the noisy night-heron that it might come true.

Night-herons were a clever species, not unlike ravens and crows, but in general more courteous and reserved. Billbaste, on the other hand, proved the exception, and insisted on teasing the smaller members of his squadron in a manner not altogether kind.

"Hey! Goat-suckers!" he cawed, taunting several nightjars with a pejorative Mankind had supplied out of their wealth of ignorance and superstition.

The tale among Men was that the nightjar and various of their cousins were wont to suckle at the teats of goats, after which the teats would first dry up, then fall off. In extreme versions of the legends, the goats might even go blind afterward. The myth, of course, was fictitious slander in every way, but as is often the case with such rumors, it flew far and wide to find a home, nestled in Billbaste's mind.

Maybe it was his own simple ignorance that drove Billbaste, or a misguided attempt to ingratiate himself with other members of the night watch, but, regardless, the nightjars did not seem amused. The smaller birds just looked up at Billbaste with steady, unflinching eyes that, though not hateful, indicated their deep displeasure.

At last, one of the larger nightjars, arriving later than the rest, flew into the clearing and circled over Billbaste, his wingbeats resounding in a loud crack as he swung them together over his back.

Clap, clap, clap, the wings beat in slow, deliberate strokes as the nightjar called down at Billbaste, "Bravo! Bravo! You *gran* bully!"

Having acquired the night-heron's attention, the newcomer swept in to land before the antagonist. A collar of red-orange feathers stood out among the late arrival's otherwise dull plumage. At less than half Billbaste's size, the nightjar nevertheless peered up into the night-heron's face, cocking his head back and forth while he assessed the larger bird.

"Oh look!" Billbaste pronounced, "A red-neck goat-sucker!"

The newcomer dropped his eyes to the ground and shook his head in quickening strokes, his body trembling with rage as he muttered an unintelligible patois.

Lifting his eyes to the sky, the nightjar pleaded, "Ay, dearest Papa, please to forgive me while I trounce this *tontoso* bird."

The bantam challenger sized up the Goliath before him, and requested, the strain in his words obvious, "Please, *mi amigo*, do not do this thing any longer. We, too, are brothers, here to help these, our Kin *pequeñito*, in their hour of need. Some respect, I beg you. Please."

Billbaste, who up until this very moment had remained oblivious to the offense he caused, at last paused and grew pensive. The tension in the bower was palpable, and Sayah positioned himself to dart between the potential combatants, intent on preventing any bloodshed in the sacred place.

The larger bird scowled, then took a deep breath, and relaxed, before bowing his head to apologize, "I am sorry. Truly. I *have* been told to watch my mouth before. I meant no disrespect. It's an unfortunate name I've heard too often given your kind. May we start over?"

The chastened Billbaste looked over at the other nightjars to implore them as well, "All of us?"

"You have my pardon," the nightjar before Billbaste responded. "And if we might avoid such discourtesy in *el futuro*, then perhaps we should know each other's names? I am called Vínculo de Sangre. And you are?"

"Billbaste," came the reply, "But you can call me Bill. I'd be happy to put this matter behind us, so long as your friends can forgive me, too."

Vínculo chuckled and glanced back at his peers to request, "What do you say? Will you pardon *mi amigo*, Billbaste, for his rudeness?"

The other nightjars were hesitant to approach Billbaste, but one-by-one they came in slow procession, their cross glowers smoothing away as the night-heron repeated his apology to each. Despite the momentary threat of escalation, Sayah sensed a cleansing between the parties as they reconciled.

Maybe the confrontation had been necessary? And Vínculo had demonstrated uncommon courage in standing up to a much larger opponent. The thought of leaving the village in the care of such as these warmed the ægle and reminded him of his responsibility in preparing them for the task.

Spurred onward by reflection and not willing to delay any longer, Sayah braced himself to lead the night watch. A rustling at his side drew his attention, however, and he found Bhean standing there, a wry grin upon his beak and a bright twinkle in his eye.

"Bhean!" Sayah hollered in excited salutation. "You're up! How are you feeling?"

"A fair sight better than this mornin'," the raven replied, "an' here Ah was jes' in time ta see tha' nigh'-heron abou'ta catch a skelping."

"You saw all that, huh? I was just going to jump in, but they worked it out themselves."

"For the best, Ah imagine. Wouldn'a been good to see blood spilt here."

The ægle nodded in agreement, stunned at the Spirit's prevalent work among them all. In some ways, they seemed to share the same mind. Even Billbaste's eventual contrition before Vínculo and the others wouldn't have been possible a few days prior. But the Kinsman's Tree changed everything. For the better.

Bhean, invigorated at night as were the others, at once asserted his authority as Watch Commander. He ordered the watch from the bower to their designated area of operations, where they launched into rigorous and, daresay, inspired exercises.

To Sayah, Bhean seemed a different bird. An excited energy crackled about Bhean that reminded Sayah of the lightning that had marked the unborn raven. The members of the watch felt it, too, and matched Bhean's smart, intense leadership with a sharp awareness of their own.

The Spirit's work was exciting to watch, but soon the ægle's internal clock was ringing its own alarm that his reserves of energy were in danger of depletion. Confident now he'd seen Bhean and his crew in action, Sayah bid the night watch farewell and retired to his own rest.

Cooling nighttime temperatures had sent Sayah seeking a warmer bed than his perch in the Tree. The attentive Rae noted Sayah's need and enlisted the help of others to find and line the hollow at the base of a nearby tree with straw and leaves. Sheltered from the chill of wintering winds, the nest was soft and warm, and as he turned in for the night, the ægle breathed a prayer of thanksgiving from a heart both happy and content.

Chapter Twelve
The Changing of the Watch

The following morning greeted a much-refreshed Sayah. The ægle was quick to rise and gather his daily portion of rhema. The Kinship had long since developed a system of rhema collection, setting the flakes picked up in the morning in tall earthen vessels for any that hungered to gather throughout the day. The jars were scattered about the clearing and those who collected the rhema in the morning would fill the container, clearing the nearby earth of the nearest wafers before moving on to the next patch.

The process proved efficient and left plenty on the ground for the rest to collect their breakfast free of worry they might trample the precious bread from the heavens. Of course, the Kin were careful to dispose of whatever remained after dinner. They had been warned the rhema would spoil if kept overnight, and that Elyon would give them each day their daily bread.

Every day but the Day of Rest, that is. After He had completed His work of Creation, the Creator had Himself rested, designating the final day of each week a Day of Rest. For this day alone, the rhema kept overnight and even those who gathered, rested.

In any case, the ægle took his meal in a pleasant spot near the Tree, savoring both the rhema and Shoym's reading of Eben'kayah prophecy while he ate. He then set out to locate Whisperweave and Blithewit. They had arranged with the Watch Commanders to work with their separate squadrons at the designated times the watches were set.

Thus, the Darlings were the first that the ægle, vixen, and fox encountered that brisk and bright morning. The starlings were as perky and intertwined as ever and Sayah put their sunny energy to work at once in gathering and mustering their troops to the staging area outside the village. The Darlings were wise to enlist their gregarious brethren in the task, and soon all members of the morning watch were assembled for duty.

To begin with, Sayah and the foxes had the watch run the prior day's simulation again, though not for any prolonged period. The idea was to develop the squadron's sense of organization, which they had spent a great deal of time on the day before. After observing the squad in action, Sayah and his advisors determined they were ready for next steps.

Without the squadrons of the other watches about, the ægle and his vulpine advisors thought it appropriate to station the crew as they would in actuality. To the great pleasure of all, the entire squadron operated with smooth, orderly precision to take their places around Endego. Oh, there were some wrinkles here and there, but these were ironed out at once without frustration.

The sense of unity that developed through even this most basic of exercises gratified everyone involved, and all the more when implemented well. Before long, they were moving into development of a system of signals for communication at distance and began to clarify the distinct leadership role the Darlings would play in directing their team.

Meanwhile, the team grew more focused and soon attempted playful engagement with non-threatening creatures in the region. Indeed, these creatures consider the miscellaneous assemblage of fowl the greater threat, and many was the rodent, varmint, or strange bird that fled upon contact with the vast screen of scouts emanating from Endego.

After a couple hours thus employed, Sayah called all members of the watch back for a break and conferred over what they'd learned as a collective. With some probing from Whisperweave and Blithewit, the group shared valuable experience from the morning's operation and from their initial contacts.

The value of precise communication soon became apparent among the entire group, as did the ability to assess their targets when encountered. Blithewit seized on the opportunity to recommend to

Sayah and the Darlings a new kind of drill to mimic the unpredictability of an actual hostile incursion.

"From this moment on," the fox began, "the team should treat every contact as a potential hostile element."

"I don't mean they should sound the alarm or be hostile themselves," he continued. "What I mean is that your team, no, every team, should apply the operating fundamentals in every instance."

"I agree," spoke Whisperweave. "There is no better training for mind and body, and everyone here needs more experience, more practice working on the fundamentals."

Blithewit concurred, "Precisely. With every encounter, the team should practice communication, threat assessment, maneuverability and maintaining contact with their targets. They'll learn how to function better as a unit, and how to observe without being seen themselves. Before long, they'll be experts, and you'll know of every last fruit-fly passing by."

Sayah inquired, "And what do the Darlings need to be aware of? How can they best help their squadron?"

Whisperweave picked up the question and directed her response at the starlings, "Your job is to remember the fundamentals. Always.

"Direct your team. Work with them to better their understanding of the fundamentals and their implementation. Be an effective hub of communication so you make the most informed decisions.

"Besides that, you just need to be present and aware. Support the team and respond to their needs. Lord Elyon will take care of the rest."

The Darlings looked at one another a moment, then responded in tandem, "We can do that!"

Sayah sent the starlings on their way and dismissed the foxes on a couple hours hiatus. He then settled in outside the village to monitor the effects of their instructions to the starlings. Not long after, the ægle spied the teams attempting to adapt to their new mandate. Clumsy though they were at first, the group was quite earnest in their efforts, and their eventual progress became clear over the following hours.

Not long after noon, Sayah spotted the white tip of a fox's bushy tail cutting through the yellowed straw. From overhead, the Darlings in their piping voices relayed Blithewit's approach, drawing a grin along Sayah's beak. The morning watch was operating just as requested. He couldn't have asked for anything more from them.

The silver fox came into full view and hollered a salutation to Sayah as he trotted to the ægle on nimble feet.

"You might take a bit of rest yourself, Sayah," Blithewit advised. "You'll be through this rigmarole twice more before the day is done."

"Will you keep an eye on things here until I get back?" the ægle asked.

"You know I will," Blithewit confirmed.

"We both will!" Whisperweave called from a short distance, "and not just now. Until you return from your journey with Rae and Nat."

Sayah marveled again at how sharp the vixen's ears were, an impression at once swallowed up by gratitude at the foxes' willingness to help in the care of the village. He thanked them both and took his leave to rest as they suggested, likewise thanking Lord Elyon as he took flight along his way.

A short while later, a refreshed Sayah returned to where he'd left the foxes, anticipating the arrival of the second watch. As expected, the eager Pteetya was first to arrive, and Sayah took advantage to call the Darlings down to the bower for a quick meeting.

Once they were gathered before the Tree, the ægle described his vision of a seamless transition between the watches. It wouldn't do in any actual scenario to call all members of a current watch away all at once when the next watch started. Such a practice ran contrary to the first principle they'd learned of continuity.

Blithewit and Whisperweave concurred and explained that the watches would need to overlap at the transition to avoid any break in coverage. Once everyone on the incoming watch was present at the Tree, the outgoing Watch Commander would join them for a short briefing.

Both Watch Commanders would be present at the meeting to review the relevant happenings of the prior watch. Establishing a continuity of both coverage and the flow of information would enable the commanders to develop any emergent issues as together they deemed fit. The layering of perspectives and skills between the two Watch Commanders as peers would also help them each to strengthen any areas of personal weakness while in the moment driving a consensus for better decision-making.

It was an effective model in which the foxes had participated while serving the Empire of Chōl that nevertheless rankled them for its connection to the Nihúkolem. The stench and stain of the oppressive regime troubled the foxes, and Whisperweave in particular. Though agitated, the vixen sensed the Spirit's redemptive direction, and responded at once.

Interjecting in the conversation, she proclaimed, "This isn't right!"

Her sudden outburst drew every eye, but she continued, "Pardon me, but I believe we ought to do something different here. These plans are all well and good, but we shouldn't just do everything the Empire did because we think it works. I don't believe that's the way Elyon would have us operate."

None heard with natural ears the Spirit speak, but notwithstanding, the waters stirred, and His voice resounded within their beings.

My thoughts are not your thoughts, neither are your ways my ways, for as the outermost heavens are higher than the earth, so are my ways higher than your ways and my thoughts higher than your thoughts.

Blithewit, in light of the Spirit's utterance and in support of Whisperweave, proposed, "It would seem that perhaps we ought to consider a prayer at each of these sessions. Let's give opportunity for Lord Elyon to speak on our plans."

"I agree," Sayah replied. "We have no idea what our enemy will throw at us. Only Elyon knows and can prepare us for it."

"Maybe," whispered Pteetya in a rare quiet moment, "maybe the point is that we *can't* without Him. Maybe we need to be humble enough to admit that He changes everything. Even us."

Whisperweave added, "All the more reason to start each meeting with His guidance, right?"

"Right!" Sayah answered, nodding along with everyone present, most of all the Darlings, whose heads together bobbed in perfect time.

By now, the entire watch crew had arrived, and the ægle contemplated the question of just *who* should pray, settling at last on Pteetya. As the incoming Watch Commander, the thrush would be responsible for not just the physical well-being of the squadron, but the spiritual as well. It seemed right for the Watch Commanders to do so as they arrived for duty, and Sayah made a mental note to discuss the matter with each of them.

Pteetya, meanwhile, requested all present join him in the water, where they gathered in a circle and bowed their heads in reverence before the Tree.

With eyes closed, the blue thrush lifted his face to the sky, and in his shrill voice implored, "Lord Elyon, Maker of Heaven and Earth and Savior to us all, please hear our cry for wisdom today. With all our hearts, we trust in You and not our own judgment.

"We submit our plans to You now that You may lead us such that we should not stumble along the path but rather seek Your way. These, our Etom Kin, have entrusted us with their protection, and we love them for bringing us before the Tree.

"Thank You for each one here. Allow us to honor our commitment to You and to one another as we grow in the duty set before us. In the precious name of the Kinsman Gaal, we so declare it."

As though to confirm His approval of their prayer, the Spirit again stirred the waters and a weighty, invisible drop struck the surface at the center of their ring. Outward from this point, a solitary ripple spread in slow, beautiful undulation.

The surge met them where they stood but did not pass beyond them. Instead, the assembly absorbed the wave, climbed their bodies in form of growing light. A dancing tongue of fire sprung up between each one's eyes to seal their minds in flame. The fire then faded from view, though they yet felt its quickening heat.

Sayah chuffed with exhilaration at the Spirit's energizing strength, then noticed the others were likewise invigorated. The eyes of some stood out in bright relief, while the feathers of another stood straight out in ruffled agitation, and still others shivered, then shook from head to tailfeathers.

"Whew!" breathed Blithewit.

"What was that?" gasped Whisperweave.

The ægle glanced their way and failed to restrain an outburst of laughter. The tail of each fox stood upraised in stiff salute. Likewise, each hair stood out in static surprise to double the size of their tails, one burnished copper and the other gleaming silver. Following Sayah's gaze, each fox looked at the other's posterior, then jumped with startlement.

"Agh! Well, this is most embarrassing," Blithewit muttered.

Whisperweave, on the other hand, strained to lower her tail and protested, "Ugh! Why won't it go down?"

The pair turned and twisted, but no matter what they tried, their tails remained pointed straight up. The effect lasted half a minute or so, and the foxes were grateful when their tails returned to a more dignified state. The ægle might have been distressed for them, if he hadn't been preoccupied with stifling his amusement.

"I'm sorry. Please, I'm sorry," Sayah pleaded while wiping his streaming eyes.

"I am *not* keen on that happening again any time soon," Whisperweave reported, her eyes narrowed with displeasure.

"Now, now, then," Blithewit reassured. "You were as lovely as ever. Don't let it trouble you. Maybe it was for our sake somehow. After all, the Spirit had a hand in it."

"And what possible purpose might it have served?" came the vixen's retort.

"Well, all Pteetya's talk of humility had me thinking maybe we take ourselves too seriously," he responded in an attempt to placate her.

"Hummph!" she sniffed, not altogether convinced, yet pensive all the same.

Despite his interest in the foxes' drama, Sayah sensed the Spirit beckoning for his attention, and followed His leading at once to confer with Pteetya and the Darlings. The transition they had worked out earlier elicited no disharmony with the Spirit or between the present leaders. As such, Sayah directed them to prepare their squadrons for the switch.

Before Sayah released them to the task, however, he had one more request.

"Today will be my last in Endego for a while. Lord Elyon alone knows how long we'll be gone, or if we'll return. I want to thank you for taking up this burden on behalf of the Kinship. It means a great deal to me that you are willing to help."

"That being said, I must ask another favor, though this one, I hope, won't be much trouble. I need to ask you all to meet with Bhean and me at the transition tonight. Darlings, I know I might be asking much, given you're starting early again tomorrow, but I have a few things I'd like to discuss with all of you at the same time. And Pteetya, it might mean you and your crew have to stay a bit later. Can you three be here, though? Please?"

"Of course!" the Darlings replied, then again shivered and shook from beak to tailfeather.

Master Darling exclaimed, "I don't know if we'll even be able to sleep tonight!"

"Yes, darling! I feel so *alive* right now. Staying up a couple extra hours won't hurt," the Missus agreed.

Pteetya raised a tiny wing and assured Sayah, "You know me. It's no trouble at all. You gotta get everything in order before you leave, right? Wouldn't be doing your job if you didn't."

Sayah acknowledged Pteetya's graciousness, "I appreciate it.".

Assuming a tone of command, the ægle turned his eyes to the perimeter of Endego, and cheered, "Now! Let's get these birds in the sky!"

The Watch Commanders burst into action, enlivened under the blessing of the Spirit, and Sayah ascended to watch. Yes, the orderly activity of the squadrons in transition held a certain beauty, for it represented the unity of their hearts and minds in the Spirit. Even in their mistakes, Sayah saw the Spirit manifest, for correction was gentle and taken with good humor.

Circling high in the clear blue sky and shining bright in the westering sun, the ægle monitored the change of watch to its completion. He'd no desire to apply unnecessary pressure to the incoming watch during transition, so he found Pteetya afterward to explain the training doctrine they'd developed earlier.

The thrush, small of stature but ever great of heart, received the news with characteristic enthusiasm.

"That's fantastic!" he declared. "I know these bums would just get bored if we didn't do somethin' with 'em. Shoot! *I* was gettin' bored. I'll get 'em started right away!"

Before Sayah could reply, the thrush had darted away on his latest orders. The ægle sighed, glad he'd had nothing more to say, and decided it was a good time for another rest. He might be up late tonight and wanted to be fresh for their parley.

This time, Sayah forced himself to sleep a while, a feat only accomplished once the sun was down. Prior to nestling down in the cozy hollow of a tree, he asked Blithewit to wake him well before they expected Bhean, and the old fox did not disappoint. The ægle felt as though mere minutes had passed when he awoke to Blithewit's hushed, gruff bark.

"Sayah! Hey there! Time to get up!"

The ægle arose, his awareness at first foggy, but clearing with each passing second. Blithewit stood nearby, obscured in the nighttime shadows, but Sayah's sharp eyes negated the gloom and picked the fox out without difficulty.

"How long?" Sayah murmured, still a tad groggy.

"Eh? What's that?" the fox returned.

Sayah marshalled himself to ask again, "How long until the night watch begins?"

"You've got the better part of an hour, though I expect Bhean may arrive early."

"Good, good. Thanks for rousing me. Have you gotten any sleep yet?"

"Nah! I've been waiting up. Didn't want to miss waking you. Did you need me tonight?"

"That's alright. I think we'll get along just fine, now we've got the most part figured out. Will you be around in the morning?"

"Of course! We'll want to see you off, won't we?"

Struck with sudden curiosity, Sayah began, "Hey, Blithewit? You and Whisperweave – are you two...?"

The ægle stopped himself, afraid to pry. It wasn't his business, but he liked the thought of the two foxes finding some happiness with each other.

"Eh? What's that about Whisperweave?" Blithewit inquired.

"Never mind," Sayah answered, then muttered, "I'm not awake yet. Don't know what I'm saying. Have a good night."

"Well, alright, then. Good night, Sayah!"

With that, the silver fox slipped into the night, his slinky figure disappearing behind the screen of Endego's staggered trees.

Sayah proceeded to the bower, which yet beckoned with a muted, amber glow. He gathered a few leftover wafers of rhema from an urn, which he consumed before stepping into the Üntfither for a dip and a drink. Blended with the flow of the Tree, the clear waters promised uncommon refreshment. An alert Sayah stepped from the stream, his thirst now slaked. He was ready.

Bhean soon fluttered into the clearing, his large, dark wings stretched wide to slow his descent. Sayah greeted the raven and informed him of the meeting. It would be the last Sayah would attend for some time, and Bhean had already guessed it was coming.

Before any others had arrived, Sayah was able to entrust Bhean with the duty of praying over the watch at the start of each night. The ægle was impressed at the clever raven's unvarnished reply.

"Ay, Ah've already been doin' tha' by ma'self. Alone, though, ye ken? Ah canna imagine startin' the night without."

Sayah wondered if Bhean's confession had anything to do with the electric energy he'd sensed flowing from the raven the night before and admitted to himself it was more than probable.

Sayah commended Bhean and added, "My guess is that it can't hurt to have *everyone* pray together before starting, then."

"Ah'd wager yer righ,' there, Sayah. We were havin' a blether, a few of the lads an' me, an' they tol' me they'd done it, too."

"Hmmph!" Sayah snorted with mild delight. "Shouldn't be a problem at all, then."

The Darlings flew into the clearing in tandem formation to land side-by-side next to Sayah and Bhean. They gave a stereo salute, then disclosed in back-and-forth fashion:

"We've just seen Pteetya..."

"...and he'll be right along."

"He's really putting his team through their paces!"

"They've come so far already..."

"...we're inspired by their progress!"

"A little jealous, too, maybe."

"Maybe a little."

"Yeah, just a little."

Pteetya swung into the bower just in time to save a grateful Sayah and Bhean. The thrush dropped into the gathering and offered his greetings then was all business. And as Sayah began to speak, the bower filled with members of the night watch.

"As you all know, I'm leaving early tomorrow. I don't know long I'll be gone, but I wanted to tell you how thankful I am for each of you. You and every member of your team is a gift from the Creator.

"That being said, I won't be leaving you without support. Blithewit and Whisperweave will help in any way they can and will provide regular reports to the Council. If the foxes are unable to help, the Council may be able, so don't be afraid to approach any of them.

"Without a doubt, however, the greatest resource any of us have is Lord Elyon Himself. He's the One who drew us to the Tree, and He has given us His Spirit to empower us for every good work. So, pray hard!

"I've discussed with each of you the importance of seeking His will as a group at the outset of each watch, but there's another aspect I'd like you consider. You are the leaders of each watch, but you should be on the lookout for anyone in your crew with leadership potential. Before long, you should each have a few candidates for a second-in-command.

"Pray over your whole team but pray most of all for these candidates – that the Spirit would point out to you which bird will best succeed you. It's important to develop your team, and these in particular. Don't be afraid to give them responsibility or allow them to lead prayer every once in a while. If, Elyon forbid, any of you are sick, injured or worse, your team will need someone to look to in your absence.

"Finally, you four are great assets to each other. Spend time together talking out what you've each learned. Your unique styles of leadership reflect your personal strengths...and weaknesses. Be humble and open to learn from one another, and don't be proud when you offer advice.

"The overall success of your mission relies not on any one of you or any one of your squadrons alone. The stakes are too high for petty rivalry to hold any sway. Lives are on the line! So, hold one another accountable, but recognize your own part in failure when you're tempted to blame another. If together you do these things, you and your teams will soar – to the glory of the Lord Elyon!

"Now, I need to direct Bhean in the changing of the watch. Pteetya, you should prepare your troops as well.

"Do any of you have questions for me? No? Ok, then, Darlings, I will see you in the morning. Pteetya, I'll see you as soon as you've completed your rounds."

The Darlings said farewell, and Pteetya flapped away on his errand while Sayah explained to Bhean the specifics of transitioning the watch. The transition would be a bit different, given the diminished coverage the night watch afforded, but the essentials were the same.

All the while, Sanctuary Endego continued to fill with the denizens of the night, and at the periphery of his awareness, Sayah perceived Billbaste and Vínculo engaged in easy comradery. The sight warmed his heart, and the ægle's hope swelled for the motley night crew.

Sayah sent Bhean to relay the outlay of deployment to his team, then awaited Pteetya's reappearance. The blue rock thrush wasn't long in returning, and joined Sayah, who then called Bhean back as well. The ægle gave Pteetya a few moments to report to Bhean the day's happenings, which in truth were not many.

Beside training exercises, little had happened, but Sayah was happy to note that Pteetya had maintained a tally of the critters his team had engaged:

2 porcupines

3 voles

7 geese

1 badger

and too many field mice to number.

Afterward, Bhean thanked Pteetya for the brief, and then invited the thrush to prayer in the pool under the Tree. The raven's rich brogue rendered his prayer almost unintelligible to Sayah, but the Spirit responded regardless.

Never redundant, the Creator demonstrated His creativity in the expression of His blessing on the night watch. The air around them grew charged and crackled with a static energy that ran through the crowd in a furcating bolt. Regardless, the one thing in common with the afternoon's sign was the transitory appearance of flame upon their heads.

Once again, the assembled squadron was exhilarated, even Sayah, who'd begun to tire as the night wore on. The memory of Blithewit and Whisperweave's extra-bushy tails forced a chuckle from him as he sent Bhean and his crew out to relieve Pteetya's squad.

The sudden burst of energy sustained the ægle as he joined the night watch over the village to observe the operation. Once again, the changeover was smooth, and the rare wrinkle handled with grace and care. Soon, the night watch was installed in full, and the others sped away home to take their rest.

Sayah checked in with Bhean a little bit later to explain how the team should proceed. The operating principle from now on would be to train the members of the night watch while on the job, just as on the other watches. The raven received the new instructions with a stoic nod and Sayah asked if he needed anything further before he took his leave.

Bhean declined but wished Sayah a good night then fluttered away to enact the ægle's orders. For his part, Sayah decided it was time to sleep, and headed back toward his hollow. He had an early day tomorrow and was a bit concerned that he might have trouble sleeping. The Spirit's quickening power yet coursed through him and the ægle hoped it wouldn't keep him awake.

As it turned out, Sayah had no difficulty at all in dozing off. Though his mind was awhirl with the recollection of a busy day, a sweet slumber nonetheless fell over him. And in the warm, dark comfort of the hollow, he slept.

Chapter Thirteen
Upward and Onward

"Sayah?" a familiar feminine voice called, sweeping away the ægle's pleasant dream.

"Sayah!" came the call again, this time more insistent.

Sayah stirred and lifted his eyes toward the voice. Just outside his sleepy hollow stood Whisperweave, her gleaming eyes alight with mischief as she peered in on him. Here was one who savored the duty of rousing the ægle.

To Sayah, the view of the village from his resting place appeared over-bright, and the shadows too short. Realizing at last that the vixen had only come to collect him because he had overslept, the ægle bolted upright with a squawk.

"Agh! What's the hour now? Is the morning watch already in? Have I missed anything?"

"Whoa! Whoa, there, Sayah!" Whisperweave raised an arresting paw and attempted to calm him.

"Everything is fine. Blithewit and I oversaw the transition this morning, and it went great. You did a fantastic job training everyone.

"Blithewit and I decided to let you rest since you were up so late last night. Besides, you have another long day ahead of you, what with the start of your journey. You'll need your strength today."

The ægle absorbed the information, appreciative that the foxes had been so quick to step in and support the reconnaissance effort.

A question occurred to Sayah, which he shared with the vixen, "Have you seen Nat or Rae yet this morning?"

"They arrived in the bower a short while ago. They looked keen to depart, but also wanted to let you rest. We decided to wake you now because Bhean stuck around to see you off, and the poor fellow is fading fast. Do you think you can manage?"

"Sure, sure," Sayah groaned as he arose.

The ægle's body ached a bit from days filled with too much activity combined with a night of too much sleep, but he started to feel better the more he moved. They weren't far from the Tree so Sayah elected to remain earthbound and walk with Whisperweave to their destination. His rolling gait was awkward alongside the vixen's light stride, but he preferred the companionship and thus endured his own clumsiness along the way.

As they proceeded, they engaged in the smallest and most polite of talk, the kind that seems unimportant for its commonplace nature, but that proves a sweet comfort when present in memory. Thus distracted, the ægle's sharp eyes did not glimpse the clearing through the trees until they rounded the great willow off Galfgallan Road.

At first sight and though his vision captured the image with clarity, Sayah's mind did not at once distinguish the swelling crowd that filled the bower. To his eyes, every Etom in the village was present, the kaleidoscope of their colorful faces peppering the scene. Of course, Blithewit stood at hand, as did the Darlings, Pteetya, and a yawning Bhean.

Perched in the branches overhead and mingled among the Etom on the ground were a good many of those fowl Sayah had trained over the past three days. Not a few of them were the nocturnal sort, and it pained the ægle a bit to see the dozing owls, nightjars, and even Billbaste fighting the sleep their bodies clamored for in daylight hours.

From the crowd broke Nat and Rae, who dashed to join the stunned ægle at the clearing's edge. Whisperweave trotted off to Blithewit and the young Etom each gripped a snowy forefeather on Sayah's either side to conduct him onward. Leery of the amassed attention of the assembly, Sayah complied with the stilted hesitance of the condemned.

Rae, Nat and Sayah approached the center of the clearing, and the Council of the Vine advanced to greet them. Several steps off, most of them stopped, while hand-in-hand Nida, Dempsey, Tram and Kehren continued. The couples glowed with pride for the young trio as they drew near, their eyes glistening with unspoken emotion.

Nida sighed, a tear at last escaping her while from Kehren fell a steady shower.

"You three," Nida spoke with affection. "How can we express just how proud we are of you? How much we're going to miss you?"

"You're the heart of us, dear ones. All of us. We're torn between the anguish of your absence and the excitement of what we *know* the Spirit will accomplish through you. To release you into Elyon's hands is ever a parent's fate, and we most pray that you do not falter in your mission. Come what may."

At this, Nida left Dempsey's side and embraced Rae then stepped back to grip the younger etma by the shoulders to plead, "Rae. Like-my-own-daughter Rae. Be the voice of wisdom when these two want to rush in, but do not quench their courage. Love them both well, and care for them. You're my favorite etma. Ever."

Nida stepped aside to stand before Sayah, while Kehren and Tram took her place to envelop their daughter in tearful hugs and kisses.

Looking up into the ægle's golden eyes, Nida raised her hands to beckon him near. His fluffy brows arched in shy apprehension, Sayah lowered his head while a grinning Nat watched on. Nida cupped the ægle's beak in one hand and caressed his soft, white cheek with the other.

"You great rascal," she chided, her voice playful. "You've changed a great deal since we met, but I still see that gawky, unfledged æglet in you. You struggled so much with your family's rejection but let me tell you a secret."

She turned her head to whisper into Sayah's ear, "You were worth it then, and you're worth it now."

Nida stepped back to avoid the great, hot tear that spilled from the ægle's golden eye, yet stayed in reach. She had more to say.

"I *know* you'd gladly lay down your own life to save either of these two, but don't you forget: Lord Elyon has plans for *you*, too – plans for you to fare well and not to come to harm; plans of hope in the age to come."

"We love you, dear ægle," she granted, then favored Sayah with a kiss on his prostrate beak before moving over to her son.

Nat looked up at Nida as she stepped before him. He'd grown quite a bit in the past months, and their eyes were almost even now. She wondered if he might return from their adventure taller than she, and the thought made their parting now more difficult. She fought back the sobs that threatened to muddle her words, aware this goodbye might be their last.

"Nat...*my* son. I call you *my* son now for the last time, at least in any sense of possession. From this moment on, I surrender you to our Lord as His child first. You're no less precious to me now than ever. No, I understand more every day how much more precious you are to Him than I can ever imagine.

"And, so, I entrust you to Him for His purposes. I know you'll do your best to honor Him like you've honored me. More so, for the Spirit of His life in you will make you able to do great things on His behalf."

Nat wept in silence, his beatific smile as ever affixed upon his face as he received her words.

"Regardless, I hope you know I love you all the more and will be praying for you three while you're on your journey. I *am* still and will ever be..."

Staring into her son's broad and smiling pale blue face, Nida succumbed to a flood of memories: Nat's peculiar birth, his bath in the latex, first day of school, fight with a bully, trek through the wilderness, escape from the Scarsburrow, deathly poisoning...

Momentous emotion overwhelmed Nida and she at last choked up, recovering long enough to spit out, "I will *always* be...your mother!"

Nat did not wait for her embrace, but leapt at her with arms wide, his own sobs ratcheting his frame as he held her.

In the immediate vicinity, all but Dempsey were reduced to a bawling mess. The assembled throng murmured with concern for their departing heroes. It wasn't long, however, before those weeping recovered themselves. Even the languid Kehren dried her tears and wished Sayah and Nat a proper farewell.

Dempsey, for his part, came last to the three. He laid a hand on Rae's shoulder, then hugged her as an older brother in the Vine. Afterward, he commended Sayah, patting the ægle's folded wing as he did.

He arrived at last to Nat, offering a strong hand as he spoke, "Nat, you're an amazing young etém. You've helped bring new life to this village, and I'm proud to call you my friend.

"If it's not too forward of me, I would like to look in on your mother while you're gone, if she'll allow it. What say you, as her son and as the etém of the house? Will you accept me as her suitor?"

Nat at first just stared at Dempsey, a curious, half-cocked grin on his face. Dempsey grew a tad apprehensive, and almost took back the request.

And then the young etém was upon him in an awkward and somewhat gangly embrace.

"Of course! Of course, Dempsey!" Nat cried through tears. "I can think of none better 'suited' to the job."

"Pun intended?" Dempsey quipped, though touched at Nat's reaction.

Nat released the older etém to drop a wink his way, the quirky smile still playing at his lips, "You better believe it."

Dempsey ruffled the youth's unkempt zalzal with a rough but affectionate yellow hand, and promised, "I'll do my best while you're gone."

He pointed a stout finger at Nat and demanded, "You just make sure to bring yourself home."

"I'll do my best, too," Nat answered, then grew introspective and added, "if Lord Elyon wills it, we'll return."

"Hey! Don't you –" Dempsey began his rebuke with a shout before shooting a glance back at Nida and continuing in a much lower voice. "Don't you talk like that. Kehren and your mother are already worried enough."

Nat just shrugged and raised his pale blue hands, palms-up as if to say, *It is what it is, Dempsey.*

Nat's gesture wasn't a rebuttal, to be precise, so Dempsey accepted it with a sigh. The kid was already well aware that the missions of Elyon came with risks.

It's best that he's prepared for anything Elyon might send their way, Dempsey surmised with a nod.

He placed a reassuring hand on Nat's shoulder and squeezed.

"Excuse me? Do you fellas think we might set out?" Rae chided. "You know, while there's some daylight left?"

Sayah remained silent, but the fiery glint of anticipation in his eyes belied his polite nod of agreement. He was more than ready to go.

"Just one more thing, please," Nat asked.

He looked around at the faces of the many Etom there, looking for one in particular. Within seconds, he spied the one he sought just beside Iver's angry orange face, the etém's distinct color drawing his attention.

Well, at least he's good for something right now, Nat quipped to himself while strolling over to Pikrïa, whose marred and scabrous face filled with dismay as he approached.

Offended and disgusted, Iver shrunk back from Nat when the young etém extended his hands toward Pikrïa, as if mere contact with Nat might contaminate him. Pikrïa, however, stood frozen at the gesture, fixed and immobile even when Nat took her hands in his.

"Great Aunt Pikrïa," Nat sighed with a smile, "I wouldn't dare to leave now without saying a special goodbye to *you*."

Beneath Pikrïa's impassive mask, something trembled when Nat glanced back at his mother and spoke, "From everything my mother has told me, we owe you a great deal.

"Without you, my mother would have never found a home in Endego after her parents died. She would have never met my father. And I...well, I would have never existed.

"So, thank you, and goodbye."

Nat breathed the words and, standing on the tips of his toes, he kissed Pikrïa's cracked and crusted cheek, where ruin had overtaken her once soft and glowing amber skin. Her trembling became quaking, and then the precious young etém was walking away, off on some fool adventure she could never understand. Just like his father. Just like Jaarl.

Pikrïa's hand flew to her cheek and it was all she could do to restrain the other from reaching after Nat, from calling after him to stop. Her elderly frame shuddered, and she took a step to one side, away from Iver, whom she appraised with a sidelong gaze.

Who is this Etom, anyhow? she asked herself. *What harm does he intend toward those here?*

From the counsel they had kept together that cold night not so long ago, Pikrïa knew Iver held a deep resentment against these who called themselves the Kinship, the members of the Vine. The Kinship that included Nida and her son.

Pikrïa's deep-seated rejection of Nat and Nida produced as a convenient by-product their utter absence from her life. In accordance with the term – "Out of sight, out of mind" – so Pikrïa had invoked their absence as a means of rendering their very real suffering a mere abstraction.

So much easier for Pikrïa to care less the less she saw Nida and then Nat, though in her heart of hearts, a still, small voice continued to inform her how they ached from the pain of abandonment. She'd made certain of it.

First Jaarl had left for Elyon knew where, then any friends or family who remained had deserted them under pressures both subtle and overt that Pikrïa had applied. Supporting a widow and her newborn hatchling was difficult enough work, and many welcomed the excuse to leave them to scrape by.

The reality of mother and son, thriving beyond their trials, and giving grace despite Pikrïa's most vicious intentions, now provoked a revolution in Pikrïa's soul. The old etma had yet to decide which faction in her civil war to side with. Overall indecision aside, she managed one choice. She no longer wished to be associated with Iver.

All that remained was how to break ties and yet find excuse to visit the bower. The people of the Tree and their place had taken hold of Pikrïa, but her pride prevented her from making any such admission. Until and unless such a time arose, she would continue to use Iver for his access to the bower. Again, the whisper in her heart of hearts told her she was free to come to the Tree as she so pleased, but Pikrïa was not yet ready to hear it.

The three young wayfarers had no idea when they might return, so the final leg of their procession took them through the waters of the Tree. A happy gauntlet of their Kin awaited them in the water, an array of Etom and fowl on either side forming a channel through which they might wade. Though the assembly varied in kind, they all shared the same kind eyes. Every last one wished them the best success.

Nat marched at the front of the short parade and was first to receive the Kinship's blessing. Shoym stood at the head of the column and, as Nat approached, he stooped to fill his ash-grey hands in the pool. Shoym raised his brimming hands to beckon Nat draw near. Grasping Shoym's intent, Nat lowered his head and stepped forth.

Shoym released the handful of water in a gentle flow over top Nat's humble head, and whispered, "I can imagine no greater blessing of Elyon but that He go with you."

The Spirit resonated within Nat, *I will never leave you nor forsake you.*

And as he, then Rae and Sayah, proceeded on their exodus through the waters, the Kin on either side, each one, blessed them along the way. Although it caused Sayah some discomfort to stoop so low as to allow the diminutive Etom and some of the smaller birds to reach his head, he suffered to receive every last benediction of his Kin. These were his people now, and he theirs.

At long last, they arrived at the far side of the water, east toward the Üntfither, where their packs had been set for them. There, Nat and Rae shouldered their provisions and mounted Sayah's back. The ægle turned so all three might face the gathered crowd, and Nat and Rae waved in departure.

Nat leaned down to whisper in Sayah's ear, "Let's not prolong this any further. What do you think?"

Sayah needed no additional signal and raised his great and shining white wings in readiness for flight. With a triumphant, keening cry, the ægle burst up from the ground, his wings beating a vibrant rhythm as they climbed into the sunlit sky.

Nat and Rae spied Kehren, Tram, Dempsey, and Nida at the front of the crowd, now far below and receding with each stroke of Sayah's wings. Not to be outdone by their peers on the ground, the Morning Watch whistled, chirped and sang in farewell, and some conducted the adventurers as far as their patrol routes permitted.

Soon, however, the grove they'd known as home shrank down to an indistinct patch of trees. Endego faded altogether in the distance as the trio sped along toward their destination, which lay far to the north and east.

Chapter Fourteen

Water in the Wilderness

For Nat, Rae, and Sayah the first day of their adventure was uneventful. Sayah flew on fresh wings, a tailwind carrying them at good speed more than half the distance to Sakkan before they stopped to rest for the night.

The three had decided from the beginning not to travel at night unless the Spirit directed them otherwise. They had no idea how long their journey might be, and thus treated it as an extensive excursion in which rest was an important component.

The Etom had packed just the necessities: a change of clothes and a bedroll for each Etom, some fresh water, and plenty of dried and preserved foods. A heavy wheel of pungent qábēs cheese encased in wax promised some comfort of hearth and home, but besides that, their fare would be seeds, nuts, dried fruit, and biscuit. And whatever they might forage, of course.

Another reason they had packed only prepared foods was to avoid the necessity of cooking. The added weight and bulk of cookware and dishes would have been greater encumbrances than they were worth. Also, the trio hoped that, to the best of their abilities, they might pass undetected along their journey, and a large cooking fire might draw attention.

Instead, they built a small fire for warmth against a steep stone. The fire didn't cast much light, but the stone reflected its heat on the trio huddled around it for comfort and shared a morsel. Keeping their voices low, the three chattered on into the late hours until at long last their excitement at setting out on their mission diminished enough they were able to sleep.

The morning greeted them with a chill frost and the hard, bright light of the early winter sun. Discomfort was fantastic motivation to arise, and the three of them, Nat and Rae in particular, rubbed away at sore, cold joints for the first few hours of the day.

The Etom had grown accustomed to sleeping in the comfort of their beds in Endego while Sayah had never known such comfort. As such, the ægle didn't need to adapt to sleeping outdoors on the ground as the Etom did. He arose with no complaint from his body but the questing gurgle of his hungry stomach.

Sayah turned about and his eyes fell on a peculiar sight that elicited a surprised cry from him, "Wha – ? Nat! Rae! Look at this!"

A few steps from their campsite lay three white wafers of what without a doubt was rhema – one for each of them. Sayah was reminded at once of his time on the Cold Vantage and fell to without so much as a second thought.

Nat and Rae, on the other hand, exchanged astonished looks. They'd heard Sayah's tale of Elyon's provision atop the windblown polar cliffs in the North but hadn't expected to see such a thing themselves.

Nat shrugged and extended an open hand toward the rhema, "Be my guest, Rae."

"Gee, thanks," the rosy-cheeked etma replied. "If it's poison, at least Sayah and I will die first."

Sayah stopped his crunching to cock a sharp, upraised brow, at once aware Nat and Rae had dragged him into the conversation.

Nat sputtered, "Well, um, I'm sure it's fine. It's just *rhema* after all."

He dashed ahead of Rae and collected one of the wafers to take a bite before she did.

"See?" he offered with a sheepish smile. "Look! It's fine. I'm not dead. Neither is Sayah."

"Hmph!" the indignant Rae huffed. "So much for ladies first!"

"Now wait a minute, here..." Nat began, then noticed Rae's cheeky grin.

"Are you pulling my leg?" he remarked with an incredulous smile.

Rae drove a stiff jab into Nat's shoulder as she walked past him to the rhema.

"Of course, you silly etém!" she quipped before snapping off a large bite of the sweet, crispy flake.

From Sayah, Nat detected the quiet "tee hee hee" of the ægle's snicker and rounded to confront him.

"Not you, too!" Nat moaned in mock distress. "Well, I'll just go eat over here by myself, then."

"Awwww, Nat! Don't go!" Rae called, racing to grab his arm and drag him back.

Smiling, he relented without resistance, and the three of them enjoyed their rhema in cheerful, reverent thanksgiving. The bread induced a deep thirst, so afterward, Nat went to the packs for water.

Coming down the gentle slope that led to their campsite, Nat spotted a shallow depression atop the stone they'd built their fire against. He stared at the smooth and sunken place, perplexed that he was drawn to it thus until a touch of resonance hinted at something more.

Nat's attention, now focused, prompted him to gather the others, "Rae! Sayah! I think you should get over here! Something's happening!"

Even as they responded to Nat's urgent summons, the Spirit out of the histories of the Eben'kayah spoke within them all.

Speak to the rock in their presence and it will produce water.

A flickering vision of the Kinsman speaking confronted Nat within his mind, the words a counterpoint to the statement of the Spirit.

"Whoever partakes of the water I give will not thirst again. No, within the one who drinks, My draught becomes a wellspring bubbling up unto life everlasting."

Nat's friends now at his side, the etém repeated the Kinsman's words.

"...a wellspring bubbling up unto life everlasting," he concluded.

Inside the dish of dented stone, a single drop of water appeared. Another appeared along the depression's curving edge and ran down to meet the first. And then another, and then another until a meager puddle had formed in the hollow.

Droplets continued to run down into the growing puddle while its surface meantime began to jitter and burble. Soon, the smooth concavity was brimming and bubbling over with a crystalline flow the trio could only describe as identical to that of the Kinsman's Tree.

Rae cupped a hand to sample the spring and found cool, clear water quenched her thirst as only the Tree's springs could. Thirsty, the two others followed suit and all three imbibed with abandon until at last they each sat back with a contented sigh.

Sayah's golden eyes sparkled with wonderous delight as he stared in silence at the bubbling spring while Nat and Rae marveled at its appearance.

"Amazing...but what does it mean?" Rae asked.

Nat shook his head and replied, "I'm not sure. My guess is that we have food and drink to spare on our journey, though."

Still fixated on the spring, Sayah spoke, "For He quenches the thirst of the thirsty and gratifies the craving of the hungry."

Nat and Rae shot a look at the ægle, surprised at his quote from the prophecies. Their involvement with the Eben'kayah had taught them a great many such verses, but the ægle had not had the same privilege.

Sayah, suddenly aware he held their attention, raised a self-conscious wing to the back his head and answered their unspoken question.

"I heard it around the Tree in Endego after returning from the Cold Vantage. I was reminded of how Lord Elyon had taken care of me, so it just...stuck."

Nat, Rae and Sayah sat in somber tranquility a long moment until Nat arose to declare, "It's time. Let's get going."

Perhaps the unhampered progress of their first day on mission set the trio's expectations of the second, but regardless their expectations were soon disappointed. In place of a tailwind, gusts struck them at the head, slowing their advancement.

The unpredictable blasts presented the danger of unseating Nat and Rae, who had spent the prior day carefree atop the ægle, occupied with the view and with excited chatter. Today, they were challenged just to lay sprawled across Sayah's back, with sore hands clutching the ægle's short feathers to prevent their flying off.

For his part, Sayah drove onward, wary of stiff opposition encountered at unforeseen moments. His wings beat with the wearisome tension that accompanied such vigilance and care that extended to his precious cargo. All three were disinclined to converse while in the turbulent air.

Right past noon, Nat clamored for a break. They needed refreshment and a brief respite from the rigors of the day's journey. Sayah identified a gravelly clearing at the bend of the river and banked toward it.

The ægle wheeled about in a shallow spiral over the clearing, his descent gentle to prevent dislodging the tired Etom on his back. When a short distance over their landing site, Sayah spread his wings and fluttered to a stop along the bank of the river.

Nat and Rae slid from his back at once to flex their hands and stretch their backs, and Sayah shook out his wings and tailfeathers. Their bodies, taxed by the duress of the flight, demanded nourishment.

Nat and Rae opened their packs at once and on a smooth, flat stone spread for Sayah an array of seeds, nuts, and fruit, a mixture they called "blend o' the track." The Etom were first and foremost concerned with replenishing the strength of their friend and mount, but likewise dug in after a quick word of thanks to Elyon for the food and for their progress thus far.

Sayah had not waited for the blessing. When Rae and Nat closed their eyes and folded their eyes to begin, the embarrassed ægle froze, seeds dribbling from his gaping beak. The staccato tick of seeds striking the rocky earth prompted Rae to open one emerald eye in time to spot the petrified bird.

She amended her prayer to offer a reassuring, "...and please accept our thanks for *all* Your provision, even what's already in our stomachs. In the name of the Kinsman Gaal, so be it."

Nat arose, his eyes and brow scrunched with incredulity as with a curious chuckle he asked, "What was that last bit, 'even what's already in our stomachs?'"

Rae remained quiet, but winked at a relieved Sayah, who returned at once to his meal, and Nat was none the wiser. The etém shrugged off his curiosity and started in on his lunch.

He had learned from experience with his own mother that at times an etma mightn't be troubled to explain herself. This seemed such a time, so instead he focused with happy intent on his handful of "blend o' the track."

Afterward, they refreshed themselves with a drink from the river and a splash of its cool flow over brow and beak. By no means did it compare with the morning's libation, but the river water met their bodily needs and they were back in the sky without delay.

If they had hoped for clearer skies following their short lunch on the riverbank, those hopes were dashed at once in spectacular fashion. Not only did the earlier squall intensify, but soon the occasional flake of snow drifted past them as they pushed on into a growing storm.

Before long, the flakes became flurries, and then a blinding blizzard. The tempest made it almost impossible to see, even for Sayah, and the chill wind cut at the three travelers until they could no longer bear it.

Rae tugged at Nat's sleeve for his attention. Squinting in the bluster, Nat made out her pale pink finger pointing to the ground.

We need to land, the gesture stated.

He concurred and crawled forward, closer to Sayah's ear that the ægle might hear. The movement along the ægle's back prompted him to crane his head back and listen as Nat roared.

"DOWN, SAYAH! FLY LOWER!!!"

Sayah could just make out the words, "down" and "lower," but it was sufficient for him to understand Nat's message. He pitched down at an easy angle, sinking lower and lower into the whiteout. The ægle's visibility was limited as they dropped, but he hoped it would clear as they neared the ground.

All at once, they fell beneath the blinding haze, and Sayah rejoiced that he could see again. His happiness was short-lived, however, as he discovered the cause for the sudden increase in visibility. They had come down over the raging river, where the spray of its rapids generated a mist that repelled and melted the snow as it fell.

Sayah and his passengers were almost in the deadly, rushing water before he was able to stop his descent and level himself over the river's frothing whitecaps.

"Are we landing? Pressing on?" he called back to Nat and Rae.

Nat looked to Rae, who gave a forward nod, and the etém shouted to the ægle, "Yes! Onward, Sayah!"

The storm was an early one, but it was almost winter, and the days were shortening with each that passed. They kept on for a good while, Sayah following the course of the river, but the sky soon darkened under waning sun and waxing cloud.

Nat looked around in the dwindling light for a good place to rest for the night, and his eyes fell on something that stopped his heart. Just ahead, on either bank, stood the splintered wreckage of a wooden bridge that once had spanned the river.

"Do you recognize this place?" he asked Rae over the roar of the rapids.

She arched a hand over her eyes as a visor and scanned their forward surroundings, her eyes wide when they returned to meet his.

"Yes! We're near Sakkan, aren't we?"

Nat nodded, and called up to Sayah, "Let's land along the eastern bank here!"

Sayah complied, finding a narrow strip of bare, flat riverbank and coming in for a landing.

"You see it too, then?" the ægle asked the others.

"Yeah, this is the place where..." Nat trailed off.

"...where that massive Nihúkolem nearly smashed me to bits," Sayah finished.

"So, the enemy may be close," Rae surmised.

Nat agreed, "Yes, and we'll need to be more cautious than ever. What do you say we make camp for the night?"

Rae and Sayah complied without hesitation and the three searched out an appropriate site in short order. They repeated the prior night's tactic in building a fire against a stone for comfort and for reduced visibility. Meanwhile Sayah took the added measure of dragging several scraggly bunches of brush around their site to screen them further from prying eyes.

They pressed in around the compact blaze and enjoyed a hunk of the cheese along with some "blend o' the track." The weightiness and fat of the cheese filled and warmed their bellies within while the fire warmed them without. The day's journey had worn them out, however, so there was little discussion after supper. Before long, they settled in close to the fire to sleep.

The night was colder and less inviting than the last, and their rest shallower for they stayed poised and alert should danger prompt them to fly. Nonetheless, it seemed the storm had covered the land with more than snow, and under the still, white blanket on the land, nothing stirred.

Chapter Fifteen
The Dimroad

Sayah, Nat, and Rae awakened to another cold but fulfilling breakfast of rhema, and sought out a fresh spring, this time with intent. Following the Spirit's prompting, they gathered near the river's edge, where they found a rotted log locked by ice and frost into earth.

The log presented to the sky a round bole in its top side. The nearby river had splashed and misted over the wooden surface in sufficient quantity that ice had then glazed it over once temperatures fell overnight.

And, thus, the wooded bole became an icy bowl that the trio clustered around with expectation. Of course, they expected a spring, but were uncertain as to how it might now appear.

Recalling the Spirit's invitation from the morning before, Nat shared his experience.

"The Spirit told me to speak, and water would come out. Then He sent me a vision of the Kinsman speaking, and I repeated what he said."

"Hmmm...," Rae mused. "Do you think we ought to pray first, then? Maybe if we ask the Spirit what to say, He'll tell us."

Nat and Sayah saw her good sense and complied.

With eyes closed, they stood in the bitter cold as Rae implored, "Lord Elyon, we don't know what exactly we should say, but we thirst. You have given us a spring that will never run dry. So, we wait for You to accomplish what You promised, for we know You are perfect in faithfulness, unlike any created being."

The Spirit returned Rae to a memory of the scrolls the Eben'kayah had kept hidden away inside the temple that once stood in Endego. In her memory, she read and recited many lines for memorization, but one script stood illumined now in her mind.

She gasped as she recognized its meaning and then spoke aloud into the frozen wilderness, "The wasteland shall become a pool, the thirsty ground a welling spring."

Drops of water welled within the ice-glazed bole of the rotting log, and soon spilled down the icy bark of the frost-encrusted tree to meet the ground. The water had a thawing effect on the hard and hoary earth, and where it struck, the ground grew soft. The land indeed was thirsty, and drank the steady trickle, which disappeared as it permeated the earth.

Nat, Rae, and Sayah stepped back to watch, uncertain what might come next. The ground surged beneath the dribbling stream – once, then twice, and on the third time, a spring erupted from the spot.

The tiny fountain bubbled from the earth, inviting the three to drink. They did so at once, careful to avoid the crumbling earth around the spring. After just a few sips, all three were sated, and made preparation to leave.

Meanwhile, the fountain sprayed, its pure, invigorating waters soaking the earth around it. Though it was mere minutes before they departed the area, the spring had carved out a small depression in the land.

The fountain no longer sprayed but bubbled beneath the surface of a small but spreading pool. It showed no signs of stopping, either, and the three wondered what kind of earth-moving force they may have just set in motion.

Today, instead of taking to the air at once, Rae, Nat and Sayah clambered up the embankment to the road off the eastern end of the demolished bridge. Nat and Sayah in particular were curious to look down the road where the elephantine wraith had once stood guard. They hadn't discussed it beforehand, but all three suspected their mission lay upon this, the Dimroad.

Back in Endego, Kehren had shared the menacing name with them, which only added to their trepidation as they stood at the mouth of the tree-ensconced road to peer down its length. The trees, stripped of most their leaves in the early winter, did not darken the road with their shade so much as they had when the wayfarers had last ventured to this place.

Notwithstanding, the overcast sky did not cast so much light as it might have under clearer skies, and less so beneath the trees. They lost sight of the road's course when it curved northward in the general direction of their destination, Terábnis. They deliberated a few moments at the eastward ruins of the bridge until Rae again proposed the obvious – they must consult the Spirit for direction.

They sensed His response in a matter of seconds– a clear and Resonant tug down the Dimroad. Without further delay, the two Etom clambered astride Sayah, who launched back out over the river to gain speed.

From above, the shining, white ægle appeared dappled with the colorful Etom and their clothes. He climbed with swift strokes of his wings, then swept back around and down toward the road. Into the dark forest they shot, disappearing into the road's dark maw and down its timbered gullet on the mission of the Spirit.

Amidst the bramble of nearby underbrush, a figure stood, screened from view but for the gleam of watchful eyes. The size of the watcher and an occasional flash of skin the color of cantaloupe betrayed the onlooker's identity as an Etom. Once Sayah was out of sight, the strange Etom dashed to follow, careful to remain concealed under cover.

What light penetrated the thick snarl of branches overshadowing the road provided little illumination to Nat and Rae, who could see but a short distance in the murk. They relied on Sayah's superior vision to navigate the dim corridor they traveled and were grateful that the ægle saw better at midnight than they might in daylight.

To Sayah, it seemed most prudent to expedite this leg of the journey. The road was wide enough for two horse-drawn carts and did not leave much room for maneuverability in the event of an encounter. His gleaming golden eyes ticked side to side as he scanned the way ahead for any sign of the enemy. And all the while, he flew along at the greatest speed he could manage on the stale and windless air.

One advantage of the dank cover was insulation; snow blanketed every bough, stifling sound and trapping warmth beneath the trees. Compared to the tumult and bitter winds of yesterday's sky, the road was pleasant. Soon, the relative coziness and tranquility had lulled the trio into a sense of security. And, forgetting the peril of their mission, they dropped their guard.

The tail Nat and company picked up at the bridge had fallen well behind, but now followed them down the road. Their pursuer wore a hooded cloak, and kept more or less to the shadows, though now the need for speed dictated he adopt increasing abandon in pursuit.

No longer did the mysterious Etom linger with watchful caution in the underbrush. Rather, the stranger pelted along behind the sparse screen of scrub beyond the trees that lined the road. Although the pursuer's breath came in great, labored gulps, the pained effort did not slow the Etom's pace.

Narrowed and focused eyes gleamed from beneath the hood, bespeaking a determined heart set on a crucial mission: his life and that of everyone in Sakkan depended on its success.

Rae, Nat, and Sayah passed their first full day on the Dimroad without event and sheltered a good way off its rutted course. The relative warmth was comfortable, though they still built a small and careful fire when the temperature fell alongside the night.

The evening held a strange and ominous watchfulness and the three spoke in whispers as they supped. Notwithstanding the odd, smothering stillness of the air, even the faintest sound carried and echoed up and down the road, bouncing between the trees.

The three were eager to take their night of sleep and be on their way as early as they were able. They retired after supper without much more than a "good night" to a slumber once again vigilant but sweeter than the night before.

In the final hour before sunrise, a loud and distant 'clack' like striking stones awakened Rae, who at first just lay still, her eyes wide and questing for the source of the disturbance. There she lay for long, tense moments in the dark, debating whether she ought to wake the others or not. That is, until she heard the grating undertone of movement, this time closer by.

Unable to identify the source of the noise, she nevertheless roused Sayah and Nat, taking pains not to startle them. The last thing they needed was a frightened shout to bring an unidentified intruder down on them.

Rae, thinking it best to prepare the ægle for immediate flight, woke Sayah first.

"Pssst...Sayah!" she called as loud as she dared.

The ægle rested on the ground with wings folded, feet tucked beneath him and head curled back to rest on his posterior. He did not budge at Rae's first attempt, so the etma tiptoed closer to try again.

Rae lifted a tiny pink hand to shake the edge of Sayah's wing and whisper, "Sayah."

The great golden eye closest her snapped open, bright amidst his snowy feathers, and the ægle lifted his head to mutter, "Eh? What is it, Rae?"

"I heard something moving out there," she explained and urged, "I think we should leave. Now."

Sayah nodded and arose, stretching as he replied, "Let's not take any chances. I'll keep watch while you wake Nat."

Relieved that Sayah had agreed, Rae went at once to Nat's side. Before she'd even crouched down to prod him, Nat's eyes were already opening.

"What's wrong, Rae?" he rasped.

"There's something out there," she whispered, "getting closer."

"And Sayah?"

"I woke him first, so he'd be ready to go."

"Alright, let's move," he yawned, and stood to roll his bedding.

Rae crept to where she'd slept to do the same, and meanwhile all three took care to make as little noise as possible. As was their practice, they'd loaded everything else into their packs the night before, and soon all that remained was to don their gear, secure the bedrolls, and climb onto Sayah's back to depart.

From just beyond the rough, dark column of the nearest tree, came the snap of a breaking twig. The trio of travelers needed no further encouragement to leave. With haste that seemed to clamor in the silence, Nat boosted Rae up onto Sayah's back with less delicacy than usual. He tossed their bedrolls up to her waiting hands and hoisted himself up.

Once Nat was secure atop Sayah, Rae patted the ægle's neck with imperative urgency. At once they were away, the blast of Sayah's wings sending the cinders of their dead fire sprawling.

"What was that?" Rae wondered aloud as she and Nat peered back into the darkness.

Nat just shook his head and responded, "I have no idea, but I'm glad we didn't stick around to find out."

Sayah, preoccupied with avoiding the trees that stood between them and the road, did not turn his powerful gaze back on their campsite. But, if he had, he would have spotted something to make them reconsider their flight.

From behind a tree near their resting place, a small, dark figure surmounted a knobby root and dropped down with a crunch into a shallow stack of dried and broken leaves on the ground. Gasping and staggering, their pursuer flailed an arresting hand after Sayah, the ægle's outline dim yet distinct in the brightening woods.

The sun rose anew, and its rays, diminished in their passage through bough and branch, nevertheless touched the Etom's upraised hand of pastel orange. Its owner, too exhausted and winded either to call after the fleeing trio or continue the chase, braced both hands to knees and brought his hooded head low in weary frustration.

The mysterious Etom's bent frame rose and fell with deep, heaving breaths until at last the stranger straightened and removed the hood. The gray and murky light revealed a young, adult etém with no visible Stain marring his cantaloupe-colored skin. His features were wily but not unfriendly, although disappointment colored them now.

The etém cocked his head sunward and issued a heavy sigh. He'd run all night to catch up with Nat, Rae and the strange ægle he didn't know. Not that he'd ever met the two Etom, but they shared a common acquaintance in Dempsey. Dempsey, who had trusted him in Sakkan to procure medical help for the young pink etma who'd just slipped from sight.

Doctor Scarsburrow had promised a heap of grains for the capture of these Etom, who had escaped the Doctor's clutches and were now wanted by the Empire of Chōl. After the mass breakout from his clinic, the Doctor had posted the reward and information on the six Etom he believed responsible for it.

Beforehand, Scarsburrow had posted a similar reward for the young, pale blue etém after the youth alone had escaped the clinic. The Doctor had surmised that, however improbable, this adolescent etém then returned with an unfledged ægle to hatch the others. Scarsburrow had been infuriated at the loss of his "patients," then fearful when he discovered the Nihúkolem also sought them for their own dark designs.

Regardless, the strange cantaloupe-colored Etom was not out for Scarsburrow's reward. Rather, he and most the region had heard rumors of strange happenings to the south in Endego. Yes, word had come to Sakkan, carried on the scampering legs of beasts and the fluttering wings of fowl who by some mysterious ability could speak with Etom. That these messengers communicated by miraculous means lent much-needed credibility to their tale, for the good news they brought was difficult to believe, but so full of marvelous hope that it bore investigation.

In addition, the Empire of Chōl began with gritty, black thumb to press all the more on its subjects in Sakkan and the surrounding forest.

Demands of tribute of goods, services and information for the military increased to the point that most could no longer bear it.

Indeed, starvation and collapse loomed over many in the shadow of the Empire. Before long, an underground network formed among the Empire's subjects to trade in what goods, services, and information the Nihúkolem had not already extracted from them.

When the report arrived in Sakkan of a pure white ægle travelling with two young Etom matching Scarsburrow's description, the underground perceived an opportunity to make contact. However, leery of defections, the Empire had restricted all travel toward Endego and monitored the movements of their subjects in and out of Sakkan through spies.

The Sakkan underground had called for a single scout who might escape to intercept the three travelers, and the young etém now on their trail had volunteered. He felt the need to atone for his earlier betrayal and here was his chance. He had discovered them yesterday just as they were departing and had not been bold enough to call out to them for fear of Imperial patrols.

He now regretted his earlier reticence. His body demanded rest and nourishment although his heart insisted he carry on. He was torn but could go no farther today.

"Well, Frenlee," the Etom whispered to himself, "this is a fine mess you've gotten yourself into. But there's nothing for it right now."

As this was as good a place to rest as any along the Dimroad, Frenlee mounded a good many dry leaves against a tree root and lay amidst the crunchy, insulating cushion. Putting his drab hood up, he was well-camouflaged among the drift of autumnal debris, and soon drifted off to sleep.

Sayah, Rae and Nat were happy to have what light the sun sent their way, and they concluded from its brilliance that the unseen sky must be clearer than the day before. Even the Etom could see much farther today than before. Sunlight glowed, muted and soft between the neat rows of trees that lined the way to illuminate the orderly beauty of the road.

The air high overhead remained crisp in spite of the sun, so the cover of snow yet lay upon the land. Down below, however, the sense of insulated, warm tranquility returned to the three adventurers, lulling them once again. For hours, they continued on the seeming peaceful road, which now was robbed of its danger and mystery.

Nat and Rae yawned in turn and Sayah shook his feathered head to clear it. Their early awakening combined with their current, pleasant course had mingled in a heady brew to make them drowsy. With all three fighting sleep, they were grateful for the gusting breeze that time to time swept in through the trees.

The dust and debris that remained of autumn swirled and danced across the road, which now ran northward straight as a beam. Enlivened in the sudden chill, Sayah focused forward through the wafting haze with renewed intent.

A good way off, but visible at the farthest reaches of the ægle's sight, Sayah discerned a brightening starburst that could be naught but an opening. They were nearing the Dimroad's end.

"I see the end!" the ægle called back.

They hadn't spoken much since bolting this morning, and Sayah's voice was deafening in the prolonged silence.

Even so, the news elicited cheers from the Etom. They were all eager to be clear of the forest and under open sky once more. Another gust of wind quelled them as it sent more debris curling over the road.

The haze grew thicker than before, and darker, too. Sayah swore the roiling dust ahead was almost black.

Black! he reckoned. *It's black!*

The instinct that hounded the ægle's thought saved them all, for Sayah banked as hard as he dared to one side, away from the dark, curling grit that issued from the trees. A vague, dark shape grazed him with a blast of air and sand that peppered his tailfeathers and almost sent him into a spin.

Rae and Nat clung with fierce and knotted hands to Sayah's back as he fought for control. The ægle's initial evasive maneuver had forewarned the Etom of potential acrobatic flight and was sufficient that they'd sprawled against the ægle's back to maintain their seat.

Ascertaining a Nihúkolem threat, Sayah recovered and flapped his wings for all his worth. The presence of his friends atop him constrained his movements, but he would not give up without a fight.

The Etom for their part looked back and relayed the enemy's position to Sayah, enabling the ægle to evade the Nihúkolem and focus his efforts forward, where their hope for escape lay. The Etom's aid soon proved invaluable, for a distracted Sayah might have missed the creeping fingers of Nihúkolem grit that wrapped around a nearby trunk.

Again, he eluded the Nihúkolem at the last instant, the scrape of its passage whipping at Nat and Rae's exposed skin. They cried out in pain at the pelting grains that cut them yet held on for dear life as Sayah dove down to skim the ground. The exit wasn't far now, and he aimed to make it.

The ægle's eyes darted this way and that for any sign of a third attacker. Meantime, Rae shrieked that the enemies at their back were closing from either side.

With care, Nat crawled forth to whisper in Sayah's ear, "We trust you, Sayah. Just listen for the Spirit. You'll know what to do."

The etém turned around, tailward, and inched back to Rae. Putting their heads side by side, the two began to pray. The advancing shadows clawed their way from tree to tree in Nat's peripheral vison, but he chose instead to close his eyes and trust in his Savior and in his friend.

Sayah blinked, unable to think of any prayer beyond a single word that pounded in his heart with frightened rhythm, *Help! Help! Help! HEEELLLP!!!*

They that wait on Me, I will strengthen. They will arise on wings like...well, like yours, My son. I made you for this. Now, fly!

Sensing the Spirit's guidance, Sayah arose from his place just over the road, glancing to either side and drawing level with the Nihúkolem in pursuit. They were almost on them now. Sayah just didn't have the speed to outpace them.

Three more leaps and the enemy would have them.

Now two leaps.

Now just the one!

The Nihúkolem pounced at the ægle and his passengers from either side, the figures indistinct yet sharp with purpose. Sayah might never snatch a wriggling fish from the water with the technique, but in that moment, the ægle executed the braking maneuver his kind employed in hunting. His great wings snapped open wide with feathers cupped to catch the air as he slowed to near a total stop.

Ahead of them, the Nihúkolem collided with one another in the empty air, exploding in a dank shower of grime. Sayah at once resumed his forward flight, and the three friends shot through the sooty cloud and up into the daylit sky, the ægle twirling as they all whooped with joy and relief at their escape.

Chapter Sixteen
Tales of Hearts at Home

In the absence of Sayah and her son, Nida discovered a deep wellspring of energy that before had been devoted to their care. Nat had long outgrown the need for Nida's direct ministrations and she'd had no such chance with Sayah, though she would have taken great pleasure in thus serving the æglet – no, the ægle, he was an ægle now – she'd adopted as her own.

Nevertheless, Nida had dedicated vast mental resources to training, reminding, and chastising both the youngsters and even Rae at times. This said, her mind yet rested on the memories of these she loved with that fervor only the best of mothers know. No, but rather, she'd surrendered their fate to Lord Elyon, and into His hands she delivered them every time hers threatened to clutch at them and bind in the entanglement of bittersweet nostalgia.

Rather, the Spirit filled Nida's open hands with the opportunity to care for many others as the Kinship prepared for the return of their once-scattered remnant. Dempsey came alongside her in the beautiful toil of making ready the village and the bower. Thus yoked, the pair saw the dormant romance between them blossom with a rapidity that took Nida's breath away.

So focused on motherhood had Nida been that now she entered a season of reflection on her identity as an etma, not just as a mother. And as an etma, she found the etém beside her attractive in the extreme: rugged, yet gentle; reverent, yet lively; passionate, yet self-controlled.

In a sober moment, she recognized these traits in Dempsey as those that had drawn her to Jaarl so long ago. She put the thought away, consigning it to Elyon's care with the grief she once carried for her husband. For their son's sake, and out of desperation, she had at long last forsaken the burden of her widowhood. She would not shoulder it again.

No, Nida breathed deep in the perfumed air of bower, and the bond between her and Dempsey strengthened as they intertwined their lives with the purposes of the Vine. With supernatural joy and fortitude, the two took the lead in arranging for the arrivals the Spirit had advised them to anticipate. And it was well they did, for the arrivals were not long in coming, and the nature of their arrival unexpected.

As the other parents in adjusting to the absence of a child, Tram and Kehren, had likewise undergone some changes in lifestyle, one of which was at Rae's behest. Before she left, Rae had given them the solemn charge of caring for the chevrotains. With all gravity, she had impressed on them the request of her friends to open out their stables, explaining the interaction she'd had with the tiny, deer-like creatures.

At first, Tram and Kehren wondered if their daughter hadn't been pulling their legs. At a very young age, Rae had formed a strong bond with the chevrotains, to the point she lamented even the use of a whip to drive them or their burdening with heavy loads. Her parents suspected Rae might be acting out of the same sentimentality without regard for the practicality of the matter.

Separated into their separate stalls, the chevrotains were manageable and could be groomed and tended without interference from others of their kind. And there was the matter of, well, excrement. Mucking out a single stable, where the animal's dung was confined to a particular area, was a much simpler prospect than searching out the mess where it may lie.

Nevertheless, Rae had made them promise at least to *try*, which her parents felt obliged to do, and so they set about the task the morning after the three youths had left. Their first surprise came when Tram opened the stable door and discovered their steeds already loose inside the stable. He slammed the door shut, put his back against it and muttered something about "that crazy kid" to the startled Kehren, who, determined they should tackle the matter together, stood on hand with her husband.

Rae had made a point of caring for the chevrotains exclusively since she'd first conversed with them, certain any of the hands about the manor would have been frightened to find them free. Of course, she also enjoyed their company, for their conversations were often over fond memories they shared.

In any case, it was the first that Tram, Kehren, or any adult on the estate became aware the chevrotains were running about the stables unrestrained. Once Tram overcame his initial shock and explained the situation to Kehren, together the pair ventured with some caution into the stables.

Instead of the chaos they anticipated, they found the chevrotains milling about in mellow contentment or standing in their stalls though nothing held them there. Indeed, the creatures took some notice of the Etom pair and stood aside when Tram and Kehren waded in toward the stables.

For their part, the Etom, wary of droppings scattered about the floor, were pleased to find none in the common area. Rather, when the Etom couple looked into the first empty stall they came to, they discovered the occupant had taken great care to keep the mess contained in a single corner of the enclosure.

"Well, I'll be..." Tram whispered.

Kehren remarked, "They're much tidier than I might have expected."

"Agreed," Tram replied and cast his gaze around the stables, "I wonder..."

"What is it, dear?" Kehren inquired.

"Do you think if we put a couple of bigger stalls at the far end of the stables, they might use them just for...you know."

Kehren nodded as she considered the proposal, "I think that might work. If they're as clever as Rae told us, they should figure it out."

"It'd make the job of cleaning out the mess a good sight easier!" Tram exclaimed with a chuckle.

Kehren giggled in reply, "Keeping it all in one place, yeah?"

The levity of the moment warmed them both, and they concluded the task Rae had "assigned" them was a blessing in disguise. Tram had been concerned that Kehren in particular would struggle at the departure of their daughter, given her difficulty in giving the matter over to Elyon at the start. The two Etom were grateful for the care Lord Elyon demonstrated in working through their daughter to give them this duty, and with shared good humor they planned together to remodel the stable interior.

Once the work commenced, the chevrotains were more cooperative than the Etom had ever seen them. Without resistance, the creatures let themselves be led where needed during demolition of the smaller stalls.

Perceiving their remarkable responsiveness, even when hitched to the carriage, Tram reconsidered the use of a whip to motivate them. Rather, he focused on verbal commands to motivate the creatures, who learned to respond at once. In their hearts, Tram and Kehren marveled at Lord Elyon's glory in working such wondrous things in their day and wondered what else might be in store.

Less than a week after Rae, Nat, and Sayah left, Bhean and his crew through curious happenstance discovered something of interest. While engaging a quartet of field mice, Vínculo flagged the nearby Billbaste over for a closer look. The night-heron landed near the large tuft of straw the mice were hiding in and waited in the darkness to ascertain their next move.

For his part, Billbaste had taken to heart the seriousness of his role on the watch as a quiet observer. He stood now stock-still and watched the patch of underbrush Vínculo had pointed out from above. The late-autumn night air chilled Billbaste while he waited, unmoving, and he prayed Elyon grant him the self-control to stay his beak from chattering when shivers threatened to betray his position.

Just when Billbaste thought he could bear to remain still no longer, a squeaky whisper floated his way on the chill air.

"Is he still out there?"

"Shhh! Yes, you dolt!" another voice peeped. "He's standing right there like a great phony buffoon of a tree. Now be quiet!"

"Be kind to the youngster," yet another squeaked in defense of the first. "He's not been out so far from the burrow before."

"And he shan't do it again if he's dead, will he? And neither will we if you two don't shut yer snouts!"

Billbaste couldn't help but cock his head to listen in, and the surly voice chastened once more, "There! You see now? He's spotted us for sure!"

Billbaste knew of those in the Vine gifted to understand the tongues of other kinds. Until this very moment, he'd not realized he was one of them and rejoiced in his heart the instant he recognized his gift. For once, the mouthy Billbaste hoped he might find honor in his speech and did not delay in calling out to the frightened mice.

"Hello there! Yes, you! The mice hiding in the clump of grass there! Come on out. I promise not to harm you!"

"Oh great! Now we're dead for sure!" a new mousy voice lamented.

"Wait a second. Can you understand him, too?" came the inquisitive reply.

Unfortunately, Vínculo had mistaken Billbaste's calls to the mice for the signal to flush out the intruders. The nightjar swept in at full speed, cracking his wings overhead in aggressive fashion. It was too much for the mice.

The four bolted in separate directions and Billbaste shouted to Vínculo, "No! Drat it all! Catch one, Vínculo!"

The nightjar pounced after one of the tiny, tawny figures speeding for cover and Billbaste swung his leg to plant a great webbed claw in front of another. With his long beak, Billbaste plucked up the mouse at his foot before it could scurry away. The mouse squeaked in jumbled protest as it hung by its tail from Billbaste's beak, then fell silent, watching in horror as Vínculo dragged another of its kin over to the larger bird.

Once Vínculo had arrived with his catch, Billbaste set his down with care, pinning the mouse's tail beneath his claw. Billbaste asked Vínculo just to hold on to his respective quarry, then addressed the creature at his own feet.

"Again, hello," the night-heron began. "You can tell what I'm saying, can't you?"

The trembling mouse underfoot held his peace, but the one in Vínculo's custody barked in piping tones, "Don't you say a word! I've heard about this. This is some evil Imperial magic. They won't get a thing out of us!"

Billbaste couldn't help but smirk and the gruff little rodent soon realized his mistake in speaking out to warn his compadre.

"So, you *can* understand me, then," Billbaste surmised.

In a gentle voice, the night-heron spoke to the mouse pinned beneath his claw, "Listen, please. I won't hurt you. I just want to talk."

With ginger care, Billbaste lifted his foot from the mouse's tail, "See? Will you talk to me now?"

The mouse ceased to shake and looked up at the large bird with curious eyes, then spoke, "Will you let my friend go, too?"

"Blast! You fool!" the other mouse raved as he dangled by his tail from Vínculo's beak.

Nevertheless, Billbaste nodded to his partner, who lowered his captive to the ground and let go. The suspicious rodent sprang away, whirling about to keep the birds under watch as he began to creep backward into the underbrush.

Meanwhile, Billbaste had built some trust with the other mouse, who relaxed enough to respond, "Thank you, Master Big Bird, er...sir! What did you want to ask me?"

Billbaste hadn't thought that far ahead, and in the moment turned a blank, questioning stare on Vínculo.

What do *I want to say?* the night-heron's eyes said.

I don't know. What? Vínculo's shrug replied.

At a loss in the moment for any other words, Billbaste's mind turned to the importance of recent events in Endego: Lord Elyon, the Kinsman, His Tree. And beginning there, Billbaste shared with the wee brown field mouse all that had come to pass in and around Sanctuary Endego over the days prior.

Soon, the little mouse stood enthralled as she listened, and her suspicious companion had crept back from the edge of the brush to stand alongside his friend. Not long after, those hidden nearby revealed themselves to join the first two mice as they listened to Billbaste's account of all Elyon had done through the Tree.

Vínculo was shocked that in addition to these field mice, a hare, a vole, and a pair of moles gathered while Billbaste spoke and that all understood the night-heron. Not only these, but other small creatures continued to congregate until Billbaste ceased to speak.

The mouse, the first to listen, piped up, "Good Master Bird, sir? May *we* approach the Tree? I know that Endego is for Etom-kind, but perhaps they'd consider sharing? Even with us?"

The mouse's humble request gripped Billbaste's heart, drawing tears from the bird. Looking back toward Endego, he weighed the potential displeasure of the Etom and his Watch Commander at conducting so many strangers through the village against the freedom of these creatures from the Stain. In that moment, the Spirit spoke boldness to Billbaste's heart, and he made his decision.

"Yes, my little friend," he affirmed, "I will take you there myself."

With confidence, Billbaste led the first group of many such strangers to take their place around the Tree. Folk of both Etom and feathered kind were aroused at the ruckus, and Nida and Dempsey were among the first to arrive at the edge of the pool. Their excitement over the long-awaited return of their friends among the Eben'kayah, had awakened these two in particular. Though they stood shivering in the cold, their teeth chattered behind warm smiles no winter chill could freeze.

Instead, confusion cooled the mood of the warm welcome Nida and Dempsey had planned when they realized that Billbaste led an escort of miscellaneous wood- and grass-land creatures into the bower. The guests that arrived now were of an unexpected kind, but the Spirit soothed Nida in her shocked concern, consoling the etma with remembrance that the Kinsman had come to free all from the Stain.

Before anyone might protest, Nida stood forth to encourage Billbaste, "Come! Bring them to the Tree, Billbaste! They are welcome! Come!"

The same field mouse who had stopped and listened to Billbaste outside the village was first to approach, her timidity apparent in her trembling. Regardless, she did not desist, but continued, Billbaste at her side, to the water's edge. A black and sullen tinge at the tips of her twitching ears proved the mouse's need of the Kinsman.

With gentle care, Billbaste explained, "Alright now, dear. You must bathe yourself tail to snout in the pool here to remove your Stain.

"The moment you arise from the water, you belong to the family, the Kinship, of the Kinsman, connected to us and to Him by the Vine. Understand, Elyon is Lord over His people and to accept His gift is to accept His rule. He is King. Knowing this, will you proceed?"

The mouse ceased to shake, her mousy brow wrinkling in determination as she twitched her whiskers, sniffed, then nodded in affirmation. Without further delay, the mouse put one forepaw in the water, then the other, and soon waded in altogether.

Looking back at her fellows on the shore, she beckoned them onward with a twitch of the head and called, "Come on in! The water is amazing! Somehow warm and fresh all at once! You don't want to miss this!"

At that, the mouse leapt, twisting in the air, and flopped down into the water with a splash. She completed her roll and stood again on all fours, drenched in the crystalline flow of the Tree.

Turning about, she tilted her ears forward for presentation and asked, "Well? What do you think?"

Her surly companion crept to shore, his Stained paws just outside the water, and examined her.

"Egads!" he exclaimed.

With a splash, he came in for a closer inspection, and this time whispered, "It's true. I don't believe it."

"Hey, you lot!" he shouted at the others. "Get yourselves in here, tails and whiskers all! What are you waiting for?!?"

Soon, he was dipping into the water and dabbing his snout with swipes of his unblemished paws. Behind the two mice, the crowd of remaining creatures swept into the autumnal oasis beneath the Tree, and a celebration of their salvation from the Stain erupted in laughter and play.

Dempsey and Nida, meanwhile, had approached the water to watch with amazement as Elyon shed His grace on these many kinds. In the glance they exchanged was inhibited excitement as they wondered if they were permitted to join these strange, new Kinfolk in their jubilation.

What I have called clean, do not call unclean, the Spirit spoke in reply to their unspoken prayer.

That was all the invitation Nida and Dempsey needed, and with a whoop and a holler, they jumped in with the others. In a movement that could only have been by the Spirit's coordination, the rest of the gathered Kinship dashed for the water after Nida and Dempsey.

Under inspiration of the Spirit, Tram on the other hand darted back to his stables and without a saddle, mounted the young Acorn. Flinging the stable doors open wide, he rode the young buck at the head of a directed stampede that followed Tram atop Acorn to the waters of the Tree, where Billbaste and a number of other such gifted Kin shared the news of what the Kinsman had done for His creatures. Not a one of the chevrotains failed to join the Kinship that night.

And all together, the Kinship of the Vine splashed and played, danced and sang until the sun arose, its rays illuminating the grove, though not so much as the Tree nestled in its midst.

From the shadows seethed Iver, who in his malice could not abide this latest turn of events. That Lord Elyon would invite all these, the unclean, the common, to consort with His people the Eben'kayah. For as long as the Eben'kayah had kept the law and the prophecies of Lord Elyon, they had also held themselves apart from the rest of the world as a holy people, dedicated to Him.

Elyon had commanded it, and so the Eben'kayah had strived to enact it. What Iver did not realize was that Lord Elyon had indeed set aside for Himself a holy people – from every kind and of every creature. The Eben'kayah had stood as an example, a society over which Elyon ruled according to His law, so when He opened the floodgates, and bid all stream to Him, these would recognize with humility the grace offered them.

Lord Elyon sought also the humility of the Eben'kayah, that in their jealousy for His grace shed upon these others, then the Eben'kayah, too, might understand their need for the Kinsman. And it was this humbling *need* for His grace that chafed against Iver, who by his own efforts had exalted himself within his self-righteous mind.

Pikrïa's desertion likewise grated against his desire to usurp the faulty leadership in Endego. As an ally, the dowager had possessed great potential, both for the vastness of her resources and for the extent of her influence in polite society. Iver had plotted to employ her wealth and influence in his cause, and the loss thereof increased his frustration.

No, he schemed, *I will have to do something far more direct now.*

Iver's eyes fell on the Tree with dismay and he thought, *But what of that infernal Tree? I swear, its power is that of the Shedím!*

In Iver's unsettled mind, the Tree represented some great evil issued from the hand of Helél to entice away the good people of Lord Elyon. Again, he mistook the obvious, life-giving properties of the Tree and ascribed to it some unholy purpose when by the very decree of Lord Elyon it had been planted. Kinsman aside, the primary benefit of the Tree was indisputable – the Stain had been removed from the Kinship and Iver had no alternate explanation.

Nevertheless, Iver's blind eyes, stopped ears, and calloused heart would neither, see, hear, nor comprehend the glory of the Kinsman or the work He'd accomplished in His people. Iver, on the other hand, saw the world trembling, rocking on edge, and he wondered if everything might go topsy-turvy before these *Kin* were finished with it. He had to do something about it, and with his mind thus bent on the destruction of their movement, he withdrew to a solitary place to brood.

Billbaste's invitation to a few new creatures inspired a change in protocol for the Watch. From that day forth, it became the duty of those on watch to assess the threat each interloper presented. Many were found among the watches to possess the supernatural gift of understanding and speaking the languages of other kinds.

These gifted ones were alerted when a team member determined the intentions of a stranger were benign, and an offer to attend the Tree extended. Most were frightened at the prospect of entering the village and shocked that the birds, many of them raptors, had not slain them for a meal outright. As such, these fearful ones did not accept the offer.

Rumor spread throughout the region, however, and soon some ventured near for the very purpose of investigation. These inquisitive souls, desiring to know more about the Tree, often probed the watch with questions when confronted. A number of these were ready to accept the invitation and, when escorted to the Tree, they found the promises of the Kinsman upheld.

The few creatures the Spirit drew to the Tree prior to the institution of the watches had since gone out into the surrounding area, spreading word of what they had discovered there. The ambient chatter that resulted from the dispersal of these Kin into the region made fertile ground of it, and the trickle of such creatures became first a stream and then a flood.

The addition of these further disseminated the good news of the Kinsman's Kingdom when they returned home from Endego. Before long, the perimeter of the watch patrols buzzed with activity as the birds admitted those seeking the Kinsman at the Tree.

Overwhelmed by the influx of such seekers, the birds enlisted help from the Etom and from those of any kind who exercised the Spirit's gift of interpreting strange speech. Meanwhile Endego transformed from the sleepy home of Etom-kind into a teeming hub for every kind, and these united in the Vine.

Amid the inflow of various creatures, the returning Eben'kayah of Endego began to appear, their eyes wide with surprise at the unexpected bustle, yet weary from their long journey. Notwithstanding, the Kinship went out of their way to welcome these Etom home and to honor the heroic efforts of each Company.

Many Eben'kayah remained absent for the hazards of the excursion, and several had been captured by Men or the Nihúkolem. Some Etom returned from such captivity with hearts and bodies broken. A few lucky souls escaped, unscathed, but for the hidden scars they bore. While most of these prodigals received the good news of the Kinsman and His Tree with gladness and open hearts, others, hardened and embittered in the travails of their trek, did not.

Since his disappointment with Pikrïa and the Kinship's invitation for all kinds to join them in the Vine, Iver had been all the more vocal in distinguishing his segregated group as the "true" Eben'kayah. He was quick to identify the Etom struggling to reacclimate to life in Endego and to collect them to his contingent of naysayers and ne'er-do-wells, a growing minority of malcontents whom the Kin loved nevertheless. And at the fringes of these, a sad and solitary young etém hung his moss-green head in lonely dejection.

And thus, he remained until, during a morning inspection of the operation she led in receiving comers both new and old, Nida spied the youth. He was broader and taller than last she'd seen him, but she knew him nonetheless.

"Rosco!" she cried with wonderment as she jogged up to greet the youngster.

At the sound of his name, Rosco had started then looked up, caution in his gaze turning to guarded hope when he recognized Nida.

"Er, hello," he muttered, and averted his eyes.

Nida lay a hand on his arm and exclaimed again, "Rosco! I can't believe you're back. When did you arrive in Endego? Have you been to see your parents?"

This last question agitated a concoction of hot, bitter emotion in Rosco, and he frowned and jerked his arm from Nida's touch in response. He'd lost a great deal through his association with the Eben'kayah and his subsequent capture by the Nihúkolem. Also, everything had changed so much in Endego since he'd been taken. That, and his best friends hadn't even been here to welcome him home. He was a child with no place to call home and no family to call his own.

"I'm sorry, Rosco," Nida apologized. "That was insensitive of me. Would you care to come with me for a bite to eat? You don't have to talk, and I can tell you what Nat and Rae are up to!"

To Rosco the sound of a hot meal and warm company was tempting, but it was the promise of news about his friends that sealed the deal.

"O-okay," he mumbled, then glanced at Nida with gratitude before his eyes flitted away again. "Thank you, Nida."

"Don't mention it, Rosco," she replied, her voice tender. "Who knows? If you feel up to it, maybe you could take Nat's bed until he gets home."

Rosco hid a shy grin as he replied, "We'll see. Maybe. If the food's any good."

Nida chuckled, "Oh ho ho! If it's any good, huh? Well, then you'll just have to find out!"

And, together, they walked the path home they'd walked with Rae and Nat so many times before, and happy memories consoled Rosco's wounded soul.

Chapter Seventeen

Taking the City Unawares

The Dimroad took a precipitous drop just north of the forest, switching back and forth over mountainous terrain as it fell toward the desert. Sayah was able to glide down on a warm updraft in much less time than taking the switchbacks would have cost them. Recognizing their advantage over anyone traveling such a road, Nat, Rae, and Sayah were happy to travel as the ægle flies.

Sayah's satisfaction was short-lived, for as they sped over swelling dunes and level grasslands, he remembered Mother and Father's warnings from his days as a chick. Terábnis was a dreadful destination not just for the Imperial presence there, but also for the desert tribe that made its home south of the city: the Hadza.

The Hadza had long been the guardian huntsmen of Terábnis' outlying areas, and all beasts feared them for their abilities with javelin and bow. Many was the creature that had fallen unaware to the Hadza, who had also mastered the art of stealth and camouflage.

Since the days of the Empire's beginning, a legend had arisen among the Hadza of a crazed and ghostly hunter who wandered the desert wastelands just beyond their hunting grounds. Often, he appeared as a mere shade behind the windswept screen of a sandstorm – a crooked, ruined figure dragging a bow.

The Hadza knew him capable with a bow, yet wasteful in his sport, for ever did he leave behind his quarry. They ofttimes discovered the corpses of his prey, all fowl, and expressed their dismayed awe at the shadowy hunter's prowess.

Not only did the poacher hunt in a storm, when both spotting and shooting a bird on the wing was more difficult, but this bowman managed a shot to the head in every instance. Afterward, the one thing he took from his quarry was a single tail feather. No meat. Nothing else.

Now the Hadza, as expert hunters, learned their craft from the earliest age, and they possessed superb awareness of their surroundings. Nevertheless, what details they had gleaned of the figure haunting the outskirts of their territory were minimal: A Man, bearded and haggard in appearance, his clothes trail-worn, and a distinctive helm upon his bent head.

Some thought they recognized the helmet for the fame of its owner but dissuaded themselves of its authenticity. Enough had seen their Emperor in sooted outline to know the Western Sorrel remained appropriately adorned in great, horned splendor. Regardless, the helm appeared its equal, despite this other fellow's lurching stride and lolling head.

Thus, the hunter's habits and appearance had earned him the reputation of a ghost, or a madman, and his proclivity to hunt fowl alone, a moniker – the Fowler. And with the advent of the Nihúkolem, the Hadza had grown ever leerier of the unnatural than even their former superstitions had prescribed. So, aside from the occasional inquisitive youth, the Hadza gave the Fowler a wide berth.

In the thirty-odd years since he'd discovered Mūk-Mudón's gear, discarded as the carapace of some molting beetle on Za'aq Ha Dam, Nimrod had devolved into a haunted Man, assigned to wander in exile from humanity.

In presuming to take up the ensign of the Western Sorrel, he'd invited also the enigmatic power behind Mūk-Mudón's ascension. Emptied of all but a trace of his dignity, Nimrod had become a vessel of the malingering curse upon a helm he could not remove, not matter how hard he tried.

The foolhardy hunter had donned the helmet without considering much the great forces that had wreaked the devastation of Za'aq Ha

Dam. For upon his final field of battle as a Man, Mūk-Mudón's last thoughts were ever stead upon the talismanic feather Helél had granted him long before.

Some dark and irrational conviction had seized Mūk-Mudón at the moment of his doom, a surety that he might acquire another talisman such as the Shedím afforded him, and the power that accompanied it. In unbroken, gibbering refrain, the helm resounded this desire, an unceasing echo that in the end had hollowed Nimrod's mind.

The feaTHER...THE FEAther! I muST HAve anoTHER! Where IS it noW? WHEre doeS it FLy? I MUST have ANOTHER!!!

Thus possessed of another Man's obsession, and that entwined with the inglorious power of the Shedím, Nimrod sought with unreasoning soul the replacement for a strength long-lost. Even now, he shambled about the wasted perimeter of the wilderness, questing, ever questing in frenzied hope of an end that held none.

In his single-minded madness, Nimrod had become ever more bestial. He ceased to bathe but under what deluge providence sent, and his beard grew long and matted. Although he stalked his prey with murderous intent, he yet ate only grass and wild produce.

About his neck, he strung the feathers of his victims in the insane belief that by such collection and adornment, he might reclaim Helél's power. As his beard, Nimrod's hair likewise grew long and feathery until almost indistinguishable from the swelling collar of feathers about his crooked neck.

The weight of the lopsided helm, its heavy antlers shorn from one side, had over decades deformed Nimrod. His neck was ever pinned to a hunched and swollen shoulder while day and night he roamed the sandswept land, one eye cocked skyward for any sign of prey.

Today amidst those very skies, Sayah warned the others of the need to climb even as he began to pitch upward. His timing could not have been more fortuitous, for at the instant he began to ascend, a swift arrow arced past his breast. The Hadza were on the hunt!

Sayah beat the air with furious wings, dipping and rolling as much as he dared while once again Nat and Rae fought with all they had to hold on. Arrows whizzed past, seeming to come from all sides, but the ægle evaded them all until at last he attained an altitude high enough they were out of range.

The ægle searched the ground for the Hadza, who had broken from cover to watch as their quarry flew off. One such hunter, a dark and slender youth, raised a hand in apparent salute, while the other trailed an empty bow.

Sayah sensed respect in the gesture and directed a keening cry down at the clustering hunters. The Hadza surprised him again when the others raised their hands as well.

What a strange people, he marveled, then turned his attention to the southern wall of Terábnis, that great city of Men, which soon loomed in the foreground.

The Men of Terábnis had stacked bricks of sandy stone high and at a slight, steep angle, giving the perimeter wall of the city a tapered look. The three travelers hadn't much discussed the approach and infiltration of the city, and Sayah didn't think it prudent to stop in Hadza lands to talk it over.

He craned back and asked, "Nat? Rae? How do we want to do this?"

Nat and Rae looked at one another with frowns of dismay. They hadn't any idea either.

The sun was now setting, and Sayah was aware that dusk light often presented a challenge to the vision of other creatures. He sensed an opportunity in the timing of their arrival and flew a broad circle around the city.

"I have an idea!" he assured the Etom.

Confident in Sayah's plan, Nat and Rae looked over the city in the dwindling light, amazed at its massive scale. The towering walls were mountainous to the tiny Etom, and the guards walking side-by-side with room to spare atop the barriers bespoke their thickness.

The sheer breadth of the place staggered their diminutive sensibilities. Scattered about the plains outside the wall, tiny firelights drew their attention to the homes on the city's outskirts.

In short order, guards were likewise kindling great braziers along the wall. When all had been lit, the sentry fires appeared a rectangular, flaming constellation unlike anything the trio had ever seen. And that was when Sayah spotted their opening.

Along one section of the eastward wall, two fires were yet unlit. In the failing light, murkiness swallowed the eastern wall, rendering it indistinct to the Etom. Sayah, however, had no difficulty examining the darkened section with perfect clarity.

Perhaps the watchman tasked with lighting these braziers was sick, or maybe the watch was shorthanded. Whatever the reason, the segment of the wall was unwatched, unguarded, and poorly lit.

The ægle called to the others, "That's our spot! That's how we'll get in!"

Sayah banked away from the eastern wall, then turned back to approach the target area head-on. He pitched down to fly level with the top of the wall. At full speed, the ægle slipped through the toothy battlements, slowing at the last moment as he crossed the far edge of the wall to drop down into the city.

Few in the tenement this side of the wall had lit their hearths for the night, so this particular corner of the city remained dark. Sayah fluttered to the ground in the relative murk and Rae and Nat slid down from him at once to get a sense of their surroundings. For all appearances, they had infiltrated Terábnis undetected.

Without a doubt, they were all three out of their element, for none had experience in the land of Men. Doubt crept over their hearts as they struggled for the next step, or even their objective in this place.

After some internal interrogation, Rae arrived at the first sensible suggestion.

"What are we doing?" she inquired in frustration. "We don't even know why the Spirit brought us here!"

Nat and Sayah shrugged, just as confounded as she.

Rae hissed with disappointment, then chuckled in amazement before answering her own question, "Of course! That's it, isn't it?"

She looked to her still-mystified companions, then rolled her eyes as though they should likewise have divined the obvious.

"The Spirit brought us here! We need to ask *Him* what to do now, don't you think?"

Understanding kindled in Nat and Sayah like the burning of a damp wick, and they nodded in sluggish agreement.

"Of course!" Nat replied. "Let's pray."

The trio gathered in the deepening shadows between tenement and wall to whisper their requests, determined to stay out of sight. They offered lengthy supplication, taking turns while awaiting the Spirit's response. After some time, neither could remember waiting so long for the Spirit to reply, but none was willing to cease in prayer.

"Oi! Whatcha' doin' there?"

The exclamation made all three jump, and Rae uttered a short scream. Though he did not cry out, Sayah shed several feathers, and meanwhile, Nat froze as though immobility might make him invisible.

The intruder spoke again, this time not so loud and from closer to their huddle, "What a strange bunch you three are – two Etom and...bless me! A snowy-white ægle!"

The travelers turned at last to confront the interloper, an indistinct but small silhouette that could only be an Etom. Nat and Rae relaxed at once while Sayah debated whether or not he might have to kill the stranger. The thought made the ægle woozy, though, so he just sat down instead.

Nat took a step toward the Etom, and greeted him, "We're travelers from the south and new to this city. Any city of Men, really. We seek safe lodging for the night. Might you be able to help us?"

"No doubt, you're travelers. Just look at them clothes, too. You must be some o' them wild Etom, eh? Not a shackle, collar or link on ya,' either.

"'Scuse me," the stranger apologized, stepping forward to offer a hand. "My name's Yeelow."

An odd clinking sound accompanied Yeelow's motions, which Nat couldn't identify until he'd shaken Yeelow's shackled hand. Their new acquaintance was in chains.

"My name is Nat, and this is Rae," Nat introduced the etma with a wave of the hand. "That over there is our friend, Sayah."

"Friends with an ægle, huh?" Yeelow asked, then clicked his tongue. "I've never seen the like of it. Usually we're food to 'em, if anything at all."

Yeelow turned his attention to Sayah and called back, "You're not the kind to peck a fella', are ya'?"

"No," the recovering ægle replied, "I don't eat meat anymore."

A pause hung over the four of them as they worked out what was out of place.

"Well, I'll be..." Yeelow breathed. "You folk wouldn't be Kin, wouldya'?"

Rae was first to exclaim, "Wait! You can understand Sayah?"

The shocked and silent Yeelow nodded, his eyes wide with surprise.

Nat jumped in, "There are Kin in Terábnis?"

The implications were staggering, but in light of the Spirit's mission, it made a certain sense.

Yeelow sidled up close, speaking with greater care than before, "I take it, then, that you've been to the Kinsman's Tree? Bathed in the waters? Tasted of the fount?"

Nat smiled in sweet relief at the Spirit's planning, and answered, "Yes, yes, and yes, my friend."

"Well, then that makes us brothers, not friends!" Yeelow exclaimed, gripping Nat's hand and shoulder with familial fervency.

Nat couldn't ignore the length of Yeelow's chain that draped over his arm, and his eyes, full of pity, fell across the links.

Nat's expression did not escape Yeelow's notice, yet he responded with a peaceable smile, "'There is neither slave nor free, for all are one in the Kinsman Gaal.'"

The Spirit replied with a Resonance that quaked rather than thrummed within the three travelers, shaking free tears of joy and thanksgiving that they'd been united with such a one. Their meeting was no mere coincidence.

Yeelow's smile broadened and he sighed, "Come now, my Kin. Better these chains than the ones I once wore around my heart.

"Besides, my freedom in the Kingdom of Lord Elyon is assured, and in this land, a hopeful prospect. But enough about me. Let me take you to the others now."

Nat, Rae and Sayah reached swift agreement to follow Yeelow, who guided them at once along a dank and circuitous path through the city.

As they walked, Yeelow in a low voice shared information about the city and the Kinship there.

"We Etom in particular are vulnerable to the blasted slavers, but they don't dare touch one in chains. These dastardly links are a sign I'm under current ownership – the one good thing about 'em...

"...and that great building over there. Yeah, the one with the columns. That's the governor's palace. Nasty happenings there and too many Nihúkolem for *my* taste. You don't want any part of it. And over here..."

Yeelow slowed near the mouth of a dark, narrow alley to caution them, "Look, we're almost there, and I don't want any conniptions once we've arrived. You should know that many of among our Kinfolk are neither Etom nor beast."

Sayah, Rae, and Nat each cocked their heads in concerted quizzicality, uncertain what Yeelow might mean. Neither Etom nor beast? What did that leave, then?

Puzzlement resolved to shock when the three realized what Yeelow was saying.

Rae was first to speak, "You don't mean...?"

Yeelow nodded, a curious, crooked grin on his face as he confirmed, "Yes. Men. In fact, our leader is a Man, if that's not too difficult to swallow. But you should know the Men of the Kinship treat me no different than their natural kind. Maybe better. Yet another miracle of the Tree."

Nat, Rae, and Sayah paused, absorbing Yeelow's statement.

"We've trusted him *this* far," Sayah quipped, shrugging in his æglish way.

Nat and Rae looked to one another, each questing for the Spirit's guidance. Their shared anxieties bled away as they considered their providential encounter with Yeelow. Sayah was right. They ought to trust Yeelow – as their Kin and as a fellow in the Vine.

"Lead away," Nat declared, pointing beyond Yeelow with an open hand.

"Right!" Yeelow affirmed and dashed to the edge of the alleyway to glance right and left before waving the others forward.

From what he had learned of the city thus far, Sayah gathered that homes lay in either direction. His sharp eyes picked up the faint glow of hearth and candle that peeked between cracks in bolted doors and through windows shuttered against the night.

"We need to slip under the gate across the road there," Yeelow indicated a weathered, wooden gate that stood straight ahead.

A high wall of that sand-colored stone common to the city ran a good distance to either side of the portal. Sayah eyed a splintered slat at the corner of the gate he thought he could slip through.

"There's a courtyard just past," Yeelow explained. "We'll be safe once we reach it, but we don't want to be spotted if we can help it. Too much negative attention and the like."

Yeelow motioned the others back into the shadows and looked down either end of the street for their chance. They waited a good while, and Rae began to wonder if they'd *ever* make the crossing.

That very instant, Yeelow hissed and waved them forward, "Come on, now! Hurry!"

Rae was caught off guard at the sudden signal and lurched forth when Nat grabbed her hand to cross. She was pleased that Nat made certain she'd not be left behind, but the start was jarring, to say the least.

Her first heavy step onto the cobbled road forced from her mouth a gagging, "HURGHK!"

Nat cast a wary glance back her way, and his trailing arm stiffened to steady her.

Rae raised her hand to communicate, *I'm alright.*

Meanwhile, from behind them a distraught Yeelow shushed, "SSHHHH!!!"

Rae got her feet under her at once and without looking back waved an apology to Yeelow. They were almost halfway across the road now and might have gone altogether unnoticed if not for Sayah's brilliant white plumage.

Several houses down, the road came to an abrupt end at a wall that surrounded a large, spreading home just past an intersection with another street. And from around the corner, torches in one hand and spears in the other, came two constables of the city, plated breasts and helmed heads gleaming in the torchlight.

They were engaged in talk of some mundane sort, else their full attention would have been on the way ahead. Rather, their eyes were turned to one another in conversation, which in all likelihood saved the four creatures scurrying across the road.

Their movement, and that of Sayah's larger, brighter form in particular, caught the corner of one watchmen's eye. He stopped chatting with his colleague at once, his brow pinched in concentration as he lifted his torch ahead to peer down the murky lane.

His mustached lip twisted as he growled, "Hi! Who goes there?"

The Etom and the ægle had arrived at the gate. They stood in shadow, pressed against the rough wooden slats, puffing with muted gasps of terror and exertion. They were torn between the fear of drawing the constabulary to their position while ducking past the gate and that of the guards regardless encountering them when they continued down the road.

After a long, desperate moment, Yeelow peeked around the corner just as the other constable began to lose patience with the first.

He jibed at his companion, "What did you see, Dikastís? Was it a ghost? There's nothing there."

Constable Dikastís blinked hard, then advanced with slow steps, his eyes boring once more into the darkness.

His colleague inquired again, "What is it? I didn't see a thing, and you're making me jumpy."

Constable Dikastís turned back to answer his comrade, "I'm not sure, Énorkoi. It was the strangest thing – a bird? Maybe a dove. But much larger...like an ægle!"

Dikastís wore confusion too well for Énorkoi's comfort, and thus he dismissed his claims out of hand.

"An ægle?!? Here?"

Dikastís remained earnest in his assertion nonetheless, and Énorkoi, knowing his partner to be an honest man, accommodated him.

"Alright, then," Énorkoi relented with a forward wave of his torch. "Let's check it out."

The constables advanced once more, one wary and the other skeptical. They had gone a few mere steps when they heard a brittle crack, and at the same instant, a flash of white to one side of the road caught their eyes.

Dikastís dashed ahead to a nearby wooden gate while the stunned Énorkoi called from where he stood, "What was *that*?!?"

As Énorkoi hurried to join him, Dikastís moved his torch about to examine gate and wall, but his investigation revealed nothing.

"I *knew* I saw something," Dikastís stated to himself, then to Énorkoi, "You saw it, right? Something was definitely here."

Énorkoi nodded while he continued to scan the area for...for whatever it was. He listened with care for any sign of activity beyond the gate, but all was still and quiet.

"Hey! Wait!" he cried out to Dikastís, who had raised a fist to pound on the gate.

Énorkoi caught Dikastís' falling hand just in time to stop him.

He breathed a sigh of relief and asked Dikastís, "Don't you know whose home this is?"

Mystified, Dikastís shook his head.

Énorkoi rolled his eyes in exasperation then filled Dikastís in, "This is the home of a hero, a soldier who served with honor in the Imperial infantry. Would you disturb such a man at this hour without good cause?"

Dikastís shook his head again.

"Good. I don't know *what* we saw, but unless we're sure it was a 'threat to the citizenry and the authority of the Empire,'" he chided, quoting from the motto of the constabulary, "we ought to leave this man alone."

Clicking his tongue, Dikastís implored, "But, Énorkoi, you *know* we saw something."

"You're right. We saw *something*," Énorkoi replied. "Maybe a *bird*, for Mūk-Mudón's sake! Hardly a threat to the Empire."

Dikastís sneered in disappointment but desisted at last. Énorkoi made a fair point, and Dikastís didn't want the others in the constabulary to see him as *that* guy.

"Alright, Énorkoi," he complied, "I concede, but let us keep a close watch on this place from now on. Perhaps something that bears our attention is afoot under cover of this *hero's* good reputation. Fair enough?"

"Fair enough, comrade," Énorkoi agreed, then stepped away and jerked his head to gesture Dikastís onward. "Back to it, then, eh? These streets aren't going to patrol themselves."

Dikastís cast one more baleful glance at the gate, and grumbling turned to follow Énorkoi. Soon, the pair receded, once more engaged in conversation, although less mundane than before, and smattered with Énorkoi's modest ridicule of his companion.

Chapter Eighteen
Kinfolk Among Men

On the other side of the gate, the quartet breathed a sigh of relief. When the more suspicious of the two constables had turned back to speak with the other, Yeelow had at once sent Rae under the gate. A narrow gap between the ground and an out-of-place slat permitted enough space for the Etom to lay flat and scoot through.

After Rae, Nat had slipped under, then Yeelow, who advised Sayah before scrambling for safety himself. The ægle caught the sense of Yeelow's plan at once, for it coincided with a thought that had occurred to him earlier. Safe in the courtyard, a worried Nat and Rae stood back at Yeelow's bidding as he reassured them Sayah would be safe if they just stayed out of the way.

On the other side of the gate, Sayah shot a sidelong look at the back of the nearer watchman, took a step back into the street, then charged the cracked slat in the gate he'd spied from the alley. When he struck it, the wood broke without much difficulty, but in that frayed and tattered manner that left a splintered comb behind.

Hung up in the raking remnants of the slat, the ægle pushed on, motivated by the slap of human feet and the jangle of their armor. The ragged wood clawed at Sayah as he pressed by, then all at once he was through and none the worse for wear but for a few lost feathers.

The feathers! If the soldiers saw those, all was lost! But Yeelow was already on the job, snaking a swift hand out through the gap to collect the evidence in rapid succession. The Etom moved with surprising silence in spite of his chains then whirled back inside to lay flat against the wall.

The ægle and three Etom followed the argument outside the gate with bated breath, uncertain if the constables would rouse the master of the house. Yeelow whispered they need not be concerned if they did. They would need to hide from the watchmen, but the humans inside the home presented no threat.

Regardless, all were thankful when the constables departed. Yeelow noted Dikastís' final words, however, and resolved to share them with their host. The added attention of one overzealous night watchman might not much increase their risk of discovery, but it was wise to be aware of the danger.

Able to breathe a bit easier at last, Sayah, Nat and Rae meanwhile took stock of the courtyard. The moon, high and gibbous, shone in the night sky to reveal in limited detail a lush desert garden that skirted both the wall of the courtyard and the home before them. Planted at regular intervals along the well-kept swath between the home and the outer wall, palm trees waved in the gentle breeze.

A path of flat, smooth stones led to the door of the house, which lay long and low but for a large upper chamber that arose more or less from the center of the domicile. No light peeked from window or door of the lower floor, but a warm glow emanated from the one visible window of the second floor.

At one end the home, an arch spanned the space between the roof and courtyard wall, atop which was constructed a pergola of long, stripped branches. Yeelow led them under the arch, past which the courtyard broadened a great deal. And in the far corner of the courtyard, the three travelers saw something that took their breath away.

It was a Tree - a Tree so like the Kinsman's Tree and the Tree in Endego that at once they knew it was the same. The same light shone beneath the Tree's boughs, and from its trunk poured a stream, pure and clear, to form a pool at its base.

And gathered around the waters knelt a good many Men, their heads uncovered and bent low in reverence. From where he stood in the ankle-deep pool, one Man spoke, his tone hushed and intense.

What was more, a number of colorful Etom stood out among the Men and some even perched on their shoulders. Men and Etom alike bowed their heads and the newcomers saw at once they prayed.

The congregation opened their eyes, and at last Nat saw the face of the Man who led the Kinship's prayer. He was a burly, bearded fellow with eyes much kinder and more joyful than when Nat had seen him last.

"Makrïos!" the shocked etém gasped.

Makrïos beckoned past those gathered in the bower to a Man who sat alone atop a large stone. Several closest to the fellow helped him stand, a crutch propped under one arm. Limping with pain, he joined Makrïos, his lame and heavy stride landing with a splash when he stepped down into the water.

At Yeelow's behest, Sayah and the Etom advanced toward the Tree while Makrïos spoke to the other Man in a voice still too quiet for them to hear. The other Man nodded, and when a young, lanky fellow passed Makrïos a modest, earthen bowl, Rae, Nat, and Sayah guessed at what came next.

Makrïos left one hand against the unsteady Man's back and leaned down to fill the bowl from the flow at their feet.

Both raised beaming faces heavenward as Makrïos proclaimed, "In the name of the Father, and of the Son, and of the Holy Spirit, we baptize this Man, Kabbet in the presence of this Kinship!"

Makrïos emptied the bowl of water over Kabbet's head and face, and all those assembled cheered his grafting into the Vine. Kabbet did not move, however, but raised his hands high to let the crutch beneath him fall into the pool.

At first, he swayed over his bent and crippled leg, and almost fell. Then strength filled his withered limb, and he straightened his leg to catch himself. Tears joined the droplets of water that yet fell from his face as he whispered praise and gratitude to Elyon. He was healed!

The Kinship there fell silent when they identified the miracle they'd witnessed, then erupted in a sweet susurration of praise like leaves stirring in the wind. Nat, Rae, and Sayah had seen many healed before, but every time, the Spirit touched them as well.

The restoration of this Man, Kabbet, was different only in the kind of recipient the Spirit had graced, which made Sayah, Rae, and Nat marvel all the more that the salvation of the Kinsman had come to all creatures. The Spirit within them drew them near the others, where they joined their Kin in worship of the Creator.

Yeelow watched the three travelers the Spirit had guided him to as they praised Lord Elyon alongside the Kinfolk of Terábnis, a soft smile on his face. He'd not know what to anticipate when he'd been sent, but he knew the Spirit's leading when he sensed it. These three were here for a reason.

Makrïos meanwhile had made his way around to where Yeelow and his guests lingered at the fringe of the bower. The pure white ægle had drawn his eye, but then he had spotted Yeelow, too. The Etom had informed Makrïos that the Spirit was drawing him to the city wall, and thus the Man surmised Yeelow's companions had been the reason for the Spirit's errand.

Makrïos appraised the newcomers, giving attention first to the ægle, certain the creature's unique plumage told a tale he was keen to hear. Beside the bird stood a pale pink etma, her eyes streaming, and hands upraised in thanksgiving. And next to her...no!

Makrïos couldn't believe his own eyes at first, for he recognized their third guest from an encounter in the woods west of Sakkan. On the word of this wee creature, Nat, Makrïos had sought the resurrected Kinsman at the place of His execution. The place where Makrïos himself had slain Him.

Instead of the desolate wasteland Makrïos had left behind, the Kinsman's Tree had stood in testimony of the Kinsman's finished work. With swelling gratitude Makrïos recalled the moment of his redemption at the Tree, and credited Nat for his courage in the woods.

But what plan of the Creator brought the young blue etém here now? No matter. Makrïos was pleased to make the youth's acquaintance again, this time as a brother, as Kin. The former Imperial Captain skirted the ægle and etma and knelt beside Nat, who with eyes closed failed to notice the Man's presence.

Leaning low, Makrïos spoke, "Nat, my friend, do you remember me?"

At the baritone rumble of Makrïos' first words, Nat's eyes flew open. Makrïos' great bearded face loomed over the etém, and he staggered back with surprise, almost falling over. Rae screeched and stumbled into Sayah's snowy breast while the ægle squawked and flapped his wings in agitation.

"Ma – Makrïos!" Nat stammered. "Yes! Yes, of course I remember you! You're the only Man I've ever met."

Makrïos chuckled, settled back onto his haunches, and offered an apology, "I am sorry to have startled you, little one. I was eager to speak with you again. After all, you're in part responsible for what you see here."

"I don't quite understand," Nat answered, perplexed. "What have I to do with all this?"

"That is a tale indeed," Makrïos replied, "but perhaps I can tell it later? Right now, there are a good many Kin I would like you to meet, if you would?"

Makrïos lay an open palm along the ground in invitation, and it was a moment before Nat comprehended the meaning of Makrïos' gesture. His golden eyes widened, and he took a step back. Rae goaded him with an elbow in the back, and Nat whirled around at her betrayal, resolute to resist her prodding.

Instead, Rae's coquettish smile arrested him as she cajoled him, "Come on, Nat. Don't you think it might be *fuuuuun*?"

The suddenly pliant Nat had replied in the affirmative and was halfway onto Makrïos' hand before he realized it. With one foot yet on the ground, Nat extended his hand back to Rae. The etma giggled and brushed a loose zalzal back as she took Nat's hand to hop on with light, dainty steps.

"You coming with?" Nat inquired of Sayah.

The ægle responded with a slow shake of the head, his brow lowered in incredulity and beak hanging mute.

"No, thank you," Sayah replied.

"Well! An ægle among the Kinfolk!?!" Makrïos exclaimed. "I've never heard of such a thing. But, no matter, Kin are Kin and will be treated accordingly."

Makrïos raised the Etom to his face to reassure them, "Don't worry, you two. I've done this plenty of times."

"Yeelow!" Makrïos hollered to the Etom below. "You've done well in finding these three! Would you mind taking the ægle around to meet some of the others?"

"Aye, Captain!" Yeelow shouted back, snapping off a passable salute.

"Hey! Hey! Watch that 'Captain' business!" Makrïos replied with good-humored affection. "I've nothing to with the Empire now!"

Makrïos turned to carry Nat and Rae over to a mixed group of Men and Etom milling near the Tree.

Yeelow followed Makrïos with his eyes, and whispered, "Makes you no less a Captain, my brother."

Sayah caught the devotion in Yeelow's tone and wondered at the miracle of unity the Spirit was working among the creatures of the world.

"What say you we go introduce you to some of our Kinfolk?" Yeelow prompted, drawing Sayah out of reflection.

Although separated during their presentation to the Kinship there, all three adventurers experienced a sense of welcoming hospitality notwithstanding. Makrïos and Yeelow were gracious hosts and introduced them as fellow Kin from Endego to the south.

A common reply that Nat and Rae received was interest in how they had encountered the Kinsman and His Tree. Makrïos understood a lengthy explanation was in order and deflected questions on their behalf.

"Let's not impose too much on their time right now. Perhaps they'll see fit to share their story with all of us at once?"

Makrïos looked to Nat and Rae with expectation, and after a brief glance at one another, Nat shrugged and answered for them both.

"I don't see why not. Lord Elyon willing, we plan to stay a while. Surely, we'll have a chance during our visit."

Nat's hedged commitment seemed to satisfy the others, who thirsted to know more not from suspicion, but from an earnest interest in their distant Kin.

The Kinship, and Etom in particular, responded to Sayah with some amazement. Besides Men and Etom, those in Terábnis had yet to add any other kind to their number. In truth, they did not know it was possible until the possibility stood realized before them in the striking form of the pure-white ægle.

For the Etom of the Kinship, as it had been with Yeelow, their concern was Sayah's predatory nature. Yeelow quelled their fears with assurances of the ægle's conduct. He was a brother and an ally to every creature in the Vine, a fact further evinced through the ægle's ability to communicate with all beneath the bower regardless of kind.

The implications of the Kinsman opening the way to the Tree to all creatures rippled through the disparate assembly, a wave that crested low yet ran deep through the hearts of the Kinfolk. They would need to reassess everything they knew in light of this news.

Yeelow and Sayah stood near the edge of the pool as Yeelow again announced his feathered friend to a new group of Etom. Yeelow declared in a loud voice the ægle was harmless to Etom and had in fact protected those in Endego.

"Endego?!?" a sharp voice shouted back over the heads of the Etom closest to Yeelow and Sayah.

Those at the back of the clustered Etom made way for the speaker, a thin, grey etém who reminded Sayah of someone, though he couldn't decide just who.

The flinty stranger's eyes were inflamed with desperate light as he inquired of the ægle, "You're from Endego? What of the Eben'kayah there? Does the temple still stand?"

"Yes, we come from Endego," Sayah replied, hesitant in the face of the stranger's intensity.

"And what of the temple?!?" came the frenzied inquiry again.

"Hold on there, brother," Yeelow interjected, standing between the ægle and his interrogator. "I know you've been through a great deal, but maybe we should start with a greeting? This here is Sayah, one of our Kin out of Endego."

"I must know if my people are safe, Yeelow!" the ashen etém cried, his form racked with grievous sobs. "Now *please* stand aside!"

The disturbance below carried up to the ears of Nat, Rae, and Makrïos, who stood nearby.

The Man leaned over the growing throng of Etom to ask, "What's going on here?"

An altercation had arisen between the ægle and a somewhat new arrival to their Kinship here. Not long ago, another etém, a stout, olive-green fellow named Kavōd, had brought the grey one here, his body emaciated and in ruin.

The two had at first attempted contact with the Eben'kayah of Terábnis, whose community the Nihúkolem had devastated after discovering they sought the Kinsman. The Empire of Chōl had persecuted the Eben'kayah – imprisoning, torturing, and killing the larger part of them.

The final stroke of the weighty Imperial hammer had been the destruction of the Eben'kayah's temple in Terábnis. Today the temple's remnants lay beneath a mounting heap of rubbish the Empire had consigned to the site.

A few Eben'kayah escaped the persecution to join the Kinship. Through these the grey etém and his protector had come to the Kin, who had taken him in and nursed him back to health. Over time, he'd regained some strength, though the scars of his imprisonment remained.

Yeelow answered Makrïos with some cheek, "He's just discovered our guests are from his hometown, and he's desperate to catch up on the local gossip."

Perhaps Yeelow might be forgiven his sarcasm, which was inappropriate, but aimed at lightening the atmosphere. Regardless, the grey etém wasn't in the mood for jest and just glowered at Yeelow.

"He's from Endego?!?" Nat exclaimed.

Rae called to Makrïos, "Would you let us down, please?"

Makrïos complied at once, and soon Nat and Rae stood beside Sayah to address the stranger.

"Hello," Nat began, soft-spoken, "my name is Nat. This is Rae and Sayah. We've just come from Endego. Do you know it?"

The flinty etém struggled to maintain his composure as he replied, "Child, I was *born* there. My father, my people are there – the only family I've ever known."

"And who are your people?" Rae asked, concerned.

"The Eben'kayah. Do you know them?"

Nat's eyes brightened, and he exclaimed, "Know them? We *are* them!"

Relief flooded the stranger's features, only to tense again as he demanded, "And what of the temple there? Does it still stand?"

Nat and Rae's faces fell at the mention of the temple, its destruction at the hands of the Empire a dark memory.

The strange etém read their expressions and with a Stain-blackened hand covered his mouth in shock, silent tears starting from his wide eyes.

Rae noted his distress and consoled him, "Please don't! What our enemies meant for evil, Elyon meant for good!"

Zeal for the Kinsman overtaking him, Nat picked up where Rae left off, "That which has replaced the temple of the Eben'kayah surpasses it in every way, for in its place now stands a Tree like this one here!"

The ashen Etom cast a skeptical glance at the Tree, his eyes yet tearful as he spoke, "I don't see how one who has known the majesty of our temple could say *this* is better.

"Where are kept the prophecies of the Kinsman? Where might we house our people in time of need? Or shelter them in time of danger? And where does the glorious presence of Lord Elyon fall if not upon the temple?"

The Spirit's prompting interrupted Nat before he could answer the inquiries, and instead the young etém posed a humble question of his own.

"May I please ask your name, sir?"

Nat's polite request stirred something in the distraught, grey Etom to disrupt his distress. His gaze became clear and introspective, as though recalling his own name likewise dredged up an identity that preceded his current shattered state.

He directed eyes clarified thus at Nat and answered, "Killam. My name is Killam."

Nat and Rae's jaws fell open when they heard the name, both stunned to learn this broken etém before them was Shoym's son, presumed lost many years prior on a mission to find the Kinsman. A mission he'd set out on with Nat's father, Jaarl.

Nat looked about with unseeing eyes in confusion at the sudden revelation. So much of what he he'd known of his father's fate was all at once pitched aloft in an uncertain jumble. If Killam had survived, then maybe...

The question erupted untrammeled from Nat's lips, "Is my father alive?"

Now it was Killam's turn for confusion, and his head tipped to one side, mouth falling open in wordless perplexity. Who *was* this child?

"Jaarl!" Nat shouted. "Is Jaarl alive?"

Killam shook his head, and answered, "Last I saw him, they were taking him out West, alone. The Empire deemed him too dangerous to keep with the others."

"Where out West, Killam? Do you know?"

"I heard rumors from time to time that somewhere near the Senter Sea the Empire held their worst in solitary confinement. That would be my best guess."

Feverish, Nat solicited Sayah, "Can you take us there?"

"I've never been that far West," the ægle replied, "but for you, Nat, I would take you as far as my wings would carry us."

"Then let's be away!" Nat cried, darting to mount the ægle.

A gentle hand on Nat's arm gave him pause, and he turned as Rae implored, "Please, Nat. Don't do this now. Let us seek the Spirit's guidance first."

Nat balled his hands into fists while he debated the matter with himself, Rae's soft fingertips a steadfast reminder of the best argument against his hastiness.

"AAARGH!" Nat growled, throwing his hands up and stalking away from Sayah and Rae.

Right now, he resented the authority Lord Elyon held over him, but the Spirit whispered comfort that took the shape of memory. Recollection of what the Creator had done on behalf of Nat and those he loved passed before his softening heart. Nat could not forsake the One who loved him, most and best.

Nat put his head down and sighed, "Ok, Rae. We'll wait on Lord Elyon for our answer. Just like we did before He sent us here."

Rae's arms enfolded Nat from behind, and Yeelow gripped his shoulder to commend him.

"Well done, young sir. You're an example to us all, especially Killam."

Yeelow's comment sobered Nat, who in passing had recognized Killam's Stained hand – and thus his absence from the Vine. He owed Killam some answers.

"Killam, can we talk a while – just the two of us? I want to tell you about what's happened in Endego."

"Will you be alright, Nat?" Rae asked.

"I will be fine," he encouraged. "An Eben'kayah of Endego has need of me. I intend to honor his commitment to his heritage and his understanding of the Kinsman.

"Please pray the Spirit speaks to his heart. It would bless Shoym to know his son is not only alive, but a branch of the Vine."

Rae smiled with admiration and nodded before heading off to collect as many as were willing to intercede for Killam. Soon, a small but diverse throng, including Yeelow, Sayah, and Makrïos, bowed together in prayer as Nat guided Killam away for some privacy.

Nat sought out a secluded spot still within the warmth and glow of the Tree's everlasting Spring, and pointed to a pair of flat, smooth stones for seats. Killam complied, and the two settled in for a quiet conversation.

"I want to answer all your questions, Killam," Nat began, "but I'm not sure I can. I will do my best, though, so please be patient with me."

Killam had calmed a great deal since his initial encounter with Sayah, and answered in a steady voice, "You have some idea of the persecution the Eben'kayah have faced under the Empire in recent days, but you should know – the Eben'kayah here and most places throughout the Empire have been devastated.

"When my friend, Kavōd, brought me to Terábnis, we found none but a few Eben'kayah, and these had joined this...this rabble. We knew a great many Eben'kayah existed among Men. Never, and I mean *never* did we come together for fear that, in their natural tendency for dominance, they would abuse us.

"That's why this union of Men, Etom, and, now, of *all kinds* is so unnatural to me. I fear the very essence of what it means to be Eben'kayah will be lost amidst all this!

"If it weren't for Kavōd, I would still be rotting away in Sakkan or dead, but because he loved me as an Eben'kayah, he carried me out of captivity and helped me find my way here. He could not bear to part with our traditions, and even now can't accept this fellow, Gaal, as the Kinsman for fear of losing what makes us the Eben'kayah.

"Don't get me wrong, he respects the work Makrïos, Yeelow and these others here are doing, particularly in the slave market, but he can't bring himself to *believe* as you do. To me, it feels like a betrayal, like choosing Gaal over Kavōd, my brother in the Eben'kayah and the one who saved my life."

"I understand," Nat answered and glanced over at Sayah and Rae. "I have friends like that, too, and Kavōd sounds like the kind who sticks closer to you than a brother.

Killam waved a worried hand over the Kinship and the Tree, and continued, "So, what frightens me the most with our temples destroyed, our people scattered, and the remnant throwing in with this lot is this:

What will happen to my people? The people I so love? What will happen to the Eben'kayah?

His point was fair, and one Nat in truth had not considered. He paused a moment in prayer and collected his thoughts before responding.

"As strange as it may seem to you, Killam, the matter has not arisen much in Endego, where it may hearten you to know a good many Eben'kayah survive. As you may remember, I still count myself as one, as does my companion, Rae. As does your father, Shoym."

"My father still lives?" Killam gasped.

Killam had not allowed himself to hope in his own father's survival, given Shoym's age and the evil the Empire of Chōl had brought against the Eben'kayah. The revelation shook him, and he wept, shuddering with emotion.

Nat lay a small, cerulean hand on Killam's spiny back and prayed in silence while he awaited the elder etém's recovery. He hadn't intended to blindside Killam with his father's fate but thought it necessary to make him aware that Shoym still lived. From Nat's very recent and almost identical experience, he sympathized with Killam, and gave him plenty of time to recuperate.

At long last, Killam straightened, his eyes pinched and brow furrowed as he collected himself and asked, "So what does my father think of all this, then?"

Nat raised his brows and exhaled before he replied, "Honestly, Killam, I can't speak for him. At least not for what he *thinks*. But I can tell you that he's happier than I've ever seen him, and more alive.

"You don't know this, but your father was the one to invite my mother and I into the community of the Eben'kayah. I love him like a grandfather, and without him and the Eben'kayah, we would likely have starved or frozen to death. No one else cared for this widow and her fatherless child.

"I know your father was disheartened at the loss of the temple in Endego, but he persevered and, in a way, saw its restoration. It could be none other than Elyon who planned what happened in Endego.

"The Nihúkolem uprooted not just the temple, but the beautiful olive tree that sheltered so many of our people. They left nothing but a hole behind. And, then, Lord Elyon sent a servant, full of the Kinsman's light and life, to accomplish His ends in Endego.

"It was my friend, my sister, Miyam, who gave her life as seed to grow into a Tree such as this one here, and in the very spot our olive tree once stood. And, under the limbs of that Tree, we've taken shelter and offered it to any who have need.

"Twice now, the Lord Elyon has granted us the Tree for Sanctuary and repulsed the Empire's attack. Mind you, full-on assaults of Nihúkolem and then their minions, defeated outright."

Killam's eyes were sharp and attentive as he received Nat's report, but something still troubled him, "That all sounds fantastic, but what of our writings? Our prophecies? Are they lost forever? And where is the Kinsman?"

"Look to the Tree. There you see the prophecies of the Kinsman fulfilled. He came. He died. Now He lives again. All to free us from the Stain and unite us through the Tree; He is the Vine that connects us, and we are the branches.

"Regarding the Kinsman, I and my Kin from Endego watched Him ascend to the gates of Lord Elyon and stand before the Tree Ha Kayim. I know Him now through what the Spirit shares, though our host, Makrïos knew Him before His death. In fact, he was present at the Kinsman's death, but that's a tale for him to tell."

Killam blew out a noisy breath, and appraised Nat.

This is the son of my best friend, my most faithful companion. But what do I know of him? His claims are beyond belief, but consistent with a certain interpretation of our prophecies.

"I need some time to consider all you've told me, Nat," Killam stated at last, "but I appreciate you taking the time to answer my questions. I may have more for you later."

"I understand," Nat offered in quiet reply. "It's a great deal to take in, and not all of it what we Eben'kayah expected."

Killam smirked, and chuckled, "That's an understatement."

The pair returned to the company of the others, Nat seeking out Rae and Sayah while Killam lingered a short while. After a bit, Nat saw Killam retreating to a dark corner of the courtyard, perhaps to retire or ponder their conversation. Nat breathed a hopeful prayer that he'd represented the Kinsman well and that the Spirit would accomplish what He desired through their discussion.

The hour was late and Nat, Rae, and Sayah were tired from the eventful day. Makrïos recognized their exhaustion and offered them a pallet inside. Accustomed to sleeping near the Tree in Endego, the three declined in favor of bedding down near the Tree here.

Makrïos favored them with a curious smile, and pointed to the Tree, "Funny thing, this Tree. You've told me of your Tree in Endego, and nothing so dramatic happened here. Nevertheless, it *is* worth sharing, if you have the time to hear it."

The three youths assented and Makrïos began his story.

"I met Gaal here in Terábnis. He had already gathered a substantial following, and rumors of His miraculous power preceded him. I'd never met anyone who at the same time was so magnetic and offensive."

Makrïos laughed, and not with modest laughter. No, he roared with great guffaws of laughter as he recalled, "Even I was offended at times, and you should have seen some of the religious folk – "

He lowered his voice to a conspiratorial whisper to relate, "The Eben'kayah among Men, that is."

Makrïos resumed his chuckling and in a normal voice quipped, "He really got their goat, their scapegoat, if you take my meaning."

His joke fell flat, but Makrïos was not deterred, "Ah. Well, I guess you had to have been there, which I was – with the other disciples of Gaal.

"Anyhow, many times I invited Gaal and my fellow disciples to my home. We spent a good deal of time here and in the upper room there," Makrïos gestured to the second floor of his home and continued.

"One morning not long after I'd met Gaal, the other disciples and I came out to find Him in the corner where the Tree stands now. He was searching for figs on the sycamore that grew there before. We were all a bit mystified, since it was *not* the season for figs.

"Of course, He didn't find any fruit, and I don't know if He was upset, but he cursed that sycamore, 'May you never again bear fruit!' We all thought He was joking. I mean, imagine it! He cursed the tree for not bearing figs *out of season*!

"Anyway, turns out it was no joke. The next morning, we came down and the sycamore was completely grey and withered, down to the roots. Even the leaves had crisped overnight. None of us dared touch it for fear of what might happen to us if we did."

"When I pointed my ruined sycamore out to Gaal, He said that the power of faithful prayer had done it. I remember everything He said then, but what stood out to me at the time were these words: 'Whatever you ask of Lord Elyon in prayer, trust you have received it, and He will make it yours.'"

"Later, after finding the Kinsman's Tree, thanks to this little fellow," he pointed to Nat, "I found myself weeping over this city. Before the Empire came, it was a bustling land for all appearances and a lively place. But like the sycamore, it was fruitless and barren of the righteousness our Creator so desires of us.

"I went to the ruined sycamore and for three days prayed that Terábnis would bear fruit, my tears watering the ground around the tree. I didn't eat, and I hardly slept. Not long into the third night, however, I fell into a deep sleep. When I awoke in the morning, a single ripe fig hung from a withered branch of the sycamore.

"I was dumbfounded at the appearance of the fruit, but the Spirit directed me to pluck the fig and plant it at the base of the dead sycamore. I did as He recommended and wept no more. Rather, I bathed and rested with my family, who had become concerned for me."

"The following day, I found this Tree in place of the sycamore, and knew Lord Elyon had answered my prayer. Since then, I have made it my goal each day to bring others to the Tree, so they may know freedom from the Stain, healing for their wounds, and abundant life in the Spirit."

Sayah was first to declare, "That's astounding, Makrïos. How did you know to pray like that?"

"I can't say that I did," Makrïos explained. "I just followed the Spirit. He set a passion for Terábnis aflame in my heart, and as far as I know, I was the only Kin in the city at the time.

"I'm happy to report my family soon joined me in the Vine, and then all those you saw here tonight. Kabbet is just the latest in a lengthening line. Not to mention the work Yeelow and Killam's friend, Kavōd, have been doing to help the slaves here in Terábnis."

When the three returned only curious stares, Makrïos continued, "By his chains, you already know that Yeelow's a slave, but you wouldn't otherwise. Our Kinship here is in the business of redeeming as many slaves as we can in Terábnis, of purchasing their freedom.

"Yeelow and Kavōd specialize in scouting out any Etom being sold at market. If they see an Etom needs our help, they sent us word quick as they can, so we can buy their release. Kavōd practically lives over there. He's that dedicated.

"And Yeelow… he's been a slave since he was born, though we could free him any time we like. Truth is, he *chooses* to remain a slave. He says it's the perfect cover to help the others."

Awestruck at the Etom slave's devotion, Nat murmured, "And *that* is how the Kinsman delivers us."

Breaking the yoke of the oppressor was an important component of the Kinsman's prophecies they had yet to see fulfilled, and Nat was just beginning to see the many ways the Kinfolk were fulfilling that prediction. Nat resolved to tell Killam in the morning. It might just be what he needed to hear to put his trust in the Kinsman Gaal.

"Well, I've kept you all long enough," Makrïos pronounced. "I just felt the Spirit nudging me to tell you about our Tree here. Beautiful, isn't it?"

Sayah, Rae, and Nat all nodded in affirmation as they gazed at the Tree, glorious in the evening glow of its vital boughs.

"A blessed night to you, then!" Makrïos called and stepped into his home.

The three travelers thought the Man had gone, but then he leaned out of the doorway and wriggled his eyebrows as he offered some final words.

"As you know...rhema's on first thing in the morning."

And then he really, truly, actually left.

The trio snickered – their host was quite a ham. He was a different man from the grim soldier and tortured transgressor Nat had met before.

In all sincerity, though, they liked Makrïos and everyone else they had met this evening – even Killam, whom they pitied for the trauma Scarsburrow had inflicted on the etém, body and soul. They agreed to persist in prayer for Killam as Makrïos had for Terábnis, then went to bed down.

Although they settled in to sleep behind alien walls built by Men, the Tree nearby, the warmth its light provided, and the gurgle of its spring provided the tranquility of home. Same stars overhead, same mellow glow all around. The three soon slept in sound comfort, and nothing there disturbed their rest.

Frenlee, the trio's pursuer on the Dimroad, had not fared so well as they. The Etom had fallen into a deep, dreamless slumber that offered little relief to his exhausted body. Regardless of his weariness, his respite lasted but an hour or two, for the dangers of the Dimroad weighed heavy on his mind – even in sleep.

His furtive vigilance aroused, Frenlee awoke in the dank, fusty air of the Dimroad to the telltale sounds of nearby skittering and scraping. He dared not move until the Nihúkolem had passed by in the shadows beyond the road. His experience with the wraiths in Sakkan had educated him on the signs of their presence, and no other creature made such a sound in passing.

Once Frenlee was assured the Nihúkolem had gone, he arose from the pile of dry leaves he'd hidden in to rest. Though out of concern he might alert the enemy to his presence, he'd taken great care not to rustle the leaves as he got up, his stomach now threatened to give his position away. The hungry gurgle was also a persistent reminder that he'd gone to sleep without sustenance.

Frenlee looked about in forlorn hope that he might discover some scrap or some morsel the three wayfarers may have left behind. To his honest surprise, a white wafer of some kind lay on the ground near the place he'd spotted his quarry before they'd bolted.

The etém wasn't one to question his fortunes and so snuck forth to take the flake from the ground. Retreating to the shadows near the base of a tree, he sampled the wafer, which broke off in his mouth with a crisp, honeyed savor. The food energized him at once, and as soon as he had finished his meal, he was ready to continue his pursuit.

Having confirmed the presence of Nihúkolem along the road, Frenlee took greater care than the night before as he proceeded. Through the long hours of the day, he crept from shadow to shadow until at last, he arrived at the Dimroad's end.

The warm, amber glow of sunset greeted the Etom as he stood outside the Dimroad's gloom, the light enhancing the orange hue of his skin such that he appeared to be ablaze. He looked out over the plains that spread beneath him, their open immensity flat and indistinct but for the great walled structure of Terábnis standing in the distance.

They wouldn't be...? he questioned of himself.

No! he disputed, dismissing the thought. *No Etom would be fool enough to venture* there *unless at great need.*

In that instant, Frenlee sensed as though a voice reminding him of the desperate lengths he'd gone to because of his own great and current need. Squinting toward the city of Men, he reconsidered, reflecting in the muted rainbow of desert sky as the sun set. A small streak of flashing orange fire arced low around Terábnis, then disappeared in the shadows of the city's eastward walls.

Could that have been them? he inquired again.

He surveyed the vast landscape before him and concluded, *And where else might they be headed? There's nothing else out here.*

Stepping to the edge of the precipice he stood atop, he looked down the sheer descent at his feet, its numerous switchbacks a grudging concession of the mountain to make the impossible merely grueling.

Men had built the road for themselves and for their Beasts of burden, and right now, Frenlee was glad to be neither. He would require no such road for his descent. His decision made, he started straight down the face of the rocky slope, his feet and hands a flurry to control his slide down the mountain.

He made good time before night had fallen in full as it was his concern to put some distance between himself and the darkening maw of the Dimroad overhead. When at last he allowed himself to rest, he was confident that the dangers he might face while he slept would not be from the Nihúkolem he'd left behind. He mounded a pillow of fallen straw, wrapped himself in his cloak, and fell asleep under the starlit sky.

Chapter Nineteen
Body and Blood

The day was in full swing following a splendid breakfast of rhema and springwater from the Tree of Terábnis. From his larder and at the behest of his wife, Makrïos had also produced a carved wooden platter loaded with sliced pear, whole strawberries, and mounds of almonds. There would be no blend o' the track for the adventurers today.

The bower's springtime warmth gave comfort against the wintery chill that encroached upon the desert land. Several other Kinfolk besides Rae, Nat, and Sayah had also opted to sleep under the Tree, including Kabbet, who as a new member of the Vine, had awoken inside a melon-like enclosure where he lay upon the ground.

Kabbet broke free of his chrysalis, and afterward the Kinship had gathered in pleasant fellowship to break rhema together. With unbelievable politeness, the two Menfolk present had restrained themselves, waiting until the smaller creatures had served themselves before they polished off the platter of food.

Nat had noted Killam's absence from breakfast and now sought the elder etém out. Nat was eager to tell Killam what he'd learned the night before, but the etém was nowhere to be found, at least nowhere near the Tree.

Nat recruited Rae and Sayah to help him look, and soon their search party had set out in all directions.

A short while later, Rae cried out, "Nat! Sayah! I've found him!"

Her voice came from near the gate that the night before they'd passed under, or in the case of Sayah, through. Nat came jogging up to Rae, who stood a few paces behind Killam. The ashy-grey Etom slouched with drooping shoulders at the gap Sayah had busted open in the corner slat.

Unwilling to risk exposure in flight, Sayah in his goofy ægle way waddled up alongside the other two.

"What are we doing?" Sayah whispered after a good many uneventful seconds had passed.

"I don't know," Rae whispered back, "Nat's the one who wanted to find Killam."

Killam raised his head to look back at them, his eyes sad, though a weak smile crinkled his lips.

"You've got some good friends there, Nat," Killam pronounced.

He gazed a moment at his feet, then through the gap in the gate, and continued, "I used to have friends like that. Well, one, in particular."

Killam turned to face Nat, his features still wistful, and added, "Your father, Jaarl. He was like a brother to me. Better, even. Now I doubt I'll ever see him again."

The hopelessness of Killam's statement pricked at Nat, emboldening the youth to challenge it.

His eyes blazing with resolute fire, Nat declared, "I don't believe that. The Spirit brought us here to find you – to find out my father may yet live! And we're not giving up until we know his fate!"

Killam flinched as though struck. An errant spark of Nat's fire drifted to catch in the remnants of hope in Killam's heart. The flinty etém gathered himself, straightened and apologized.

"I'm sorry, Nat," he said with a remorseful frown. "I shouldn't write your father off. I was left for dead in that reeking hole, yet here I stand.

"Of the two of us, he was ever the stronger. If there's any chance he might still be alive, I would like to help you find him. What say you? Will you let me help?"

Quiet tears of gratitude graced Nat's cheeks as he responded, "I would gladly accept your help, Killam. However..."

"Yes? What is it?"

"However, we answer first to Lord Elyon," Nat disclosed with some anguish. "We are not at liberty to do as we please. We must consult with His will and not act out of presumption."

"Surely, Lord Elyon would have you find your father?" Killam replied with incredulity.

"The part we play is His to dictate," Nat replied. "As Author of all existence, He composes our fates as well. And, I, for one desire an ending that makes the most of Him."

Killam shook his head in awful disbelief, unable to muster a response. The law among the Eben'kayah was clear – one should honor father and mother. Nevertheless, Killam knew the highest law also commanded a love of Elyon that surpassed all others, an impossible feat, but one these children seemed to have accomplished.

But how to love One you've never seen, let alone know *Him?*

"I wish that you knew Him," Nat uttered in a low voice that shook Killam once again.

It's as though he sees my heart, Killam speculated with mild terror.

Rae stepped forth to place a gentle hand over his breast, and whispered, "*We* don't see it, silly."

"No matter how sharp our eyes might be," Sayah concluded with a gentle nod.

Killam's knees buckled, and Nat dove to assist Rae in catching the elder's sagging form as he collapsed.

"What *are* you three?" he moaned through tears.

"Merely vessels for the Master's use," Nat stated, matter-of-fact as he shouldered one of Killam's arms.

From the other side, Rae joked, "We hope for His *honorable* use."

Killam snickered while they set him upon a rounded stone, but Sayah did not comprehend the joke.

"What is it?" he squawked in telling ignorance of a vessel's various uses in an Etom home.

Decanter, pitcher, dish pot, chamber pot – the use mattered, but neither of the Etom could manage an explanation without breaking down into fits of embarrassed giggling. At last, the ægle resigned himself just to join in the infectious laughter and didn't think the worse of his friends for it. When they had collected themselves, Nat remembered what he'd wanted to tell Killam the night before.

"Killam, I know you were curious about the prophecies of the Eben'kayah that foretold deliverance from our oppressors. Well, I want you consider that we three and any other Kinfolk already have our deliverance."

Killam gave him a confused look and asked, "The Empire of Chōl still holds dominion over the entire world. How are you any different? Are you no longer subject to the Empire?"

"Our King rules a land no earthly empire can touch," Rae answered, placing a hand on Killam's chest.

"Wha – what do you mean?"

"The heart," Sayah interjected. "The Kinsman Gaal rules the kingdom of the heart."

Nat picked up the ægles' thread, "And in our hearts lie the treasures of His kingdom, and a hope that never dies, no matter the circumstance."

"How else could we know what your heart spoke?" Rae inquired.

Nat proclaimed, "Even now, His kingdom has arrived among us! And we welcome His rule and reign in our lives!

"Indeed, many righteous and prophets of the Eben'kayah longed to see what we have seen and hear what we have heard, but they did not live to see this day. So, today, do not harden your heart in rebellion. For your creaturely heart is a wilderness, fallow and full of stony places, and this is the day of your testing.

"By the Spirit, we have cast the seed. Do not allow it now to be snatched away, neither deceive yourself and receive it superficially or become distracted by the worries of this life. No, we three beseech the Creator now to make the soil of your heart soft, rich, and receptive to our words, so that they may bear much fruit in you."

"But I was left for dead!" Killam returned, "Left in the hands of that brute, Scarsburrow."

"Surely, you don't believe that any of that was by chance," Nat replied, "when I was the one that Elyon used to free all the Etom imprisoned at his clinic? All but one, that is – a funny, older fellow."

Killam gaped, amazed at how the Creator had orchestrated events, using mere children to liberate Scarsburrow's victims, his friend...himself. Nat took Killam's silence as opportunity to continue.

"Killam! You stand now at the precipice of a decision that will change the course of your life. What say you now? Will you be free of the Stain and live as an etém free from the bondage of the Empire of Chōl? What say you?!?"

Killam shook his head with a soft chuckle and replied, "You remind me so much of your father, right down to the preaching. And you make a compelling case.

"How could I resist such an invitation? After seeing Elyon's provision and how he used you to save me from captivity? Take me there now. I wish to be loosed of this burden!"

Killam stood and raised his lank hand, fettered and blackened by the Stain. He no longer needed assistance as they marched toward the Tree, where they welcomed their friend into the Vine as a brother. Beneath the flow of the Tree's springs, Killam was restored and brought into new life. No longer a slave, he arose, unshackled from the Stain that had withered the strength of his hand and the strength of his soul. Bright face shining, he looked forward into days full of hope, as he once had in his youth, though this hope would not be shaken.

Following Killam's induction into the Kinship, the three Etom and Sayah spent the rest of the day waiting on Elyon to direct their next step. Foremost in their minds, Nat's in particular, was the prospect of finding Jaarl, and they prayed the Spirit might release and enable them to do so.

The three remained in prayer well into the evening, taking the most modest of breaks to refresh and relieve their bodies. During one such intermission, Makrïos had learned what they sought of Lord Elyon, and joined them in their prayers, recruiting many other Kinfolk besides.

The sincere involvement of the Kin of Terábnis touched the three youngsters from Endego, and together, they pleaded with greater fervency for the Spirit's will and the power to obey Him.

The sun had set in full and Sayah, Rae and Nat remained at water's edge before the Tree, their heads bowed as they inquired of the Creator. A gentle hand fell on Nat's shoulder and squeezed for his attention. Releasing his anxieties to the Kinsman, Nat exhaled and arose to face Killam, who had come to summon him to supper on Makrïos' behalf.

"Come," Killam beckoned, "Makrïos says he has something special to share with us upstairs. Sayah and Rae, too."

Grateful for a moment's respite, Nat gathered his friends and for the first time they entered the house of a Man. Through the door beneath the pergola was a room with a small, rough table and four worn seats for dining.

The dining space opened into a kitchen, where on a counter covered with a rough cloth rested several steaming loaves of bread. Fighting the distraction of the delectable smell, the four creatures looked ahead to their destination.

"There," Killam pronounced, pointing to the staircase that lay before them.

The glow of many lamps shone through the doorway at the top of the stair, inviting them onward. Nevertheless, the prospect of the stairs was daunting to the Etom, and at first the wondered how they might ascend them.

"Oh! Hello there," a young voice called from behind.

They turned to find Kabbet, the fellow they'd seen baptized the night before, now standing behind them.

"I don't suppose you need a lift?" Kabbet asked, crouching low with hand extended.

Rae replied, "If you don't mind, we'd very much appreciate it."

"Of course, I don't mind!" Kabbet declared and brought his hand nearby.

The Etom stepped on and Kabbet lifted them to chest level, then inquired of the ægle, "Will you be alright on your own, then?"

Sayah nodded, and to demonstrate, hopped up onto the first stair without delay. Kabbet chuckled and followed Sayah up the stairs.

They entered the upper room to discover Makrïos and a number of Men on cushions around a low table with a squared horseshoe or 'U' shape. On the table itself were many Etom, who took their places opposite and between the settings for the Men.

As host, Makrïos was seated to the left, but arose to welcome Kabbet and the others.

"Ah! There you are! We didn't want to start without you. Why don't you take a place here with me?"

Makrïos gestured to a cushion at his side for Kabbet and pointed out three settings on the table for the Etom next to Kabbet's place.

He motioned Sayah to a stool at the end of the table adjacent Kabbet, and apologized, "I am sorry, my ægle friend, we have never set a place for your kind before. I hope you will be comfortable here."

"I am honored that you considered me, Makrïos," Sayah replied as he hopped onto the stool. "This will do quite well."

On Makrïos' other side sat a quiet Man, who in place of his table setting had laid a sheet of parchment and a small brass inkwell beside it. Sitting altogether still, he held a quill out over the parchment, lost in apparent thought.

"Makrïos?" Rae inquired. "Who is that next to you?"

"My goodness!" Makrïos replied. "I can't believe I haven't introduced you. This here is Dowid, our resident scribe."

At the sound of his name, Dowid stirred, and offered in a quiet, confident voice, "Hello, there. I am Dowid, a disciple of the Kinsman Gaal. Makrïos and I were with Gaal since the beginning of His ministry, along with a few others.

"After the Kinsman left us, the Spirit impressed upon me the importance of recording His words and deeds so that others, too, may know Him."

"Like the law and prophecies of the Eben'kayah?" Nat asked.

"Precisely, yes," Dowid answered. "Among our people, the Eben'kayah, we maintained the Word of Lord Elyon so that we would recognize the Kinsman when He came. And now that He has gone, we must do the same so that we and many others may know Him still."

"I hate to interrupt, my friends, but it is time for the meal to be served," Makrïos interjected. "Are you quite ready to eat?"

All those nearby gave their hearty assent in reply.

"Splendid!" Makrïos exclaimed and clapped his hands, rubbing them together with savor. "Let us begin."

The marvelous aroma wafting from the bread downstairs had whet their appetites, but when Nat, Rae, Sayah, and Killam looked around the table, they saw no refreshment but a few pitchers of water and some dishes of rhema.

Makrïos followed their gazes and promised, "Do not worry. We will eat soon enough, but first I wish to share the words Gaal spoke at His final meal with us, His disciples."

The three travelers looked around the table once more in surprise that these Men had lived alongside the Kinsman. Makrïos did not delay in offering a dish of rhema to his guests.

"Please, take one, and wait a moment for me to bless the meal."

They each took a wafer of the bread and Makrïos passed his dish to those nearby, so others gathered may do the same.

Afterward, Makrïos held one of the wafers between thumb and forefinger as he recounted, "The night before the Empire took Gaal to execute Him, we met in this very place for what would be His final supper.

"Taking the bread, Gaal gave thanks and broke it, saying, 'This my body, given for you. Take and eat in remembrance of me.' And, so, we take and eat of the bread in remembrance of His body, broken as a gift to us all."

Sayah and Nat flinched as those gathered around the table broke the bread, each crackling snap a reminder of the blows the Kinsman received the night of His demise. They wept in silence, and Nat chanced a glance across the table at one who had delivered many of those blows to find none wept with greater bitterness than Makrïos.

Indeed, not an eye remained dry at the table. For though most had not been present for Gaal's abuse, report of it had spread far and wide, even at the behest of the Nihúkolem, who had been keen to make an example of Gaal. The Spirit now resonated in the deepest hearts of the Kinfolk who heard the account afresh, bringing to life the truth of the gift that Gaal had given to the world.

After they had eaten, Makrïos lifted the pitcher that stood at hand, prompting the others at the table to do the same.

In the other hand, he took a cup and through his tears, pronounced, "In that moment, Gaal also gave thanks and offered us His cup saying,

'This cup is the new covenant of my blood, poured out to abolish the Stain of many. Drink, all of you.'"

From the pitcher, Makrïos poured water so pure it could have no other source than the spring of the Tree and the slender stream sparkled on the way down. Halfway down the twisting trickle, the water became as wine, blood-red when it fell into the cup.

Afterward, Makrïos turned to fill the wooden thimbles set as makeshift cups before his smaller guests as all around the table, the others received their draughts.

Soon, all sat with wine before them when Makrïos signaled them to partake, "And so, we drink now in covenant of the Kinsman's blood, shed for us."

Each one raised the cup to drink, but Nat paused, awestruck as he recalled his vision of the chalice Gaal revealed within the depths of His being. He had drunk of this cup before! Memory of sorrow and offense set the Etom shaking, but he closed his eyes and once more raised the draught to trembling lips. Would he again be overwhelmed?

Instead of filth and grief, Nat tasted instead wine, sweet and warm, then a joy and innocence that suffused his limbs. An artless smile spread across his face, and he opened his eyes to discover his expression reflected on dozens of beaming faces.

Sadness no longer shaped any countenance, nor did tears darken any eye. And from some corner of the table, laughter erupted.

It was infectious.

Before long, every last one present giggled or guffawed in celebration of the freedom that Gaal had purchased for them. And none could think of a joy more unshakable and enduring than that which strengthened them now. They feasted on mirth and made merry with fellowship a long while before their appetites provoked them to consume anything else.

Without notice and a spry as a youth, Makrïos darted for the stairs with Kabbet at his heels, returning within moments with loaves of bread and seasoned oil for dipping. It was uncommon for the host to serve at his own meal, but Makrïos did just that, returning several times with different dishes: cheeses, fruits and vegetables and lentil stew with more fresh bread.

Nat cautioned himself to pace his consumption, and took note of Rae and Sayah, who bore no longer the strain of the day's entreaties. They were at rest, and he sensed the same ease within as the Spirit brought a psalm of the Eben'kayah to mind.

Those who sow in tears will reap with joy.

The Comforter's words served to shore up Nat's peace of heart, and he allowed himself to relent at last from all worry over his father's fate. If his father were alive, Lord Elyon had sustained him thus far, and would continue to do so if it so pleased Him.

In the warmth of their communion, the revelers continued their revelry well into the night. Many stayed the night in that place, whether stretched across the floor of some corner of the home or reclining beneath the boughs of the Tree outside. And within each one's heart, they held a deeper sense of home when together than they ever did apart.

Once again, Frenlee might have been disappointed to know how he had fared this day by comparison to those he pursued. The cold wind that swirled across the mountain's face woke him earlier than he would have liked. His dreams had been fearsome, full of difficulty and peril throughout. That is, until he'd reached the end, when the most comforting presence he'd ever felt had bid him nigh.

And right at the rewarding finale of the arduous dreamscape he'd traversed, a biting blast had torn away the comforting veil of sleep. Growling in protest, Frenlee stretched and blinked his weary, care-lined eyes against the whipping wind. His stomach growled a pained reply, but though Frenlee cast his gaze about, no such fare as he encountered the day before was present this morning.

With no food forthcoming, Frenlee continued at once with his downward climb, determined to spend the last of his remaining strength finding the three he'd followed thus far. He held out hope that he might encounter a morsel on his descent, and so kept his eyes open for anything he might forage.

He was well down the mountain when he spied a flash of red beneath an outcropping below. Aiming for a better look, he skittered across the slope, scrambling until he could confirm his hopes.

Success! The bit of red Frenlee had spotted were the bright berries of a rowan shrub. The berries weren't known for their delicious flavor, but one of the tart, bitter orbs could sustain an Etom, so long as he didn't overindulge.

Frenlee dropped down beside the shrub and plucked one of the berries, setting it in his hood for safe keeping, then grabbed another for immediate consumption. He took several minutes, taking small bites and chewing the berry with care so as to give his empty stomach time to adapt to the acidic fruit.

He knew he would be sick if he wasn't careful, but that the nourishment the berry provided was too rare a commodity to pass up in the wilderness. Little by little, he ate until he'd eaten over half the berry. His belly rumbled in warning, this time to tell him he'd had enough.

Frenlee took the warning to heart and tossed the rest of the berry away. He felt somewhat strengthened as he checked that the berry in his hood remained secure, then set out down the mountain once more.

Due to the directness of his path down, Frenlee made very quick progress despite his small stature and stood at the bottom well before sunset, looking out over the broad plains toward Terábnis. Before setting out across the expanse for the city, Frenlee ate the other berry, this time finishing it.

The Etom was aware any number of predators would make short work of him if he wasn't careful, so he darted from cover to cover as he made for Terábnis. Meager clumps of dry grass and leafless, scraggly shrubs were allies along his route, poor friends who extended only empty limb and frond in aid, but Frenlee was grateful for them nonetheless.

Compared to the mountainside, the weather was warmer down here on the plains, and drier, too. Frenlee mulled over the change in climate and the likelihood that he might encounter unfamiliar dangers in a place so strange to him. He wondered now if even snakes might still be active so late in autumn.

Despite the relative warmth, Frenlee shivered at the thought. He hated snakes. His eyes flitted back and forth with sudden anxiety, but it was his ears that cautioned him of danger. The alien cry of some unknown creature, perhaps a bird, trilled over the expanse and finished with a dry click.

The sound was unlike anything Frenlee had heard before, but something in its nature struck him as false. The call was too rich and throaty for a bird, and the Etom saw no such creature in the sky. Another such cry arose nearby, just out of sight – trill trill trill and click.

Frenlee didn't wait to hear the next signal but bolted away at once. He crossed a small clearing with a thick screen of tall, yellowed grass covering his passage from one side. Ahead, another such screen barred his way.

Panic gripped Frenlee for a moment until he spied an opening between the bunched stalks, a tight and cozy lane that might just accommodate an Etom. Yet again the call arose, this time closer than before. Frenlee ran for all he was worth, certain some fell beast stalked him.

Sprinting at full speed, he dashed into the gap, which ran straight as beam as far ahead as Frenlee could see. The Etom knew he was still in danger but considered himself safer here than he'd been in the open. At the thought, relief fell over the Etom – an instant before the net did. Writhing to escape his entanglement, Frenlee felt himself rising from the ground and sought some sense of what had happened.

Before the Etom, a large pair of gleaming eyes appraised him with curiosity. The Man, a member of the Hadza, looked the Etom over, muttering in contemplation. Frenlee gaped in horror. He'd heard the tales as a child. He'd had the nightmares as he'd grown. Now the reality of Man confronted him.

Another of the Men called for Frenlee's captor, who produced a wicker cage and without ceremony dumped the Etom into it. The Man hooked the cage to the end of a pole and slung it over his shoulder to carry the apparatus. The Man hailed his partner in the hunt and set out to join him on the road to Terábnis.

Frenlee, meanwhile, dangled within the jouncing confines of his cage as in shocked dismay he contemplated his sudden enslavement. He despaired that he had not caught up with those he pursued. All hope for himself and for his people failed him and, in his helplessness, he cried out to his Creator for help.

Chapter Twenty

Bound for Home

Nat, Rae and Sayah awoke to a loud thrumming that at first disoriented them. It took them a moment to recognize what caused the disturbance, and soon identified the Tree as the source. The Tree shook with incredible frequency, sending regular ripples through the pool at the base of the trunk.

At the edge of the water, a sheet of mist arose to circumscribe the pool in a luminous arc and cast a rainbow across the courtyard. The three travelers were quick to investigate, as was Killam, who soon stood alongside the others in curious confusion. The Spirit made no idle manifestation, so what did it mean?

The strange phenomenon subsided a few moments after the four of them had gathered at the shore, though it was no clearer what purpose it had served. The nearby door into the house banged open and Makrïos issued forth, his expression intent as he swept his gaze across the courtyard. The Man's eyes settled on the quartet and he directed his steps their way.

"Just the four I wanted to speak with!" he bellowed as he strode up to them. "I've had a dream that I believe the Spirit sent to me on your behalf. But, please, test my words for yourself to see if they indeed are from Him.

"In my dream, you four departed for Endego this morning with all haste. In my consideration, the Spirit is counseling urgency, and desires you set out at once to locate Nat's father."

Nat just gaped at Makrïos, too skeptical of his own motives to trust the Man's words. Rae and Sayah cheered while Killam nodded, his flinty face determined as he considered the challenges of their quest.

"I know you doubt my words, young one," Makrïos consoled Nat, "but as I said, test my words by the Spirit. If they are true, the Spirit should confirm my counsel to each of you."

"Alright, then," Nat concurred, then addressed the others. "I know we often pray as a group, but in this instance, I think we should take some time alone and come back together after we have the Spirit's answer. I don't trust myself in this matter, so it's very important to me that you three help me stay honest."

"Of course," Sayah complied.

"You're the most honest Etom I know, Nat," Rae replied, "but I understand why you want to do it this way."

She leaned in to whisper, "I can't imagine how you feel, but I'm praying for you, too, and not just for an answer."

Killam gripped Nat's shoulder before taking his leave to pray, and offered some encouragement, "I'm sure your father will be proud of you, whatever your decision. You're an upstanding young etém."

Nat alone knelt at a distance from the Tree while the other three opted to enter the water. The sky blue etém bowed his head for but a moment before a ruckus near the Tree drew his attention.

Screams, shouts, and squawks of surprise resounded in the bower as a concurrent wave lifted Rae, Killam, and Sayah out of the pool to deposit them on the shore. Rae stood to dangle a toe over the water, which arose to challenge her entry.

Mystified, Nat wondered what was happening until the Spirit spoke to each of their hearts.

Have I not commanded you? Be now strong and very courageous. Do not be fearful, neither be dismayed, for I am with you wherever you will go.

From his chuckle, Nat surmised that Makrïos had likewise received the message. The Man stood otherwise silent with arms folded and a self-assured smile on his face.

He winked and clicked his tongue before chiming in, "Well, I've never seen it done quite like that before, but He *is* the Creator. We might expect Him to be creative."

A sopping Rae sloshed up to Nat with an equally soaked ægle and etém in tow.

Shaking great drops from her hands, she inquired in a sweet falsetto that belied her irritation, "Well, then...was that confirmation enough for you, Nat?"

Nat's face wrinkled in a suppressed smirk as he nodded in affirmation. Words would only betray the snicker he held back by force of will alone.

Rae rolled her eyes and slapped his arm with a wet sleeve.

"Silly etém," she muttered, then shouted up to Makrïos. "Hello up there! Would you happen to have any towels handy? We're likely to catch cold if we try to fly like this."

Makrïos smiled and held up a finger before heading into the house. He returned at once with three towels large enough to dry human hands. They were more than sufficient for the two Etom, but Sayah declined.

While the Etom began to towel off, the ægle took a few steps away to puff and then shake his feathers from beak to tail. The maneuver flung droplets from his water-resistant feathers, rendering him altogether dry in seconds.

Once everyone else had dried off and Nat and Rae had strapped on their packs, they prepared to take off. The added weight and bulk of another rider atop Sayah was something they hadn't considered until the moment arrived. Sayah was confident he could carry everyone but let them all on board up to reassure them with a trial run. Sandwiched between the two younger Etom, Killam's eyes were wide with fright and his fists clenched Sayah's feathers with a grim ferocity.

Sayah knew he'd have to keep his flight beneath the height of the courtyard wall to stay out of sight. He anticipated more of a fluttering hop across the courtyard than a true flight, but the exercise would allow him to gauge his abilities under the burden of an additional passenger.

"Ready!?!" the ægle called back to the others.

"Ready!!!" Nat and Rae barked with confidence.

"R-R-Ready!" Killam stammered with a considerable amount less.

From the far end of the courtyard, Sayah pointed himself at the gate, crouching low and level in readiness to launch. He raised his wings, paused, then sprang into action. The extra weight was noticeable, but manageable. He compensated with a flurry of wingbeats, gaining altitude until he reached his apex just beneath the level of the wall.

Once aloft, Sayah for the most part was able to glide but for a miniscule flap of the wing here or there to adjust trajectory. He fluttered to a stop near the gate, touching down with ginger care out of consideration for his first-time flier.

With practiced poise, Nat and Rae slid off Sayah's back, but Killam stayed atop him, frozen.

Sayah craned his neck to check on the Etom, "Killam, are you alright? We've stopped now. We're on the ground."

Killam shook his worried head, exhaled a shaky breath, and then smiled.

"That. was. AMAZING!" he shouted.

Killam shifted and dropped from Sayah's back with much less care and agility than the youngsters, then darted in front of the ægle.

With eyes full of wonder, he looked up at Sayah, shaking his head again as he exclaimed, "I never thought I'd live to see the day I'd ride an ÆGLE! Thank you, Sayah! Thank you!"

Nat and Rae smirked with pleasure at Killam's reaction. They'd been a tad anxious at his initial catatonic response but were happy to see hc had in the end enjoyed the experience. Given the length of their journey back to Endego, it was the best possible outcome.

Makrïos approached them near the gate, a small bundle of cloth in his hand. He bent down on one knee and opened the bundle before them. In it lay five pieces of rhema – one for each of them.

"I know you didn't get breakfast this morning, what with all the ruckus," the Man offered, "and I wanted one last opportunity to break bread with you before you left. After all, we've no assurance we'll see one another again."

They each took a piece of the rhema, and Makrïos blessed the meal. By comparison to the somber and weighty atmosphere at supper the night before, the mood was light. Nonetheless, even this most basic act of fellowship among the Kin hearkened back to the joy they had shared.

Reflecting on the experience, Nat inquired of the Man, "I was wondering if we should serve a supper in Endego like the one last night. What do you think?"

Makrïos gave the question some thought before responding, and when at last he did, it was with deep seriousness.

"I think all Kinfolk should partake of the Kinsman in this manner. Indeed, He commanded it. However, some have partaken without sufficient care, without regard for the sacrifice of the Kinsman or for the dignity of those He purchased with His body and blood.

"It's a weighty matter, and one we've discussed at length. The Spirit granted insight to one of our number, Pávlos, and we've abided by the recommendations he received.

"Whenever we eat of the bread and drink of the cup, it demonstrates the Kinsman's death and the manner in which He died. You told me once that you were witness to His death, and I was party to it, so we both know well the gravity of it.

"For this reason, we have a responsibility to convey how meaningful His death is, and challenge everyone who wishes to partake to do so with a serious mind. For whoever eats and drinks in an unworthy manner will be guilty regarding the body and blood of Gaal. As one who was once guilty on both counts, I understand the weight of the matter.

"The supper is a time for reflection, when each one of us should examine ourselves for any remnant of the Stain's influence in our life. It is a chance for the Spirit to show us the error of our ways, so we may turn and be washed clean.

"If anyone is flippant in consuming the bread and the cup, it is to their own judgment, for they have failed to recognize Gaal's body as broken and his blood shed on their behalf. It grieves me to say, but some have fallen ill, and one has even died after partaking without reverence.

"That is why you must take care, little brother, if you intend to serve our Kin in Endego thus. It is a ministry most sacred and comes with the warnings I have given.

"Now! As much as it pains me to say, I think I've delayed you quite long enough. You've still a great journey ahead of you, and the sun is rising in the sky."

With sincere tears, they said farewell, and the Etom once more sat astride Sayah in preparation to leave. Makrïos told them it was safe to leave the city without concealment, so long as they didn't linger. Birds of all kinds often came and went, just none carrying passengers.

A direct and speedy departure was the best course of action, so Sayah once more stood ready at one end of the courtyard. This time, he launched with the intent to clear the wall and continue on their way back home.

Like a flash of light, he burst over the wall, climbing high and swift to exceed the reach of any slings and arrows that might come their way. Before long, they soared over the great walls of Terábnis and into open sky once more.

Before they left, Killam had counseled them against a return journey on the Dimroad. Instead, he suggested they fly west until Endego was due south from their position, and then make a beeline for home. The others agreed without objection, and soon they were heading west, the ascending sun at their backs.

No winged creature had stirred Nimrod's interest in a good while, but from the forest west of Terábnis, the Fowler spied something quite remarkable at last. From over the city a shining arc etched the sky, a bird of snowy plumage like a dove, but too large and with the form of an ægle.

Nimrod had never seen the creature's equal, and within his heart bloomed the wild hope that this ægle bore the talismanic power he sought. Alas, the ægle flew too high for the Fowler's arrows, and he could only raise a hand in futility and follow the progress of his prey with eyes askew but unflinching.

The feaTHER...THE FEAther! I muST HAve THat oNe! tHEre IT is! THerE iT flIES! I MUST have THAT PRIZE!!!

The constant chanting of his otherwise empty mind quickened with excitement over the ægle overhead. Nimrod twisted about and lurched for his bow. He returned his eyes to the sky at once to track his quarry, and for the first time since insanity gripped him, the Fowler left his haunt to pursue the pure white ægle.

Chapter Twenty-One
On Wings Into the West

For Sayah and his passengers, flight was refreshing after time spent confined to Makrïos' home, no matter how gracious their host had been. The adventure had borne various fruit already, not the least of which was the discovery that Nat's father, Jaarl, may yet live.

The winter sky was clear, bright, and cold and provoked Nat to reflect. He hadn't thought of it before, but the course Killam proposed would take them past the Kinsman's Tree, that very Tree on which Gaal had died.

To proceed without stopping at Sanctuary just seemed somehow wrong to Nat, and he promised himself he would bring it up to the others once they had stopped for the night. It might require a slight detour, but he guessed the others would feel the same nonetheless.

A village of Men lay west and a bit south of Terábnis. Killam had told Sayah to keep an eye out for it, since it stood as the landmark signaling their need to turn south. An hour or two past noon, the ægle spotted a cluster of low structures made of wood and stone and warned the others of his maneuver before banking southward.

At the edge of the village stood a tall, wooden watchtower, and in it a pair of lookouts facing either direction. The Man looking Sayah's way turned to nudge his partner, then pointed right at the ægle. Sayah lamented he'd flown close enough to be spotted. They didn't need that kind of attention. Without much sunlight left for the day's journey, the ægle intended to get well clear of the village before they made camp.

Carrying all three Etom was manageable, but the added weight wearied the young ægle and he was relieved they would soon stop for the night. Though thin for an adult etém, Killam was double the weight of the others, and had alone thus doubled Sayah's load. Sayah's struggle to endure his current burden brought to mind his family's flight to the Cold Vantage.

While a bitter memory, Sayah appreciated anew Father's strength and tenacity in carrying him there. The journey could not have been easy, and the driving headwind they had flown through must have presented particular challenges. Even now, Sayah saw afresh the love Mother and Father had expressed in leaving him so far afield, out of the Empire's reach.

Sayah set down before much longer, and Nat, Rae, and Killam worked to build the fire while he kept watch. They then settled in for some good ol' blend o' the track and a bite of cheese. After dining, Nat proposed they visit the Kinsman's Tree. Everyone was pleased at the thought of it, and Killam was excited at the chance to see Sanctuary for himself.

When they awoke in the morning, they found again the rhema Nat, Rae, and Sayah had come to expect while in the wild. Killam, however, stared at his flake with wide eyes, turning it over and back as if expecting it to reveal itself as a counterfeit else dissolve in a puff of dust. They decided it was best not to stop for a drink until they arrived at Sanctuary. Rae didn't know if Killam's mind could handle that particular miracle just yet.

Up to their afternoon arrival at the Kinsman's Tree, the day was otherwise uneventful. Of course, Sayah was first to spy the Tree, or rather the aerie atop it that had once been his home. His time as an æglet there had not been pleasant, but the wistfulness he once felt for it was now gone. The transformation the Spirit had accomplished was from the inside out, and the wounds inflicted there He had altogether healed.

"Do you see it?" he cried to the others.

Taller and greener than its neighbors, the Kinsman's Tree stood out. Regardless Nat and Rae could naught but recognize it and Killam sensed the vibrant swell of the Spirit within him as they drew near.

Sayah circled to find a good place to drop into the clearing below, his wings a billowing, silken sail as he drifted to the ground with ease. As soon as they entered the bower, the verdant, springtime vitality of Sanctuary's essence filled their transfixed view. Regardless, the ægle caught movement from the corner of an eye, and, startled, he whipped his head around to confront a perceived threat. But what awaited him surprised him more than his initial shock.

"Sayah?" Mother asked, her voice tender toward him in a way he'd never known before.

Mother stepped over a gnarled root and approached her son with affection in her gaze. Sayah recoiled, almost pitching the riders from his back. Their startled shouts brought him back to the moment, and he ducked low to let the Etom disembark then returned his attention to Mother, who was a few paces distant now.

"Sayah?" she said again. "It *is* you, is it not?"

All at once, Sayah was an æglet again, longing for her approval, her love, and he shook himself to steel against the inevitable disappointment that ever greeted this particular desire. He had all the love he'd ever need in the Spirit and among his Kinfolk. But...but here love was...with feathers on.

"Mother! You're here!" he responded at last. "I mean you're *here* of all places."

Mother answered with a gentle smile, "Well, son, it *is* rather close to home. And how long did you intend to keep this secret?"

Her soft chiding was a playful caress that stunned Sayah more than the harshest rebuke.

"I...I didn't have the chance, you see. We were – we were separated, and I *wanted* to tell you and Father. I wanted to tell you more than *anything*, but I didn't...I didn't think you would..."

He trailed off, but she completed the thought, "You did not think we would listen. And, at the time, you were right. But much has happened since then."

Sayah intended to introduce his friends just then, but noticed Mother looking back in the direction whence she came. Her eyes lingered there with a meaning Sayah caught at last.

"Father? Is Father here, too?"

"Yes, son," she blocked Sayah's way with an upraised wing as he darted to pass her, "but you should know – he is not well."

He met her eyes with tearful concern and saw the care reflected there.

"Why? What has happened to him?" he cried, the long-dormant affection for his Father awakening.

"Let me take you to him," she coaxed. "Please."

Sayah nodded, and glancing back to his friends, pleaded, "May I have a moment?"

Nat and Rae had not seen their brother so forlorn since he was an æglet, malformed and rejected. Without hesitation, they assured him to take as much time as he might need, and in the meantime knelt in prayer for Sayah and his family.

Together, the ægles walked away, their tottering walk and synchronous swish of their receding tailfeathers a testimony to their familial likeness.

They were rounding the Tree's trunk when Mother stopped Sayah once more.

Her eyes now stony, but brittle as slate, Mother adjured him, "I need you to be strong, Sayah. Father is not well at all. He may not survive his injury."

She lowered her head in heaviness but did not allow herself to weep as she added, "In truth, it would be a miracle he did."

Sayah swallowed, determined to brave this trial with the strength Mother asked of him. He nodded for her to conduct him onward, and soon they approached a familiar stand of grass. This was the very patch Sayah had fallen into the day he'd met Nat. The day his life had changed. And, here, it would change once again.

They crept around the far side of the grass, and in its midst, Sayah saw at last Father – that fixture of stern stability who always stood within his memories, holding a distant standard aloft and ever out of Sayah's reach. But now, nestled in the grass, Father was diminished, his breast rising and falling in short, desperate breaths, and one wing dangling askew, black and bleeding on the ground.

Windspanne had known at once that Imafel had shattered his wing. He would never cross the sky again. But that had been his initial comprehension of his wound, and the seep of blood had caught his attention only after he and Stromweise had been in the strange bower a good while. He had been too busy tending to his near-strangled mate to notice otherwise, but a crimson streak across the grass alerted him of injury.

At first, he'd checked Stromweise over from beak to tail, so fixated on nursing her to health that he ignored the gritting pain that radiated from his splintered bones. Swooning fatigue made him see at last the blood-sopped feathers trailing from the end of his ruined limb.

Stromweise had regained much strength, so Windspanne thought it safe to tell her, "I fear I am destroyed, my huntress. My wing will never spread the same again. And...and...I bleed."

Stromweise had recoiled in horror when she saw the blood draining from her mate, but she regained composure at once, as every noble ægle ought. This would be no end for them, her hunter's soul contended, but they knew no medicine that might mend Windspanne's wing or even forestall his end.

Nourishment! Nourishment was what he needed, and she looked about for food. In the peaceful clearing, though, she found no prey for meat, and a clear and heavy foreboding hung overhead. In the apprehension, she perceived that just those acts that lent to life might be permitted there.

Nevertheless, need compelled her to seek *something* for her spouse's help. The oddest spring she'd ever seen flowed pure and bright from amidst the nearby Tree. The spreading pool it formed beneath its boughs offered a more appealing a draught than any, and thus she hurried to its edge.

Stromweise leaned low over the crystalline surface but hesitated at its mirror sheen. The ægle she saw there was haggard and hopeless, not at all worthy of the drink she sought.

But it is for another! she disputed, her heart shrieking at the empty wind.

But then the Wind spoke back.

If anyone is thirsty, come! Come and drink! There is no cost.

Stromweise froze in uncertainty, then decided to take a chance and trust the Voice she'd heard. Dipping her beak into the flow, she tasted the peerless waters, cool and delicious. But she did not swallow. No, she carried the sip to Windspanne, draining her shallow beak dry of every drop for him in a journey she repeated over and over and over again until a portion of his vigor returned.

To Windspanne, he'd tasted nothing so sweet, nor had he seen a form so beautiful as his huntress leaning over him in continual delivery of swallow after swallow of the elixir he disbelieved was water. Every drop he imbibed fortified him more than any meat he'd consumed and quickened him more than any blood he'd drunk.

Though his bleeding did not altogether stop, he soon arose to express his gratitude to Stromweise and to insist she drink some herself. His mate slaked her thirst, then began again her circuits on his behalf, this time to clean the wound.

One beakful at a time, Stromweise dripped water over Windspanne's matted, bloody wing. After a great deal of time, she succeeded in cleaning the wound of the dirt and grit clumped within the scabbing blood.

She proposed moving Windspanne to the water's edge to clean it there, but he refused. He felt to enter water so pure and sweet with an open wound would defile it, and so Stromweise continued her ministrations until exhausted. She knew her mate appreciated her efforts, and that his heart was devastated in his inability to contribute more in their situation.

Which reminded her – what *was* their situation? She took in their surroundings, surprised at the verdant trove that lay hidden beneath the very aerie they had occupied for so long. This place was abnormal in most every aspect.

And then there was that Tree, so like The strange Tree that had eliminated most their airwing during an attack on what should have been an easy target, a cluster of undefended Etom. And Sayah standing beside the wee creatures, shining bright as he and the others without fear observed the coming of their doom.

Windspanne dozed nearby, safe and content to rest for the time being. Stromweise crept to the edge of the pool, where the water lapped in mellow rhythm. She screwed up her eyes and cocked her head at the Tree, uncertain what it signified, but drawn nonetheless. And without end she might have remained thus, squinting at the inscrutable, but for the curious interruption of a spark, floating toward her in a most deliberate arc.

Stromweise had never witnessed such a thing and flinched back from it when it stopped just shy of her beak. With a jingle and a chime, the spark spun this way and that, casting multicolored light in all directions before settling on a vibrant pink that somehow excited the ægle's mind.

...t...ny...æ...les a...rou...here...ou...ldn't...y chan...know...yah?

Though broken, the speech of this...this *thing* in her mind regardless conveyed the sense that it was intelligent, and Stromweise marveled at the existence of such a creature. Even now, it bobbed and twirled without a sound as if...as if awaiting her reply.

Ægles weren't known for their social graces, but failure to respond to direct address was the height of disrespect. And *that* Stromweise would not abide.

She blinked, swallowed and made her best attempt to communicate, "I am most sorry. I don't quite understand."

With another tinkle and a flashing twinkle, its color shifted to a something a touch more purple, and Stromweise detected its words with perfect clarity.

Oh my! I hope this is better. Let me just say it again: There aren't many ægles around here. You wouldn't by chance know Sayah?

Stromweise was stunned. No! More than stunned! Not only had this sparking...whatever talked, but it seemed to know Sayah!

Her maternal instincts drive her to interrogate the strange creature, "What do you know about my son? And how come I can hear you talking *in my head*?!?"

Oh dear, I've upset you. I'm a friend of Say – your son. My name is Astéri Ha'vimminkhulud of the Malakím, a messenger of the Lord King Elyon.

Recalling Nat's confusion over his name at their initial introduction, he added, *You may call me Astéri. Yes, Astéri is just fine.*

Stromweise's eyes pinned at the revelation of this information. It was a lot to take in. The Creator was real, and not in some distant, unknowable way. No. One of his servants, a Malakím was shining before her, and *knew her son*. They sounded like the best of buddies, in fact.

"I am sorry," she blurted at last. "This is too much. You want to tell me you know Sayah? Well and good. I can accept that. But..."

She hesitated, scowling in frustration that she had to broach the topic of the supernatural, which up to this point, she hadn't believed existed.

Notwithstanding, she pressed on, her eyes boring into Astéri's dancing gleam, "But you want to tell me that you work for Lord Elyon, the Creator of all things? And where has He been all this time? While His creation falls into ruin? Eh?"

Ooooo, you're rather hostile, aren't you? No matter. But how do you explain me without Him? What am I if not what I told you? Eh?

"Fair point, *Astéri*. I might concede that you are a Malakím, but you haven't answered my other questions. What has His Lordship been up to while we all suffer and die in this world He created?"

Well...this, Astéri replied, waving a concentrated beam of light over the bower. *This is what He's been up to.*

Stromweise threw her wings wide over the clearing and spat, "And what is this, exactly? What good does it serve? How does *this* help anyone?"

*This...*Astéri began, then sighed with the sound of a wan and forlorn horn and faded to a sad and murky blue.

This is the Kinsman's Tree, and upon it, the Kinsman was slain. 'For Elyon so loved the world that He sent His Son, the only begotten One, so that whoever believes on Him shall not die, but rather receive life everlasting.'

Most know the tale as I assume you do, but you may not know that this was the Tree Ha Datovara, the very tree from which was plucked the fruit forbidden Mankind. This is where the Stain and downfall of Creation originated. This, too, is where the Son of Elyon died to free the world from the power of the Stain and the inevitability of death.

So, nailed to the crooked ruin of the Tree Ha Datovara, the Kinsman of Lord Elyon and of Mankind paid the price for all offense. Do you see how tall and straight the Tree now stands!

Astéri flared a brilliant orange that dulled to a pulsing, heated glow as of embers while Stromweise stood in dumbstruck silence.

Few know that in the original tongue, the Tree Ha Datovara means the Tree of the Knowledge of Good and Evil. How twisted in form that old and desolate tree became, to the death of all creatures.

For the perversion – root, trunk, limb and fruit – of the Tree of the Knowledge of Good and Evil manifested in the Stain, and none knew the true way of life anymore. And how could they, since to know Elyon is the way?!?

In His holiness, Lord Elyon could not abide the Stain, and destruction was the judgement of those who bore it. Rather than destroy His creation outright, however, He separated Himself from it in the Sunder.

In the same moment, and at great cost to Himself, Elyon promised a Redeemer – His own Son, the Kinsman. You ask what good the Kinsman's Tree serves, and I say it serves the Source of all good. You ask how the Tree helps anyone, and I say to you, that the Son did not die in vain, but died for your son! Your very own!

As the resurrected Kinsman transformed the wasteland that once stood here into the vibrant forest you now see, so too did He transform the wretched æglet who was your son into the singularly brilliant creature he became. I hope you'll agree that Sayah is much better for it.

Now, did I answer to your satisfaction? Or would you prefer a lengthier exposition? Believe me, friend ægle, there is more. Much *more.*

Stromweise shook her head. She did not, in fact, wish to hear more. Not right this second.

"No, thank you, Astéri," she replied, mollified for the time being. "I am sorry. This place is wonderful, and we are grateful for the safety it grants us."

She looked up through the foliage to the crown of the Tree, "It is difficult to believe this was right here under our beaks all this time.

"I hate to impose further, but is there any food here? My mate has suffered injury, and I fear he will not recover without nourishment."

Astéri blinked and flashed his reply as he turned an uncertain shade of peach, *Um, well, that is, we've had this problem before – with your son, no less – and we don't know that we have anything that will suit your kind.*

"Please, Astéri!" Stromweise implored, "We will take whatever you can give us. My mate must eat."

Alright, then. I will see what I can scare up, and don't be surprised when I come back with my friend. I can't actually carry anything to you, except maybe messages. I'm just a little ball of light and all.

Astéri sped out of sight beyond the trunk of the Tree, and Stromweise returned to tend to Windspanne. His slumber had deepened, and he even snored, a light, whistling through the nares on his beak.

Across the clearing, Stromweise detected movement, the tracing light of Astéri's approach accompanied by...by what to be exact? She had no category for what she saw, which is why, even with the prodigious vision of her kind, she could not describe it.

Alongside Astéri's glow glided what appeared to be a miniature tree. Its leafy crown shook as it bustled along, carrying a tall stack of irregular white wafers. Stromweise detected neither feet nor legs on the creature, but instead its meager trunk plowed through the rich, crumbling soil.

However the thing moved, it was all happening out of sight, beneath the earth. The creature wandered this way and that in a distracted manner, held to a general course by Astéri's continual reminders.

They weren't too far away when the creature hailed her with a voice that emanated from behind the stack the creature carried.

"Hello there! Astéri told me you were hungry, so I brought some foooooood!"

The voice was male, but young – very young, as evinced in his cavalier greeting and his energetic wandering about. Astéri shushed him out of consideration for the wounded ægle he knew rested, and the strange creature quieted as he ground to a halt nearby, chastened.

Astéri sounded a gentle flute to offer the white flakes to Stromweise, *This is called rhema. Despite its bland appearance, it is quite edifying. Please, eat.*

Astéri's companion set the stack of wafers down before her and stood to back away, revealing a pleasant, nut-brown face with liquid green eyes. He was fidgety to begin with, but exploded with activity as the food teetered, then began to topple. The youth bent at the middle and dove in to save the doomed tower, his leafy, branch-like hand catching one falling side.

The wafers flipped and rolled every which way, which set the creature off in a frenzy of even greater activity. He hustled to and fro, plucking the helter-skelter rhema from the forest floor until he'd reassembled the original stack. This time, however, he stood nearby with a hand atop it to prevent it from falling again.

With delicate care, he removed his hand. At once the tower started to lean, so he replaced his hand before repeating the process again. And again.

From behind him, Astéri dropped a dubious whistle.

At last, the creature grabbed the stack halfway down and set the smaller stack beside the first. These did not waver, so he backed away with slow, deliberate care to point at the stacks with open hands.

Distracted in the disarray, he had forgotten the sleeping ægle and announced in a loud voice, "May I present your rhema!"

Stromweise winced as Windspanne sniffed then shook his head, blinking his eyes before they landed on the newcomers his mate had befriended while he slept. He was unsettled at the presence of the strangers, so Stromweise did her best to calm him while Astéri made introductions.

Ummmm, hello there. My name is Astéri, and this is my friend, Yebul.

"HALLOOOOOO!!!" Yebul called, waving a branch-like arm in salutation.

We know we're not your typical woodland creatures, so please let me explain. I am a Malakím, a messenger of Lord Elyon. Yebul here is a Sprig, which is something like a tree, but, as you already know, a whole lot louder.

"Yup!" proclaimed Yebul, who hadn't quite gotten the hint. "I AM loud!"

The Sprig began to dash about, his trunk raking the clearing as he played, and his arms spread wide so that the breeze fluttered his leaves while he shouted.

"Whoosh! Whoosh! Woohoo!"

Please accept my apologies, Astéri pleaded, his glow alternating between an embarrassed blush and a contrite apricot.

He is, well, he is a bit Spriggier than most Sprigs I introduce to guests, due to his age. But no one else is around right now, so what choice did I have? Elyon knows I wish it otherwise.

He arose right before Windspanne's crossing eyes, prompting the uncomfortable ægle to balk.

I hope that you can take some food now. It's all we've got, but it should help you regain your strength.

Windspanne looked to his mate, and Stromweise nodded to assure him. When he still didn't move to take bite of the rhema, she elected to be first to try the strange food. She neared the two piles and lowered her open beak in awkward, breathy posture to collect a single flake.

With slow and delicate effort, she closed her beak around the wafer until she bit through it with a ginger crunch. The rhema had no aroma, so Stromweise didn't know what to expect, and her eyes brightened as a pleasant sweetness like honey met her tongue. It was no meat, but it was good.

"Come! Windspanne, come!" she demanded. "It is good, and you need your strength."

Windspanne stirred at last to drag his wounded wing to where the rhema lay. In an odd, precise parody of his mate, he collected a sample for himself and likewise bit down with care until he could taste the bread.

"Sweet!" he cried as his energy returned. "It *is* sweet, but not too much so."

He and Stromweise dug into the piles of rhema, and now Astéri had another reason to be happy that Yebul had separated the food into two stacks. The ægles were so ravenous, that otherwise they might have hurt one another competing for a share of the food.

Within a matter of seconds, the pair of ægles had demolished their portions and now scoured the earth for crumbs, each with a single great eye cocked over the ground. From time to time, one would find a speck and, in a flash, peck the spot to recover the morsel. For Astéri, the meal was frightening from start to finish.

Once the ægles had finished eating, Astéri invited them to stay in Sanctuary as long as they needed. The Malakím knew cleaning Windspanne's wound with the waters of the Tree would slow the creep of Stain and Blight, but unless drastic action was taken, he would succumb in the end. Regardless, this was the safest place in all the Empire for the pair of ægles to convalesce, and a steady diet of purest water and sweet rhema would do them a world of good.

The ægles passed the following twelve days in Sanctuary under the ministrations of Astéri and Yebul, who were ever servants to Windspanne and Stromweise. While she recognized that she'd find no place better for her mate to recuperate, Stromweise nevertheless concluded that Windspanne was slipping away. In his wounded state, he inched on toward an inexorable fate.

Regardless, the numerous mercies received over their almost two weeks in Sanctuary were a gentle downpour softening her heart. She and Windspanne did not deserve the blessings offered them, but they came nonetheless.

With each passing day, the experience caused her to question her outlook, in which the stronger ate the weaker and thrived. Yes, perhaps there was another way, a better way by which all might thrive, and she wondered if maybe this was the way that Sayah and his friends now followed.

Although comforted in the peaceable provision of Sanctuary and the growing comprehension of a higher order that sought the best for all, Stromweise notwithstanding experienced great sorrow at the looming loss of Windspanne. She saw no hope for his future, just the dark and weeping Stain that crept out beneath bloodstained feathers.

The arrival of Sayah and his friends had interrupted Stromweise's deepening cycle of despair over her ailing spouse. She was likewise grateful to see her son again. The last time they'd been eye to eye was at the Cold Vantage, and that had been a bitter parting for them both. Today, for them, was sweeter.

Doubtless, however, the sweetness of their reunion comingled with the acrid sting of mortality when Sayah saw Father. Sayah blinked hard and looked away, fighting back tears. This could not be Father! Yet it was.

"Sayah," Father sighed, "Look at you now."

He paused for a heavy breath and continued, "Fledged in full like no ægle I have ever seen. Amazing."

Now it was Father's turn to look away, but he didn't fight the uncharacteristic tears that slid from his eyes. Sayah just stared. He'd *never* seen Father weep.

"I was wrong about you," Father lamented, his voice weak and trembling. "I was wrong."

Sayah went to him then, gracious and full of forgiveness, and beckoned Mother join them as he at last told the tale he'd longed to tell his family most of all. From start to finish, he recounted his plunge into

Sanctuary, the vision of the Kinsman, and his part in rescuing the Etom from Sakkan.

Mother and Father listened, transfixed, and did not interrupt. They were amazed to discover the secret life and adventures of the son they had all but written off, and it stung them to hear their part in the tale, though Sayah made no accusation against them. The charges were clear, and the pair stood convicted for the coldness of their love.

Nevertheless, to hear Sayah tell it, his abandonment at the Cold Vantage had become his greatest blessing. Without the need his solitude there precipitated, he may not have grown in his dependency on the Spirit. He had fought the despondency that plagued him since birth and achieved victory by the power of the Spirit.

The trusting bond that the Spirit had developed in Sayah through the trial on that cold and lonely precipice is what had enabled the then-æglet to answer the Spirit's call to leap from the stony heights. And rise again on wings of glory, granted to him for his faithfulness in waiting on Lord Elyon. Indeed, his strength had exceeded renewal, and had overflowed as a testimony to the vultures in the North and to Gael in Endego.

Mother and Father exchanged glances at this part of the tale, certain they had misjudged their daughter as well. Her story had not been altogether false, despite her apparent lunacy. They cared for Gael still, but no longer held out hope for her now that they'd betrayed the Empire.

The most difficult moment in the conversation arrived for Sayah, and although he was hesitant to begin, he knew it would be of greatest benefit to his parents.

"By the Spirit of our Creator, I live now in wholeness. The Kinsman has cleansed me of the Stain and raised me up in new life despite my own deficiencies. For all bear the Stain, in nature and in deed, and fall short of Elyon's glory and of the glory He intends for us.

"But even in all this, He does not condemn any who would come to Him with the same expectation as I had: that He would wash me, that He would restore me, and that He would transform me by the power of His blood. And, so, I ask, would you come with me before the Tree?"

Stromweise's heart leapt with excitement at the invitation. How deep her longing for just this very thing had been, without her even knowing of it. Windspanne, on the other hand, was reluctant.

"Sayah, my son," he replied, "I am so very proud of who you have become, but I do not believe this 'Kinsman's Tree' is for me."

He swept an eye over his ruined limb and resumed, "Look at me! What hope have I in this Tree? Will I ever hunt again? What of my honor, forsaken in my betrayal of the Empire?

"As an invalid and one bereft of dignity, I do not deserve such deliverance. No, I will take the death that comes to me before I accept something I did not earn with my own two talons."

After a moment's consultation with the Spirit, Sayah responded, "Father, this is not the kind of thing you *can* deserve or earn. If it were, then none ever would. No, this is a gift, something uncommon among our kind, yet known to us nonetheless.

"I remember every morsel you brought back to the nest, and every time you covered us with your wing in a storm. Those were no less a gift than what is offered here, and from One many times greater than an ægle is to a chick.

"Yet, here you are by virtue of such gifts your own father and mother gave you, and none the lesser for it. Perhaps the memory is so distant that you can't recall, but if you might, know this, none comes before the Kinsman but as a chick, dependent on the gifts of a Father who longs to nurture and to shelter in His wings."

Sayah ceased to speak but turned within to plead the Spirit drive the words he'd spoken home into the heart of his father. The three lingered in the brilliance of the bower, the buzz of bees and twitter of songbirds a soft symphony to accompany reflection.

In the quiet solace of the clearing, Windspanne appeared to nod off, his eyes closing and head drooping to his chest in slow rhythm with the rise and fall of his breast. The stillness was broken when he cried out, wincing with a pain that prompted him to speak at last.

"Agh! My love, it hurts so much!" he cried in unabashed vulnerability.

Sleep had taken him, but the eventual drowse that came with prolonged loss of blood. He was on the brink of falling into a slumber from which he would not awaken.

Father affixed Sayah with a penetrating gaze and implored, "Please, son! I wish to know the Kinsman as you do. Take me to Him now!"

With great care, Sayah and Mother helped Father up and conducted him to the water's edge. Together, they waded into the pool, Sayah supporting Father beneath his one functional wing while at his side Mother reassured him. Nat, Rae, and Killam had let the family of ægles alone until they saw them emerge from the grass. Now, they watched from a short distance as the raptors entered the lapping flow.

The three Etom apprehended the dire state of Sayah's father at once, and Nat urged, "Come on. We should go with them."

The Tree towering over them all, the trio went to the shore, and hand-in-hand, strode into the water to bear witness. Sayah and his parents stopped in the midst of the spreading pool, inside a shaft of sunlight falling through an opening in the branches overhead.

While he swept his spreading wings beneath the water's prismatic shimmer, Sayah asked Mother to support Father. Nearby, he detected the approach of his friends, and bowed his head to acknowledge them. The fragile smile on Sayah's face forewarned his friends the occasion was bittersweet.

With wings yet spread beneath the surface, Sayah looked into Father's eyes and asked, "Are you ready, Father? Ready to be rid of the Stain?"

"I am ready, son," Father rasped, his breathing ragged.

Sayah declared, "Then in the name of the Father, and of the Son, and of the Holy Spirit, be joined to the Kinsman in the Vine!"

Sayah raised his wings high over Father, his feathers cupped into an overflowing chalice that burned as firelight amidst his plumage. Golden eyes closed in reverence, Sayah released the deluge in a crystalline cascade over Father's upturned face. Father gasped, his brow furrowing as he winced then stared down at his contorted wing as it straightened. The blood that seeped from his wound dissolved in the waters, and the Stain that streaked his feathers disappeared.

Hopeful from the numerous healings he'd witnessed at the Tree, Sayah watched for Father's recovery. But, alas, it was not the Spirit's will to mend all wounds. Instead, an assurance filled Sayah that Father's spirit would soon ascend on wings unseen to Lord Elyon's side to await the arrival of his Kin.

"Sayah," Father croaked. "Thank you. You were right. This is the greatest gift I have ever received.

"Now, will you give your Father one last gift? You and Mother?"

"Yes, Father!" Sayah assented through tears. "What is it?"

"Will you let me see the open sky again?"

"Can we?" Sayah asked Mother, uncertain.

Mother, likewise weeping, offered her resolute answer, "We will, son. We will."

Father lifted wings full, yet frail and bent his legs to spring into the air. With the greatest flap he could muster, Father lifted from the pool, beating the air with dwindling fury. He foundered and began to list to one side.

At once, Sayah was beneath him, bursting skyward to catch his weakened Father.

"On my back, Father!" Sayah keened. "This time, I will carry *you!*"

Father relented with furling wings falling to drape over Sayah's shoulders as Sayah bore up under Father's frame.

How light he seems, Sayah wondered while bearing Father upward with Mother right behind.

Above the Tree, the day's final light was fading fast as the sun set on the western horizon. Sayah carried Father to their aerie and helped Mother point Father into the sun's failing brilliance.

Father's eyes were wide and bright though his breath came in short, quick gasps, "heh...heh...heh."

Mother and Sayah stayed beside him as he stared at the westering sun, a noble trio of ægles standing tall with wings furled.

Father's breathing came faster and faster, "heh heh heh," but his eyes never left the blazing orb as it sank behind the horizon.

And still he stared, his eyes widening on the skyline as he spoke through ragged breath, "I, heh, I-I see it heh heh...heh."

Then Father breathed no more.

Chapter Twenty-Two
Of the Desert and of Dust

Mūk-Mudón upon his ascension had set the seat of the Empire's power amidst the crumbling ruin of a great tower in the desert. Though long since abandoned during construction, it was impressive nonetheless. Rumors ancient in their inception told of the great king who had attempted to reach the heavens themselves by way of the tower.

Now Mūk-Mudón haunted its darkened halls and slouched upon a jeweled throne in the heights of the tower. While he was never certain as to when Helél observed his movements, Mūk-Mudón suspected it was quite often. He was the lynchpin to the dark contract of the Shedím, signed in his own blood to subjugate the world. Helél dare not leave him unattended.

Alas, for Mūk-Mudón and company, things had gone from a tad askew to altogether sideways. And Mūk-Mudón was not happy. Not at all. Neither was Helél, making any semblance of happiness for Mūk-Mudón an impossibility until matters were resolved to the Shedím's satisfaction.

What had begun as rumors among the Eben'kayah, who Helél despised, had erupted into a full-blown insurrection. Raised among roving warlords, Mūk-Mudón had heard nothing of the Kinsman until Helél brought the prophesied figure to his attention. But ever since Helél had dominated the amassed armies of the East and West at Za'aq Ha Dam, the Shedím made clear to Mūk-Mudón that destroying the Kinsman was top priority.

Mūk-Mudón was curious, but understood he was not at liberty to investigate the Kinsman unless Helél granted him leave to do so. Thus, the clever fellow bided his time so as not to appear too eager, then constructed a plausible pretext for his research.

After several years had passed, Helél came to him with the compelling demand to find the Kinsman once and for all. The time of His advent drew near, and the Shedím were leery.

If I may be so bold, milord Helél, how is it that you know the time is near? Mūk-Mudón demurred.

Prattling fool! Helél spat. *Do as you are told!*

While I appreciate your desire for privacy, milord, the cavalier Emperor began, *your business in this regard is my business as well. At your request, no less. I seek only to serve you, master. Would you not prefer I understand who it is we seek as well as where and when?*

Pah! hissed Helél, *I will tell you what you need to know.*

Mūk-Mudón persisted, *You hold dominion over all, lord Helél. What has you so preoccupied? Would you not allow your greatest servant to aid you as best he can? Perhaps if you told me how it is you came by your information, I might be of yet greater use.*

A cold stillness crept over the high, dark chamber of the tower where Mūk-Mudón communed with his benefactor. The air itself ceased to move, and not the smallest grain of sand stirred. What seemed dim grew yet dimmer and sound failed to travel in the gloom. Mūk-Mudón doubted himself for an instant, but then his confidence grew. He'd had enough of sitting in the dark.

Master, what have you to fear from me? Mūk-Mudón implored. *You hold my very fate in your hands, as you have since my youth.*

All the more reason to hate me, though I gave you everything you asked, the voice slithered from corner to corner of the hall.

Lying through the silty remnants of his teeth, Mūk-Mudón replied, *Nay, milord. How could I love you more? You are and ever were as the dawn, the morning star, breaking over the land. I could never hate you.*

Flattery was pivotal in dealing with Helél, as Mūk-Mudón had learned, and was no less influential in this instance.

Why is it you seek to know this? Helél's voice floated down, sweeter now.

As I said before, lord Helél, Mūk-Mudón continued his pretense, *I wish to serve you, and how else but by finding the Kinsman for you to do with Him as you will? Is He in some ancient text? I will read it. If among a certain people, I will slay every last one. Only allow me the honor to seek His end on your behalf!*

273

The room warmed, and the darkness subsided as Mūk-Mudón anticipated Helél's favorable answer.

Very well, Helél assented, *I will point you in the right direction for your research. But tell no other! You must keep this to yourself.*

Mūk-Mudón cheered within his heart but offered a cool reply, *As you wish, milord. I have shared nothing of your existence with even my closest advisors. Consider this an extension of the same discretion.*

Without delay, Helél began to describe the distinct people who maintained the law of Lord Elyon and the prophecies of the Kinsman. Mūk-Mudón listen with care, resolved to suss out the whereabouts of the mysterious Kinsman, no matter the cost.

Decades later and Mūk-Mudón had found the Kinsman, Gaal, and had succeeded in finding and executing the fellow at Helél's behest. The lord of the Shedím had made clear the location and manner of Gaal's death. Something about that particular Tree being where it had all begun.

No doubt, something had been strange about the Kinsman, but nothing Mūk-Mudón hadn't anticipated. His years of research had pointed to a paradoxical figure, at once a servant afflicted for the sake of all and a powerful king with authority over all Creation.

After viewing the Kinsman through the prophetic lens of the Eben'kayah, Mūk-Mudón had been underwhelmed at meeting Him. However, since their meeting at Gaal's execution, the Kinsman had haunted Mūk-Mudón's thoughts, His eyes full of surrender to a power the Nihúkolem did not comprehend. For everything in Gaal's posture had revealed a confidence that He went of his own volition to His doom.

The concept disturbed Mūk-Mudón, who had only ever known the power of the sword's edge, wielded to avoid his own destruction or to threaten that of another. That the Kinsman would willingly surrender to death confounded Mūk-Mudón. The implications shook the foundations of the Emperor's thinking and with each passing day, he grew more unstable.

Then to suffer not one but two consecutive defeats in some backcountry village of those vermin, the Etom! Not even a worthy foe, but creatures not much higher than a grasshopper had stood firm against his forces and won. Of course, they were not alone in their victory. No, some mighty force contended on their behalf.

What Mūk-Mudón had witnessed through the eyes of his Nihúkolem the night they first encountered the strange power had astounded him. Not long before, his forces had demolished the miniature stone temple of the Eben'Kayah and uprooted the olive tree that sheltered their homes.

With a suddenness that belied the laws of Nature, a different Tree had sprung up, shining with a frightening light that had drawn the attention of the Empire. After losing two of his scouts to defection, Imafel had feared further desertions among the foxes and sent all available Nihúkolem against the Tree in their stead.

Mūk-Mudón recalled the harrowing and helpless dissolution he'd experienced through those dashed against the light, which had then pursued Imafel, leaving the general a listless pile of dust. In his shock, the Emperor had been unable to contain the spread of the experience to the minds of all Nihúkolem, who were terrified at their vulnerability to the power of the Tree. Even now, he felt the unexpressed trepidation among the wraiths, who for so long had been immune to injury.

But that had not been the end of the Empire's humiliation. No. The plan to assail the village with battalions of Men and Beasts had been sound, even in the hindsight of their failure. What had occurred afterward was beyond imagination, even for one familiar with using magical arts in warfare. They had lost all their infantry to the depths, and the better part of their airwing in the thrashing of the Tree's limbs. It was as though heaven and earth had conspired against the Empire to their defeat. Or Whoever ruled them.

Throughout his study of the Eben'kayah's texts, Mūk-Mudón identified a common thread, the acknowledgement of One called Elyon as Creator of all things. This claim intrigued the heathen king, who had heard mere whispers of such a Being or ribald mockery at the mention of His name. This fact, coupled with the discovery and eventual execution of the Kinsman, set his mind ablaze. Gaal had claimed to be the Son of Lord Elyon, and Mūk-Mudón had slain Him!

If there were any truth to the claims of the Eben'kayah's prophecies, then no wonder Creation itself warred against the Empire. A sense of dread fell upon Mūk-Mudón, driving him further down into the sinking sand of his shattered presuppositions. With the evidence stacking up against him, he began to suspect he'd made a terrible mistake.

When Imafel had suggested an investigation of the Tree where they had killed the Kinsman, an alarming disquiet clamored within Mūk-Mudón. He'd been defensive and had prohibited Imafel from poking around the Tree before retreating from their council.

Contrary to the suspicions of his generals, however, Mūk-Mudón had not retired to seek audience with Helél. Rather, he had retreated to brood over the significance of the resistance they had met and that had proven insurmountable thus far.

Imafel's apparent insubordination in examining the site of Gaal's execution had confirmed for Mūk-Mudón that without a doubt a connection existed between this Tree and the one in Endego. What had happened to the decrepit wreckage of a Tree to which they'd nailed the Kinsman? And what had happened to His body?!? Did He yet wander the earth as a ghost? It might explain some of the strange happenings in recent days.

The two Trees shed the same light and poured forth the same pure water, filling their bowers with life and power. Mūk-Mudón realized it was too late to keep the matter altogether secret from Imafel and decided he must chance bringing the general into his confidence.

A calculated risk, but Mūk-Mudón was beyond fretting over the particulars of the matter when potential ramifications were on a cosmic scale. He detected more and more proof, mounting to the heavens, as it were, and to his own demise.

In the days following these events, the certainty of his conviction ballooned into his primary concern, and he fell into disinterest with the affairs of Empire. Notwithstanding, he managed to relate a great deal of what he knew of the strange Tree to Imafel, keeping a few important details to himself.

Mūk-Mudón's explanation of the issue worried Imafel, on one hand due to the off-handed manner of its delivery and on the other due to the fact that no punishment was forthcoming. The Emperor's behavior was beyond uncharacteristic and once released, Imafel had fallen into anxious meditation as he planned how he might compart what he knew to Cloust and Belláphorus. Meanwhile, cloistered in his lofty chamber, the weight of concern pressed down on Mūk-Mudón with unrelenting gravity.

This present day, a certain small relief came to the Emperor in the form of news from a distant eastern outpost at the edge of the Takla Makan, a region of the Shamo Desert. With surprise, the Nihúkolem garrison broadcasted the approach of a large Imperial military contingent – the troops lost in the waters at Endego!

A collective cheer went up among the Nihúkolem, followed by sullen reminiscence of the dread they had all felt at the Empire's defeat. The recollection sobered the whole army of wraiths, and those stationed in the East sped to receive and debrief the incoming cohort.

The recovery of the Endego contingent turned out to be a tale in and of itself, and a consistent account soon developed out of the survivors' reports. What Mūk-Mudón learned in the aftermath left him perplexed and more curious than ever regarding the power behind the Tree.

To begin with, while a great many had been wounded, not a single member of the company died, during or after their defeat. All described a momentary panic when the water had encapsulated them, exacerbated when the ground overhead sealed them in. This had turned to near-instantaneous relief when the earth opened up to belch them onto the desert sands, water and all.

The great volume of water sent flowing across the desert had given immediate rise to foliage and formed lush oases in all directions. While a great many had been anxious to set out at once to rejoin the Empire, others had vied to treat the wounded so that travel was more feasible. Besides, they had reasoned, no one knew for certain where they were, and they would be striking out in vain until they did.

The impatient throng saw the reason in taking the remainder of the day to dress injuries and to scout the land. Past the spreading greenery of their immediate surroundings, a great sea of dunes swelled to meet every horizon. Given the rise and fall of the landscape, birds were the most sensible choice for scouts, though the number that were not too injured to fly was limited. They recruited a supplement of wolves to make up the lack of fowl, and the scouts set out in all directions with instructions to return before nightfall.

Upon their return to camp, each group of scouts greeted the great company with bitter disappointment. In every direction, they had discovered dunes, dunes, and, surprise! more dunes. Following a heated debate amongst the leadership of the camp that lasted far too late into the night, they arrived at no conclusive agreement as to a course of action for the following day. Rather, they retired, intending to awaken over fresh arguments until they reached a consensus.

Lo and behold! In the morning, no contention was necessary, for in the night, a westbound wind had carved a lane through the dunes, and the pools of water had coalesced into a stream running through the midst. While many in the camp shunned superstition, the overt sign granted them was difficult to dispute, and all among the leadership but one agreed to follow the clear course before them.

Alongside the level road that cut through the strength-sapping rise and fall of the dunes ran a stream of fresh, life-sustaining water – in the desert no less! Once they had made the determination that any way was as good as another, their decision now was clear.

The one dissident was a contentious honey badger who, for obvious reasons, was called Termagant. She was displeased to follow the path provided, but in most cases, her displeasure was inevitable, so the others pursued it nonetheless.

Thus, the lost of Endego were led beside quiet waters to their restoration from the wasteland. Slowed by the transport of their wounded and the desert heat, the trek had taken them a couple weeks. The water had sustained them to the last day, when after breakfast, the stream had subsided at first to a trickle, then to a languid drizzle, and at last to naught but dust.

In that moment, panic was close, and would have consumed them but for the outcry of an ægle scout high overhead. The troop strode out at last from the wall of dunes on either side into open plains, hazy and streaked with the chalky residue of salt.

In the distance lay what could be none other than the towering architecture of an Imperial fort. The company cheered at their deliverance from the desert, muted though it was at the prospect of returning to Imperial service. Regardless, they were excited to rejoin civilization and marched at double-time for the open gates.

Intrigued, Mūk-Mudón absorbed the reports of their return, which did nothing to quell his disquiet. Rather, he was troubled at the apparent mercy bestowed his army, for it brought to mind once again the strength he had detected in the Kinsman at His vanquishment. A strength that stood in opposition to the power of death and destruction. The power of life itself. And that disturbed Mūk-Mudón more than anything else.

The disturbance did not stop at the Emperor, however. Amongst those who had returned from the desert lands, from the certainty of a drowning death, frenzied rumor stirred. They had seen too much, and now knew of a power that could overcome the Empire of Chōl.

In the hearts of the most grateful returnees from Takla Makan, the seeds of hope found good soil and, taking root, bloomed into courage. This courage became the impetus for many to desert – not en masse, but in the quiet of the night, and just one or two at a time. Those others, who had seen the hand of Elyon at work but were not brave enough to defect, remained quiet at the desertion of their comrades. They understood their peers' reasons and many longed for a courage sufficient to do the same.

Some time passed before the Nihúkolem noticed the desertions and the extent thereof, but that any had been so bold sent further shockwaves throughout the Empire's military. Not since the Empire's inception had anyone defected. Those that had dared, the Nihúkolem tracked down and executed, their tortured bodies left on display outside the gates of cities throughout the Empire.

The penalty for such treachery became knowledge common to every subject of the Empire, and so it remained to this day. Those who now abandoned their duties to the Empire had signed their death warrant, but the foregone penalty for their desertion hadn't deterred them. Even among the Nihúkolem, the matter provoked consideration, and soon the Imperial rumor mill ground the grist of its greatest scandal to date.

The plentiful lower ranks of Nihúkolem buzzed with excitement over the latest wave of defections, almost all of whom had been those presumed lost after Endego. The speculative static generated among the Nihúkolem charged Imperial air with a renewed anxiety not felt in the world since the wraith army had first conquered it, and gave perfect cover for Cloust, Imafel and Belláphorus to meet.

Mūk-Mudón had retreated from recent events to muse over their implications, and even should the three generals feel his presence, they gambled that the overwhelming drone of their subordinates' gossip would interfere with Mūk-Mudón's senses.

We all know the happenings of these past days, Belláphorus began, *but what do we propose to do about it?*

Cloust, ever diplomatic, offered, *Perhaps we should just go to Mūk-Mudón – in person and together – and let him know our minds on the matter.*

In a retort punctuated with explosive coughs, Imafel rebuked Cloust.

Blast it, Cloust! He'll never abide such a parley. He would only see it as insurrection. You know this!

Imafel had not been altogether himself since he first encountered the power of the Tree in Endego, in that he'd not been able to pull himself all the way together. The bits and pieces that comprised his frame continued to slip away if his concentration failed him for an instant, and neither could he contain the sporadic cough that now plagued him. The malady likewise eroded his vain image, and though the duress of maintaining his form proved a heavy burden, he wearied himself with the load regardless, unwilling to surrender his vanity.

Belláphorus cocked a sooty brow and observed, *Have you fallen ill, Imafel? You look a mess!*

I've not heard of such a thing among the Nihúkolem before, Cloust added with a touch of concern. *What could it possibly be, I wonder?*

Again, you play the fool, Cloust! Imafel snapped. *Can't you two see this is the power of that accursed Tree at work? What else could it be?*

Imafel's two peers regarded what they'd learned of the Tree with curiosity, which was further piqued at Imafel's declaration.

A power that can loose our bonds? Belláphorus mused. *What say you, Cloust?*

I say we might know more of this Kinsman and His Tree, yes? Cloust replied.

The Kinsman? Imafel asked, incredulous. *What has he to do with the Tree?*

Methinks that now is your turn at playing the fool, Imafel, Belláphorus jibed. *Have you forgotten? We were there. It was under Imperial orders He was slain, and was it not to the very Tree where you lost your ægle escorts that He was nailed? Who else might be responsible?*

Bu – but that's impossible! Imafel spat. *He's dead!*

Of all who roam the world, oughtn't we best understand the flexible nature of what's possible, Cloust quipped. *Eh, Imafel?*

True, true, Imafel answered, lost in reflection.

Also true, rejoined Belláphorus, *is the unhealthy interest Mūk-Mudón has in the Kinsman. Why else do you suppose he's gathering up every last scrap of information on Him?*

Aaah! exclaimed Cloust with relish, *So that's why he's going after the Eben'kayah...*

The who? Imafel inquired. He'd heard very little of the Eben'kayah and thought even less of them.

The Eben'kayah, Cloust answered. *The keepers of the law and prophecies of Elyon, the purported Creator of all things? Is this truly the first you've heard of them? They were quite numerous in Terábnis.*

Ah, yes, the fellows with all the funny rules and such, Imafel recalled. *I never paid them any mind. But you say they are the key to all this?*

They may be, Belláphorus responded, *but we must move with care else tip our hand to Mūk-Mudón. He already has a substantial lead, and little may remain out in the world for us.*

Indeed... Cloust pondered the matter, then inquired, *but though their writings may be in Mūk-Mudón's hands, the Eben'kayah themselves yet live among our subjects, yes? Given how important their holy writ is to them, the Eben'kayah are our next best source of information.*

Well judged, Cloust, Belláphorus returned, *and though Mūk-Mudón has made a rout of them, certainly some remain within Imperial lands.*

Imafel, felling a tad left out, interjected at last, *And how do you propose we find them?*

It's quite simple, really, Cloust proposed, *They will come to us.*

Chapter Twenty-Three
The Welcome of Family and Friends

Back in Sanctuary, the three Etom did their best to comfort Sayah and his mother in their grief. The loss of Windspanne was profound but hope in the Kinsman buoyed the survivors. Though his body remained in the aerie, Windspanne had gone on to the presence of Lord Elyon, and was no doubt soaring higher than ever before.

Out of respect, yet another pair had waited to make their appearance – Astéri and Yebul. Astéri had difficulty restraining the Sprig, who desired to greet the newcomers in typical boisterous fashion. The Malakím had taken the opportunity to teach Yebul something about timing, and it had not been the time for noisy introductions.

Astéri was grateful that Yebul had received his instruction in the moment, for now the time was right to greet the others.

Quietly, though, Yebul. Quietly, Astéri cautioned as they neared the band of Etom and ægles.

Hello, Sayah. Stromweise, Astéri saluted the ægles.

"Hi there," Yebul offered, then lowered his eyes, unsure of what else to say.

"Astéri!" Sayah replied with surprise, and at once the Etom likewise thronged about the Malakím and his friend.

Sayah. Stromweise. May I offer my condolences for your loss? Astéri began. *I did not know Windspanne well, but from what I saw of his conduct the day you both entered Sanctuary, Stromweise, I would say he was a brave and noble ægle. I hope you both are proud of him.*

"I see him there," Yebul in his innocence pronounced, placing a hand beneath each eye then lifting them toward Sayah's.

The gesture caught the grieving ægles unawares, and Sayah, wincing, dropped his head to hide his tears.

Stromweise, on the other hand, exhorted her son, "Sayah, do not hide yourself!"

Sayah raised his teary eyes to meet Mother's.

"This little Sprig is right, son," she continued. "You have the eyes and the bearing of your Father. Do not be ashamed, even in grief. He would not desire it."

Recovering, Sayah thanked the Sprig.

I am sorry, Astéri apologized. *I haven't had the opportunity to introduce my young friend here. This is Yebul.*

Nat, Rae and Sayah were all very pleased to meet another Sprig, since Miyam was the only other they had met before. The stunned Killam was a tad more hesitant to greet both Malakím and Sprig, but he soon warmed to them. Reality was turning out to be much stranger than he had come before to know, but he was adjusting.

They had all been so concerned with sending Windspanne off that they had forgotten an important detail, though Stromweise soon reminded them.

"Ahem!" she interjected, "I should very much like to join my mate and my son in the Vine, if you would please."

"Mother! Oh, my goodness! How could we have forgotten?" Sayah moaned, and all the others bustled her off into the pool.

Night had fallen, but the clearing glowed with the warm amber light of the Tree as Sayah repeated his earlier ministrations. Fresh memories of Windspanne elicited tears amongst the gathered Kinship while they celebrated Stromweise's adoption to their number. The occasion was bittersweet, but joyful overall and left everyone ready for the slumber that overtook all but Sprig and Malakím.

In the morning, ægle and Etom alike gathered for breakfast and a discussion of their plans moving forward. Nat was certain that the Spirit had business for them in the West but wondered if Stromweise might be best off in Endego for the time being. The Kin there would be sure to receive her well, and she might find a place among the watches.

Sayah was excited at the idea but wondered if it was what Mother wanted. She hadn't yet expressed it, but she must be reeling from the loss of her mate and the uncertain fate of her daughter. Maybe some time alone here in Sanctuary would be best.

"Nonsense!" she sniffed when Sayah proposed she stay put. "I will go with you to Endego. I like very much what you have told me of the place. I want to see it for myself."

And that settled it. Stromweise was a headstrong bird and none could convince her otherwise once she'd made up her mind. After breakfast, they met with Astéri and Yebul to say goodbye, and the Malakím had a warning for the travelers.

Be wary of what you find in the West. All is not what it seems there, and you will undoubtedly encounter resistance of a kind you never have before.

As if that weren't quite cryptic enough, when Nat asked for clarification, Astéri replied, *That is all I am permitted to tell you. Be vigilant in the Spirit.*

"I'm going on a journey!!!" Yebul interrupted, his gleeful fronds waving in the air.

"What does he mean?" Rae giggled.

Astéri grew red and bright, which the others interpreted as a smile, and the Malakím answered, *He means Sakkan, Rae. He is going to Sakkan.*

"No!" she protested. "Not there! What can one so small do in that horrid place?"

Why, what every servant of Elyon, great or small, should do...grow.

Rae could muster no further argument, but instead embraced the tiny tree. A rather rugged and prickly affair it was, but she insisted.

Yebul seemed to appreciate the gesture, and whispered, "I like you best of all, Rae."

Then they were off again, on adventures uncertain yet meaningful. Once they were aloft, the winter winds favored their flight southward. Stromweise offered to share Sayah's burden and carry Killam. She was less practiced than Sayah as a mount, and the experience held some frightening surprises for Killam at first.

Nevertheless, after almost dropping the etém a few times, Stromweise adapted and everyone was able to enjoy the journey a great deal more. Indeed, the remainder of their flight to Endego was gratifying. Although they still stopped for another night, the tailwind had carried them closer to their destination than they anticipated, and the last leg of the trip would be several hours shorter.

Late the following morning, Sayah called out, "Endego! Dead ahead!"

To the south stood the familiar grove, and circling about it were the many fowl of the First Watch.

From the perimeter of the Watch, a cry arose, "They've returned! With guests!"

The message traveled back toward the village, and greetings met the returning adventurers from every side as they neared the village. They dropped down into the village grove, gliding unhurried toward the Tree and coming to rest at last in Sanctuary Endego. They were home.

Nida heard the call go up announcing the imminent arrival of Nat and his friends. Without delay, she hurried to the Tree, sure that's where they'd set down. Just outside the bower, Dempsey waited, ready to support her as she went to meet her son. Hand in hand, they scampered into the clearing just in time to see not one, but two ægles touch down.

Nat and Rae slid from Sayah's back while a strange grey etém debarked from the other ægle with some difficulty.

There's something familiar about this etém, Nida thought as they neared the gathering that grew to welcome the travelers home.

Nida and Dempsey were still a way off when she observed Shoym at the outskirts of the throng. The elder etém appeared agitated as he removed his top hat and dove into the crowd, shouting something indistinct as he plowed through the assembly.

"Is something wrong?" Dempsey wondered aloud.

"I don't know," Nida answered, "but I intend to find out."

Hands still linked, the pair increased their pace, determined to get to the heart of both the matter and the crowd. Over top the bobbing heads of the gathering, they heard Shoym's voice again, but still could not make out what he said through the din.

They broke into the clearing about the wayfarers, where Shoym was embracing the strange etém, and at last they could hear his cries, "Killam! Oh, Killam! My son, my son!"

"Killam?!?" Nida exclaimed in shocked surprise.

Nat appeared from around Sayah's alabaster breast and ran to her, "Mom! Can you believe it? Shoym's son is alive!"

"And that's not all," he rasped once close, "He says he knows where dad might be."

Nat's words slammed a door on Nida's senses, and the world around her grew dim and distant but for her son's words.

"Mom? Did you hear me? Killam says dad is probably still alive. And he knows where he might be!"

Nida dropped Dempsey's hand and stumbled back a step in shock.

"Mom!" Nat shouted, "Are you alright? You look sick!"

Nida *felt* sick. And sick at heart, she grasped for the singular remedy she knew for such an illness.

Elyon! she cried out in desperation, *is it true? Is my husband still alive?*

She glanced at the concerned Dempsey, who stood beside her, and implored, *Why now? Why this?*

An upswell of strength carried her upright, and she managed to respond to her son, "I'll be fine, Nat. I'm just...surprised. I told myself that your father passed away long ago. It's a lot to take in."

"I understand," Nat sympathized, laying a comforting hand on her arm. "We're going to find out for sure, either way. And soon."

"Does that mean another trip, then?" she asked. "I don't know that I can take it."

Nat looked up as he contemplated his response, "Uuummmm, then let's just pretend that it's all one trip. We only came home to bring Sayah's mother here and reunite Killam with Shoym."

"Sayah's mother?" Nida inquired. "Is that who this other ægle is?"

Nida looked the unfamiliar ægle over, seeking a resemblance to the other. For one thing, the ægle was the larger of the two and thicker through the breast, but Nida didn't know if that was due to age. Of course, their plumage differed, since Sayah had pure white feathers all around while his mother's were brown except for her neck and head, which were white like her son's.

Though Nida couldn't quite put a finger on it, something about the ægle's gaze was fiercer than Sayah's, but in that instant, those piercing eyes fell on Nida, and she blanched.

The ægle chuckled and asked, "Well, are you just going to stare? Then I will proceed with the introductions. I am Stromweise. You must be Nat's mother."

"I'm very sorry, Stromweise," Nida recovered, "I was spying a bit. You are correct. I'm Nat's mother, Nida."

"I am very happy to meet you," Stromweise returned. "Your son has helped my family more than you know."

Right then Nida realized that Sayah's father was absent, and out of concern asked, "Where is Sayah's father? Is he well?"

Stromweise tipped her head and stared into the distance for a moment, then returned her gaze to Nida and replied, "We met with treachery from the Nihúkolem. Father and I were harmed but he managed to drag me to the safety of the Kinsman's Tree.

"I am grateful. He saw Sayah once more and met the Kinsman before succumbing to his injuries. He died with honor in our aerie, a free ægle."

Nida was shocked at Stromweise's forthright announcement, and tears leapt to her eyes as she glanced over at Sayah. She knew he had never given up hope that his family would join him in the Vine. That he'd seen his father to the Tree was a blessing, though Nida imagined it was one mixed with sorrow.

"And you, Stromweise?" Nida inquired. "I see no Stain among your feathers."

"Quite right. I, too, have joined the Kin, as we are called. That is the exact reason I am here. I wish to be among my own kind and learn more of our ways."

Nida was impressed at the Spirit's work in the ægle. Stromweise already identified on a deep level with the Kinship, something that took others a good while to do. The etma suspected she and Stromweise would be fast friends.

"I hope I can help with that," Nida offered, favoring Stromweise with a warm smile.

The ægle blinked and bowed her head in reply but was otherwise silent.

Meanwhile, Killam's reunion with Shoym had captured the attention of all but Nida, Dempsey, and Stromweise. Even Nat had returned to the scene as father and son began to catch up on all that had occurred.

Greatest on Killam's mind was the absence of the temple, and he asked with trepidation, "Please, father, what became of our scrolls? The sacred law of Elyon? The prophecies of the Kinsman?"

Shoym shook his heavy head with disappointment and replied, "I am sorry, son. The Nihúkolem destroyed or took almost everything away, even our writings and the beautiful tapestries Nida made."

"But!" Shoym added, "We managed to save a single scroll, the scroll of the great prophet, Yeshayahu. Every day, we read the scroll aloud and make it available for certain, trusted individuals to study. We are protective of our only remaining text, so very few are allowed to handle it."

Killam was heartened to know that not all had been lost to the Empire of Chōl. As ever, Lord Elyon had preserved a remnant for His purposes – a remnant of His people and of His Word. Killam look around the home he'd left so long ago and saw that Elyon had already been faithful to multiply His people. A certainty filled the etém that Lord

Elyon would likewise increase His Word and soon joy came alongside the surety within him.

Killam smiled as his eyes swept over the bustling bower.

What a blessing to live in such a time!

Kehren and Tram had since arrived to reunite with Rae, and Kehren took the opportunity to smother Rae with hugs and kisses. Tram just put a soft hand on her back and lowered his head to thank Elyon for his daughter's safe return. Nat watched on with interest, content to share in his friend's happiness from a distance.

A thick mossy-green hand fell on Nat's shoulder, causing the engrossed etém to jump.

"Agh!" he shouted as he spun around, though the face he met then shocked him into momentary silence.

"R-Rosco?!?" he stammered once he'd regained himself. "By Lord Elyon, it's good to see you!"

Nat threw his arms around the larger etém, who lifted wooden arms around Nat in an awkward embrace.

"I want to thank you, Rosco," Nat announced. "Without you, we mightn't have made it out of Endego. And Elyon has used us to accomplish so much since we left."

Rosco still in his embrace, Nat expressed his gratitude for the sacrifice of Rosco's silence when the Nihúkolem had captured him. Rosco had not betrayed his friends to the enemy.

Releasing his friend at last, Nat inquired, rapid-fire, "Where have you been? When did you get back? We've missed you so much!"

"You're happy to see me then?" Rosco chided as he lobbed a meaty fist at Nat's shoulder.

At the time they parted, the impact of the punch might have staggered the then-smaller Nat, but his exploits in the wilderness had toughened the pale blue etém. With the passage of time, he had shot up and now stood almost eye-to-eye with Rosco. As a result, Nat absorbed Rosco's shot without so much as flinching.

Rosco's eyes went wide and with a crooked grin he exclaimed, "Look at you, Nat! Taking it like a grown etém!"

Nat's cheeks flared at the praise, and he answered, "Well, I've a way to grow still, but thanks, Rosco."

Rosco tipped his head at Rae, who had yet to extricate herself from Kehren's grasp, and asked, "You two have been on some kind of adventures, eh?"

"And what's been happening here..." Rosco looked around the clearing and exhaled through pursed lips, "it's wild, isn't it?"

"You don't know the half of it, Rosco," Nat replied, "but I'd love to catch up. What are you doing right now? Have you had lunch yet?"

"Not yet, but I could definitely eat."

"Great! Let me see if Rae and Sayah would like to join us."

"Sayah?" an uncertain Rosco queried. "Who is that?"

"Oh ho ho! He's the white ægle there. Just wait until you meet him! I bet you two will be great friends. Let me go get them and I'll introduce you."

Nat turned to pelt away and didn't catch the dismayed frown on Rosco's face. Rosco scowled and took a deep breath to shake off his vexation. Before long, his features had smoothed to present a placid mask of contentment while he awaited Nat's return.

In her distinct style, Rae caught Rosco in an affectionate garrote of a hug, which Rosco endured without complaint. In truth, he enjoyed the warm reception, but hesitated a split second when confronted with Sayah. To be honest, it was a common reaction among Etom, who were accustomed to shaking hands when meeting someone new.

Rosco made a weak pantomime of a handshake, then dropped his hand and lifted his chin in a short nod to the towering ægle.

Sayah understood the etém's reticence and attempted to ease the interaction, "Hello, there. My name is Sayah. Don't worry, I don't bite...anymore."

With a rumble, Sayah's hungry stomach signaled lunchtime.

Rosco snickered and responded, "As a potential meal, that's good to hear, Sayah.

"I'd hear that birds and other creatures here could talk, but you're the first for me. I'm Rosco. Good to meet you."

Nat chimed in, "We have a lot to talk about. How about we go pick up some food and chat."

"I could do that," Rosco complied, and the quartet set out for some lunch.

The ægle and three Etom found plenty rhema in a nearby collection jar and took their meal to a pleasant place in the sunlight to sit down.

They each spoke a word of thanksgiving before eating and Nat went last to close the prayer with, "In the name of the Kinsman, Gaal, so be it."

Nat's final statement draw a cocked brow from Rosco, who inquired, "What do you mean, 'in the name of the Kinsman Gaal?' Your mom told me about finding the Kinsman, but not a whole lot more."

"Oh. my. goodness!" Rae blurted out. "We have *so much* to talk about."

Rosco sent a sidelong glance at Sayah, and agreed, "You're right. We do."

"I don't even know where to start, Rosco," Nat declared. "We were all so worried about you when the Nihúkolem carried you off…"

"Right! That!" Rosco barked with awkward curtness. "You don't need to worry about that. I was just *fine*."

Something in Rosco's behavior troubled Nat, but Rae was first to pose the question, "But what happened? Where did they take you, Rosco?"

"Where did they take me?" Rosco asked, his voice almost shrill. "Let's see…where *did* they take me?"

"Oh yes!" came Rosco's near-manic reply to his own question. "They took me somewhere down South for what the Nihúkolem and their Etom minions call an 'education.' My school was a tower of black, glassy stone and I would've traded my instructors there for Headmistress Kehren on her worst day.

"Sometimes, they didn't let me sleep. They would keep the lights on or splash dirty water on me and shout the most horrible things about the Kinsman and the Eben'kayah."

Rosco reached a fever pitch as he continued, "Then they might make me get up and run or jump in place under threat of a beating, or they might not feed me for a few days. All the time, one of their goons would yell at me or ask me questions about Elyon, about the Eben'kayah, about you guys!

"If I answered wrong, they would beat me or keep me awake or not feed me. You know, the usual. It was fantastic," Rosco spat, his tone bitter and resentful.

"Why do you ask, Rae?"

Rae didn't respond, but just wept over the pain of her friend's experience while Rosco continued.

"And what have you guys been up to? Seems like it's been pretty great! Just look at you now, gallivanting around the world on a flippin' ægle for the sake of all Creation!"

Rosco's anger dissolved into heaving sobs, and Nat went to wrap an arm around his friend's shoulder. He could think of nothing to say that was worthy of the moment, so instead he prayed in silence for the Spirit's help. Rae came around Rosco's other side and did the same, while Sayah, cued by their bowed heads, joined in the prayer.

After a bit, Rosco sniffed and lifted his head to speak, "Nat. Rae. I'm alright now. Really. I'm sorry I got so upset. The worst of it all was that I started to *believe* what they were telling me. All those *lies*.

"That, and just how alone I was. You weren't there, and after a while, I didn't think even Elyon was there anymore. And after all I went through, I don't know if He's even real anymore.

"No! That's not right. I know He's real. I just don't know if He'll ever forgive me for what I did to survive. For what I *said* about Him. I don't know if I can forgive myself. I'm still working it all out."

"If it helps," Rae began, "I *know* that He'll forgive you, Rosco. He wants to. That's the whole reason the Kinsman came."

"I don't think I'm ready to hear this right now," Rosco asserted, shaking his head. "I'll be fine. I would rather hear what you've been up to."

"For real?" Nat asked, doubtful.

"For real," Rosco affirmed, "I want to hear it all. I've missed you two so much, the thought of you out there, somewhere, doing something, anything. It was what kept me going."

Given how wrapped up their lives had become in that of the Kinsman, Nat couldn't help but think that Rosco was going to get an earful about Him whether he wanted it or not.

Oh well, he thought and, shrugging, found a matching expression on Rae's face.

At least he would not be alone in the telling of this tale. He smirked and winked at Sayah to signal him to be ready to tell his part when the time came. At that, the three set to weaving the tale of the Kinsman's Tree, the thread that had woven all their lives and, indeed, the lives of all creatures, together.

With attention rapt and hand floating from rhema to mouth and back again, Rosco listened.

Chapter Twenty-Four
Rosco and the Diamonds in the Rough

"...and that's how we came to arrive in Endego this morning," Nat pronounced, at long last.

The account of their adventures had lasted well into the night. The ægle had assumed a natural responsibility for recounting the larger part of the story that involved flight or any other matters in which he had been directly involved. Rae had taken on a similar role in providing particular insight into those initial encounters with those outside their kind.

Nat had been the most involved of the three throughout most events and thus the task of chief storyteller fell to him. Without a doubt, however, the trio hoped the Spirit had been most to speak, regardless of which one told the tale.

In the meantime, Nida, Kehren, and Tram trickled in to sit with their children, eager to spend time together before they departed once again. The adults, curious to learn about more recent events, sat in rapt attention for the later parts of the adventure in particular.

For his part, Rosco had been enthralled for the length of the tale, interjecting from time to time with surprised exclamations or questions to clarify what he'd just heard. Now the story was over, though, he just sat with blank eyes staring at the earth before him, altogether silent while the adults bid their children a good night and left for their own beds.

"Rosco?" Rae prompted, once her parents had left. "Are you OK?"

But for the slow up and down motion of his head, Rosco did not at once respond. Howbeit a second later, a smile crept across his face, and he looked around at his friends with renewed courage in his eyes.

"I get it!" he called out with a fiery zeal. "The whole time I was shut up in that dungeon, you were all out here doing something important. Something so fantastic, that if the Nihúkolem had caught you when they caught me, it might have never happened.

"It makes all I went through mean something. It was all part of Elyon's plan. And totally worth it!"

"What was meant for evil," Rae declared, "Elyon meant for good and so that many could be saved."

"Exactly!" Rosco shouted, jumping to his feet and clapping his hands together. "That's it! That very thing!"

Nat grinned and joined in, "I'm starting to think that's one of Elyon's greatest themes. Just look at what happened to His Son, Gaal. What the Empire meant for evil became our greatest good."

"Too true," Sayah added, then he looked up into the stars and sighed, "He is unstoppable."

At the ægle's words, all four shivered and goose pimples wrinkled the Etom's skin while Sayah's feathers stuck straight out from his body to render him a white and fluffy puff of ægle.

The hour was late. Later than they had intended when they had begun their tale. Notwithstanding, Nat thought it important to add at least one more thing.

"Rosco, you've heard what we witnessed. You know now the promises of the Kinsman. Would you tonight join us in the Vine?"

Rosco huffed once as he thought, then replied, "I don't know if I'm ready yet. I would like to sleep on it."

"That's fair," Nat answered. "I want you to be sure about your decision. Know this, though. Whatever you decide, we are still your friends."

"C'mon, then, you sappy etém," Rae interrupted to razz them, "let's get some sleep. Plenty to do tomorrow."

Involuntary stretches and yawns signaled their agreement, and the three Etom settled against the ægle's soft plumage under the warmth of the Tree. Within minutes, all four were sound asleep, exhausted from their adventure and its retelling.

Nat awakened the next morning before Rae or Sayah and stretched a balled fist skyward as a yawn forced his eyes into a squint. Through his bleary gaze, he strained to make out a not-too-distant figure at the edge of the Tree's pool. A few blinks later, he identified Rosco, his round, moss-green head hanging low over the water.

Nat left his other friends sound asleep and made his way over to Rosco at the shore. While yet several steps away, Nat spotted the telltale patter of falling tears in concentric ripples along the water's surface. He stopped, uncertain if he should interrupt until Rosco spoke.

"You can come over, Nat. I don't mind."

"Rosco, is there anything I can do to help?"

Rosco swung his head back and forth in low, heavy arcs, "I don't know if there's *anyone* who can help me now. After all I've done."

I thought we got past all this last night! Nat reasoned with himself.

He fought down the urge toward exasperation and instead asked in as gentle a voice as he could muster, "Rosco, what happened? You were so excited last night. Like you understood the part you played in Elyon's plan. Why do you doubt Him now?"

Rosco stooped to scoop a handful of water and let it drain out between his outspread fingers, declaring, "It's like this water, slipping from my grasp. Whatever I do, I can't seem to hold onto the joy I felt last night. The joy I feel around you, Rae...even Sayah now."

Nat looked down in thought, then came forward to crouch beside Rosco at water's edge.

"You're right, Rosco," he began. "Joy isn't something you can hold onto like that."

He reached down to gather a handful of the water for himself, and continued, "Joy is something you carry inside, hidden where the world can't touch it."

Before the water ran from his cupped hand, Nat drank what was left and turned to Rosco.

"And once it's there, you can never truly lose it. No matter what. Because it's true. Because it's real. Just like everything the Kinsman promises."

Nat took up another handful of the pure flow and presented it to Rosco, asking, "Will you taste now and see that He is good, Rosco?"

Rosco was a tearful shambles as he asked with trembling lips, "Is He, though? Really?"

"Better than you could ever imagine, my friend. Come with me, won't you?"

Together, just the two of them entered the pool, and in the crisp, quiet hour of the winter sunrise, Rosco first partook of the Kinsman's goodness. Nat had detected no visible Stain on Rosco's frame, but as he came up from the water, he was wracked with a frightening cough.

After several deep and throaty hacks, Rosco discharged a dark saliva. He winced with embarrassed disgust as the dank and stinking sputum struck the water. In the cleansing flow, however, the blackened mucous altogether disappeared and the sacred spring was no less so for it.

Nat clapped Rosco on the back and congratulated him as they made their way out of the water.

"You've taken your first step on the most important journey of your life," Nat encouraged. "I hope you already sense the new strength, the new life that's inside you. The resurrected Kinsman comes to life in us and through us by His Spirit. You are now a member of His family, His Kin."

"That's good," Rosco replied with wry humor, "since I doubt my own family wants anything to do with me."

Nat hissed through his teeth as he recalled Rosco's final moments with his father Rufus. In an act of selfish greed, Rufus had given Rosco over to the Nihúkolem, betraying both his own son and the Eben'kayah of Endego to the Empire.

"I'm so sorry, Rosco. I didn't even think about your parents."

"Don't worry about it, Nat. It *has* been a while, and a lot has happened since then."

"The Kinship takes care of their own, Rosco. That I know. You will have a place here, and who knows? The Spirit can do amazing things, even in your father."

As he thanked Nat, Rosco's smile was no longer dampened by the excess of sorrow he had carried in his Stain. The two of them went to awaken Rae and Sayah, who were ecstatic to learn what they had been up to.

"Woohoo!" Rae cheered as she threw her arms around Rosco. "I'm so happy for you, Rosco!"

Sayah was more restrained, but no less excited as he offered his congratulations. Rosco had taken some time to adapt to interacting with the ægle, but the Spirit brought unity over the time they spent together.

They gathered breakfast and as they shared a meal, Nida and Kehren approached with Shoym and Killam not far behind.

"Hey there!" Nida called from a distance. "Good morning! Did you all have breakfast yet? I got a little worried when Rosco didn't show up at my dining table this morning. He's been taking Nat's seat at every meal since he got back."

"That reminds me, Rosco, you never did tell me *how* you got back to Endego."

"Well, to be honest, ma'am, that's a story I haven't even told them yet," he replied and gestured to his friends.

Nida plopped down with the others and exclaimed, "Let's hear it, then! I'm sure they want to know how you made it home."

Free of the weight of accusation he'd felt before, Rosco inquired of the others, "How about it? Do you want to hear my story now?"

The others expressed immediate interest so Rosco sat down with them again and Nida invited Kehren, Shoym, and Killam to do the same.

After a long moment clutching his chin in thought, Rosco began, "When the Nihúkolem carried me off, the one thing I was sure of was the direction they took me – South. During the trip, I got to know more about the Nihúkolem than I ever wanted to. That buzzing sound, it just never stops when you're close to them, even if they aren't talking. Not that the wildcat or whatever took me away was the chatty sort.

"No, the whole time we traveled, it didn't say a word to me. Didn't offer me food or a drink of water. Didn't even stop. Just kept on with me in its mouth, running. We were all night like that before we got where it was taking me.

"Petragróktima is what the Etom there called it. The night it brought me to the tower there, I saw just a barren, rocky field with nothing much else around. I learned later that several Etom lived around and even under the larger stones.

"You wouldn't have known it, but there was water there – bitter stuff that made your mouth feel drier and dustier than before you'd drunk it. They dug their wells deep there and minerals or something seeped into the water. Whatever. It was either drink it or die, I suppose.

"In any case, the Empire forced the Etom who lived there to feed and support the Proctors who ran the 'school' where they sent folks for 'education.' I don't care to talk about it again, but it was nasty, and I was alone. You know it's bad when you look forward to seeing the etém who's supposed to torment you just because it's another face.

"I'd been there a few months when all of a sudden one night I heard the Proctors running all over the place outside my cell. They were shouting, and it sounded like there might have been a fight, but then everything went quiet. I didn't hear much of anything for a long time, but then the other prisoners started calling out to each other.

"I don't think any of us could make out what the others were saying, but it felt good to hear the voice of another Etom. Etom who weren't shouting all kinds of nastiness at us like the Proctors did. Now that I think of it, it almost sounded like singing.

"That went on a while, and I was just sitting with my back up against the door of my cell, so I could hear better when the whole place started to shake. It was pretty scary, and it felt like the whole tower lifted and tipped to one side, then split in half.

"The quake set a few prisoners free, and they went and found the keys for the rest of us. The place was kinda topsy-turvy, but we all worked together, climbing all over what was left to make sure every Etom made it out. They didn't come for me until just about everyone else was already out, but I felt like no matter what we weren't leaving anyone behind.

"When they opened my door, I almost fell out of my cell since the whole place was leaning, and I didn't know what to think of what I saw at first. There was no sign of the Proctors anywhere, but what seemed strangest at the time was the great tree root that ran through the building. Like it had grown up there in a matter of seconds just to break open the prison.

"Water was starting to fill up the bottom of the tower and at first I just assumed that some kind of underground spring had welled up there. Then it hit me that it didn't feel like nighttime, exactly. I could see the stars in the distance, but we had plenty of light to see our way out of the prison.

"And I started to recognize some of the Etom once we'd gotten clear of the tower. They were Eben'kayah from Endego. Company Diamond, I found out later. I went to them right away and then we all – all the prisoners – we all tried to figure out what to do next.

"Most of them were Eben'kayah from all around the Empire, though a few weren't. Not that it mattered much right then. We were all just happy to be free and looking to get somewhere safe, to get home if we could.

"The adults talked until they figured out where we were – on a map Company Diamond had, that is – and then started working out how to leave. Petragróktima was more or less in the middle of nowhere, so we'd need food and water before we set out.

"Everyone started looking back at the village, hoping the Etom there would be willing to help us out. Some didn't care if they were willing or not. They were going to take what they needed. Those Etom in the village had helped to keep us locked up, they said.

"Some Etom figured the villagers had just as little choice in helping the Empire as we had in getting locked up. They started arguing with each other, and there was almost a fight then. But it turned out that they didn't need to.

"While everyone else was arguing, one of the prisoners spotted a bunch of the villagers coming our way. By the time everyone heard her shouting to stop bickering, the villagers were right on top of us. The more aggressive prisoners were ready to pounce on them because they thought the villagers had come to make sure we didn't get away.

"The villagers didn't try anything like that, though. It wasn't every last Etom from the village, but it was close, and wow! did they surprise us. They came with armloads of clothing, food, skins of water, whatever we needed, really. I don't think they were Eben'kayah, but what the villagers did for us reminded me of the Eben'kayah. It was something I couldn't put my finger on until this morning, if you know what I mean.

"We prisoners took what we needed for our journey, and the villagers just apologized over and over to us while practically giving us the clothes off their backs. They cared! They really did! Most of us thanked them for the help and then got ready to leave.

"The sun was almost up by the time we were ready to go. I had joined up with what was left of Company Diamond, and when we all took one last look back at Petragróktima, our jaws about fell off. None of us had paid the roots any mind the night before, but now we saw a massive Tree, all by itself in that barren field.

"It hadn't been there when they brought us to Petragróktima, and we figured it hadn't been there until the night before. What was left of the tower was poking out of a pond around the Tree, and the field, that field full of stones, was just covered with grass, flowers, shrubs, even tiny sprouts of more trees!

"At the time, none of knew what it meant, but we were dead-set on getting home. It took us over three months, three *hard* months, to get here, and now I know just what that Tree means. I know exactly what it means. Just like back then, that Tree means freedom."

Rosco finished his tale, and this time the others had questions. He appreciated the attention but didn't think himself qualified to answer all they asked. Rather, they turned with wonder to the Tree of Endego and praised Lord Elyon for all He was accomplishing.

The implications staggered the adults, who hadn't had time to mull the matter over as the Rae, Nat and Sayah had. They had taken their recent experiences in Endego and with Miyam at the Kinsman's Tree for something of a local phenomenon. However, Elyon was revealing what they had witnessed as a single harmonic strain amidst a worldwide symphony of His power.

A Tree three months to the South? And another in Terábnis? Where else did they have Kin? The thought served to increase their admiration and adoration of the One bringing life into the world unparalleled since the time of Gan.

The direct confrontation that had already occurred in Endego aside, the Kinsman's Tree posed a real threat to the Empire of Chōl! Nida's head spun, and she asked Kehren to remind her that they needed to bring this information to the Council.

Right now, however, another matter, this even more urgent, clamored for Nida's attention. She hadn't paid Killam any mind when a few minutes earlier, he had gone to Nat and Rae and whispered something to them. But now she understood why he had done so.

Nat, Rae, Sayah, and Killam yet had a mission in the West. The night spent in Endego had been to rest and let the Kinship here know what they had learned in Terábnis. Time had again come for them to go, and Nida's heart ached, though the pain was not as sharp as their prior departure.

The pain was keen for Kehren as well, and she went to fetch Tram to say goodbye before they left. Nida wondered if Stromweise might want to wish her son farewell and asked Sayah as much. The ægle was at first bashful at the suggestion, then rallied to seek Mother out. And although Killam was a grown etém, his long absence from Endego likewise prompted him to find Shoym, leaving Rosco, Nat, Nida, and Rae to wait for the others to return.

An awkward moment passed before Rosco declared, "I can't believe you two are leaving me again!"

The statement was half in jest, half not, and Nat and Rae understood his frustration. The things they'd seen while apart from Rosco boggled the mind, though they thought his account had also been noteworthy.

Nat was first to answer the feigned accusation, "Rosco, I hope we return to find you stronger, more whole than ever before. The Spirit has some healing yet for you here in Endego. I have my father to find, and perhaps you have yours."

Rosco growled with exasperation, but Nat continued anyhow, "You should not count him out, Rosco. You've heard what the Spirit can do, and you've seen for yourself, within yourself."

Rae chimed in to add, "No doubt your mother needs to know about the Kinsman, too, Rosco."

Whether she spoke by the Spirit or not, Rae's words hit the mark, and Rosco gritted his teeth as he considered his mother's fate. A long time she had stayed by his father's side, though he knew not why or how she had managed to do so. The marriage could not have been easy, given Rufus' greed and foul temper.

The thought of a mission closer to home gave Rosco a purpose in staying behind and kindled his resolve. He would see his duty in Endego through before setting his eyes on the next.

"Very well," Rosco relented, "I will stay and do what I must for my family. But I'll be praying for you – that Elyon will give you success and that He'll protect you from our enemies. You never know what you're going to find out there, especially these days."

The others were returning from their errand and their assembly began to grow once again.

Nat and Rosco embraced as Kin and Nat offered, "Be blessed in the Spirit, my brother. If the Lord Elyon wills it, we shall return safe with my father.

Around them, the Kinship gathered to say farewell and pray the Spirit's blessing on their journey. Soon, the time came to launch once more, this time into the West and for the deliverance of Jaarl. They were on their way well before noon, the sun at their backs as they sped into the horizon.

Chapter Twenty-Five
The Strangled Stream

From the information Killam had provided them, they knew to seek the sea to the West. Once they had reached the sea, they were to hug the coastline and head North. Somewhere near the coast was the dark and tangled wood where Killam suspected the Empire held Jaarl.

None from Endego, Killam included, had ever visited the sea. The Etom there knew only that it lay a great distance away and that the perils between rendered such a sojourn prohibitive. Doubtless, the ægle and his Etom passengers would be wary of all manner of hazard they knew, but it was the kind they did not that occupied Nat's meditations.

The young cornflower etém fell into deep prayer amidst the cloudy heights of the heavens, his mind ever bent on preparation for the danger Astéri had warned him of in Sanctuary.

Lord Elyon, Creator of all things, let us be sensitive to Your Spirit and discern Your will in every situation. Only You know what lies before us, and that we are absolutely dependent on You. Grant us success in finding my Father and deliver us from evil.

I wish to heed the warning of Your servant, Astéri. You do not act without purpose, and if You desire anything of me, of us in our response to Your warning, please help us to know it.

In the matchless name of the Kinsman, Gaal, so be it.

Nat opened his golden eyes, taking in the majesty of the undulating tapestry beneath them as Sayah flew above the clouds. The etém sensed resonant confirmation from the Spirit within as his confidence in their mission grew. Whatever they met, they would do so in the power and wisdom of the Spirit.

The morning of their third day on the westward journey, they broke camp and departed at once. From low along the eastern horizon, the sun struck the ubiquitous glaze of snow and ice, setting it ablaze with winter fire. The first hour of the day was blinding in its brilliance, and Nat was glad that the sun was at their back.

Over the past couple days, Sayah had forced himself to fly faster and harder than he might under normal circumstances. Since their departure from Endego, the additional weight of Killam on his back stood as an ever-present reminder that if their mission was successful, he would be carrying yet another adult etém home. Thus, he hoped to strengthen himself through increased exertion in the interim, and they made exceptional time due to his efforts.

From time to time, they had encountered the occasional flurry or bluster, but these had lasted no longer than a few minutes. Today, however, the western skyline filled with mounting thunderheads, a roiling bulwark against their advancement.

Sayah also noticed a change in the distant landscape, a recession of the white and snowy borders of winter. By all appearances, they approached a warmer, wetter climate indicative of the sea. But first, they would have to master the storm that sped their way, spreading in all directions to fill the sky.

Some darkening hour of the late afternoon, they met the storm's fury. Beforehand, the consensus was to weather the storm and press on through. Nevertheless, once the dark mantle of the maelstrom had settled over the adventurers, they began to question the wisdom of their initial strategy. The anxious eyes of all four wayfarers were on the turbulent clouds overhead, their churning mass shot through with dangerous flashes of lightning.

Thunder all about concussed the very air, and the storm with abandon seeded the sky, scattering it with volatile and unpredictable pockets of turbulence that threatened to overturn the ægle. Regardless of his strength in flight, Sayah could not foresee every twist of the wild winds and grew concerned he might lose one of his friends to the dark unknown below. And that was before the rains struck.

The rains arrived without prelude in a sudden deluge that presented an icy-cold wall of heavy droplets. Their initial encounter so shook the party that all three Etom almost lost their hold on Sayah, which would have spelled certain doom for any of their poor souls.

Sayah made an executive decision without consulting the others, certain they would forgive him his initiative later if they disagreed. From their terrified screams and shouts of horror, he did not anticipate resistance to his plan. At as steep a decline he deemed safe, he dove for cover under a grove of trees.

The near-freezing rain pelted them, and gusts of wind buffeted them but neither stopped their descent. Within seconds, Sayah fluttered under the shelter of the trees – to the gratitude of his precious cargo. The leaden sky let almost no sunlight past, and the shadows of the glade were so deep that the ægle's powerful gaze alone penetrated the murk.

With great caution, Sayah landed and peered about the wood for any sign of danger while the breathless Etom astride him awaited his assessment in the gloom. The grove was roomy in the sense that the trees were spaced apart at regular intervals. The trunks of the trees were thick with smooth, silvery bark, and no branches whatsoever sprung from their lower extremities.

Indeed, the boughs that spread overhead all started from the trunks at the same height and came together with the branch of its neighbor to form neat, symmetrical arches. Sayah looked deeper into the wood to find ranks of such arches in each direction. A species of flowering vine twined about each intersection of the branches, and upon closer inspection, Sayah saw the vines had so enwrapped the uppermost branches of the trees that the overgrowth kept out most the rain.

Someone has tended these trees, Sayah concluded as he coiled for flight, *and we are not alone.*

"What is it, Sayah?" Nat asked at last, sensing the tension in Sayah's frame. "What do you see?"

"Shhh!" the ægle hissed. "Listen!"

A vague rustling approached them on all sides, and Sayah was just going to spring back out into the storm when, maybe a dozen steps before them, a torchlight bloomed. The torch's flame illuminated the face of an etém, a mellow smile on his face.

"Hello there," the stranger greeted them, his voice sweet and inviting.

"Guests, everyone!" he called back into the gloom. "We have guests!"

The flare of a great many torches blossomed to either side of Sayah and his Etom, a blazing procession that began at the foremost and spread back into the grove along two orderly lines. The bearers of the flames in lockstep closed on their spokesetém, who now spoke again.

"Welcome! Welcome, travelers! Welcome to Shug'shug!"

"Welcome!" the others intoned as with one voice and took their place in neat rows behind their spokesetém.

The newcomers marveled at the coordination of their hosts, though something indefinite at the same time chafed. Nat, Rae, and Killam slipped from Sayah's back and stood beside him.

"I am Posher," the one who had greeted them now strode forward and extended a hand.

As the one adult present, Killam stepped forth and took Posher's hand, "Killam. Pleased to meet you."

"As are we!" Posher exclaimed.

"As are we!" echoed the rest.

"We just came in to get out of the storm," Killam explained. "We won't be any trouble. We can wait right here until the weather clears, if that's alright with you."

"Nonsense!" Posher answered, flashing a toothy smile. "You *must* come with us. We have the most amazing sight to show you! It'll make all *your* dreams come true! Guaranteed!!!"

Neither Rae, Killam, nor Sayah detected any threat, but Nat wondered if it was wise to follow these strange Etom. Something wasn't right here, but he couldn't place it.

Killam sensed Nat's hesitation and requested a moment of Posher to confer with his companions. They gathered behind Sayah's bulk to keep the discussion discreet.

"Well, folks," Killam prompted. "What do you want to do?"

"Let's pray," Nat suggested at once, prompted by his disquiet.

"That's a good idea," Rae concurred as did Sayah with a silent nod.

"OK," Killam agreed, and the four bowed their heads to listen for the Spirit's voice.

Go with them, but be careful, the Spirit answered. *I have work here for you.*

They turned to find Posher waiting with smile intact and unwavering.

"We'll come with you," Killam answered.

"Awesome!" Posher shouted. "They're coming with us!"

"Awesome!" the others intoned with enthusiasm.

The torchlit parade of voices turned about with choreographed precision and began to move off back into the trees. Posher beckoned for the travelers to follow, and they were soon on their way. The dancing light of the torches revealed to Nat, Rae, and Killam at last the eerie tidiness of the grove that Sayah had noted before.

The ægle too now realized with some foreboding that the ground beneath them was level and altogether void of any random stone or miscellaneous blade of grass. The earth itself was flat and spotless. Sayah had only ever seen its like in the paved streets of Terábnis.

At the head of the procession, the forerunners disappeared behind a curtain comprised of the same flowering vines that bound the trees together. Something in the familiar glow that peeked through the opening heartened the wayfarers, but as they drew near to pass through, what struck them first was the cloying sweetness of the flowers on the vine.

Almost choking on the fumes, they swept aside the draping vines and, coughing, entered the warm light of the clearing. Nat was first to recover and after sweeping his eyes about the bower, he gasped in horrified shock.

"What is this?"

"This, my friend, is the Kinsman's Tree!" Posher exclaimed with excitement.

Rae, Sayah, and Killam had likewise recuperated from the sick, sweet perfume of the vines to come alongside Nat and take in the sight. It was, in fact, a Tree like that in Endego, like that upon which the Kinsman had given Himself to redeem all from the Stain.

Yet, these Kinfolk here had accomplished something rather odd. First of all, they had draped every entryway to the clearing with vines, all but containing the light that radiated from the Tree to the confines of the bower. Next, instead of allowing the everlasting stream of the Kinsman's Tree to flow free as it may, they had built a high and peculiar wall to keep the waters confined to the bower.

At one side of the wall, a steep stair arose that even now the Etom that had preceded Nat and the others into the clearing struggled to climb. Atop the steps was a wide platform over the water, where waited a large etém in flowing robes, his doughy pink face fixed in an expression of jowly earnestness.

The Kin from Endego watched in silence until Rae piped up at the sight of the etém on the platform.

"Who is that at the top of the stairs?" she inquired of Posher.

"That's Kliarós," Posher replied, beaming with pride.

The first to reach the top, an etma, strode out to the edge of the platform, then turned her back to the water. She and Kliarós were too far from the Kin of Endego to hear what words were exchanged, but they were close enough that Sayah saw her pass something to Kliarós.

"Was that a...a purse?" the ægle asked, confused.

Posher was either too enthralled with the activity at hand or chose to ignore the question. Shouting aloud, Kliarós lifted one hand high and held the other against the etma's back as she closed her eyes, clasped her hands, and raised her face heavenward.

Nat and company were yet too distant to hear Kliarós, and what they heard was indistinct, though they gathered that Kliarós was going to immerse her for cleansing from the Stain.

"Awww," Rae sympathized. "She must be so excited. I remember when I was first immersed."

"Oh, she's been washed before," Posher informed with a zealous smile. "We all have. Every night."

"Wha – ?" Nat began but didn't finish the question.

Kliarós was finished...yelling...and now brought his hand down on the etma's forehead with a meaty slap that sent her falling back into the water. Or so Nat and the others hoped. They had yet to see if indeed any water lay behind the towering dam.

A faint splash met their ears and they breathed a sigh of relief, though they wondered how the etma might get out.

Killam noted, "It's quite a show."

His chalky commentary slipped by Posher, who just smiled and nodded, "Isn't it, though?"

Meanwhile, the procession up the steps continued, and the next Etom repeated the process: go to the edge of the platform, turn around, hand Kliarós...something, get in a prayerful position, then wait for Kliarós to deliver the finishing blow.

"What are they handing him?" Killam inquired.

"Those are offerings, my friend," Posher answered, his eyes wide with excitement as he explained.

"Our offerings secure the blessing of Elyon. We know He wants to bless His Kin, so our offerings pay for the Blessed Barrier you see around the Tree. We wouldn't want any of the blessings He means for us Kin to leak out now, would we? But you know that! You're one of us, and just look how blessed we are!"

Killam shot Nat and the others a sidelong glance. The party from Endego was beginning to get a clearer sense of what might be wrong here, though they hadn't seen the half of it yet.

"Well, I had better get going myself," Posher declared. "Would you like to join me?"

The travelers exchanged looks of dismay but decided they should at least examine the situation up close. The Etom followed Posher up the steps while Sayah waited below.

He was just tall enough to peek over the so-called Blessed Barrier and called out to the others as they struggled up the stairs.

"Be careful up there! You're going to want to see this!"

Posher whispered something to Kliarós as he handed over his offering, then assumed the position of penitent patience. This time, the Kin of Endego were close enough to hear the bellowing words of Kliarós. "Oh, Lord Elyon! We are grateful for all You have bestowed on us. Your blessings are Your gift to us, given for our pleasure. We know Your servant Posher is a faithful etém, and so we claim the desire of his heart, which he has shared with me, the minister of Your blessing. And, so, bless him in the name of the Kinsman!"

The wayfarers had surmounted the platform and were close enough now that the heavy slap of Kliarós' hand against Posher's forehead elicited winces from each of them. They dashed up next to Kliarós to watch Posher fall, the ever-present smile affixed on his face, and what they saw below disturbed them more than anything else in Shug'shug.

The Kin of Endego were struck first by the smell, a pungent odor as of rotted eggs wafting off the stagnant water. They realized now the stink had always been present, but that the sweet perfume of the flowering vine had concealed it.

The water itself was an unhealthy greenish murk, but greener and murkier at the perimeter near the dam in particular, where it had filled the reservoir almost to the top. The visitors were stunned to find the interior wall plated with precious metals and encrusted with jewels. No wonder it took so much in the way of offerings to maintain the Blessed Barrier of Shug'shug. Notwithstanding, the scrim of scum that lined the ornate wall tarnished whatever beauty might have been present in such a display of wealth.

Seeking their attention, and no doubt their offerings, Kliarós offered his blessing to the travelers, who refused. Momentary suspicion passed over Kliarós' puttied features, but then he elected to just bless himself and be on his way.

In rote repetition, Kliarós as the others had and pronounced the generic benediction he'd prayed for all who had presented their offerings this evening. The Kinfolk of Endego noted that Kliarós gave no such offering, thought it would have just passed back to himself regardless. Coming to the end of his noisy invocation, Kliarós yet raised a hand high and brought it down with a loud smack against his own forehead before falling back into the brackish pool.

Disgusted, the adventurers turned their eyes ever closer to the Tree, following Kliarós as he paddled toward the trunk behind Posher. There the water grew clearer and purer. Indeed, a modest puddle right under the dribble of the Tree's spring resembled the draught they had come to know at the Kinsman's Tree and again in Endego and Terábnis.

Following the meager flow of water up the trunk of the Tree of Shug'shug, they spied a travesty of a spring. The water did not so much flow as drip, as if just enough to confirm that this Tree was, in fact, authentic but under protest to the errors of the Kinship here.

Alongside the Tree's dwindling falls, the Kin of Shug'shug had embedded a ladder, and up its meandering rungs, they now clambered to the branches of the Tree. The Kin of Endego observed the different Etom as they crawled along the boughs with singular purpose. Even Kliarós disembarked from an arduous climb onto the lowest branch and shambled to take his designated place closest to the trunk.

About the branches, the Kin of Shug'shug had wrapped more of the pervasive vines, and from them hung some kind of flaccid, leathery bags. The visitors spied Kliarós struggling to fit first one leg into an opening in the contrivance, then the other, and last he pulled his trailing robes in behind him. And all over the Tree, the others swarmed to do the same, settling at last into their slumber as false fruit along the fruitless vine of Shug'shug.

The Kin of Endego were at first too stunned to speak on what they had seen, but Nat was first to turn his back on the spectacle and start down the stairs. The other Etom followed suit while Sayah awaited them at the bottom. Nat did not leave the bower but found a spot at a distance from the Tree. There he sat and just stared at the trappings the Etom here had erected to contain the unique and vital conduit of the Kinsman's life-giving power.

Nat didn't take his eyes from the Tree, and though the others exchanged the occasional word, the mood among them was somber. No one had the heart for conversation, so grieved were they. Rather, they followed Nat's lead and with him fell into deep, fervent prayer.

Several hours passed as they sought the Spirit's will, and Nat in particular strove for a precise understanding of just what about this place grieved the Spirit so much.

Lord Elyon, I don't know what happened here. I just know You are so displeased by it that my heart aches for these Etom. For Your Tree. If You are willing, would You tell me how these Etom have grieved You so?

Nat, My son, you are tender of heart and have both heard My voice and followed Me where I have led you. Not so with these Etom here. They have fancied for themselves a lord who exists to do their will. The resist Me, their Creator, who has redeemed His creatures for His own purposes and according to His own will.

The selfishness that rules from the throne of their hearts has enticed them to keep My blessings for themselves alone. But my blessings are not to be kept thus, for in truth I bless giving more than I do receiving.

Alas, the one called Kliarós has led them astray, for he understood the waywardness of their hearts and took advantage. Appealing to their weakness, he manufactured a false blessedness, a false vine, and, worst of all, a cheap imitation of Me.

Nat absorbed the Spirit's words and asked, *What would you have us do?*

You must destroy that detestable barrier and cut the bonds that have seduced them into slumber. Awaken the Kinship by the truth, and do not cease to speak. The rest I will do by the might of My power. Now go!

Nat opened his eyes and shook his head, uncertain.

Without thinking, he spoke aloud, "Now? Like right now?"

The others lifted their heads as well, and their gleaming eyes gave answer. Then they got to work.

314

The dam that ringed the Tree in Shug'shug was a fine bit of engineering, but it had not been designed to withstand sabotage, which is just what Nat and company intended. All around the wall, wooden struts were dug in and propped against the wall to offset the outward pressure the water within exerted.

Each of the Etom had brought a blade, and they now put them to use in preparing for the destruction of the encircling wall. Sayah's razor-sharp talons served as blades and his size would be a tremendous asset in the demolition of the structure.

The ægle carried the Etom to the top of the vines that served to enclose the clearing. The three Etom leapt from his back and clung to the tendrils, hacking at the lengths beneath them until the individual threads comprising each curtain began falling to the ground.

Meanwhile, Sayah went to another such drapery and tore it to shreds. By the time he returned to the others, they had cut theirs down as well. In this manner, they soon opened the entire bower up to fresh breezes that carried the smell of rain in the aftermath of the storm.

Next, they took the lengths of vine they had cut loose and tied them to the struts encircling the wall. Once each strut was attached to a vine, Sayah draped the attached vine over the branch above the strut. The Etom then tied these vines into those wrapped around the branches.

The process took a good while, and although the hour was late, they each worked with supernatural haste, buoyed by the Spirit. In the end, several lengths of vine were tied to each individual strut below. These vines they had connected to the ones that supported the Etom of Shug'shug as they slept above. Once they were finished, they stood back to survey their work and breathed a collective sigh of satisfaction. They were ready.

Sayah and the Etom each took their positions atop a different branch, and with blade and talon upheld awaited the signal. Nat gave the nod, and they each began to cut away the vines wrapped about their designated branches. With slow resignation, the vines holding the Kin of Shug'shug sagged and drooped as Sayah and his Etom friends cut the sections away. The loosened vines and the Etom they held acted as a counterweight to pull taut the vines attached to the struts below.

With Sayah's help, the Etom sped to the next bough, working their way around the Tree, until they had cleared the vines from every branch that held Etom. And as the weight of the descending Etom pulled against the struts below, their plan began to have the desired effect. From the lowest branch of the Tree, the saboteurs watched on with hopeful expectation.

One support below lifted a bit, skidding out somewhat before stopping again as the end of it fell and dug back down into the ground. The wall there sagged, distorting the circular shape of the barrier. Water sloshed at the movement, and the disturbance sent ripples out in all directions.

Another strut creaked and groaned as if it might snap, then ceased its complaining – to the disappointment of Nat and his party. At once, an altogether different support lifted out of the ground and the Etom providing the counterweight drooped toward the pool below. The dam did not budge.

However, the cantankerous strut from mere moments before resumed its complaint, though not for long. With a dry crack, the beam snapped, and the barrier split, flooding the forest with a sheet of the fetid water. All at once, the rest of the struts either broke or came out of the ground and the corresponding section of the dam fell flat onto the earth.

Considering the ruckus the destruction of the barrier had caused, Sayah and the Etom were surprised at how long it took the sleeping Etom to awaken. Even after his odd sleeping skin had settled down into the shallow water, Posher was a while to emerge, bleary-eyed and perplexed at the sudden change in scenery.

"Hello there!" Nat called down. "Are you alright?"

Posher flashed his patented smile and with squinted eyes replied, "I'm great!"

Standing in knee-deep water, he looked around again at the once-pristine and level clearing, devastated in the destruction of the dam and the subsequent violent passage of water.

"Hey!" he shouted up to them. "Did something happen while we were asleep? The place looks different!"

Brooding in the sandswept ruins of his desert palace, Mūk-Mudón was unused to visitors, save the oppressive, lurking presence of his dark patron. For his part, Helél sensed he'd almost spent the use of his pawn, who reigned now with listless disinterest.

Helél had seen these symptoms in his puppets before, and knew that most times, this unmotivated malaise was the final stage of their utility. Helél had exhausted every leverage in manipulating Mūk-Mudón and none, not even the fear of destruction, remained now this deep-seated apathy had taken hold of the "Emperor." Never one to waste an asset, however, Helél would extract the last drop of worth from Mūk-Mudón before disposing of him.

After all, the rebel prince of the Shedím had never had access to a specimen of such potential before, nor had he accomplished such a feat before through a proxy. The entire world lay beneath Helél's taloned feet and he intended to keep it that way. Indeed, Helél's baleful gaze had landed on an untamed, wild brute who had come to his attention when the fool had donned Mūk-Mudón's imperfect helmet at battle-scarred Za'aq Ha Dam.

Helél had made inroads into the imbalanced mind of one they called the Fowler, substantial inroads that might yet grant Helél control of his tarnished soul. Already, a single-minded lust for power had possessed the Fowler, a vestige of Mūk-Mudón's amplified ambition that by Helél's craft yet haunted the broken artifact upon his head. He was unstable, but pliable, and full of an unrelenting vigor that Helél could use.

His attentions thus diverted, Helél left Mūk-Mudón to his own devices for a time, unconcerned to leave his indifferent pawn unattended. And perhaps something more than coincidence set that very time for Imafel, Cloust, and Belláphorus to come to the seat of Imperial authority.

Regardless, the three generals were set on learning more of the Kinsman and His power. Thirst for freedom from their haunted existence compelled them on their way, three dark stars shooting across the sky, a shared purpose in their minds.

The three generals had predetermined to comport themselves with easy nonchalance, as though their visit were a run of the mill occurrence amidst the everyday workings of the Empire. Nothing to see here, milord. Just going about the business of running the world.

In any case, their sudden appearance in Mūk-Mudón's murky court did not seem to surprise the Emperor, who laughed and welcomed his old friends. So disquieted were they, Cloust in particular, that they almost broke from the plan for fear that somehow, the jig was already up.

When it became clear they had only caught mercurial Mūk-Mudón in a benevolent mood, the generals resumed their scheme. They were here on Imperial business, a plan to get to the bottom of what was causing the appearance of these strange Trees throughout the Empire, the desertions, all of it.

Belláphorus was the spokesperson and proposed the plan. They would gather a substantial portion of the Eben'kayah's captured materials – not enough to endanger Mūk-Mudón's collection, mind you, but enough – and store them in a location near Endego that was not well-defended. A leak that the trove just waited for the taking would draw the apparent devotees of the Kinsman into the trap. Once they were in Imperial custody, the Empire could interrogate the captives for all their worth.

Of course, the generals proposed to oversee the entire operation, which would give them access to whatever information was garnered. With uncommon conviviality, Mūk-Mudón agreed to their proposal, and his generals for a moment caught a glimpse of their old friend, which only made them question their own disloyalty.

Notwithstanding, Belláphorus, Cloust, and Imafel proceeded with their plan. Now they had presented it to the Emperor and he'd approved it, they were committed, and so set about making preparations to ensnare for their own purposes members of the Kinship.

Chapter Twenty-Six
Beauty for Ashes

Even several minutes after awakening, Posher remained in his drowse as did the others who emerged from their sacs. Kliarós was last to arise but first to comprehend the magnitude of the change that had occurred. His pasty pink jowls trembled with a combination of fright and fury as he stomped and splashed about the pool, surveying the clearing.

The floodwaters had spread in every direction, turning the sterile, well-packed earth to mud. The released torrent had likewise sent the stench once contained within the barrier all about the clearing with no cloying perfume left to cover up the stink.

At the instant of the dam's destruction, the outpouring of the Tree's spring had increased to healthy proportions such that the overflow of the pool's shallow banks continued. The flow gained purchase in various places to dig shallow trenches that deepened with the passage of more water.

With time, a number of brooks developed, each one stemming from the pond beneath the Tree. The pool grew clearer and clearer with each passing moment until at last it resembled the genuine article. Soon, the distributary brooks also ran with pure water. Along their banks sprang up fresh grasses and wild flowers that did not conceal the boggy stench that had saturated the ground, but, rather, dispelled it.

Life was returning to Sanctuary Shug'shug and the Kin of Endego were pleased to have been a part of it. Nonetheless, they knew their work was far from over and now turned to the more difficult task. All four prayed their words would be full of the Spirit's grace and power as Sayah carried them down to where Kliarós, Posher, and several others assembled in the waters below.

The ægle touched down and the three Etom dismounted with a light splash. They approached the growing crowd, out of which emerged a visibly disturbed Kliarós to confront them.

"YOU!!!" he bellowed and strode toward them, his forceful steps kicking up jets of water despite the wet robes that encumbered his movements.

Kliarós' cheeks, blotched with an angry red, jiggled as he shouted, "You *ungrateful* peasants! We welcomed you in and were nothing but gracious to you. Now look what you have given us in return!"

"Devastation!" he howled, waving an arm over the flattened wall.

His broad and sopping sleeve whipped around to slap him in the face, which did nothing to improve his mood. Their responses sluggish and their movements sleepy, those behind Kliarós joined him at last.

Sidestepping Kliarós, Nat spoke past him to address the Etom in the crowd, "Awaken! Awaken and stand, you Kin of the Kinsman!"

Kliarós sputtered in protest, then ceased at once for at the young etém's first words, the earth trembled, and the eyes of those gathered opened wide to hearken to Nat as he continued.

"You have drunk the draught of a false vine, a cup filled with the fury of Lord Elyon. You have drained it to the dregs, and it has left you reeling!"

Killam, recognizing the passage from the scroll of Yeshayahu, sensed the Spirit strengthening him also to speak. Stepping forth, he placed a hand on Nat's shoulder in solidarity and proclaimed.

"Awaken! Awaken and clothe yourselves with strength! Clothe yourselves in garments of splendor, Oh you holy people! For no longer will the Stain be found in your midst."

At Killam's declaration, many in the burgeoning throng straightened, and their eyes grew yet clear and focused. Killam's words sent sparks blooming in Rae's mind and she, too, bounded up to Nat's other side to grab his arm and pronounce.

"Arise! And shine with the light that has come to you! For the glory of Lord Elyon has arisen upon you!"

The Tree's light intensified from the usual nighttime amber glow to rays of clear, penetrating light that shot through them all. Kliarós and a few others in the crowd winced and held up a hand to protect their eyes, but most stood fast and did not shrink back from the brilliance. Rather, these, with eyes unblinking, shed tears of grief over what they'd allowed to pass in Shug'shug.

On contact with the radiance, what remained of the sweet, stinking vines on the Tree withered and turned a deathly brownish-grey. The scourge spread throughout the entire grove of Shug'shug, desiccating the vines wherever they twined, but leaving all other life unscathed.

The Spirit prompted Sayah last, and the ægle stood behind the others to declare, "Over you who fear His name, a righteous sun will rise with healing in its wings. And in your freedom, you will dance and make merry amidst the lush, green abundance of His provision."

After he had spoken, Sayah straightened and spread his wings wide in blazing reflection of the Tree's light. At the same time, the vines that had so enwrapped the village dissolved altogether in holy flame and ash began to drift down from above. The whole of the grove seemed to sigh with release from the fetters that had bound it, the trees throughout relaxing their boughs from rigid arches to natural form.

The long night was over, and the sun had arisen over Shug'shug, its rays now piercing the once-constricted and overgrown canopy to illuminate the forest floor once more. With faces upturned, all watched as bits of ash floated down amidst the shine of sun and Tree. Upon the Etom who yet wept over their part in the grievous mockery they had made of Kinsman, Tree, and Vine, the flecks of ash settled between their brows.

Sensing again the Spirit's inspiration, Nat spoke once more, "To those who mourn among the people of Elyon, He will give a crown of beauty in place of ashes, the oil of joy in place of grief and the raiment of praise in place of heaviness; that they might grow into oaks, just and upright, planted by Him for His glory."

At once, the flecks upon their heads turned from ash to oil, spilling over upturned faces to run down the necks and garments of the ones who wept. Sobs turned to smiles and they wept no longer, recognizing the restoration of peaceable fellowship with the Kinsman that followed their repentance.

All about the grove entire, where the ash had landed sprang up now life, a verdant and vibrant crown of exultation. And among the people of Elyon arose the ancient verse, a song of renewal for those who trust in Him:

> When Lord Elyon restored us from captivity,
> we were as those who dream.
> Our mouths poured forth laughter,
> our tongues sang songs of joy.
>
> Then every nation declared,
> "Lord Elyon has done great things for them!"
> And so, we sing, "He has done great things for us!
> Our hearts are filled with joy!"
>
> Oh Lord, restore us as streams in desert land.
> Those who sow in tears will reap with joy.
> Weeping, they depart, carrying seed to sow,
> But singing, they return laden with the harvest.
>
> He has done great things for us!
> Our hearts are filled with joy!

All around the singing Kinship, the waters effervesced, and tiny spouts shot up into the air. Kliarós and a small contingent had started away from those who sang but were yet in the pool when the it began to bubble. When the surface erupted, the spray caught Kliarós altogether by surprise.

"Agh!" he shouted. "What is th – ?!?"

A spurt of rising water hit Kliarós square in the mouth, interrupting his shocked exclamation. Sputtering and disoriented, he tripped over his wet robes and fell face-first into the pool. He arose in indignation to slosh and stumble to the shore, his cohort struggling to contain bemused snickers as they followed close behind.

After the song concluded, the recovery effort in Shug'shug got into full swing. Over the course of mere hours, the Endego contingent was surprised to see Posher emerge as a leader among the Kin there. Perhaps they hadn't been altogether fair to Posher in presuming of him a commitment to Kliarós' faulty order. Notwithstanding, the Spirit used the events they had set in motion at His direction to affect great change in the Kin of Shug'shug, Posher included.

The etém who greeted them now did so with humility, his smile absent in place of an authentic joy that the Spirit alone could provide.

"I want to thank you all," Posher offered. "At the beginning, we worshipped Elyon as we did today – in Spirit and in Truth. But then something happened. I think we started looking to each next big experience, and if Elyon didn't deliver, we made up what we wanted.

"Kliarós saw that and had all these amazing ideas on how we could get what *we* wanted from worship, as if it was ever about us. More and more, we crowded Elyon out until it was *all* about us."

"I think we knew deep down that Elyon wasn't pleased with us. That's why we didn't sense Him anymore with us. We got desperate and decided to keep the waters for ourselves, thinking we'd be blessed if we just held on to more and more and more.

"We started thinking that the blessing was in the having and in the big production we made of it all. But we were wrong. Close-to-dead wrong. So, thank you. Thank you for listening when we couldn't or just wouldn't anymore.

"I know some folks are upset, but they're going to have to get over it. We're *never* going back. And we'll make sure the ones who still care about that sort of thing get their due from that monstrous wall."

Posher hooked a thumb back to the remnants of their "Blessed Barrier" and quipped, "I never realized until now what an awful eyesore that thing was. We're taking it apart as soon as we can.

"Maybe we can do some good with it. Don't know how yet. You can't eat the stuff, but we might be able to build a few ridiculously fancy houses for some poor souls. Make them feel like a million grains."

"Posher," Nat started, but stopped when the other etém put up a hand.

"Sorry, I forgot to tell you. The name's not Posher anymore. After everything that happened here, I'm a new etém. The name is Shakōn now, and I'm not the only one who decided on a fresh name to go with our fresh start.

"We even decided to change the name of the village. It's not Shug'shug anymore, it's Amityot. From false prosperity to true abundance, I'd say this place has changed as much as we have."

Shakōn looked them over with welling eyes and expressed again his gratitude, "And it might not have happened without you."

"Po – ," Nat stopped himself this time, "Shakōn, we have just done our duty to the Spirit and to you, our Kin. We hope that the Kinship here remembers what happened and doesn't hesitate to obey the Spirit when He commands you.

"Now, you may have been wondering what brought us out here, so far from home. The truth is, we're looking for someone. My father, to be exact."

"We have reason to believe the Nihúkolem have a prison out this way," Killam added, "a place they would send only the most undesirable."

"A prison?" Shakōn wondered aloud.

He thought long and hard before a smile once again graced his lips, and with a snap, he shouted, "That's it!"

The others looked at him with expectation.

"It's not what you'd call a jail, exactly. It's the most solitary confinement imaginable, if the rumors are true. A single prisoner with a single guard near the northern shore of the sea. But, again, if the rumors are true, you will need to be very careful, even with your escort here.

"By all accounts, the one posted to watch your father is a ferocious, bloodthirsty predator. Few have survived to carry away the tale, and those that did told of a fearsome sentinel, an all-seeing and merciless raptor."

Sayah shuddered at how much Shakōn's description resembled his sister, Gael, but he set aside the concern, certain the Empire wouldn't have wasted her talents on such a backwater assignment. Nevertheless, he meditated on how they might meet and overcome such a formidable foe, especially if he was carrying the others. Without a doubt, it bore further discussion later.

For the moment, he was drawn back to the conversation in progress as Nat requested, "Can you tell us how to get there? We're eager to find him after all these years."

"I think I can help," Shakōn affirmed, then asked. "How long has he been gone?"

"I – I've never met him," Nat admitted with sudden tenderness. "He left right before I hatched, and the Nihúkolem captured him not long after."

"I was with his father, Jaarl, when they took him away," Killam offered, stepping in to shield Nat. "I, too, was a long time in captivity, but the last I heard was Jaarl had been taken out this way."

"I see," Shakōn replied, now aware of the matter's great sensitivity. "As I said before, the place is not too far from the northern shore of the sea. You should follow the coastline until you come to a long tract of forest. If the rumors are true, search northward along the eastern edge of the forest. That's where you may find your father."

Now was Nat's turn to reciprocate, "Thank you, Shakōn. We are happy to have helped here. I hope you understand why we must be off so soon after arriving."

"You're welcome back anytime. All of you. May the Lord Elyon bless your journey with success."

"Sayah?" Nat inquired. "Are you fit to fly?"

"You know it!" Sayah squawked.

After a night without sleep, the four adventurers were still wide awake. To their surprise, they brimmed with supernatural energy, a blessing of the Spirit to sustain them. The ægle dipped down for the others to mount, and once they were all astride him, they bid farewell to Shakōn and to the Kinship of Amityot.

Pikrïa's appearance in Sanctuary Endego had rekindled in Shoym a spark of the smoldering interest in her that he'd once tended with care. Though long ago the blizzard blast of Pikrïa's rejection had almost put out the flame of his love, a flicker ever remained.

Like fresh air across a bed of hot coals, the Spirit breathed inspiration afresh across the glowing embers of Shoym's heart. The flames of Shoym's passion sprang up, dancing within him as from afar he plotted his approach of the lost love of his youth.

Even at a distance, Pikrïa noticed Shoym's attentions, though she might have died rather than let on. Since her initial encounter with Nida and Nat, she sensed the daylight pressing in through cracks in the brittle, crumbling architecture of her funereal fortress. Ever more difficult was it to scrape together enough of the cloying, embittered mortar to seal out the warmth she sensed in the hearts proffered her.

Shoym's tender affection, a sunbeam in which Pikrïa had basked before, searched for purchase in the once impenetrable barrier she'd striven so long to reinforce. The restless rage that had empowered her struggle over the years to keep others out now failed her, and she sensed her desire for vengeful isolation waning.

With the aplomb of a long-time suitor, Shoym at last made his move. On a rare occasion when Iver had left Pikrïa's side, Shoym hurried up behind the lover who had left him in his youth. He cleared his throat from several steps away in hope the distance would diminish Pikrïa's startlement at the sudden sound. Despite his best intentions, Pikrïa nevertheless jumped, her shoulders bunching with surprise as she uttered a strangled cry.

Pikrïa pivoted with slow, tense deliberation, her ire present in the sharp narrows of her eyes. However keen and cruel her gaze began, it grew softer and kinder as she turned, blunted against the stalwart passion that met her in Shoym.

By Elyon! she gaped. *He's never given up on me, has he?*

The answer was clear in the willing devotion of the gentletém before her as he spoke, "Pikrïa..."

That one word, his utterance of her name, was freighted with a lifetime worth of longing, undiminished by the burden of age or hardened by the callous passage of time. No. This was love at full heat, a fire whose strength would endure any trial for the sake of the beloved.

Nothing but her tortured heart, unwilling to receive its warmth, had kept the blaze at bay so long. The furnace blast of Shoym's affection now threatened to overwhelm her cold insulation, and Pikrïa realized if she remained nearby much longer, she might capitulate to his advances. And so, she stood, stock-still, and let love do the work that she could not.

"Hey there!" a petulant shout came from beyond Pikrïa.

Iver, his face in color resembling a brick in his fury, was closing fast, the diseased clamor of his heart heard on his lips, "You let her be! I'll have none of your bunch corrupting my good folk."

Iver stood beside Pikrïa to address Shoym, whose gleaming eyes hadn't left Pikrïa's in spite of Iver's interruption.

Rather, his eyes asked the question that the gaze of lovers had ever asked since time began.

Do you see me, my love? I see you, and I would take you, whole and entire. Would you take of me the same?

With a nod she herself had difficulty perceiving, she gave her assent. And then again, she nodded, with greater certainty, and tears started from her eyes, so long dry they stung now to weep.

Iver, sensing a tidal shift of Pikrïa's loyalty, gripped her harm above the elbow and growled, "Come now, Pikrïa."

Pikrïa looked down at Iver's hand with incredulity. Not since her father, Savaal, had anyone laid a hand on her thus, and the recollections Iver's hand now evoked did not sit well with Pikrïa.

"Unhand me, Iver," she demanded in all her patrician dignity.

"You're coming with me, you old hag," Iver persisted, and turned to leave, yanking on Pikrïa's arm to drag her with.

With a quickness that belied his age, Shoym darted forth and spun about to place a meaty, work-calloused hand against Iver's chest.

Thus checked by the sudden obstruction Shoym presented, Iver attempted to menace the gentletém, "You'll be wanting to get out of my way."

"NOW!!!" Iver bellowed when Shoym did not at once move.

Instead, the flinty elder etém just cocked an interested brow, a smirk tugging at one side of his mouth.

"I think the etma would prefer to stay," Shoym replied, addressing Iver, then to Pikrïa, "Isn't that right, my lovely?"

At the term of endearment Shoym directed at her, the long-forsaken kindling of Pikrïa' love for him at last ignited.

With renewed zest, Pikrïa cried, "Yes, yes! I want to stay! I want to stay!"

Shoym's words ignited an altogether different kind of blaze in Iver, however, and thus incensed, he released Pikrïa's arm to strike out at Shoym. The blow was looping and clumsy, but dangerous all the same. The fist sailed toward its mark just in front of Shoym's ear, and if it made contact, could well have been a deathblow.

Shoym's expression didn't change a bit as he awaited the stroke. At the last instant, he stepped aside and brought his own fist up into Iver's descending chin. Iver was fortunate that, though his mouth stood open as he swung, he'd managed to keep his tongue inside his head. The resounding click of Iver's teeth slamming together from Shoym's counterpunch was proof he might have lost his tongue from the force of the blow. And it might have better for them all if he had for all the evil Iver produced with the tiny organ after.

For the time being, however, it was sufficient that Iver was sent sailing up and back onto his tail, where he collapsed, flat as a corpse on the ground. Even amongst his followers, who had come at the ruckus of the confrontation, none was concerned enough to come to the unconscious Etom's aid.

Shoym, taking pity on Iver now he was incapacitated, knelt down to check on him. Shoym placed his hand before Iver's nostrils and, feeling the breath there, called some of the malcontent's lackeys to help. When none at first were willing, Shoym demanded they assist. Though hesitant, a couple younger etém came and picked Iver up to carry him off, leaving Shoym and Pikrïa alone at last.

Together, they toured the bower, Shoym relating to Pikrïa all that had happened there before Iver had led her back into his life and that of Nida and Nat. While Shoym would have enjoyed strolling all day with his long-lost love on his arm, he soon recognized that Pikrïa had been almost altogether silent during their walk.

"What is it, my lovely?" he asked with concern.

Pikrïa no longer upheld her dignified masquerade, and as she turned to Shoym, her tortured countenance appeared doubly so for the grieved expression there.

"How can you say that to me now?" she bawled. "Just look at me!"

She held a wrinkled hand up to her ruined face, "What's lovely about this? About me?"

"You know, my friend Nida once told me a secret. Even when she was at her lowest, when it seemed no one else loved or valued her, she would hear one word, a name given her in the secrecy of her heart – *Lovely*.

"She received her name and the strength it gave her without knowing who exactly had spoken it – until at last she met Him in a place very much like this."

Their route had taken them to the edge of the pool, and Shoym pointed a hand at the Tree.

"Nida found the Kinsman at the Tree, where He had drawn her through His loving kindness, where He had called her by name. Not the name given by parents or peers, but the name the Creator speaks into Creation, to His every child – *Lovely*. And so, He awaits those who claim the gift of adoption, of those who cry out in response, 'Daddy! Father!'"

"I myself heard the call, Pikrïa. I believed and answered with all my heart. Right here beneath this Tree. And He has clothed me in the Kinsman's righteousness and made me lovely in ways I could never be without His gift of the Kinsman's glory. And, He will make *you* lovely, too."

Pikrïa wept as Shoym spoke and in shame held her face behind her hands until Shoym took them in his own.

At his touch, she raised her face to his and he looked into her eyes with tenderness to speak, "Pikrïa, do you hear Him calling you? Calling you to be His *Lovely*? Will you answer Him now?"

In a single word torn from her chest, Pikrïa replied, "YES!!!"

"Then come with me, my lovely, and be free of your curse."

With a gentle hand, Shoym led Pikrïa down into the water. Word of the earlier confrontation with Iver had at last reached Nida outside the bower, and she now dashed for the Tree, Dempsey on her heels.

Although they hadn't yet discussed the impact of Jaarl's survival, Dempsey no longer pressed his suit with her while they awaited news of her husband's fate. Nonetheless, they continued to work side by side as though nothing had changed.

When from across the clearing Nida spied her estranged Great Aunt Pikrïa and Shoym descending into the pool, she sprinted all the harder for the Tree for the joy of what she saw. Dempsey did his best to keep up, but Nida ran as though carried on the wind, arriving at the water's edge before Shoym and Pikrïa were yet waist-deep in the flow.

"Wait!" Nida cried, prompting the pair of Etom to turn around and reveal Pikrïa's transformation had already begun.

Pikrïa's face was radiant, though veiled by the Blight that covered her features. Even still, Nida perceived the softening of Pikrïa's eyes when she saw Nida sloshing toward them with Dempsey not far behind.

"Nida..." Pikrïa gasped.

"Yes, I'm here," Nida responded, as, all dignity aside, she splashed up beside Shoym to face Pikrïa.

"I'm here, Pikrïa."

Shoym and Dempsey beamed as they watched the two etma after all these years reconnecting much as a mother and daughter might. Already, the Blight's grip on Pikrïa was loosening, but Shoym, Nida and Dempsey knew it would not let go altogether until Pikrïa had joined them in the Vine.

"Shoym," Nida began, "will you do the honors?"

Shoym looked as excited as a groom on his wedding day when he replied, "Yes! Absolutely!"

"Hold on to me, dear," he whispered to Pikrïa, who gripped the arm he placed before her as with the other he supported her back.

Then in a voice much louder, he proclaimed, "Long have we loved our dear Pikrïa, and today our love finds its greatest expression in bringing her to the Kinsman. In Him, we put to death all offenses of her past so that she might arise, forgiven, as member of our family, our Kinship."

"Are you ready at last to meet Him, my love?" Shoym whispered to Pikrïa, who with eyes closed around streaming tears, nodded her head with fervency.

"Then in the name of the Father, and of His Son, and of His Holy, Life-Giving Spirit, we so baptize this etma!"

With the delicate grace of a dancer, Shoym dipped Pikrïa back into water. Pikrïa rested there beneath the flow, the blissful, helter-skelter smile on her face visible under the crystal-clear water. While she waited with breath abated, she sensed the scabrous mask of Blight loosening. With barbed, intrusive fingers sent deep into her flesh, the Stain had long held a grip on Pikrïa. A grip that now first slackened, then retreated altogether.

To the surface floated the remnant of the horror that with slow inevitability had overtaken her countenance. The bloated crust dissolved at first into a frothy scrim, then disappeared altogether.

When Pikrïa arose through the purifying flow, the smile she wore proclaimed her liberty from the Stain and Blight. Though age yet wrinkled and crinkled her skin, her face glowed with the youthful shine of a hatchling. For born anew she was, and forever would she live on in the Vine.

Chapter Twenty-Seven
Free at Last

In contrast to the wet and gloomy skies that had sent Sayah and his riders ducking for cover the day before, the skies now were clear and bright. Clouds lay in a lengthwise column of silver over the sea to the West, but they neither darkened nor grew to threatening proportions as the travelers glided toward them on the fresh, moist air.

The sea itself began as a leaden thread draped on the horizon that soon stretched to fill it. They smelled the salty brine long before they heard whitecaps crashing as they descended around noontime for a bite to eat.

Once they had landed on the beach, the sea astounded them in its breadth, and its apparent emptiness filled them each with a peculiar loneliness, provoking silent reflection amongst the quartet. They ate without much conversation, then left the shore and its vast sadness behind.

For his part, Nat was reminded of the depths of Gaal's sorrow and wondered if He'd created such a place as a mirror of His attributes.

In confirmation of the thought, the Spirit brought to mind a verse, *The heavens declare Lord Elyon's glory, and the skies above display His craftsmanship.*

The words sent Nat's mind reeling at the implications – if sea and sky revealed His qualities, so then did all of Creation, right down to...down to Nat himself. Or at least that what Lord Elyon had desired since the beginning. Since before the fall of Gan.

Nat's mind thus occupied with his meditations, time passed for him without so much as a single tortured thought of his father. Whether he admitted it or not, Nat was anxious to have a definitive answer as to Jaarl's fate. Now hope had been rekindled, Nat clung to it with a ferocity that might have been unhealthy but for the restraint the Spirit granted him within.

As the sun began to sink over the western skyline, Sayah called out, "Forest, dead ahead!"

Not long after, the Etom also spied the dark green line of trees to the North. The ægle had maintained the same swift pace he had since their departure from Endego, and before nightfall, they were near enough they might camp within the forest's bounds.

Nat signaled the ægle to land before they got too close and they held a brief parley concealed amidst the shrubbery outside the woods.

"What do you think?" Nat inquired. "Should we stay in the woods?"

"Uuuuh...I don't know," Rae replied. "They look pretty dark. Remember the Dimroad? It feels a bit like that."

Sayah concurred, "I agree. I don't imagine the Nihúkolem this far out of the way, but there are other things..."

"Too true," Killam opined, "We don't know what might be lurking in there. At least out here, we have clear line of sight in every direction. Hopefully, we'll see any threat coming."

"And the underbrush here is thick enough we're unlikely to be spotted," Rae added.

"OK, then," Nat surmised with a nod of the head. "Sounds like everyone is agreed. We'll stay out here for the night. But I don't think we can chance a fire."

"We haven't had any rain or snow all day, and the sky looks clear now," Rae observed. "We should be fine with just our bedrolls. Will you be warm enough, Sayah?"

Sayah smiled, touched at her consideration, and replied, "So long as I have my Kin nearby, I'll be satisfied. Besides! Since the Cold Vantage, nothing much seems cold by comparison."

"That's because your little æglet tushie didn't have any feathers on it back then!" Rae jibed.

Sayah was plenty amused and agreed he was much warmer since fledging. The exchange warmed them all despite the lack of fire and soon they settled in beneath the shrubs to share in voices kept low the warmth of food and fellowship.

A gloomy, drizzly morning greeted them when they arose. The day was of the kind that sat atop the landscape like a dark, damp blanket, though it failed to dampen the spirits of the four adventurers. The weather had no impact on the happy mood of their breakfast, and they partook with gratitude of the rhema that awaited them upon waking.

They found extra rhema that morning, at least enough for an extra portion for each member of the party. Strange enough, no matter how many times they ran back through the weekly calendar, each time they figured the next day was not the Day of Rest. In the end, they chalked it up to a mystery of the Spirit and hoped He might reveal His purposes in time.

While the forest before them was less intimidating in the daytime, the gloom of the overcast sky shrouded its depths in shadow. Before they had broken camp, Sayah noted that an overgrowth of the same vines that had covered Shug'shug likewise infested these woods. This stock must have been much older for the thickness of their stalks and the wild ubiquity of their tangles. So tight was their constricting weave amidst the branches that very little light indeed reached the forest floor.

The party took some pleasure in the fact they mightn't need to enter the wood at all, depending on where they found Jaarl. The Spirit had supplied them a measure of faith in finding the lost etém such that, in their minds, it was a foregone and certain conclusion. The one question that remained to them was just how his deliverance would play out.

They delayed no further in taking to the air, and soon they glided along the eastern border of the forest. Sayah stayed level with the tree branches and neither rushed nor dallied while his passengers scanned the foliage for any sign of the captive Etom. Preoccupied with detecting the presence of the Empire's hostile warden, the ægle was unable to lend his eyes much to the search, though from time to time, he flicked a glance that direction.

After an entire morning spent in fruitless research, the quartet elected to picnic at a distance from the forest. Again, they found some brush to screen them from the woods, which seemed to leer at them from cavernous eyes between the trees. The feeling of the place was altogether unwholesome.

Regardless, the sense of foreboding did not impinge on them as they broke bread together. They determined that, with its tendency to spoil, the extra rhema would not go to waste, and indulged once more in the fortifying fare. And although their practice was to dispose of what remained after a meal, Nat asked that they saved the piece that was left, though he himself was uncertain as to why.

Before they took again to the sky, they gathered in prayer and asked the Spirit's help and guidance in their search.

"...in the name of the Kinsman, Gaal, so be it," Nat concluded.

After the prayer, Rae lifted her eyes to a sky unchanged but for an unnatural whirling in the bank of dark clouds overhead.

"Uhhhh, that's abnormal," she stated, matter of fact, as she pointed out the disturbance to the others.

"Isn't it?" she asked.

"Yes," Sayah replied. "Definitely, yes."

The eye of the twisting clouds opened wide, boring through the bulging grey mass, and a bright shaft of sunlight shone through. Like a finger, the light pointed to an outcrop of the overgrown forest, and amidst the tangle, a flash of reflection. Something was there!

"Sayah!" Nat cried, his face flushed and eyes bright. "Do you see it?!?"

"Yes!" the ægle answered and ducked low for the Etom to mount. "Let's go!"

The three Etom were up at once and Sayah sprang into the air, his wings flashing as they climbed toward the pressing rays. And once aloft within the shine, he flew as if a silver dart, onward to the mark.

Long months on the fringe as sole warden of the little blue bug had further unbalanced Gael, who now sulked about her days in disconsolation. No matter how much she tortured the prisoner, no matter how long she starved him or rained screeching fury down on him, he had persisted in his friendly overtures – to Gael's great displeasure.

However, after a time, not even the captive had excited a reaction from Gael. She became all the more withdrawn from reality, ever meditating on the moment she had fallen from so great a height to where she dithered now.

She traced her demise back to her brother, who in Endego had thrown off the yoke of her dominance in an act that defied all her prior considerations. And present there had been Something else altogether. Something that had overturned her towering pride in an instant of effortless power. Something she cared very little to think about.

Thus, she went 'round and 'round: Sayah the runt, ever at her feet. Sayah the luminous, overpowering her. The overwhelming weight of presence before the Tree. Shriek after shriek of denial!

Sayah was the runt, always at her feet. He could *never* overwhelm her. The sense of hated, unassailable strength. NO!!! And on and on it went until the path paced on feverish feet within her mind wore down first into a rut, and then a steep and insurmountable trench she could no longer escape.

Months. So many months Gael was alone in burdensome meditation, stripping meat from bones with bloody dispassion – killing just to kill, eating just to fill the belly. The beast that beat behind her breast now sagged and slumped with erratic, dwindling interest, its form bloated from slaking Gael's bloodthirst and feathers clotted with the gore of her victims.

No color remained in the world, not even the once fresh and invigorating claret of that vital flow. All had turned to ash, smudging the world a desolate grey.

The day's weather hadn't helped either. Gael wandered this way and that, picking apart an unfortunate rabbit, and then smashing some poor vole against a rock. She destroyed with wanton disregard, hoping to elicit within herself some sense of...anything as her wanderings took her ever eastward.

Around noon, Gael turned an indifferent eye to the west, where for the first time in a very long time, a different thing occurred. Something interesting, perhaps. She could see the sun breaking through the leaden cloak of the sky in a most peculiar way, its beam shining with odd precision on the location of her hostage. Most peculiar, indeed.

And then she saw him. A gleaming figure who in an instant set her heart pounding and the craven creature within howling with fury once more. Sayah. There he was, blazing again with strange light and speeding toward *her* prize, the justification of her singular duty here on the western frontier. The entire world seemed to slow, and Gael arose on thunderous wings that beat heavy for her vindication.

Sayah sensed the driving compulsion of the Spirit behind each stroke of his wings, a revisitation of the Spirit's power as at the Cold Vantage, speeding them to the deliverance of Nat's father. They all felt it, the absolute certainty of success now, and the Spirit's jubilation to set the captive free at last.

They were short seconds on the wing before arriving at their destination, a rusty, creaking cage that swung from a vine-enveloped tree. The thick branch from which the cage depended had so long supported bore its chains that the rusted links had sunken down in the bark to embed the encircling length in the bough.

Sayah had not altogether alit atop the limb before Nat was bounding from his back. The way the cage hung presented a minor obstacle to its access, but Nat, ever the accomplished climber, had no trouble scaling down the chain to the cage.

Is this really *where my father spent the last decade?* he asked himself as he descended to the enclosure. *Is he even here now?*

Upon his heart, the doubt fell heavier than the links of chain in hand, but Nat took the thought captive by the power of the Spirit. Persevering, he reached the cage and clambered down the rough slats, his eyes peering through the gap for any sign of the prisoner.

He was almost to the bottom of the cage and had yet to spy an occupant within its shadowy recesses. The weighty doubt threatened once more, but the vigilant Nat thrust it aside and continued to the bottom. Above, the others watched with expectation for any sign they had indeed located the long-lost etém.

Nat reached the bottom of the cage and placed his feet through the gaps on either side of a slat with care.

Gazing through into the darkness, he ventured, "Hello? Is anyone there?"

No response. Undeterred, he worked his way around to another spot, glancing into the gloom as he did. He stopped at last at the sunward side of the cage, where a sliver of the warm rays pierced the dank interior of the cage.

The streaming light illuminated a swath within, where Nat's shadow danced along the floor. Across the cage, Nat spied a dark and huddled form, a shape he might have mistaken for a misshapen pile of rags. And then it stirred.

"Hello!?!" Nat called again with greater urgency. "Is someone there?"

The wispy figure, no more than skin and bones wrapped in threadbare tatters, arose and staggered forth on unsteady limbs, a shambling mummy embalmed in the cruelty of the Empire of Chōl. As the prisoner drew near, he became more distinct: an etém of deep blue skin and a broad smile upon his lean face.

"Jaarl?" Nat called, his own smile a reflection of the father he'd never known. "Are you Jaarl?"

Jaarl arrived at last, falling against the cage with weary joy as he looked into Nat's gleaming, golden eyes.

"Yes. I'm Jaarl. And you are? Have you come to set me free?"

Happy shock registered in Nat's widening eyes as he replied, "I – I'm Nat. I'm your...son."

Jaarl's face contorted with emotion as he began to weep with joy, "My son? My own son has come to take me home? How can I ever thank Lord Elyon for this blessing?"

Strength returned to Jaarl and he straightened against the slats to extend a thin arm through them.

He stroked Nat's cheek with affection as he cried, "My son, Nat! *My son!*"

Nat closed his eyes and frisked under his father's caress. He savored the first touch of his father's warm hand, reaching up to feel the strength present even in the emaciated fingers. His father was alive! And here!

A sudden intensity filled Nat and he lifted shining eyes to announce, "We must get you out."

"I would like that, son," Jaarl sniffed, "Very much."

"How? Is there a door? A lock?"

Jaarl pointed toward where he'd sat and offered, "They thrust me through that gate many years ago and locked it tight behind me. It's not been opened since."

Nat worked his way around to the gate while Jaarl moved across the interior to meet him there. Vines obscured the aperture and rust had covered both lock and hinges. Nat peered at the corroded mechanism, uncertain it would turn even if they possessed the key.

"It doesn't look good," he admitted to his father. "Do you have any other ideas?"

"Well..." Jaarl pondered, then stomped against the floor, his face alight with a smile. "The floor! It's wooden. And very old. Maybe your large friend up there could lend a hand? Or should I say, a wing, eh?"

Of course! In his preoccupation with finding his father, Nat had forgotten the others. Sayah was big enough he might break through the bottom of the cage.

Nat looked up to where the Sayah perched atop the branches. The ægle alone was visible from Nat's vantage, and Nat was just about to call him down when something fluttered in the corner of the young etém's eye. And then all the world stood still but for the shrieks of warning on Nat's lips.

Gael had flown high and circled wide to avoid both Sayah's incidental gaze and the light that, as a javelin cast from heaven, pierced the sky. Her heart pumped with lunging fury in time with the powerful beat of her wings. She attained the height of the clouds, then folded her form into a silent missile directed at her brother's shining form below.

She dove in quiet and complete commitment to her brother's destruction. She would not cry out in challenge nor would she give him opportunity to defend himself. This was her opportunity to obliterate the one who stood as a symbol of her failure, a reminder of the unspeakable power her mind could not comprehend.

Down, down, down she dove, accelerating with reckless abandon. With just the feathers of her tail, she adjusted her course. Until, at the last moment before collision with her target, she flared her chestnut wings, her gleaming talons snapping forth with bloodthirsty intent.

A string of high-pitched squeaks from below distracted Gael for a split-second and alerted Sayah to her assault. He slipped aside as her talons slashed at his neck though he didn't altogether escape her grasp. A splash of red stained his shoulder and he dove beneath his perch in search of room to maneuver.

The frenzied Gael, however, gave no quarter but pressed Sayah this way and that, her larger form blocking every route of escape from the snap of her beak and the reach of her claws. Sayah's injury reduced his agility by the merest measure, but it was sufficient to prevent him outpacing Gael.

With a brutal leer curving her hungry beak, Gael roared with laughter that to the nearby Etom seemed the most dreadful cackling. Today, she would taste her brother's tepid blood and feast on his simpering heart. Today, she would be victorious. She was gleeful in his torment and neither Father, Mother, nor any other force would hinder her this time.

In her fevered state, she gave voice to her glee, "Ha! Do you see now, Sayah? There is no one to protect you here. No Mother! No Father!"

Gael's mention of Father kindled in Sayah's heart a resolute rage, an indignant and righteous fury at her disrespect. In a sudden reversal, Sayah went on the attack, looping forward to catch Gael under the chin with the rear hook of a talon.

Gael shrieked with incredulity and tumbled back, rolling with the force of the blow. Sayah had made contact with her beak and thus had not drawn any blood, but the stroke staggered Gael, who had been unprepared for any such reprisal.

And now Sayah was shouting back at her, his voice firm as he declared, "Father is *dead*, Gael! How dare you dishonor his memory? Have you no honor of your own?"

If Sayah's first blow had stunned Gael, his words were second in a combination that set her up for knockout. The wailing brute within her didn't just slow its pace. It froze altogether, and in the stony stillness, fell. Gael likewise plummeted to the earth, landing in a clumsy stance that betrayed her perplexity.

"Dead?" she whispered as if to herself.

Sayah heard and answered, "Yes, dead! But *he* died with honor, cleansed of the Stain, an ægle free of the Empire's oppression, though it was at their hands he died."

Sayah hovered between Gael on the ground and the cage overhead as he continued to adjure her, "And yet you continue in the Empire's service. So, again I ask, where is *your* honor?"

Despite her shock at Sayah's revelation, Gael had enough of her brother's high and mighty tone. The beast within howled against the charges he laid to her account, rattling its cage with increasing fervor.

Opportunity presented itself as Gael plotted Sayah's demise, her brow furrowing over a ferocious gaze as she watched him. Overhead, he drifted in subtle, lateral arcs beneath the cage, and at just the right moment, she lunged.

Gael burst from the earth, her wake behind scattering the leaves and various detritus of the forest floor. She crossed the span between her and Sayah like a bolt fired from a bow, slamming into him with a force that carried them both upward.

She surprised Sayah with her rapid advance and pinned him between herself and the bottom of the cage. For a brief instant, he was concerned his bones might be broken in the impact. Indeed, the tender snap that came from his backside worried him at first until he recognized the cracking sound had come not from his body but from the cage's wooden base.

The cage lurched upward and canted to one side as the two ægles drove into its base, flinging Nat from the cage on a lofting trajectory, where he was grateful to catch hold of one the ever-present vines. For his part, Sayah spread his wings wide, determined not to let Gael stuff him into the enclosure, where she would have him altogether at her mercy.

A small, stifled cry from behind him confounded Sayah for a split-second.

Jaarl! his mind informed him at last. *He could be hurt as well!*

The weight of the cage overcame the initial upward thrust of their collision and began to fall, jerking back and forth in shortening, chaotic arcs. The violent jostling cast Gael aside and gave Sayah a bit of breathing room.

In that brief moment, he sensed his opportunity, and with care began to work himself loose.

"Sayah!" Nat shouted from where he hung. "Can you catch my dad?"

Sayah stopped and looked for Gael, who had fluttered to the ground below to regroup. She stood, shaking her head, but didn't look ready to rejoin the fight quite yet.

Sayah called back, "I'll try. Can you ask him to get ready?"

Nat was perplexed at the ægle's request until he remembered his father mightn't be able to understand Sayah.

"Yes!" he replied, then shouted to his father. "Dad, can you get ready to drop onto my friend Sayah's back?"

"Ok, son! I'll be ready," Jaarl affirmed, then added, "but are you just going to repeat everything he says?"

Nat chuckled and just shook his head in reply as Sayah removed himself from the cage. Flapping hard to maintain his altitude, the ægle circled back to catch Jaarl as splintered bits of the floor fell to the ground. A large, irregular piece fell crosswise across the end of the cage, obstructing it somewhat, but leaving a narrow, slanted gap under Jaarl.

The etém did not hesitate to drop onto the tilted floor and work himself feet-first through the opening.

"Is he ready for me?" Jaarl called to Nat.

"Ready?" Nat asked Sayah, who nodded and arose just beneath Jaarl's dangling bare blue feet.

Jaarl looked over his shoulder in preparation to drop down, then spotted behind Sayah the rising form of Gael approaching fast.

"Look out!" Jaarl shouted.

Without waiting to look, Sayah dropped, diving and spinning around in the same moment to meet his attacker.

Gael, frustrated in her attempt to assault Sayah, turned her ire on Jaarl, who, kicking his feet, pulled himself back up onto the skewed and precarious plank positioned across the bottom of the cage. The raving ægle rammed into the shattered base, sending Jaarl aloft. He landed with a hollow thud as Gael tried to reach around the board for him with piercing talons.

Gael's questing claws left deep scratches in the wood, but Jaarl crouched low on all fours and steadied himself as Gael shifted the floor in her search for him. Toying with her prey, she was altogether preoccupied when Sayah struck her broadside with his shoulder.

As she fell away, Gael's swinging foot knocked the base of the cage altogether loose at last and flung Jaarl against the slats. By the grace of Elyon, he caught hold along the rusty edge and began working his way down to see if he might climb out somehow.

From the perch he had attained since hurled to another tree, Nat foresaw the challenge his father would face before Jaarl reached the bottom of the cage.

"Rae! Killam!" he shouted to the others. "Can you drop a vine down to my father!?!"

Jaarl overheard Nat and, stunned with happiness, peered up toward the branch where the other two Etom waited.

"Killam?" he inquired with hopeful eyes. "Killam's here?"

The answer to his question came in the form of a vine unfurling alongside the cage, followed by the grey etém himself, who came sliding down with a cheery cry on his lips.

"Jaarl! My friend, you look a bit worse for wear!"

Jaarl chuckled, and replied, "And you look better than I remember. A sight for sore eyes, you might say!"

Their brief levity ended when Killam descended beside Jaarl and locked eyes with his old friend, a fervent intensity in his voice as he pledged, "It's your turn now, brother. Time to set you free."

Jaarl looked down through the open cage, the heights below dizzying and the clamoring screeches of ægles locked in combat disconcerting.

"How are we going to do this, Killam?" he asked.

"I'm going to swing underneath," Killam replied. "You'll have to drop down onto the vine when I do."

"Is everything alright down there?!?" Rae called down from above.

The fighting between the ægles had intensified and the ruckus concerned the young etma that they might not be able to get Jaarl out to safety.

"Yes, Rae!" Killam called back. "We're just about to spring him now."

"Ok, um, just hurry. I don't know how much longer Sayah can hold out."

"You ready, Jaarl?" Killam asked. "We get just the one chance at this. When I swing under, you need to jump down onto the vine."

Killam winked and offered a wry grin as he added, "Try not to knock me off, OK?"

"I can't make any promises," Jaarl chortled, "but I'll do my best."

"Well, then, let's get this show on the road," Killam declared.

Killam met Jaarl's eyes and he gave short nod of his head before kicking hard off the cage. He swung out a good distance from the creaking enclosure, rappelling several body lengths and widening the arc of his swing as he did. Jaarl stood poised on the inner edge of the cage, watching Killam as he began his swing back. Just before Killam drew even with the cage, Jaarl jumped.

Jaarl timed his leap just right and fell astraddle a curving length of the vine. Gripping for all he was worth, he held on until the vine fell still.

From below, Killam cried, "You'll have to climb, old friend! Do you think you can manage?"

"Just try and stop me!" Jaarl replied and hand over hand began to scale the makeshift rope.

A furious Gael shrieked nearby at that very moment, prompting Jaarl to revise his statement, "Not you!"

Killam was right behind Jaarl when the pair at last surmounted the branch where Rae awaited them.

"You must be Nat's dad!" she exclaimed. "I'm Rae, his...friend, a good one."

Killam glanced over the edge, where the ægles scrapped it out and commented, "Doesn't look good for our friend, Sayah. Do you think we should have just gone all the way down?"

Rae gave her head a solemn shake and answered, "I don't want to go down there. Do you hear them?"

Nat shouted from his place in the neighboring tree, "Do you think there's anything we can do to help him out?"

"All we have are vines, Nat," Killam responded. "Unless we can convince the other ægle to..."

Killam trailed off, his face pensive until he exclaimed, "That's it! Nat, can you get Sayah's attention? We'll need his help if this is going to work."

"I'll try!" Nat replied. "What do you need him to do?"

"We need him to draw Gael over here by us when I say so."

"I'll see what I can do!" Nat called back, then set about the task of signaling Sayah, a feat made difficult while he was preoccupied with fending off Gael's attempts on his life. The other Etom, meanwhile, began gathering vines together in preparation to implement Killam's plan. While they worked, Killam explained his intent, and Rae and Jaarl began to feel hopeful they all might escape intact.

In the meantime, Nat waved, jumped, and shouted for Sayah's attention, and his efforts were at last rewarded when the pair of dueling raptors flew past. In that instant, Sayah's eye fell upon Nat, who beckoned him nearby. Flitting this way and that, Sayah outmaneuvered Gael and was able to fly past Nat again a bit slower.

"What is it, Nat?" he huffed through his exertion. "I'm a tad busy right now."

"See if you can get her to fly under the branch the others are standing on!" Nat shouted.

Nat was aware Gael did not have the help of the Spirit in interpreting the tongue of the Etom, and thus had no regard for secrecy or lowering his voice. The Spirit had provided a distinct advantage, and Nat intended to take it in full.

"I'll do my best!" Sayah fired back over his shoulder and then dropped into a sharp dive to avoid the sweep of Gael's next assault.

"He's going to do his best to bring her to you!" Nat told the others. "Get ready!"

Rae, Killam and Jaarl worked non-stop to prepare their trap, and were almost finished when Nat called to them again.

"Sayah's coming your way! Now's our chance!"

Killam was not altogether confident they were prepared, but urged the others on nevertheless, "Get those last two tied together, Rae! Jaarl, can you pull that bit back up here?"

Killam worked with a frenzied passion while continuing to direct the others and believed they just might make do with what they'd readied. Not that his opinion mattered much now the two ægles bore down on them.

Their trap aside, however, he spotted another problem with the plan – Sayah's pursuer was so close behind they might catch the both of them if Sayah couldn't pull away a bit. Nevertheless, Killam was undeterred and prompted Rae and Jaarl to join him in egging the snowy-white ægle on.

"Sayah! You've got to put a little room between you two!" Killam cried. "You can do it!"

"Yeah, Sayah, I know you can! Fly faster!" Rae echoed.

Jaarl, for his part, cheered Sayah on with unintelligible chirps that, together with the others' exhortations, seemed to get through. Sayah sped their way with Gael in hot pursuit, and in response to the Etom, gave an almost imperceptible nod.

Bellowing for all their worth, all four Etom cheered him on while in their hearts they pleaded the Spirit's aid. In reply, the indwelling Spirit quickened Sayah to a velocity unlike any he'd known since his miraculous flight from the Cold Vantage.

This time, Sayah sensed his wings loosened to a degree that exceeded even the strength he'd found anew in carrying the others. A lightness of frame accompanied the beat of Sayah's wings, their movements now effortless and swift under the incredible transition as he pulled well ahead of Gael.

Like a bolt of silver fire, Sayah streaked beneath the Etom, his passage so tremendous that it almost blew the wee creatures off their feet. Then the single-minded Killam was shouting to spring the trap and Rae and Jaarl forced themselves to act, despite their unstable footing.

Together, they forced the snarl of vines before them from atop the bough, and the apparent mess of tendrils unfurled across Gael's path to reveal a crude net. At top speed, Gael punched into the draping snare, a surprised screech of rage emanating from her beak.

The momentum of the angry ægle dimpled the far side of the net as her head slipped into a green collar and her shoulders rucked up against the net. Her talons likewise fell into the rough, square crosshatch of the snare while her wings, though free, flailed to no effect under the encumbrance of the trap.

"Quick!" Killam hollered. "Get the other side!"

With another concerted effort, the three Etom cast an identical weave off the other side of the branch, sandwiching the angry bird between the lank and heavy nets.

"Let's go!" Killam directed once more. "Final step and we're home free!"

He was already at work on his section of the branch, sawing away at the vines with his blade. Rae was quick to follow suit while the unarmed Jaarl helped separate the stretches she severed and drop them over the edge. With each falling vine, the net curled and tangled ever more to enmesh the raging ægle, who predicted her downfall with increasing displeasure expressed in the waxing cacophony of her cries. Within seconds, the net dangled by a single tendril, its taut length charged with weighty potential.

"Give me a little room, you two," Killam cautioned.

Rae and Jaarl stepped back and Killam braced himself square before the final vine with blade upraised. With a decisive blow, he severed the tendril, which, whipping, sprang away.

Below, the ægle keened with rage and displeasure until gravity knocked one last shriek from her snapping beak when she met the ground. Although more than a tad spent, Sayah had not been idle in the meantime, but had collected Nat so that now two of them join the others on their perch.

From beside Rae and Jaarl where he stood and watched the ægle below struggle in her bonds, Killam looked up to greet Nat and Sayah.

"It looks like it worked," he sighed, then asked of Sayah, "Are you well, my ægle friend? That was quite a scrap."

Scarlet streaks crisscrossed Sayah's form, their presence all the more visible amidst his white plumage.

Sayah did not seem too much the worse for wear as he replied, "I'll be fine. Nothing more than few scratches, and I have to say I got my licks in, too."

Rae looked up now and offered, "It's so sad that you had to contend with her. It's a tragedy when family fights, especially when blood is spilled."

This last bit caught even the attention of Jaarl, who to that point had stood enthralled watching Gael struggle below.

The freed captive turned to the others, then asked Sayah, "Family? Who is this ægle to you?"

Jaarl learned of Gael's relation to Sayah, and in the end nodded as he meditated over what he learned. The revelation confirmed for Jaarl what he suspected he must do, and so he made a request of Sayah before they departed for Endego.

"I must see her one last time," Jaarl shared and pleaded, "Will you carry me to her?"

Sayah nodded in agreement and added, "It was in my heart as well to have a word with her. It pains me to leave her so, though I know she will see her way to freedom before too long. We seek a head start alone in her current captivity. No more."

Soon, they were landing near the struggling ægle, who for all her efforts did not desist in her fury. Sayah allowed the Etom to dismount, then he and Jaarl approached Gael while the others waited, their lips lively with prayers for the ensnared ægle.

As her brother, Sayah was first to speak to Gael, and he kept a safe distance as he began, "Gael, I am sorry for any harm I've done you here. I hope you understand I fought only for the freedom of my friend's father, a prisoner the Empire unjustly imprisoned."

In her rage and disbelief at being capture thus, Gael's speech had deteriorated into mindless shrieks and howls, which were her sole reply to Sayah's words.

Regardless, he continued, "Gael, you're my sister and nothing is going to ever change that. I hope you find your way back to the honor you left behind – to the honor Father and Mother exemplified.

"I hope you, like me, find your way to be rid of the Stain. I hope you find your way to the Kinsman, Gaal. Gaal will change you and give you life itself and that in abundance. I will continue to pray He meets you where you are and draws you to Him. That's the greatest kindness, the greatest love I can ever show you.

"I hope you're not long in this place, Gael. I hate to leave you so, but you've not left me many options. I must protect my friends and carry them away. I know that you'd try to stop me, and so I will take my leave now. Goodbye, Gael."

Sayah turned his back on his squawking sister and went to join the others while Jaarl lingered to address the ægle trapped beneath the heavy, verdant coils.

Jaarl held out no foolish hope that the ægle would understand his words but hoped and prayed that by the power of Lord Elyon, she might comprehend his intent. He approached her without trepidation, drawing close enough he was just beyond the reach of her snapping beak.

He stood in plain view, right before her enraged and piercing eyes and began in a gentle voice, "I've just learned your name today, Gael, but long have you been in my prayers so that you would know you were created for much more than this. I see such a strength in you, but the Stain has twisted it into something cruel.

"All this time you have watched me and served me out of duty to and fear of the Empire that now I almost hate to say farewell, though I pray that you do fare well."

Gael opened her beak and screeched at him, the force of her utterance causing the fabric of Jaarl's garments to twitch.

Undeterred, he resumed, "I want you to know that I don't hate you for all the harm you've done me. No, I want you to know that I care for you very much."

Jaarl took another step forward, placing himself within Gael's reach, and all fell still. Behind him, Nat forced himself to stifle a warning. If anyone was aware of the danger, it was his father. Even Gael waited, unmoving in her uncertainty, as Jaarl extended a hand toward her.

Jaarl set his deep blue hand upon Gael's bloodstained beak and spoke just these three words, "I forgive you."

And then without fear he turned around and walked away, leaving the stunned Gael to contemplate what had just occurred.

Jaarl rejoined his deliverers, who had been in breathless prayer while he hazarded his encounter with Gael. While Sayah was yet somewhat wearied from his confrontation with Gael, he understood the need for urgency. The ægle was refreshed enough he thought they could depart at once, if only at a bit slower pace.

Jaarl, on the other hand, had almost reached them when he swooned and stumbled. Nat called out and dashed forward to catch his father, who was no heavier than Rae or himself. He held onto his father and attempted to think of how they might help him regain his strength.

Recognizing the need before her, Rae exclaimed, "I've got it!"

She hurried to open her pack and soon produced the leftover portion of rhema.

Offering it to Jaarl, she declared, "Now we know why Elyon left us the extra today!"

Nat smiled, thankful for Rae's presence of mind and informed his father, "Please, eat it. This is our daily bread, given from the hand of Lord Elyon."

Jaarl took several careful bites to allow himself to adapt to the food, any food whatsoever. Without complaint, he told the others that it had been a few days since he'd eaten his last morsel, which explained the sudden faintness that had overtaken him. In moments, his eyes brightened, his strength returned, and soon he was the one to call for their departure. He'd had his fill of the place.

With some help, Jaarl managed to mount Sayah, then the others followed him up and they were off without delay. Every one of them wished to be shed of the place, and as they took to the sky, Sayah's eyes lingered on Gael's prostrate form while Jaarl's were fixed on the cage.

A pensive Jaarl gave utterance to his thoughts, "Strange. All that time, she was the one in a cage."

"And now, at last, you're free," Sayah returned.

"Not quite," Nat chimed. "We have much of the Kinsman and His Tree to discuss with you, father. I'm happy we were able to deliver you from your long captivity, but if the Kinsman sets you free, you are free indeed."

Epilogue

The adventurers, now homeward bound, obscured the route of their departure by circling high and to the north in view of Gael. Once out of sight, they looped back along the western edge of the forest to head south toward Amityot.

Nat, Rae and Killam meanwhile shared what they had learned of the Kinsman with Jaarl, who had a plethora of questions.

"So Yeshayahu's prophecy of the suffering servant is fulfilled in the Kinsman, no?" Jaarl cued Killam. "And what of the conquering king? We know Him now as the Lamb, but what of the Lion?"

As a new believer, Killam answered as best he was able from what he'd overheard of conversations among the Kin in Terábnis and Endego.

"Jaarl, in His sacrifice as the Lamb of prophecy, Gaal has conquered the Stain and death itself. How else do we explain His resurrection? And what greater victory is there than that over death?"

Slapping Killam on the back, Jaarl chuckled and replied, "I have missed these conversations of ours, my friend. You are right. The Kinsman you describe must be mighty indeed to repel the advance of the Stain.

"Up to now, the only way to avoid the curse of the Stain and the Blight that follows was by careful observation of the laws and commandments Lord Elyon passed down through the Eben'kayah. And no one is perfect in such observance. Not one."

Jaarl unbuttoned his tattered shirt, spreading the lapels to reveal the dark blue skin stretched over his emaciated chest. Over his heart stood a small dot, dark in its punctuation of Jaarl's flesh.

After a long moment, Jaarl offered an embarrassed plea, "Please don't think less of me for the depth of my iniquity. This blemish is my greatest shame and I look forward to its removal."

"How is it so small?" Nat asked.

His own experience with the Stain was that it tended to grow, in particular when the bearer underwent the times of duress and trial that often drove a heart to bitterness. And trials his father had experienced in plenty.

"No matter how small the Stain may seem to us, it leads to death in the end," Jaarl returned. "Even this is sufficient to incur Elyon's judgement, though I have since my youth strived to keep His commandments."

Nat understood. He'd been mere moments in unbelieving despair before encountering the Kinsman's Tree, and that had been enough to mar his face with the Stain of faithless tears. But thanks be to Lord Elyon, who in that very instant had been gracious to bring him to the foot of the Tree and wash all Nat's Stain away. And now he stood beside his father, ready to guide him to the Kinsman. Nat couldn't be any more grateful.

"None but the Kinsman is so pure, so holy, my friend," Killam answered Jaarl. "See now my hand, once so Stained it was on the verge of Blight. Now, it is clean as the day I was born. Cleaner. Spotless and without blemish. Unless the One promised had come and fulfilled the law, this would not be possible. You know that."

"And you, son," Jaarl prompted Nat, "what do you believe?"

With respect, Nat began, "Father, more than any other knowledge I possess, my knowledge of the Kinsman is certain. He is the Son of Lord Elyon, the perfect Lamb who takes away the Stain from the world.

"If you had seen the hundreds of creatures of all kinds cleansed of the Stain that we have, you would believe. Or if you had known the communion we have with the Creator through His Spirit dwelling in us and the fellowship we share with one another, united in the Spirit.

"Not just that, but the power of the Kinsman is unstoppable, transforming the landscape of this broken world no matter how the Empire tries to suppress it. Not to mention the transformation of those who have submitted to the King who conquered their hearts by His gracious and self-sacrificial love."

"Look now at these miraculous wings upon which we fly!" Nat exclaimed, pointing to Sayah. "When I first met Sayah as an æglet, he was destined not to fly. From his hatching, he had known only the frailty and disfigurement of one would die early of the Blight.

"Now look at him! A more majestic ægle you will not find, and not because of his own glory. No! It is due to the power of the Spirit, glorified in Sayah's life in surrender to His will, that this ægle shines so!"

Jaarl listened to Nat with a crooked smirk on his face, and when Nat finished, Jaarl clapped him on the back as he had Killam earlier.

"Son, now I *know* beyond a doubt you are mine!" he cried. "What a preacher! What a sermon! You have convinced me. I wish to know this Kinsman by His Tree.

"To be honest, I decided a while ago, but I was so encouraged to hear more, that let you all keep sharing what wonders the Kinsman is working in our world.

"I owe my life and now my freedom to Him, and sense in Him the fulfillment of my lifelong desires to know Lord Elyon. I have awaited this day for many years and would like nothing more than to join you all in the Vine."

So engrossed in their conversation were they that the travelers had failed to notice the swift accumulation of silvery, sunlit clouds about them. Sayah carried them into the banks of a mass so brilliant that his form, enrobed in silver mist, disappeared beneath them.

Soon, the Etom felt they floated along unassisted amidst the glorious cloud. The caress of the mist refreshed them with its coolness, fragrant with an unidentifiable yet invigorating scent. Together, those Etom in the Vine sensed the presence of the Spirit all about them, and they were inspired to a hushed reverence.

"What a wondrous thing to fly among the clouds," Jaarl marveled, "but I would give now my very life to stand before the Kinsman's Tree."

"We will take you to the Tree in Amityot at once, father," Nat promised, hidden in the cloud.

Their discussion of the Kinsman tapered off and they wondered in collective silence as the luminous cloud in which they rode grew thicker. So dense was it that it rendered the travelers invisible to one another, and if not for the tranquility of the moment, they might have been frightened.

Moments later, they broke through the other side where high overhead the sun greeted them with brilliance. The Etom blinked at one another in awe amidst the open sky, quiet until Killam called out in surprise.

"Jaarl! Your chest!"

Jaarl looked down to where he'd left his ragged shirt open, his Stain bared to the others. Instead of the dark, puckered blemish, his taut, blue skin stood, clean as the day he was born.

Unable to restrain himself, Nat reached out to with a curious hand to touch Jaarl's chest. No evidence of the Stain remained upon his father's skin.

Together they crossed the sky, their awe unanimous that by faith alone in the Kinsman and his work upon the Tree, Jaarl was delivered from the Stain amidst the clouds rather than beneath the Tree.

Look for
The Climactic Final Volume of *The Kinsman's Tree* Series
Summer 2019

Author Biography

Timothy Michael Hurst continues to pursue God's call and is working hard to finish *The Kinsman's Tree* trilogy by the end of 2018. He holds a bachelor's degree in Foreign Languages and Literature from the University of New Mexico, and currently resides in New Mexico with his wife and four children.

In the author's own words:

"I am a writer who believes that the life lived best is lived in service to God and that only under the guidance and power of the Holy Spirit one might produce a worthwhile work. I seek to craft entertaining, enriching, and inspiring tales that glorify the Lord in confidence that the Holy Spirit will use them to change lives and draw people closer to Jesus Christ.

In simply offering myself in surrender to the Spirit, I have discovered the satisfaction of worshiping the Lord as an instrument of the writing process. I believe my experience be confirmation of God's calling on my life and pray that each and every person is as deeply transformed in reading these stories as I was in writing them. To Him alone be the glory."

—Timothy Michael Hurst

Made in the USA
Las Vegas, NV
27 November 2021